380

ST. MARTIN'S

MINOTAUR

MYSTERIES

AN EYE
for
GOLD

SARAH
ANDREWS

St. Martin's Paperbacks

AN EYE FOR GOLD

Copyright © 2000 by Sarah Andrews Brown.

Excerpt from *Fault Line* copyright © 2001 by Sarah Andrews Brown.

Library of Congress Catalog Card Number: 00-031735

ISBN: 0-312-97792-1

Printed in the United States of America

St. Martin's Press hardcover edition / September 2000
St. Martin's Paperbacks edition / December 2001

10 9 8 7 6 5 4 3 2 1

To my readers, especially
Clint S. Smith
and
Carlos Eduardo Gomes de Souza Santos,
without whom mysteries would just be so much ink on paper

Acknowledgments

I WOULD LIKE FIRST TO THANK THE KIND PERSONS who arranged for me to tour a working gold mine and mill during the fall of 1999. I found their disciplines fascinating, and observed that they carry them out thoughtfully and with utmost respect for the forces of nature with which they work. I wish dearly to name them here in gratitude for the care they took to educate me and keep me safe; however, I have been asked not to do so for reasons of proprietary interests, and shall instead honor them by respecting that wish.

I thank Thomas J. Casadevall for taking me through the underground workings and mill at the Sunnyside Mine, an event that taught me more mineralogy than a full semester in college. That tour occurred in 1977, and I report it here for two reasons: first, the contrasts evident in care taken for personal and environmental safety. While that mine was operated with a high standard of care for that era, mining safety standards have since come a long way. Second, because I borrowed mining procedures used at that location. In creating a work of fiction, I routinely composite myriad observations of people, places, and things in order to create an interesting story with all of its attendant tensions. Mines and mining procedures vary as infinitely as the rocks they seek to address. The Gloriana Mine does not exist, nor does the specific mining and milling scenario that I have depicted.

My thanks to Jon Price, Nevada State Geologist, and the members of the Geological Society of Nevada for their raucous assistance in helping to familiarize me with the geology of Nevada; in particular, Earl Abbott, Alan Coyner, and Deana Banovich. They are not to be blamed for any places where I got things wrong.

I thank Robert B. Kayser, scion of the Spur Ranch, Douglas, Wyoming, and gatherer of great stories, for putting me in touch with Marcia Murdock, wildlife biologist. Sorry to bump off the wildlife biologist, Marcia.

My thanks to Sarah George, mammologist and Director of the Utah Museum of Natural History, for her boundless enthusiasm and assistance with mouse detail and lore, including an unforgettable Thelma-and-Louise-esque tour of Antelope Island. Likewise thanks to Marjorie Chan, professor, Department of Geology and Geophysics, University of Utah; John Middleton, geographer; and Vicki A. Pedone, professor, Department of Geological Sciences, California State University Northridge, for their details of the natural history of the Great Basin.

I am indebted to David M. Abbott, Jr., consulting economic geologist, formerly with the Securities and Exchange Commission, for his careful critique of this manuscript. Thanks for other essential technical details and ideas go to Erich P. Junger, forensic geologist, Fauquier County, Virginia Sheriff's Office; Steven R. Murray, geologist; Robert E. Moran, consulting geochemist; Richard Louden, geologist; Donald Rasmussen, paleontologist; Carlos Eduardo Gomes de Souza Santos, small-arms expert; Priscilla Lane, agricultural inspector; Pat Bagley, editorial cartoonist, the *Salt Lake Tribune*; Mark Lea, machinist; Doug Rustad, professor, Department of Chemistry, Sonoma State University; and last but heavens not least, Artemas Yaffe, who defies description.

My thanks for literary reviews go to Mary Hallock, Thea Castleman, Ken Dalton, Jon Gunnar Howe, and Susan Ball.

In preparing this work, I found the following published works to be essential resources (in the order they lie on my nightstand and other dusty places): *Life Among the Piutes,* by Sarah Winnemucca Hopkins; *The Silver State,* by James W. Hulse; *Seven Arrows,* by Hyemoyohsts Storm; *The Art of Happiness,* by His Holiness the Dalai Lama and Howard C. Cutler, M.D.; *Mammals of the Intermontane West,* by Samuel Zaeveloff; *The Chemistry of Gold,* by R. J. Puddephatt; *Karnee, a Pauite Narrative,* by Lalla Scott; *Geology of the Great Basin,* by Bill Fiero; *The Nevada Desert,* by Sessions S. Wheeler; *Mines of Humbolt and Pershing Counties,* by William O. Vanderburg; *Nevada Ghost Towns* and *Mining Camps,* by Stanley W. Paher; *The Gold Companion,* by Timothy Green; *The Gold Book,* by Pierre Lassonde; *The U.S. Gold Industry 1998,* by John L. Dobra; and *Misuse of Water Quality Predictions in Mining Impact Studies* and *Cyanide in Mining: Some Observations on the Chemistry, Toxicity and Analysis of Mining-Related Waters,* by Robert E. Moran.

I wish to acknowledge the wit and wisdom of "Ol' Three Toe" and "Club Tail" (not your ordinary fossils), whose column "The Great Basin Experience" in the *GSN Newsletter,* February and March 1999, is quoted herein.

I am indebted to my editor, Kelley Ragland, and my agent, Deborah Schneider, for their superior efforts on behalf of this work, and as always to my husband, Damon, and my son, Duncan, for supporting me in the writing process.

WHEN HE HAD FINISHED ASKING HIS QUESTION, HE put one elbow on the table, rested his chin in his hand, and waited for me to speak. He was old enough that such a gesture pushed the skin up on one side of his face, cocking one of his superbly graying eyebrows into an inquisitive angle.

I didn't answer right away. Instead, I distracted myself by trying to calculate his age. Fifty? Fifty-five? Certainly the progress of at least that many years lay about him, imbuing his pleasant looks and rangy build with a comforting gravity.

He added cream—without stirring—to the coffee the waiter had just brought him and raised it to his lips, pretending to find great interest in this short view of the universe. Swirling steam. Black and white churning slowly into brown. He took a careful sip, and, content with its temperature, followed with a long, satisfied draw of the acrid brew.

The rich scent of coffee rose from my own cup, too. I stared at him gape-mouthed. He worked as an undercover agent for the FBI. I didn't know his name. And if I understood him correctly, he had just offered me a job. Sort of.

I glanced away, hoping to see Ray returning from the men's room. Seconds passed, half a minute. Feeling the agent's eyes on me again, I squirmed, realizing that he was too confident in his work, and too calmly intelligent to be deterred by silence. "What's your real name?" I asked, trying next to avert the subject of the job by getting off the hot seat and offering it to him. "On the phone you said Tom Latimer, but that's not your name, right? I mean, that was just the name you were using on the dinosaur job, right?"

"You help me with this job and I'll tell you my real, honest-to-gosh, no kidding name," he said, beginning to smile.

I wondered if trout see smiles like that on the faces of

fishermen who feel their hooks sink home. I tried not to thrash, but hooked fish have no dignity. Shifting uncomfortably in my chair, I wondered why he had waited until Ray left the table to ask his question.

With proper flourishes, the maitre d' seated a couple at the table to my left, arranging their heavy cloth napkins on their laps as if American culture had a place for such groveling displays of class consciousness. I watched, playing for time. The man searched around for a place to hang his cream-colored Stetson, and wound up resting it on the tablecloth. He kept a hand on it, fiddling nervously with the grosgrain ribbon at the edge of the brim.

Ignoring the waiter and the menus he artfully placed before them, the couple fell into a tense minuet of banal conversation and missed eye contact. The young blond woman said to the remarkably fit gray-haired man, "Well, like, I've known him like two months, but it's like, so *real* when we're together." She shifted her slender torso constantly as she spoke, and twisted a ring set with a huge stone, trying in vain to make it a casual motion. "I mean, we can, like, talk about *anything*. It's really a *great* relationship. I'm really, *really* thinking this is something *special* this time, you know?"

The man drew his elbows up onto the table, folding his hands over his mouth so that his face was less readable. He bobbed his head a little, distractedly indicating that he had heard her.

Discomforted by his minimal response, she said, "I like, *love* to sit up late with him. It's okay with him if all we do is *talk*. You know? But of course, I suppose *you* wouldn't have anything to talk about with him, because you're all, like, into the *environment*."

The man's hand tightened on the brim of his hat.

The FBI agent took a noisy sip of his coffee, retrieving my attention from the other table. "So Em, was this a bad time to ask?" he inquired.

I switched my gaze from the couple to him, and caught an impish glint in his eyes. I hadn't seen this side of him before, and I didn't like it. Where was Ray? Just how long could it take a man to pee? "Well, um, I'd have to think about it," I answered lamely. There, it was out: the preliminary put-off. The stall. The What-in-hell-am-I-doing-with-myself-anyway? pit gaping open at my feet.

The man who was not named Tom Latimer set down his cup and leaned toward me, bringing his salt-and-pepper crew cut within twelve inches of my own first threads of gray. "So, Em," he said, keeping his voice down to a murmur so that no one would hear over the clatter and clash of restaurant noise, "you've been in Salt Lake a week now. I was thinking you might be getting bored. You don't have anything pressing back in Denver. You've been laid off yet another job with this latest 'consolidation' in the oil business, and considering how many thousands of petroleum geologists are out of jobs this time, you have little hope of finding another. You keep telling yourself you're a geologist, not a detective, but when you get down to it, the only real difference is in the time scale, right? I break a sweat over fresh evidence of crimes that happened yesterday and you think fragmental evidence for events four and a half billion years past are a walk in the park."

I began to fiddle with my napkin. He was right, geologists are just a kind of detective, but his flattery was finding a disquietingly easy way to its mark.

He continued. "It's been a while since you helped us with the George Dishey murder. Almost a year. All those months sitting behind a desk, then standing in line for your unemployment check. Ray's been over to Denver four times courting you, and you just didn't know what else to do with yourself, so you came here. If I understand you at all, you're itchy for a break from the ordinary."

I shot him a warning look. How did he know so much about my doings in the past months?

He went in for the kill. "About now I'll bet you're wondering what you're doing being a polite guest at his mother's house when what you really want to do is—"

"That's enough!" I snapped. It was nobody's business but Ray's and mine if Ray wanted to stay true to his Mormon upbringing and not bed me outside of wedlock.

He leaned back. "You're right. That's getting a little personal. I apologize. But I've been keeping an eye on you. And don't get paranoid; I've only been talking to your pal Carlos Ortega. Nice guy, Carlos. Good cop."

I glanced into his gray eyes for a moment, then once again regarded the tablecloth.

I set to work corralling stray bread crumbs with a pinkie. As always, I had dropped at least five times as many crumbs as anyone else at the table. It seemed to be a special talent of mine. I wondered longingly if somewhere on Earth it was considered good manners or perhaps a subtle clue to a superior intelligence.

The blonde at the next table continued her dissertation on her new boyfriend as she scanned the menu, her spine straight as a ballerina's. "It's like we've known each other *forever,*" she informed her companion.

I clenched my teeth, fighting the urge to say out loud, Oh come on, honey, you can come up with a better line than that!

"So tell me how you met him," her companion asked. I glanced over toward him. He looked bored. No; blank. I wondered what their relationship was. May-December lovers? No, if that were the case then he would not be suffering to hear about her new swain as calmly as he was.

"Well," the blonde said, lifting her chin with trumped-up dignity, "I was at a *concert.* I met him at the *bar* during *intermission.* He had flown in just for that day in his *jet;* like, he flew it him*self.* And, well, we were drinking the same brand of *Chablis.* It turns out he knows à *lot* about wine. *Quite* a lot." She asserted this last with a horizontal chopping motion of her left hand.

She's a southpaw, I thought abstractly, then cursed myself for automatically collecting data about a total stranger.

"What do you see?" the man across from me asked softly. "You're a good observer, Em."

Their waiter appeared and asked, "Are you ready to order?"

The agent tapped my hand. "Em, I need your help."

Silence hadn't worked. Changing the subject hadn't worked. Sulking hadn't worked. I tried skirting the issue. "For an endangered species case?" I said. "I mean, what's that got to do with me? I'm a geologist, not a biologist. You remember those major divisions they taught you in science class? Animal, vegetable, mineral? Biologists do the first and second parts. I do the third."

He leaned forward again and dropped his voice so low that I had to strain to hear him. "Sure, there's a biologist on staff who could do the little fuzzies. It's the setting. Gold mining, out in the middle of nowhere. Geologist's heaven, eh?"

"You got that one straight," I said nervously, trying to cover just how little I wanted to consider options just now. "The only place I like better than the middle of nowhere is the back of nowhere." I rolled my eyes at the fancy appointments of the splendid urban restaurant in which we were seated, all dripping with coordinated colors and restrained centerpieces. The chow was fine, and the coffee was terrific, but sitting on the ground eating straight out of the cook-pot with a stick suited me even better.

Where *was* Ray? And what good was a boyfriend if he didn't come and save me from uncomfortable moments like this? After all, half the reason that I was uncomfortable was the fact that he had butted his way into this meeting, asserting his presence as an unspoken reminder that he had a proprietary interest in how I spent my time.

I stared at my hands, recalling our conversation earlier that day. "I'm having an early dinner with that guy from the FBI," I'd told him. "I'll be done about when you said you'd pick me up to go to the reservoir."

Being economical in his use of spoken language, Ray had said nothing, but his eyes had grown dark with sudden annoyance.

"Not a big deal," I'd added defensively. "He just kinda called me up and said how are you, and suggested that we get together."

Ray had come back with, "And just how do you think he got your phone number?" Leave it to Ray to grab the one

loose thread in my thinking and give it a yank. And he had
insisted on joining us.

The FBI agent now jerked my attention back to the present
moment, saying, "Here comes Ray."

I swiveled my head, searching the crowd for him. There
he was, just outside the hallway that led back to the bath-
rooms. Some bald man I'd never seen before had stopped
him, and was talking with his hands swinging so wildly that
he looked like he was polishing the air. Ray stood straight
and gorgeous, his lithe, muscular build the perfect foil for the
dark blue uniform he wore as one of Salt Lake City's finest.
It took a trained eye to know that he was jumping with nerves.

"You can come along on a recon," the FBI agent whispered conspiratorially. "We'll catch a hop out there tomorrow,
meet with one of the other operatives. It's just an hour or
two's flight into Nevada by light plane. . . ."

I squeezed my eyes shut. I loved flying. He knew that.
What was so urgent about this case that he needed to seduce
me into it? *Or does the seduction lie in another vein?*

When I opened my eyes again, Ray had turned a shoulder
toward the man who'd buttonholed him and was storming
toward the table. The bald man followed in his wake, still
talking. The FBI agent across the table from me said, "Here
he comes. What'll it be?"

"Why are you doing this outside his hearing?"

The agent shrugged. Smiled. Feigned innocence.

My pulse quickened.

Ray reached the table. Looked at his watch. Looked point-
edly at me.

You possessive so-and-so, I thought irritably.

Ray's lips tightened. He had read my face. I stared at my
hands; thought, *I should never play poker.*

The FBI agent introduced the bald man who had detained
Ray. "Em Hansen," he said. "This is Tom Latimer. Ray, I see
you two have already met."

Ray glowered.

The bald man gave the FBI agent an inquisitive look,

shrugged his shoulders, stuck out a hand to me, and said, "Glad ta meecha."

I glared at the man across the table from me. "Very funny," I told him. Then I shook the bald man's hand and said, "Amelia Earhart. Glad ta meecha yourself."

Ray took my jacket off the back of my chair and held it for me. I stood up and put it on. The bald man slipped into my place. The FBI agent told him, "I'll be right back," rose, and followed us toward the front door. On the way, he caught my elbow as we shuffled through the maze of tables, artfully setting up eddies in the flow of human traffic until I was walking a distance behind Ray. He murmured, "What was your take on the couple at the next table?"

"He's her father," I answered, falling too easily into the game of analyzing miscellaneous data. "He and her mother split when she was a toddler. She's seen very little of him since. She wants him to make it all up to her, just as soon as she's done turning him on a spit. But he's just a shallow, self-obsessed old pretty boy." When the agent smiled, I added, "And she's inherited his shallowness. Why?"

"And you know this how?"

"They look alike. Same nose, same angles to the face. At least fifty percent Scandinavian blood; they stay baby-faced and fit past ninety, but his thatch is gray. She craves emotional intimacy, but because she hasn't known him all these years and because she's deep down extremely pissed at being abandoned, she throws it all in his face by offering it on a channel most daughters don't use on their fathers. Ha-ha daddy, I'm all grown up and you missed it. I talk about sex right to your face. He's stunned that he's even in the same room with her, and hasn't a clue how to behave, except to be about as available as he ever has been, which is not at all."

The FBI agent grinned. "Like I said, you're a natural."

I threw him a sideways glance. Ray had reached the door and was holding it open, his lips drawn into a straight line. I said, "Why do you ask?"

He replied, "Because it bears on the case. The only thing you missed is the possible connection between the boyfriend and daddy, but I haven't yet proven there is one."

"Oh, sure," I said sarcastically. "We're in a restaurant, and the people you want to observe just happen to sit at the next table. How'd you do that, Houdini?"

He gave my elbow a squeeze and smiled more broadly. "Prior planning and agreeable maitre d's. If you want to avoid suspicion, you find out where and when your quarry's eating, and make your reservation just ahead of them. The man who's now sitting in your chair, looking ever-so-casually like some big witless slob ordering creme brulee and another cup of coffee while he listens intently to their conversation, works with me. Cheap tricks. You'll pick them up quickly."

I could hear Ray tapping his ring against the handle of the door. The ring his deceased wife had placed on his finger. Tap, tap, tap. Hurry up, Em.

I wanted to spit. "My truck's in the shop," I said. "I'd need—"

"I know," said the agent. "I'll pick you up about a quarter to six tomorrow morning. Don't worry about breakfast. I'll have doughnuts and coffee with me. You take yours black."

I glanced at Ray. He was glaring at me. "I'm particularly fond of those cream-filled guys with the chocolate on top," I said.

"A good choice. Wear hard-toed boots," the FBI agent replied. "Where we're going, the Mining Safety and Health Administration rules the road. And tell Ray to calm down. I'll have you back in time for dinner."

PAT GILMORE SAT AT HER COMPUTER, HER FINGER-
tips lightly tapping at the keys, so lightly that no letters appeared on the screen. This was her habit, her nervous tic, a
world of energy drawn up tight and idling. *What am I going
to do?* she was wondering, as her fingers failed to jitter away
her nervous charge. *I can't just let this happen. It's not right.
He's lying and I know it. The data's right here in front of
me.*

She jumped up from her desk and marched back and forth
across the tiny office, stumbling into the overflowing wastebasket in her haste. Grace had never been one of her attrib-
utes. Pat was a tall, large-boned person, the kind of
heavy-muscled woman men call a "big girl." The men's work
chinos and short-sleeved shirts she wore did nothing to ame-
liorate that image. To say she didn't care how she looked
would have been inaccurate; it was more that other things in
her life took priority over grooming; and while painful, other
peoples' opinions were not quite important enough to moti-
vate her to consult a fashion advisor, or change her haircut
to something softer and more feminine, or, God forbid, mess
around with makeup. There were simply too many things to
be done.

Right now pacing topped that list. She moved like a
penned bull, her hands balled into fists, crossing the small
trailer that housed her office in three long strides. The opposite wall fetched her up with a thud. She knew the wall
was there and could have avoided it, but the collision felt
good next to the chaos that writhed within her. Forcing her
breath out with a roar, she crashed both fists into the tack
board she had slammed into, tearing a photocopied announce-
ment regarding employee rights. She yanked a push-pin from
elsewhere on the bulletin board and jammed it ferociously

into the center of the memorandum, turned, then stormed toward the opposite wall.

The telephone on her desk rang, a loud jangling that jostled her already over-tight nerves. She snatched up the receiver in one large hand. "Well?" she roared into the instrument. Her eyes went huge with rage as she listened to the voice at the other end of the line. "Bullshit!" she shouted. "No *way* I'm going to keep this quiet!" Without saying goodbye, she slammed the phone back into its cradle.

Growling in frustration, she bent over her desk and yanked a hidden group of papers from underneath the blotter, then rummaged violently through the wastebasket for a reuseable manila envelope large enough to hold the pages. Finding one that would serve, she jammed the pages into it and raised it to her lips to lick the unspent shreds of adhesive that remained along the flap. It would not stick. Cursing violently, she got after it with a wad of package tape. Turning to the front, she grabbed a marking pen, crossed out the old return address, wrote "from" next to her address—Patricia Gilmore, Staff Biologist, Intermontane Biological Consultants, c/o Gloriana Mine, Winnemucca, Nevada—and then in big letters below it wrote, "To KREN News, Reno," then added, in the lower left corner, "John Howell, eyes only." She allowed herself a bitter laugh over the paltry likelihood that she could get her way in even this one small request, but kept moving. There was no time to be wasted fussing over the unfairness of life, the universe, and newsrooms. She had to keep trying, that was all. Yes, try. End this distortion of everything she by God dressed in chinos to protect.

With these thoughts firmly in mind, she snatched her jacket off its hook, flicked out the overhead lights, and headed outside into the rumbling drone of the mill, the setting sun, and the scent of sage. She rushed across the fresh smooth blacktop toward her ancient pickup truck, for once cursing how quickly this ostentatious armoring of asphalt would give way to the miles of graded dirt that lay ahead. It would slow her transit, and tonight she wanted speed.

To my way of perceiving things, Ray's jet ski sounded more like an angry bee than any kind of enhancement of a summer's evening on the reservoir. But he looked happy enough. His perfect white teeth flashed in the lowering light. Smiling and waving back as if I, too, thought it was neat to make that much noise by way of entertaining oneself, I lay back on the blanket he had thoughtfully provided and tipped my straw cowboy hat over my face.

The cooling breezes worked playfully at the hairs on my arms. With sunset, the day's heat had quickly begun to lift from the mountain air, but I was warm enough and well fed, the granola bar Ray had supplied for my dessert blissfully masticated in my stomach. As I let the sweet thought of the next morning's flight over the desert beyond this jazzed-up mountain playground occupy my thoughts, the incessant buzzing of Ray's craft began to fade from my attention. My contentment might even have coasted into a happy little snooze if Ray's dog had not decided on a moist inspection of my chin, dislodging my hat. "Shoo," I said, swatting at the long, wet hairs that drooped around his muzzle. The dog had the couth to go away. I put the hat across my face again and tried to find my way back into my daydream.

A moment later, the thrill of rancid dog breath was topped by the high-pitched insistence of a child imitating an alarm clock. "Ring-a-ling-a-ling!" said Ray's nephew Teddy, about three inches from my left ear. "Ring-a-ling-a-ling!"

I whipped the hat off my face and gave him a narrow-eyed stare. Irritation was immediately followed by humiliation, as I realized that I was trying to intimidate a five-year-old. Worse yet, he seemed pleased by my reaction. Attempting to save face, I muttered, "You rang?"

"Ring-a-ling-a-ling!" he sang triumphantly. "Want to play

chasies?" He leered at me brightly, all freckles and mischievous intent. He had purple stains on his lips and chin from eating popsicles, and I wondered briefly if the synthetic red and blue dyes that had combined to make that color had short-circuited his brain.

Rather testily, I said, "Thank you, no. I thought I'd just lie here and enjoy the evening."

"You're supposed to be looking after me."

"Me? Ah ... no. That would be Ray. I'm just along for the ride."

"Uh-uhn. Unca Ray's out there on his jet ski. That means *you* get to play chasies with me."

Ray buzzed past in the fading light, a grinning symphony of wet muscle and athletic flair, one hand pumping in a thumbs up gesture. I began to get the picture. This was his subtle way of getting me to sample the joys of child care. We were, after all, thinking of making our relationship a serious commitment, which in his—Mormon—universe meant marriage and progeny.

I sat up and regarded the specimen who was now shooting me with one index finger (*pschew, pschew!*), and tried to decide how I'd feel about him if he were mine. He was an engaging enough child, but a little hyperactive for my tastes. A little too let's-throw-sand, and definitely too let's-make-ringing-noises-in-Auntie-Emmy's-ear.

Teddy grinned more broadly. He was in charge of what was happening, and he knew it. I didn't like that. I cursed the inexperience that had left me as ignorant as I was about asserting authority over small children.

Teddy danced from foot to foot. "*Nah*, nah, nah-*goo*-goo," he sassed.

I took a deep breath that soured into a sigh. "I'll give you a lead of five," I informed him as I lumbered to my feet, "then you'd better run like hell, because I'm from the great state of Wyoming, and we grow up chasing the wind!"

Teddy's eyes popped wide.

"One-two-three-four-*five*!" I roared.

He turned and ran. I dashed after him, suddenly caught in

the glee of the chase, my bare toes digging into the sand. He accelerated like a jackrabbit, his slender little legs working like pistons, but my legs were longer and I gained on him, my lungs sucking in the warm air, the full blood of the hunt yanking my over-intellectualized brain from the heights of morose self-consciousness to a nub of ego. I wanted to *win*. My arms windmilling, I caught him by the shoulder, tumbled, scooped him into my arms, and rolled along the shore. He was squealing incoherently. I presumed that this meant he was enjoying himself, but when we tumbled to a stop, he broke free of my grasp and turned to face me, his little eyes tight with contempt. "I'm going to tell," he said.

"Tell what?" I asked.

"Unca Ray!" he squealed. "Unca Ray!"

"What's the matter?" I blustered, once again getting to my feet. I put an arm around him and brushed the sticky sand from his yellow hair.

He planted two tiny hands against my ribs and wrestled himself away from me. I let him go. He ran down the beach, screaming and waving his hands until he caught his uncle's attention. "Unca Ray!" he cried again and again, his voice rising.

Ray cut the engine on his jet ski and sluiced the machine to a stop near his nephew and knelt, lowering his eye-level to the child's, and spoke to him in words too soft for me to hear. The boy tumbled into his uncle's embrace and buried his face against the wet life vest. Ray patted his hair, pursed his lips in soft cooing, then stood him up straight and chucked him under the chin like a good soldier. Ray then crossed the sand to me. "He says you said a bad word," he said sharply. I couldn't see his eyes behind his wrap-around sunglasses, but his lips had drawn tense.

"A bad word? What bad word?"

Ray's chin lifted in challenge. "He's been raised not to repeat such language. What did you say to him?"

I peered up at my twin reflections in Ray's sunglasses, incredulous. "Say? I counted to five and chased him. What's so bad—" Then I remembered. "I told him he'd better run like hell. Aw, Ray, it was just an expression!"

Ray took off his glasses and rubbed his eyes. He left them closed for a long moment and then opened them again. Examined his glasses. Wiped at a smudge that had marred their mirrored surface. Looked at me, his face flat. "I repeat—"

"Fine," I said, cutting him off. "I get the message. Now watch, I shall apologize to the child." I turned toward Teddy, clenched my teeth, and said, "I'm sorry. I didn't mean to upset you. Where I come from . . ." I let that sentence trail off. It didn't matter where I came from. I wasn't there now. My rough-and-ready ranch heritage was his social screwup. I felt deeply embarrassed, but at the same time angry. I turned to the west and watched the scattered clouds turn to gold, my mind slipping easily to the happier prospect of what the morning would bring.

"It's getting late anyway," Ray said.

"Exactly," I replied.

4

IN LOVELOCK, NEVADA, SHIRLEY COOK COUGHED
and slipped her feet out from under her quilt, searching with
her toes for her worn old slippers. The day was coming—she
knew that, as she always woke at the same time, but her world
stood always in darkness. She had been blind since girlhood.
She knew the event that had blinded her had hurt her looks,
too, but the march of the years had one by one plucked loose
the threads of her blossoming vanity, and she had found that
life without the hope of men held other interests far more
perplexing and in their own ways just as satisfying. By long
habit, she ran her right hand along the wall until she found
the door and loosed her bathrobe from the hook near its top,
wrapped it around her aging body, and cued her mental map
for transit into the kitchen.

She moved to the stove. The sun would soon rise and
warm the house, but in the meantime, she would have a cup
of tea. Plucking a match from the tin holder on the wall to
the left of the stove and striking it, she delicately felt with
her smallest finger for the edge of the burner and turned the
knob with the other hand. Then she pushed the kettle into
place, turned, and moved across the room to where the cat
now stretched itself awake in greeting. So sensitive were her
remaining four physical senses that, had she needed to, she
could have reached out and found the cat by the tiny warmth
it cast into the air around it. Or she could have listened for
the minute smack that accompanied the opening of its mouth,
or the whispery purr it emitted as it now rolled sensuously
onto its back, baring its fur-lined stomach to be patted, or she
could have flared her nostrils and tracked the ancient feline
by the funk of its breath.

But Shirley used a different sense for locating things that

were living. She had learned, with practice, that she could sense the animal's presence. To find the cat, she simply thought about it, then followed her sense of it, of what that cat seemed like to her—selfish, self-indulgent, and loving, compactly packaged—as mariners might follow a beacon, narrowing her search as the signal grew stronger, almost prickly, with increased proximity. On the rare occasions that the cat wasn't there, there was simply no sense of its presence, and Shirley would call to it, or clink together two cans of cat food until it came.

Shirley flicked on the radio that rested on a shelf above the sink, then grunted as she bent to reach a fresh can of kidneys-'n-bits out of the lower cupboard. She had worked hard to fight the ravages of her advancing years, forcing herself to walk down the street with her cane each day, but with each decade she had nonetheless gained an inch or so in girth, and now, at sixty-eight, there was simply too much flesh in the way of her hinges for them to move efficiently. She fed the cat. "There you go, you old mooch," she murmured affectionately. "You don't do a lick of work around here. I don't know why I tolerate you."

The twanging strains of country and western music on the radio gave way to news on the half hour. "A Winnemucca woman died last evening when the pickup truck she was driving left the road near Lovelock. Patricia Gilmore was twenty-eight years old, and was apparently driving home from her job near the Gloriana Mine when the accident occurred. And in the nation's capital today—"

The droning voice on the radio stopped short as Shirley yanked the unit from its shelf, ripping the power cord from the wall socket. Sucking in her breath on a tide of fury, she wound back and hurled the contraption as hard as she could against the floor. Shards of plastic ricocheted off the adjoining cabinetry. "Shit!" she screamed, so loud that the cat, who was already cowering, scattered for its hatch door and disappeared into the yard. "Shit! Patsy, Patsy, I *told* you to keep your goddam mouth shut!"

*   *   *

IN DENVER COLORADO, Gretchen MacCallum sat on the edge of her bed, running a boar's-bristle brush through her glorious dark hair. Continuing the rhythm of the strokes with her right hand, she turned over the handset of the bedside telephone and dialed a number in Lovelock, Nevada, then pinched the phone between her shoulder and her ear and listened to the far ringing. Fifty strokes she gave her hair each morning, as she readied herself for sleep. It was her habit to phone her husband before turning in. If she had just come off duty from her night shift work as a nurse, she would have placed this call from the hospital, such was the timing necessary to catch him before he got in his vehicle and headed out into the mountains to look for gold.

Gretchen worked night shifts by preference. That made things awkward sometimes, during intervals when her husband was home and they wanted to have a connubial moment or two, as he was early to bed and preferred to rise by six so he could make a good breakfast for the kids and discuss soccer practice and geometry and laugh about what was being taught under the label "History." But sometimes on Saturdays or Sundays he would open one eye as she slithered in between the sheets, and would muster up some middle-aged nookie and then fall back asleep with a long, hairy arm resting warm and sweaty across her freckled skin. They didn't talk much, and didn't need to. In fact, the phone call she placed to him each morning when he was away in Nevada—or the e-mail she sent to him in South Africa, or Chile, or Australia, or wherever else the world of gold exploration took him—was but a habit and a formality borne of the comfortable affection of almost thirty years of marriage and the smoothness that comes between two pebbles of differing shapes if they rub together long enough in the stream.

This morning he was in Lovelock, a blip on the map along Interstate 80 ninety miles east of Reno. The phone rang six times before a voice answered it. "Desert View Motel," it said nasally.

"Donald MacCallum, please. Room two-twelve."

"Oh, good morning, Gretchen," said the motel receptionist. "I'll transfer your call."

As Gretchen pulled the brush through her hair a twentieth time, a twenty-first, and on and on to strokes number twenty-seven and -eight, she heard the impersonal clicks and buzzes of her call being transferred, and the line in her husband's room ringing. Before the ninth ring, the line switched back to the front desk, and the nasal voice said, "He ain't answering."

"Oh. Did he go out early this morning, Rita?"

"No, I ain't seen him."

"Oh. Is he out at the mine, then?"

"Wait, I'll ask Kyle here." The voice got weaker as the desk manager swung the boom microphone away from her mouth, opened a window, and shouted, "Hey, Kyle! You seen Don?"

"MacCallum?" a male voice volleyed.

"Yeah, yer Scottish buddy. He out drilling or something?"

"Haven't seen him. I'm thinking maybe he's gone home to Denver."

"Wait. Gretch? You hear that?"

"He's not here," Gretchen answered. "Otherwise why'd I be calling you?"

"Oh, yeah. Here, you talk to Kyle."

A baritone voice came on the line as Gretchen completed strokes thirty-eight and thirty-nine. "That you, Gretchen? Has he called you since yesterday? I'm—I'm kind of wondering where he is."

Gretchen paused in her brushing and thought a moment, considering the hint of anxiety in Kyle's voice, then continued, giving special attention to the hairs at the nape of her neck that seemed to always catch on the sweater she wore over her nurse's uniform. "Oh, come on, Kyle. He's probably gone out early to check some idea he had during the night. You know him. He woke up early and didn't want to wake you or something."

"Gol, Gretch, I wish I could find a woman as cool as you

are. Both times I was married, if I didn't call in twice a day the little woman would get crazy."

"They shouldn't have married a geologist, Kyle. It comes with the territory, right?"

"Right," he said. "Gone more than home sometimes."

Gretchen heard the self-pity in his voice, and decided to deflect it with humor. "Yeah, I've heard all the jokes. 'If your wife not only knows what a thermocouple is, but knows how to replace one on the water heater, you might be a geologist.' "

Kyle said, "Yup. And, 'If you wake up at home and can't remember what motel you're in, you might be a geologist.' And if it's Tuesday, I must be sampling saprohites in Australia."

"Oh, quit griping, Kyle. You guys have been cozy there in Lovelock on and off for years now."

"Yeah, if the desk manager at the motel knows not only your name but your wife's and kids', you might be a geologist."

"Yeah, well . . . listen, if you see Don, tell him I called, okay?" Gretchen fought off a yawn. She was done with her brushing now, and even if she had reached her husband, she would be hanging up the phone now, switching off the light, and lying down to sleep. "G'night, Kyle."

"Yeah, sleep tight, Gretch."

Kyle's final salutation faded as Gretchen's hand drifted with the receiver over to its cradle. As her eyes closed and the fatigue of eight hours carrying needles, pills, and thermometers up and down the hard vinyl floors of the hospital pushed her underneath the first wave of sleep, she dully wondered why her wandering husband hadn't been in his room to hear her say she loved him on this, the fifty-fifth anniversary of his birth.

5

THE MORNING LIGHT ON AVA RAYMOND'S BIG, lovely house had already shifted from liquid gold to the fuller spectrum of day when I walked out the front door to wait for the FBI agent. I was staying with Ava during my visit to Salt Lake City. She's Ray's mother. Strict Mormons observe such niceties of chaperonage. So anyway, when the man who called himself Tom Latimer pulled up in front of her house to pick me up for the flight to Nevada, she was just returning from her early morning jog. "Tom!" she called out, somewhat breathlessly, as she had just taken her fifty-two-year-old frame up and down a few hills that still lay in the shade of the towering Wasatch Mountains. "How nice to see you. Are you joining us for breakfast?" She gave him one of her efficient, take-charge, but surprisingly hearty smiles of welcome.

"Ava," he replied, "you are a sight for sore eyes. Wish I could stay, but I'm just here to spirit your star boarder off for a field trip. Can I take a rain check?"

I looked back and forth between the two of them. They had not seen each other, to my knowledge, since the strained circumstances in which we had all become acquainted, a murder case that had involved me, the FBI, Ray, and because of Ray, Ava. Now I mapped the flush that was coming to Ava's cheeks and the twinkle that was lighting the FBI agent's eyes and wondered if more than good exercise and early morning sunlight were causing them. Yes, definitely: Ava shot me a look that said "back off" and the agent's smile grew broad enough to uncover his eyeteeth.

The tightness in Ava's expression now shifted from defense to pending disapproval. "So this is your mysterious appointment. Yes, I suppose we must be discrete when working with the FBI, but does Ray know about this?"

I gritted my teeth. I could go along with staying with her

instead of Ray if that's what they all needed to feel kosher, but I was damned if I was going to hold still for cross-examination of my choices of how to kill time while he was working.

The FBI agent said sweetly, "I asked Em to keep the object of our, ah . . . excursion mum. And it's outside of Ray's jurisdiction, so—"

Ava cut him off. "Shall we expect you for dinner, Em?"

I gave myself a moment to remember that I was a grown woman in my thirties, then answered, "Thanks, Ava, but as I said last evening, no thank you. I'll be gone all day."

Out of the corner of my eye I saw the FBI agent's eyebrows rise. I did not acknowledge his puzzlement. It was none of his business what I planned to do after we returned from Nevada. It would be something simple, like taking myself to a movie. Or to a bar, where I'd down a nice, cold, micro-brewed beer. I needed a little time to myself. To think about the row I'd had with Ray the evening before. To cool off. To ask myself what in hell's name I was doing here, and with the rest of my life.

Ava turned toward the FBI agent and gave him a calculatedly polite smile. She said, "Have a nice excursion," then went inside her big beautiful house to continue her inviolate life as widow of a beloved husband and reigning matriarch of a sprawling clan crammed full of personalities as strong as her own.

I moved quickly toward the agent's nondescript car. With more than a little venom, I said, "So that's why you were so pleased to pick me up. You wanted to see Ava."

He grinned clear back to his molars. "And she was a pleasure to behold," he replied.

A HALF-HOUR LATER, the small twin-engine Piper Cheyenne II the FBI agent had chartered lifted smoothly out over the high desert, its shadow running ahead of us down the lake shore and out across the breeze-dappled waters of Great Salt Lake. We rose over the brown slopes of Antelope Island and continued westward, our airspeed rising as we leveled off at twelve thousand five hundred feet. As always, the world seemed softer and more comforting from the sky, a well-integrated stanza of poetry in which details that seemed daunting from close up—scorpions, quicksand, potential mothers-in-law—were brought as if by magic into a more comprehensible calibration. Down there was civilization, with burger stands and scurrying cars and stop lights and corporate concepts of aesthetics; up here was a limitless sky over arid landscape so beautiful that my heart recalled peace.

The airplane cruised at 283 knots, which is something over three hundred miles per hour. About fifteen minutes into the flight, we passed over the western shore of the lake and headed out over the Bonneville salt flats, a stark white veneer of minerals that were precipitated from the lake as it shrank from its ice-age vastness to the relatively small, shallow expanse it is today. The twin ribbons of Interstate 80 and the Union Pacific Railroad ran straight as dies across the white expanse of salt. The flats are so smooth and so immense that motor daredevils have used it as a track table on which to test their capacities for demon speed. Far to the south I could see still other lands that God had left dry and open and which man had transformed into sere gardens for testing bombs.

As I breathed in the parched air, I searched the ground below for any traces of the wagon trains that had crossed the flats a century and a half before, winding slowly along a spur of the Emigrant Trail toward dreams of greater fortunes in farming and mining. Then, the land I was flying over had been still part of Mexico, which had only recently wrested itself from Spanish colonial rule. Those who traveled the trail were from the eastern states truly emigrating to a new land. I knew well its trace where it passed from Nebraska through my native Wyoming. Most emigrants had skirted around what is now called Utah, passing instead through Idaho. A few, notably the ill-fated Donner party of 1846, had staggered across this salt desert, their oxen already ruined from crossing the Wasatch Mountains east of present-day Salt Lake City. For all, the challenges of the western two-thirds of the Great Basin still lay ahead.

The Donner party was part of the first pioneering trickle of emigrants. In 1848, the United States took these territories from Mexico in the Treaty of Guadalupe-Hidalgo. That same year, gold was discovered at Sutter's Mill in the Californian foothills of the Sierra Nevada, and the flood gates of emigration opened. During the summer of 1849, twenty-five thousand people poured along the trail.

As I stared out across the parched expanse, I was, as always, amazed by the determination of those pioneers, men and women and children who had walked across this barren wilderness beside their oxen, sparing their weights from the exhausted animals' loads. They had passed with painful slowness, taking six months to cross these landscapes. Twenty years later, a railroad would have carried them the entire distance in a matter of days. Now, a century and a half later, I looked down at four lanes of blacktop which carried bored motorists at seventy-five miles per hour in air-conditioned comfort, and at long snakes of freight trains hurrying as quickly on steel rails; I touched the earth with nothing but a shadow, and manned spacecraft overhead saw these longitudes roll past several times a day. My world was contracting.

I lifted my gaze from the whiteness of the salt flats to the staggering challenge that had met the emigrants further west: four hundred more miles of desert cut north to south by rugged mountain ranges. Every fifteen to twenty miles, they had climbed long grades toward a pass, or added leagues to keep their passage close to the life-giving waters of the Humboldt River which rose in the valleys of northeast Nevada. This river they had followed westward for several more weeks to the place where it vanished under the desert sun. There, already pushed to the edge of survival, the wayfarers had set out parched and hungry across a final forty miles of cruel, waterless heat, lured on by the heartless dance of mirages. The lucky ones had found life and hope at the banks of the Carson and Truckee Rivers, which flowed east to meet them from the final, towering challenge of the Sierra.

The waves of mountains and valleys that rose before me may have seemed a wasteland to most emigrants, but to my

geologist's eye, it was heaven. I found the sweeping emptiness and frank rhythms of the brown topography infinitely
soothing. Out of the soft dryness of the high desert basins
before me rose long fins of bald mountain rock, ramparts tens
of miles long and thousands of feet high, naked crests of
eroding earth. Each range lay collared by a ramp of its own
discarded sediment, alluvial fans fed by laceworks of arroyos
which spread outward into sagebrush-studded barrens or
phantom seas of brilliant white salt. The mountain ranges
marched toward us like massive swells in an ocean made of
rock, wave after cresting wave as far as the haze-laden atmosphere could disclose. I coughed. "Smoke," I said, to no one
in particular, speaking into the microphone on my headset.

"Pretty bad visibility," the pilot said, her voice seeming to
originate just inside my ears thanks to the excellent noise-
attenuating headphones I was wearing. "I can usually see
clear across the state."

"Where's the smoke coming from?" I asked.

"Another range fire. Been a lot of them already this year.
Lightning starts them, or some tenderfoot playing with
matches again. They rise up from their Barcaloungers, buy
themselves a thirty-five-thousand-dollar four-by-four, load it
up with beer and tortilla chips, and think they're Davy Crock-
ett. There ought to be a law."

"Yeah," I said, "but somehow you just can't legislate common sense."

The dark pall hung in the air like a dingy smudge of
poorly-erased graphite.

"Word has it you're a geologist," the pilot said.

"Guilty as charged."

"So how were all these mountain ranges formed?" She
asked.

"Word has it that Nevada is being stretched on a rack. Or
at least, that's the theory that most people currently agree on."

"Could you enlarge on that?" she asked, smiling wryly.

"Well, you see, Nevada hasn't always been this wide. Fifteen or twenty million years ago, it was one-third narrower.
It's been stretched, kind of like an accordion."

"Oh, sure," the pilot said doubtfully.

"No, really," I said. "The process happens so slowly you wouldn't hardly notice it, except for the earthquakes, but they're far enough apart that you'd feel few of them in your lifetime."

"What luck. Because I hate accordion music. So who's playing this accordion?"

"Giants," I said, "and they have perfect pitch. No, seriously, there are several theories about that, but they all have to do with plate tectonics."

"Which is?"

"The earth is made up of concentric spheres of differing materials. It has an inner core of very hot, solid iron, an outer core of—"

"Simplify it for me. I'm trying to fly an airplane here."

"Okay, imagine a peach. You have your pit, the earth's core. It's solid. You have your flesh, or mantle. And you have your skin, the earth's crust. Okay, now the theory is that the insides of your peach is made of molten rock that is dispelling heat, which sets up convection currents in the flesh. These currents drag on the skin. Your skin is rigid and brittle relative to the flesh, so it fractures into sections, called plates. Okay, now there are places where you have upwelling convection, lots of hot flesh rising to the surface. The plates slide apart, and flesh from below fills in as new peach skin. This is called a spreading center. Got me so far?"

"I'll never eat another peach."

"Good. Well, if one part of the skin is being spread apart, then it follows that in another place it's being compressed, because you only have so much peach. In the case of the earth's crust, sometimes that results in a pressure ridge, like the Himalayas, but in other places one plate is sliding under the other, like Peru sliding over the Pacific Ocean floor."

"Peach. You were talking about a peach."

"Keep flying the plane. Okay, the evidence in the chunk of the peach we're flying over says that North America slid right up over a spreading center, just like a Buick going over a speed bump, and that hot upwelling place is now right under Nevada."

"Should I turn around?"

"No. There are hot springs around here, but you're not likely to land in one. Anyway, so the theory is that all that upwelling heat is forming a bulge, which is heaving the middle of the state upwards. The crust is being stretched east and west, so it fractures north and south, splitting into parallel chunks which slide east and west away from each other. Voilà, mountains and valleys."

"How'd the gold get there?" she asked.

"That's also there because of the heat," I said. Gold is—at least initially—a hydrothermal deposit. I have oversimplified these faults. There is a network of fractures. Chunks move up and down, back and forward, and there are many pulses of movement and heating. As these rocks crack and move apart, hydrothermal fluids—superheated water with dissolved minerals—move through them. As the waters cool, minerals fall below their freezing points one by one, and solidify, filling the fractures."

"Voilà," said the pilot. "Gold deposits."

"In essence," I said. "But not all will have gold. Most have other minerals. Sometimes the vein—the filled fracture—will have been fractured again, cross-cutting, and a section will drop down. That's why the old sourdoughs finally had to just take their best guess and dig. Even today, the miners sometimes stop digging inches away from the gold. It's all a crapshoot," I said.

The pilot nodded appreciatively, but changed the subject. "Want to fly her for a while?" she asked, lifting her hands from the yoke. "Word has it you're also a pilot."

"Just try to hold me back," I said, gingerly taking the controls. I had never flown anything as fancy as this. The Cheyenne had dual controls and a panel encrusted with aeronautical dials and widgets including GPS, radar, and a radar altimeter. It was long and sleek and had twin four-blade props, wing-tip auxiliary fuel tanks, and full de-icing equipment.

I glanced over my shoulder. Behind us, the FBI agent lounged in one of four beige leather seats, his long legs up on the opposite seat in front of him and his coffee forgotten in its walnut burl cup holder. His eyes were closed, and his chest rose and fell in a deep, slow rhythm. But an odd tension in the muscles of his face told me he wasn't really asleep.

Had he sat back there specifically so I could sit up front? Was this further seduction in whatever game it was he was playing with me? Should I fly the plane and play along, or pass up the offer and see what happened next?

Still uncertain, I turned back toward the pilot. What had she said her name was? Franci? No, Faye. Faye Carter. She was the kind of woman I wished I was; tall, confident, and amused by life. She wasn't beautiful, exactly, but she had a vigor that outshone anything a whole box full of cosmetics could do for anyone who lacked it. She had rich hazel eyes, a splattering of freckles on milky skin, and a thick brush of auburn hair that curved nicely toward the nape of her neck. I wondered how she fit into the picture. The embroidered patch on her breast pocket read SPECIAL DELIVERIES FLYING SERVICES, which meant that she wasn't an employee of the FBI, and I knew that pilots worked for years before they made a halfway decent wage. Yet her pilot's uniform—a light blue shirt with epaulets, and navy slacks—fitted her extraordinarily well, as if they'd been custom-made. The twill of the slacks were of summer-weight wool gabardine, very fine and fancy for a lowly charter pilot. And she seemed quite at ease with her client; no trace of the obsequiousness that comes with normal levels of dependency. I speculated that she had a second source of income, and wondered what that meant.

"I'd love to fly it, Faye," I answered finally. "But I've just got the basic license. Single-engine only. Never flown a twin. Is it much different from a single?"

Faye's laughter filled my ears. "I wasn't suggesting that you should try anything fancy. Just keep her straight and level and keep your hands off the throttles."

I nodded and put my feet on the pedals in front of me. They felt stiff. I moved the yoke a fraction of an inch clockwise as a test. Not much happened. I moved it back. "This thing has more guts than the machine I trained in," I said. "Not so quick to turn."

"She's pretty stable," Faye said. "A little heavy on the left rudder. I'll put her on autopilot for a minute so you can feel the size of the corrections you'll need to make."

I felt the yoke and pedals shift slightly as we met lifting air beyond the crest of the first range inside Nevada. After a moment I said, "Shall I maintain this bearing?"

"Yeah, until we pass the next beacon." Faye showed me the instruments she was using to track our position relative to nearby navigational beacons. She unclipped the air chart from her knee board so I could spot their positions.

I unfolded the chart and ran a finger over the route she had penciled onto it. We were following a narrow slot defined by a daisy chain of small airports that served small towns along Interstate 80. Our route was further constrained by the requirement that we dodge between a series of military munitions test and practice ranges which lay to the north and south. I smiled. Just like the emigrants of the 1840's and 1850's, the railroad builders of the 1860's, and the highway builders of the twentieth century, we would follow the Humboldt River.

"I'll switch off the autopilot now," Faye said.

"Okay, Cisco."

"You got her, Pancho."

I tried the controls again, and this time I began to feel the movements of the plane match my intentions. I flew along for a while in peaceful rapture, feeling the sleek plane and the power of flight as an extension of my own body. The thickening haze offered further detachment from the earth below, and I began to dream an eagle's dreams.

A few minutes later, I was distracted by the sight of an enormous hole in the ground off to the north of our track. It was so big that it stopped my breath in my throat. It was clearly man-made, and at least half a mile wide and a thousand feet deep. "What's that?" I asked, pointing it out to Faye.

"Doesn't that just fry your mind?" she said. "They're supposed to put all recognizable features on the air charts, but somehow they left that one off. I'll bet you can see that puppy from space. The faintest little road gets marked, but a big, honking mine like that . . . nothing, or at best they give you this little pick and hammer symbol which just means 'mine.' "

"I *know* it's an open-pit mine," I said, "Meteor craters don't have access roads and tailings ponds. But what are they mining?"

The FBI agent's voice suddenly came through the headphones. "That, my dear Em, is the source of what brings us here today."

I whipped around in my seat and looked at him, startled, even though I had known that he was awake. His eyes were still closed. "They're ripping a scar like that for gold?" I asked, covering my surprise with my annoyance over the view. "The stuff's worth hardly anything these days. And all that just to make pretty stuff to hang around peoples' necks and fingers?" I felt almost sick. My beautiful desert symphony of sweeping curves and dust-brown vistas, all gone *thunk* so a few people could decorate their clavicles and metacarpals.

"Sure, jewelry still uses up seventy percent," the agent said, "but there's also gold crowns for your teeth, and of course the little matter of corrosion-free electrical contacts in computers and cell phones and lovely little widgets like that."

"Bah!"

The agent opened his eyes and looked at me. "That's my Em," he cooed. "Get that moral outrage up! Take sides!" He ran a hand through his short salt-and-pepper hair and yawned. "But while you're at it, please keep in mind that part of your nation's might and stability resides in a nice, big pile of gold bars stored at a quaint old fort called Knox."

"I thought we'd gone off the gold standard," Faye said.

"Yes, that's true," he replied. "And you can no longer turn in your greenbacks in exchange for silver from the U.S. Treasury. But there's still a mountain of gold in reserve, and while it might not back all of our currency, it acts like a sea anchor for the nation's economy."

"How?" I asked. I knew there was a stack of gold in a

vault at Fort Knox, but I had no idea how it linked to the value of a dollar, or, for that matter, where Fort Knox was. Kentucky? Tennessee? Somewhere back there in one of those states I had never seen.

"Consider the fate of a banana republic with no bullion," he replied. "They have a military dictatorship. They start a war with their neighbor, or an uprising of some kind. It costs the government to wage that war. They have no natural resources, so instead they buy their weapons from us, or from China. They don't really have the money to pay for those weapons, so they just print some. Galloping inflation follows, people rolling wheelbarrows full of paper money down the street to buy a bag of flour. We don't get that here in the U. S. of A., because we enjoy a stable society, both because we have a strong Constitution, but also because we have true wealth in minerals and productive land."

"That's quite a little speech," I said.

He opened one eye and looked at me. "Germany tried to mine gold from sea water to pay off its debt after the First World War."

"We had a little trouble after that war, too, as I recall. A little thing called the Great Depression," Faye countered.

He smiled. "Yes, and things got tough for a while. But Roosevelt got us through it by putting us to work on the land we had, rather than by starting another war to try to grab the wealth next door."

"But he didn't keep us out of *that* war, now *did* he?" Faye said. "And that was what really dragged our economy out of the Depression. The old military-industrial complex saves the day."

His smile spread into a grin. "*Touche.* But my point is that, overall, we've enjoyed a relatively stable economy with no runs of hyperinflation. In part because we have gold reserves."

I was following little of what was being said, so I switched to something I did understand. "So back to that hole in the ground. You said we were out here to look into an endangered species thing. Are you saying that the species lives in an open pit gold mine?"

"Not an existing mine, not yet," he answered. "Just one that exists in the hearts of investors and the imaginations of geologists like you." His clear eyes rested on mine for a while, measuring my reaction.

"Okay . . ." I said, not quite certain to what I was agreeing. Was he pointing out the conundrum geologists try to live with—that the resources we are paid to locate are sometimes ripped from the ground in ways we'd find both amazing or horrifying—or was he inviting me once again to forsake my profession for his?

He nodded, apparently satisfied. "Good. Because we have work to do."

6

STEPHEN GILES GAVE THE CLASPS ON HIS BLACK leather suitcase a buff with the heel of his right hand. The clasps were fashioned of a lustrous bronze, which stood out to good effect against the richness of the leather. But it wasn't just the appropriateness of the metal that pleased him: even their shapes were perfect. Quality, they said. The owner of this bag has style and class.

But today even the perfection of the clasps could not save him from the sea of frustration that engulfed him. He was going to have to postpone his trip, and the use of this splendid suitcase, and . . . It was fine that the FBI had started their investigation; it was their *timing* that was a problem. But he would do his job, and *then* he would go. Be gone, at last, into his real life. Release. Freedom to be who he was, if only for a while. . . .

Sighing, he flicked the clasps open one more time and again lifted the lid. Inside lay his summer-weight gabardine slacks. They would look excellent on him, draped like silk over the leg muscles he had developed to just the right balance of strength and sleekness at the gym. Beside the slacks, the perfect hundred-and-fifty-dollar boat shoes winked through the little plastic windows in their protective flannel sleeves. The sleeves had been a good investment. They would keep everything else in the case neat and clean once he'd actually walked in those shoes. The sleeves had been an extra expense, yes, but expense had no meaning when it came to quality. He understood quality. It was wasted on so many, but not on him.

He ran a hand over the smooth fabric of the slacks, touched the nubbly knit of the deep burgundy sweater beside it that would so exquisitely set off the ruddy tones of his skin. Cashmere. Beneath that, more slacks, pristine white leather running shoes in another set of sleeves, a stack of perfectly folded shirts—all silk—his leather toilet kit, and underwear—all brand new, but pre-laundered, so they would hang just right. Boxers, not jockey shorts. Jockeys were for boys, and for men with no class.

He sighed again and closed the lid of the suitcase. All this would have to wait. How long? A week? Lucky that his first-class ticket could be so easily exchanged for a later date; no, on second thought, luck had nothing to do with it. An absent smile curved his lips. First class was just exactly that: full and complete recognition of his place in the universe, at long last. First class was, "Of course, sir, Mr. Giles, sir, we can change your reservations, no problem," and "Let us look after these other niggling details so that your day can be more comfortable. . . ."

He slipped the suitcase back inside the heavy plastic bag that protected it from the gray dust that filtered insidiously in from the desert through the joints in the steel walls of the storage locker. Using quick, sure motions, he taped the bag shut and replaced the roll of packaging tape in the cardboard box he kept there to hold such little necessities. He looked around the otherwise empty storage locker, thinking. The case really deserved a stand of some sort, something beyond this film of plastic to keep it up off the cement floor. But it had to be something special. A mahogany luggage rack, perhaps. He would look for one on his next trip to San Francisco, or L.A. Perhaps he could slip away over the weekend, and in some small way release himself from the agony of the wait.

He nodded to himself, affirming that plan. Then he straightened up, cracked open the door, and looked to see if anyone was coming. The pavement beyond his storage unit was empty save for his car, an eight-year-old Honda Civic. Stephen curled his upper lip in disgust. That car was an abomination, but a necessary camouflage. As if to keep it in its place, he had parked it several doors away.

Taking care to open the door to his unit no farther than was necessary, to prevent sudden passersby from seeing what he kept so carefully hidden within, he slipped out and applied his heavy-duty padlock to the hasps. Then he hurried across to the Honda, got in, fired the ignition, and pulled away, following a circuitous route in and out through several aisles of the storage facility before cutting through the electronically-controlled gate and back into the world of mediocrity that waited beyond it.

As he turned onto the road that would lead him back into Reno, his job at the Bureau of Land Management, and another day as John Q. Nobody, he felt the familiar pressures rise.

EARLY MORNING SHADOWS cast by ranging pickup trucks still reached like fingers down the main drag of Winnemucca, Nevada as Umberto Rodriguez, Ph.D., strolled into The Griddle, a homey little cafe where everyone who was anyone in the mining industry took their breakfast. He was in a good mood, an expansive mood. With the extinguishment of Pat Gilmore from among the breathing, his plan had become much simpler.

He had timed his arrival well—not too early and not too late—to make certain that there would be many people already there eating their eggs and hash browns and sucking up their coffees like the silly pigs they were, but still few enough that he could easily chose from among several still-empty booths and tables. That way he could nod graciously to anyone of importance, even raise a hand in casual salute, but command his own place in the room. Let them come to him.

The Griddle was a gathering place in part because some mines provided minivan transit from and to Winnemucca for their employees, and using a cafe as a gathering point meant they arrived at work well fueled. Such peasant accommodations were not for Umberto Rodriguez; he would drive to his office at the mine himself in his own elegantly appointed Ford Explorer, at a per-mile price to his employer, of course.

On this morning, Umberto found several booths filled with scruffy geologists and unimaginative engineers from the local mines. Along the counter he recognized a few of the miners who were content to spend their lives moving loads of ore for the rich investors who would profit by their sweat. *Like so many burros*, thought Umberto, and then, without realizing the ambiguity in his own thinking, he gave over half a second to despising them for how well their work actually paid them. *More than I make*, he thought bitterly. *I who am educated . . .*

One of the geologists did address him. " 'Lo Bert," he said, but did not invite him to sit down. Umberto stared at him, trying to recall his name. He could not. Ah well, if he couldn't remember, then the man was not important. But the husky man seated to his right was. Virgil Davis, superintendent at Gloriana Mine, a high-ranking employee of Granville Resources. He rarely saw Davis here, probably because the man lived up near the mine.

Umberto's interest in the occupants of this table rose. Was this a breakfast meeting, called in reaction to the crisis they faced after the previous night's events? Or did they know yet that Pat Gilmore was dead? Regardless, he would let them raise the topic first, but must look suitably grave. He must give Davis just the right greeting, a peer's acknowledgment of his prominence within the corporation; bowing his head slightly, he passed his upturned right palm from left to right at the level of his navel. Yes, that was perfect.

Davis nodded, and continued to chew his toast.

Rodriguez lingered just an instant longer. Far more interesting than Davis was another mine worker present, Laurel Dietz. Laurel was *una rubia*, a choice young blonde with blue eyes as big as lakes. To Laurel he presented a sympathetic smile. She blinked back distractedly and took a suck at her orange juice. *Perhaps she has not yet had her morning coffee*, thought Umberto, as he passed onward, now wishing indeed that any of them, especially Laurel, had invited him to sit down. *Que lástima*, he would seat himself at the center table to the left, just as he had previously planned.

He ordered the Cajun scramble and ladled sugar into his coffee, still thinking about Laurel. Perhaps she screamed at the moment of orgasm. The quiet ones often did, a kind of inverse relationship between the profane and the profound, fueled by the release of repression. Ah, she was looking his way. He smiled slightly, and nodded to her over his cup, making certain to keep his face impassive should she feel the need to cover her interest in a married man—but no, her eyes flicked away again, without so much as the tiniest dance of flirtation. She was a tough one, but worth the chase.

Virgil Davis and another man rose from their booth and came over to Umberto's table, but remained standing. Virgil coughed. "Sorry about your coworker," he said.

It was time to look grieved. Umberto lowered his gaze and let his lower lip sag from his swarthy face. "Yes. It is terrible. So young."

"Yeah. Well, these roads are dangerous sometimes."

"Yes," said Umberto. "Perhaps a trucker fell asleep at the wheel and drifted across the road, or perhaps she herself fell asleep." He made a long, trailing gesture with his hand, indicating the trajectory of the hapless biologist leaving the road and thus exiting this existence.

"She wasn't on the highway," the other man said, staring at him blankly.

Virgil glanced at the man out of the corner of his eye. "Oh. Umberto Rodriguez, this is John Steinhoff, our metallurgist."

Rodriguez inclined his head in greeting. Steinhoff continued to stare.

Virgil coughed again, a deep, phlegmy rumble.

"That cough sounds bad," Umberto said conversationally.

"It's the smoke."

"Yes, I heard. Range fire over by Lovelock."

Virgil's eyes slipped out of focus, then sharpened again. "Well, anyway, it's sad about your biologist, but here's the thing: you think it'll slow the project down any further?"

Umberto set his wrists at the edge of the table and steepled his fingers. He wanted to say, with some annoyance, that with someone as incompetent as Pat gone their pitiful project would most certainly speed up, but such a display of candor would not do. Instead, he said, "We shall redouble our efforts. You may depend on Intermontane Biological Consultants as always."

Davis smiled vacantly. "Great. Because we want to start drilling that property ASAP. How close are you to pushing the permits through the BLM?"

"Very close, I am sure. I foresee no delays." Umberto had in fact no idea where they were in the permitting process. That had been Pat's domain. Damn her obstinacy, she had managed to conceal the paperwork somewhere, and his contact at the BLM had been less than forthcoming this time.

"How soon? I'd like to start grading the roads. I got a cat skinner just sitting up there cooling his heels."

"Let me make some inquiries for you. Give me your card, okay?" This was good; he was moving in already on what had been the irritating Ms. Gilmore's territory. "And don't worry," he murmured soothingly. "I'll take care of this for you."

WHEN THE TELEPHONE rang in Scarface Pete's mobile home at Pyramid Lake Indian Reservation, his middle-aged daughter Hermione answered it. She had sensed that a call would be coming, a bad news call, and had come quietly across the desert soil from her own small trailer to wait. Shirley Cook's voice rose angry and exasperated from the other end of the wire. "I got rotten news," Shirley said.

"Yes," Hermione replied.

"Pat Gilmore is dead."

Hermione said nothing.

"You hear me?"

"Yes."

"This is really the limit. You get any word on this from anyone else?"

"No. You're the first."

"I have to assume it was a road accident." Shirley grunted. "Or not an accident, know what I mean?" she added darkly.

"Yes."

"Shit, 'Mione, this is no moment for your inscrutable Injun stuff. I called the sheriff's office, they ain't talking. I called the coroner's office, same run-around. I called the paper, they're asleep at the switch. Now you're doing your yes-no act. Cut the shit; this is a disaster."

"For Pat."

"Of course for Pat! We'll all miss her, boo hoo, we'll hold a wake and grieve her later. Right now we got work to do!"

"I hear you."

"Good," Shirley said, her voice dropping promptly into the sadness she had not heretofore let herself feel. "You heard from the Salt Lake group?"

"I'll get back to you," Hermione said.

"Do that." Shirley's voice was on the edge of breaking down.

Hermione heard a click as Shirley hung up the phone. She rose from the straight-backed chair on which she had been sitting to await the call, moved to the narrow bed where her father rested, and touched his shoulder. He lifted one great hand that had grown glassy smooth with the disuse of extreme age and closed it around hers. Even trembling slightly with the slow disintegration of his nervous system, his hand was, as always, cool and dry, and comforting. "What?" he asked, the sound coming as a concussive huff from his disease-riddled lungs.

"A warrior died," she said softly.

"Ah. A loss. Pat Gilmore?"

"Yes."

"Did she tell?"

Hermione stared out at the stark, beauty of the dry landscape, at the morning sun glinting off the glittering surface of Pyramid Lake itself. "I hope not," she said.

7

FAYE BANKED THE PIPER TOWARD RENO'S AIRPORT. I had seen Reno only once before, or more precisely, had seen it fleetingly. I had been one of five squealing eighteen-year-olds packed into a Volkswagen, amped on caffeine and junk food and a mistaken sense of immortality. It had been a Saturday night, and we had turned off the highway on a whim and zipped down Virginia Avenue, right through the heart of "the action." I was in my freshman year at Colorado College, it was spring break, life seemed like one big smorgasbord of weird experiences, and we were on a road trip to California, another five zit-faced wackos aiding and abetting each other in misspending our youths.

Then, the excesses of a state and city which upheld gambling and other such compulsions as a manifesto of liberty had struck me differently. Then, I had found it extravagant and exciting to cruise past the dizzying displays of neon lights. Then, I had marveled at the sights of slot machines spilling right out onto the street and skinny rubes with cigarettes hanging out of their mouths skulking the sidewalks, and had wondered which of the tarted-up women counted themselves among Nevada's legion of hookers. Then, life had seemed one big carnival of independence, and I had greeted each day with the impressionableness of a baby chicken. Now, I was almost three years past thirty, that age past which giddy eighteen-year-olds could no longer trust me. Now, life had shown itself to hold fewer possibilities and harsher repercussions. Now, I approached a Reno caught naked in the cool glare of morning, and the idea of gambling and all its attendant self-indulgences touched me with fear.

My headphones crackled with radio calls to and from the tower as Faye brought the twin expertly down into the landing pattern, dodging between a Boeing 727 inbound from San

Francisco and a private Lear jet outbound for who knew where. The air was bright and clear now; a hundred miles or more back out over the empty desert, we had passed to the south of the obscuring pall of smoke that still belched like billowing ink from the range fire. I gawked with cowgirl frankness at the jumbled Reno cityscape, amazed by the dimensions of this clutter of passion-palaces that sprawled across the desert floor and sloshed up against the blue rampart of the Sierra Nevada. I noted the notch in the mountain front through which the 1849 emigrants had labored, whipping their flagging oxen up over the final grade toward the waiting gold fields and farmlands of California. South along the mountain front lay Virginia City, home of the Comstock Lode, the center of Nevada's first rush for precious metals. Silver had been mined there first and foremost, winning Nevada the title of the Silver State.

We touched down and taxied to the private transit terminal, where the FBI agent found his local contact waiting with a car. The Reno man was young, slender, and broad-shouldered, and had flint-black hair and skin tanned the color of strong tea. The two men stepped aside and spoke in voices too low for me to hear, their heads bowed. By the increasing tightness of my host's brow, I gauged that something was amiss. After mulling his new information for a moment, he turned to Faye and said, "We'll be here a couple hours longer than I expected, and will need to cover more ground. I had thought to have you pick us up in Lovelock, but you'd better make it Winnemucca. Prep a flight plan and head back there whenever you're ready. We'll arrive there by car by say, three P.M."

"You got it," Faye answered, snapping him an off-handed salute.

The Reno man walked up to me and offered me a hand to shake. "Tom Latimer," he said, grinning at the joke the more senior agent had obviously just put him up to. "And you're?"

"Eleanor Roosevelt," I growled, turning toward the older man. "Good joke you're playing on ol' Emmy. What's your real name? Something embarrassing, like Basil Frisby? Or

Fauntleroy Fangmire. Or does the FBI only hire men named Tom?"

He grinned. "I knew this job would be more fun if I brought you along."

"And I let myself believe it had something to do with my peerless capacities as a geologist!"

"Well, that too."

A third man was now approaching us. He was about forty-five or fifty but boyishly lively in his looks. He was dressed in European-cut slacks and a knit silk short-sleeved shirt, and carried himself with an easy pride and a smiling presumption of command. He came straight up to the elder of the two FBI agents and stuck out a hand to be shaken. As he did so, I saw a fourth man a few strides behind him come to an attentive stop with his hands folded just below his muscular chest. He reeked of bodyguard. The man who had approached us said, in a crisp British accent, "Roderick Chittenden here, president of Granville Resources. I came just as soon as I heard of the trouble. I understand from your man here that you're in charge of this investigation into the species business at my prospective mine."

So this was a corporate big-wig, just arrived by private jet. I wondered at the exquisiteness of his timing.

The senior FBI agent said, "This is Em Hansen, a geologist. You've already met 'my man' here."

I stuck out my hand to be shaken. Chittenden moved his hand toward me, flicked his gaze my way and scanned my face. His eyes were confident, sharp, and shrewdly intelligent, and he had a dashing sort of good looks and sense of mischief about him. Having all this aimed at me was unnerving. Luckily, it lasted only a split-second before he made a decision about my potential usefulness (none) and turned his attention back to the older FBI agent. "So. What do we think here?"

The agent smiled a heavy-lidded smile I had come to know meant he was suppressing annoyance. "We have just arrived. How can I reach you if I have questions for you?"

Instead of looking rebuffed, Chittenden's face took on a look of robust pleasure. He raised a finger in signal to his second. "My man will give you some telephone numbers." He clapped the agent on the shoulder, said, "Very well then, carry on, my good fellow," turned, and headed away, calling instructions to his bodyguard. "Get the car, James; our first meeting is in ten minutes."

The redoubtable James produced a card, palmed it to the agent, and tore after him, bounding along with athletic grace to open the door for his master and hand him into the backseat of a waiting silver BMW.

As I watched them leave, I had the nasty sense that I was playing a game in which I was privy to only a few of the rules.

As WE LOADED into our own U.S. government plain-Jane car, I said, "So we're going to Lovelock *and* Winnemucca? Is that why you rented a plane instead of flying commercial, so you could zing home from wherever you wind up? Or was it so you wouldn't have to explain me on the expense account?"

"All that and the job just heated up," the agent replied, his smile vanishing.

"Oh. Because Chittenden just—"

"No. Because the woman we were supposed to question was killed last night."

I snapped to attention. "Who? The biologist?"

"Yes."

Making a turn past a staggeringly tall and opulent pile of hotel with jazzy lights advertising all-night breakfasts, the local operative said, "We don't know much yet. They're saying it's a one-vehicle roll-over accident."

"Bullshit," I said. "The timing's too cute. And Chittenden obviously—"

The older agent raised a schoolmaster's index finger in caution. "Hold on, Em. Some days a cigar is just a cigar. Sometimes people make life very inconvenient for everyone around them by having a road accident. And it's natural that what's-his-name would want to make an everything's-fine appearance."

"Garbage." I wiggled out of my shoulder restraint so I

could lean forward onto the back of his seat. I was annoyed at the way I'd been written off by the president of Whatzis Resources, and more annoyed yet that the FBI agent had once again managed to wiggle out of telling me his real name. That made me reckless, which in this case meant pushy. "So who are we going to see here?"

"The BLM agent who brought the biologist to our attention."

"How long has he known we were coming?"

"Since yesterday afternoon."

"Bingo. He files something on her, you say you're following up on it, he's a sieve for information, she's dead. Chittenden probably had him on the payroll."

"No, Em."

" 'No Em,' why?"

"Because it is not in the best interest of our smiling Brit that the biologist be dead."

"Why?"

"You will shortly know all."

"Well, okay, so then why's Chittenden here?"

The older agent turned his eyes heavenward and sighed. "Em, I'd say that with you along, I'm out of a job, except I'm not here to investigate a murder."

"What do you mean? You're here to investigate a biologist. Now she's a dead biologist. That makes it a murder investigation."

"Murder comes under local jurisdiction."

"Are you trying to tell me the FBI never investigates murders? Come on."

"Only on federal lands."

"Most of this state belongs to Uncle Sam. Maybe five percent tops is private. What's not BLM is military testing ground or Indian reservation. Just how federal do you need it to be?"

He sighed. "Yes, a lot of this state is government land of one sort or another, but let me put this another way: I'm here to investigate an alleged fraud against government policy. The death of this biologist—murder or not—is at present just a new sidelight which may or may not have anything to do with this *possible* fraud."

I moved slowly back against my seat again, frustrated. Murder was much more intriguing than fraud. Murder was high stakes, a vicious rending of the ultimate human taboo. Fraud was by comparison impersonal and tepid. "Fine," I said testily. "You mess with your fraud, and I'll look into the murder."

"Tom" turned to look at me over the back of his seat. He was smiling again.

I HOPED THAT when we got to the Reno office of the Bureau of Land Management, the two FBI agents would introduce themselves by their real names, but they showed their identification to the receptionist rather than speaking their names. "We're here to see Stephen Giles," the younger agent said.

The woman picked up her phone and dialed. A few minutes later, the man they had asked to see appeared at the front desk and led us down a hallway to a small conference room.

From the first moment, something about Stephen Giles struck me as odd, or at least unusual, but it took me some minutes to analyze exactly what. I suppose I was already looking for even the slightest support for the theory I had formed in the car on the way from the airport, and he was handy; except that after meeting him, I promoted him from information sieve to possible murderer.

I couldn't help staring at him. He was just below average height, about five foot eight, and though he held himself as straight as a dancer, he lacked a dancer's poetry of motion. He was dressed in chinos and a polo shirt, and wore white leather athletic shoes. And this last he appeared to fill honestly. He was not athletic, exactly, but fit. Healthy, or should I say, lacking in physical ailment. His legs were nicely shaped, and his slacks fit him exceptionally well, but for some reason the effect did not appeal to the woman in me. That was odd, but what really set my mental buzzers off was something in his expression and overall bearing, an oddity of affect which seemed to hang over him like a mist: he seemed weirdly absent, like a pre-recorded holographic projection rather than the actual man.

"Hello," he said dolefully. "I'm Stephen Giles." As he spoke, he looked anywhere but at any of us, and his face was pinched up with the pensive, slightly pained expression of a man who is here but dearly wishes to be somewhere—or sometime—else; in fact, he seemed to have already faded halfway there.

The effect was not just visual. As the agents asked questions, his answers consistently lagged a beat or two behind the moments I expected them, as if his voice was being relayed from outer space.

The man who called himself Tom Latimer asked, "Have you come up with anything new since we last spoke on the phone?"

Stephen Giles paused. "I hadn't expected you to follow up so quickly. I hope you haven't come all this distance for nothing."

"You just let me worry about that, Mr. Giles," the agent replied. "This is nice the way you have the file all laid out on the table for us. Very pretty. No, you stay," he added, as Giles began to fade toward the door. "We'll need you every inch of the way."

Giles hung his head despondently. I wondered at his lack of interest in a case he had brought to their attention.

"Why don't you give me a thumbnail on this situation," I suggested. "I'm a geologist. I'm here because this case connects with gold mining somehow."

Giles looked directly at me for the first time—at my nose, my clothes, my ears, but not my eyes—sadly mapping me into some provisional anteroom of his universe. He glanced quickly at the two FBI agents, who nodded. He sighed. Then he said, "Well, yes, this involves geology—gold mining—but only peripherally."

"Just how peripherally?" the younger agent asked.

Giles stared into space. He seemed so preoccupied that he had, in a matter of seconds, forgotten we were there.

"How is the BLM involved?" I prompted.

Giles took a breath and let it out. "Granville Resources bought up the old claims to the mineral rights on the property in question, but it's federal land. The BLM manages it. They want permits to drill exploratory holes. Look for precious metals." He laid a hand almost passively on a map that lay in the center of the conference table, then pushed his hand forward until the index finger lined up with the boundary of a smaller area marked "Phase I: Proposed roads and drilling positions are marked in red."

I glanced at the index map near the edge of the map. Phase I lay at the south end of a range marked Kamma Mountains, which lay about fifty miles north of the town of Lovelock, and about a hundred miles northeast of Reno.

"In order to develop their claims, they need to drill test holes, and test holes require access roads and drilling pads," Giles said.

I took a step toward him, purposefully crowding him to see what happened, and said, "The claims are on federal land, so the General Mining Law of 1872 governs the mineral rights, correct?"

"Yes," he replied, stepping sideways away from me.

"Any Tom, Dick, or Harry can claim the minerals, but they have to prove out the claim," I continued, taking another step toward him. "But Granville has bought up old claims, presumably ones that have already had some mining activity."

"Yes." Having fetched up near the wall, Giles began to stiffen, as if contracting into a protective shell. He continued to avoid eye contact. "Yes. But nowadays we require that certain environmental measures be observed. Especially for potentially large projects like this one, we require that an environmental impact report be filed. Granville hired a consultant to make certain that the project would pose no threat for endangered species."

"And Patricia Gilmore was that consultant." I took one more step closer.

"Yes. No."

"Which was it?" I said, now extending my neck toward him. I peered into his face.

"She was part of a team," he said, a piquant whine slithering into his voice. His defensiveness screamed to me that he had something to hide. I turned up the heat even farther. "I saw a lot of smoke from a range fire as we were flying in today. It was near Lovelock. Is that where Ms. Gilmore was working, perchance?"

My question got a clear reaction. Stephen Giles stopped breathing for a moment.

The older FBI agent now stepped toward him and asked his own question, his tone unnaturally soft. "Is there something about that fire that's bothering you, Stephen?"

Giles stuttered slightly as he replied. "Th-there have been a lot already this year. Cheat grass."

"Cheat grass?" the older agent inquired.

Giles' face contorted into a sickly ghost of someone trying to be winning, and his voice carried the slight sing-song of one reciting a prepared script. "Yes. Big problem. It's a short-lived annual, an exotic that came in with the cattle. It makes a poor forage for the antelope and other native fauna."

I said, "Endangered native fauna."

Giles did not reply. His head pitched forward and he stared at the section of floor that lay a few inches in front of his shoes.

"So Patricia Gilmore was part of a team?" I persisted.

Giles spoke to the floor. "It has the potential of being a very big project."

"Open pit?"

After a moment, Giles said, "Perhaps."

I pondered this. Another hole in the ground like the one I'd seen from the air would indeed be a big project. "If that open pit happens to replace the favored nesting ground of some dwindling species of bird or fox or lizard, or worse yet, the only known habitat of same, then there will be no project, eh? Scratch one source of jewelry and cell phone connections."

A subtle riffle of anger swept across Giles' face.

The older FBI agent said, "Quit beating up on the witness, Em."

I didn't care what Mr. FBI What's-his-name said, this guy bothered me. And yes, I was beginning to behave badly. "So tell me why you wanted the FBI to talk to Patricia Gilmore," I insisted.

At this question, Stephen Giles turned quite pale. He stared forlornly at the maps and memos he had spread out on the table. His eyes went out of focus. Then he flinched slightly, as if awakening with a start, and said quickly, "She had in fact found an endangered species, or one we think might be endangered. But her reports here say it's not." He sighed again, a long, pitiful exhalation of breath, and his voice slipped back into a whine. "In fact, her numbers say it's increasing its range."

8

M GRETCHEN

KYLE CHRISTIE BRAKED HIS RENTED FORD EX-
plorer to a stop and contemplated his next move. This was a
novel activity for him, because without Donald Paul Mac-
Callum, he had no next move. Up until now, he had successfully obscured this fact from the management of Granville
Resources, and it was important that he kept that deal going.
Up until now, he had been able to stay in the game by keeping
track of MacCallum. But this morning—of all Goddamned
mornings to choose—MacCallum had vanished.

MacCallum had not been in his room at the Desert View
Motel in Lovelock—Kyle had peered through the open curtains onto his empty, unruffled bed, just to double check. No
Don, and Rita had confirmed that he hadn't paid up and left,
and neither had he been across the road in the cafe at Sturgeon's Casino. And, as Gretchen's early morning call would
attest, MacCallum was not in Denver. Inquiry by telephone
had also proved that he was not at Granville Resources' re-
gional offices in Reno. And he was not in the hospital, or the
morgue. These last Kyle had deduced from a conversation
with the Pershing County Sheriff's deputy who had inter-
rupted Kyle's own breakfast at Sturgeon's.

"What do you know about Patricia Gilmore's death?" the
deputy had asked, rather nastily. R. WEEBE, his name-plate
read. He was a short man with a spreading waist. Even standing up with some rather high-heeled cowboy boots on, the
deputy's eye level had barely matched Kyle's.

Kyle had slumped slightly on his cafe stool to see under
the brim of the deputy's hat. Weebe's jaw muscles had tightened. Kyle's pulse had raced as the sure knowledge that he
had already blown this interview hit his brain stem. How he
hated short men who hated him for being tall. Little did this
one know that, no matter how short or tall, officers of the

law, just like officers of corporations, had, even on the best
of days, only one effect on Kyle: he wanted immediately to
find a dark place to hide until whatever was happening was
over.

"It was an accident, wasn't it?" Kyle had asked Deputy
Weebe in answer, slipping reflexively into the "don't ask me,
I'm a dumb shit" tone of voice at which he was so adept, and
which now, reviewing his performance in the relative safety
of the vast open desert landscape, he realized angrily must be
part of why dregs like Weebe so easily pushed him around.

Kyle's mind nattered at him like a chattering monkey, continuing to replay the scene at Sturgeon's Casino. The deputy
had not replied to his question. Instead, after an unnervingly
long moment, the deputy had demanded to know, "Where's
this guy MacCallum this morning?"

Kyle's stomach had loosened half a notch as he deduced
two things: that MacCallum was not sick or dead, because
deputies tended to be up on such statistics, and that the deputy
was more interested in MacCallum than he. So Kyle had replied with yet another question: "Why do you guys need to
talk to Don P. about Pat?"

The deputy had been chewing on a toothpick. He had
moved it around so dexterously that Kyle had recognized the
artistry of long habit, and had watched with tense fascination
as the deputy's toothpick du jour worked the rubbery folds at
one corner of his mouth. Kyle's overheated brain had struggled abstractedly to match this grotesque effect to previously-
observed patterns that now niggled at the edges of his
memory. MacCallum had explained this phenomenon to him:
"Us geologists are wired that way, Kyle. It's how the intuitive
mind works. Our brains gather data—in any order, and it
doesn't have to be complete—and we're constantly trying to
form a coherent pattern from the random information we're
seeing. Little glimpses of things. And *bang*, as soon as it
looks like anything we've ever seen or heard about before,
we have a pattern. Or *wham*, if the picture is entirely new,
then *that's* our pattern. Brain files it away for reference. Compare, contrast. Themes and variations. This is like that, only

a little bit different, but still it fits such-and-such category. It's qualitative, Kyle. Screw the numbers. If you want to do gold exploration, you've got to be loose."

Confronted with the way that toothpick creased the sheriff's cheek, Kyle had taken a quick breath and let it out, as MacCallum had taught him, trying to kick his conscious mind out of the loop so that the intuitive levels MacCallum swore lay beneath it could rise and advise him. For once, MacCallum's exercise had worked, as Kyle realized with a jolt that the deputy's skin was deforming exactly the way Kyle's deflated bicycle tire had when he had tried to pop it over the wheel rim with a screwdriver. That was just before the screwdriver had slipped and gouged a ragged hole though the palm of his hand.

That image was so discomforting that it had taken Kyle several seconds to return mentally to the cafe and the rubber-faced deputy, only to discover that the intimidating little shithead was belligerently asking, "I *said*, why do you want to *know*?"

To which Kyle had replied, "Huh?" letting his own mouth sag open.

The deputy had responded with a dose of the old yo'-in-a-peck-o'-trouble-boy stare. "You interest me," he had said. "Pat Gilmore's dead. Sheriff Obernick tol' me he figgers it for an accident, bad luck, *que lástima* Pat Gilmore. But I ain't so quick to dismiss such a tragic end to a life so young and full of purpose. And now here you sit lookin' kinda uneasy about the whole situation. That bears watching."

Kyle had tried looking less stupid and more innocent, but had managed only to look like his breakfast was giving him gas. *Hell*, he thought, *I was born guilty, the way these assholes treat me*, but he said, "Well, we can all be thankful that she was on your side of the county line when she flipped that pickup, or her death would have been dismissed before lunch time. I admire that in a law enforcement individual, Deputy Weebe, sir." He pronounced the name "weeb," one syllable.

Weebe's toothpick had stopped in mid-gyration with a crunch. With heavy contempt and a spicing of menace, he

had said, "That's Wee-be," and had added, "son," even
though the deputy was at least fifteen years younger than
Kyle. "Get it right."

"Thank you, Deputy," Kyle had answered. "I'll keep that
in mind."

"You do that," the deputy had said, then strolled off to a
table, where he'd sat down and ordered three eggs scrambled,
toast, and a rasher of bacon.

Kyle had made a show of taking his own sweet time eating
the rest of his hash browns, toast, and eggs, even though they
now went down like plaster of Paris, and he had even ordered
a lingering third cup of coffee to make certain that this Weebe
creep got bored and left before he did. Because Kyle could
not stand to tuck his tail quite so far between his legs as to
slink off like a flea-bitten dog. And because he had not
wanted to be followed as he drove out here to look for
MacCallum.

Now, as Kyle set the parking brake, stepped down onto
the dirt road, and relieved himself of the daughter products
of that coffee onto an anthill, he meditated bitterly upon his
meeting with the deputy and tried to decide which of the
narrow, twin-rut dirt tracks that left from here to try first. Kyle
found himself hurrying as he rebuttoned his fly, his fingers
as stiff as if the Deputy were standing there watching him.
He'd definitely fucked up somehow, he decided; the memory
of the interview was sticking to him like a booger he could
not dislodge from his finger. Furious, Kyle fantasized that he
could fling the sticky little deputy into the anthill and watch
the hungry little insects rip him to shreds.

Forcing his mind back to the business at hand, Kyle
scanned the sweeping curves of the yellow and brown landscape, again just as MacCallum had taught him. He turned
slowly in a full circle, examining the flanks of the mountain
ranges that surrounded him. MacCallum was out here somewhere. He knew it. He could feel him like he could smell a
woman's scent long after she had left a room. He spat, dis-
gusted with himself. First bicycle tires and now women's perfume. MacCallum had always had this discomforting effect

on him. Sweat beaded up on Kyle's forehead. He swiped at it impatiently and told himself that the day was already getting hot.

MacCallum was here. Kyle scrambled mentally to classify this awareness as not a sexual connection, but a sensual one. A whore at the Bronco Betty had explained the distinction to him once, as she had first bumped his hand and then caressed it. As he'd looked into her vixen eyes, he had seen that she was playing with his mind. Yes, that was it, MacCallum had the same fucking quality as perfume—pervasive and teasing—and, just like the women who wore such scents, seemed always to have gotten there before him, no matter where 'there' was. He had known MacCallum for decades, had worked with him in Mexico, Bolivia, Australia, and all over Nevada; and always, *always* The Don had found whatever precious metal they were looking for like it had been lying on the ground while he, Kyle, stumbled about like a blind man. The goons up the corporate ladder fucking *loved* MacCallum, let him wander in and out as he pleased, whacking at a rock sample here and there, and leave the details to some poor shithead down the line. *And*, Kyle thought bitterly, *I am that shithead. They seem to forget that I'm his partner, not his assistant!*

At the same time, I love the son of a bitch. Kyle shook his head, exhausted by his thoughts. He squeezed his eyes shut, trying to fathom this. *Whether they know it or not, Granville needs me*, he told himself. *Because without me, MacCallum would never stay focused. Just look at him. Things get a little hot, and he wanders off somewhere.*

Kyle opened his eyes again and scanned the desert basin in which he and his vehicle stood, hoping for the telltale wisp of dust that would indicate the movement of another vehicle. He saw none. He faced west. Short, sparse grasses danced in the wind, and the cobalt blue sky stretched on past the dry mountains toward the Black Rock Desert and California and Oregon beyond. He crouched down and squinted sideways at the grasses. By following subtle interruptions in their dance, he could trace the faint trails left by the passage of even one off-road vehicle, a trick who else but Don MacCallum had taught him. On this day he could discern only the local branch of the Emigrant Trail, the Applegate-Lassen spur that led over to Rabbithole Springs, and that was a well-beaten track. He scanned the mountains once again. He saw the divots left by an earlier generation of gold exploration, tiny interruptions in the pattern of desert scrub that could only have been made by some mad prospector's feverish scrabbling with pick and shovel. But he could not see MacCallum's beige Ford Explorer. The crafty old piss brain always rented beige, the better to blend in with his surroundings. He'd laughingly told Kyle it made him harder to spot.

Kyle cursed under his breath, climbed back into the dark green Explorer that he had rented, and turned the vehicle to the north, choosing the graded dirt road instead of the faint track. Why risk getting stuck when he really had no idea where the son of a bitch was?

As the air conditioner whooshed into action and cooled his brain, he impulsively spun the wheel, veering off onto a road that led to the west into Rosebud Canyon. Perhaps the old squatter who lived up there would know where MacCallum had gone. Then he hesitated, once again braking the vehicle to a stop. It would take him a while to prepare himself for a conversation with that old crapper. Pulling the Explorer to the edge of the road, he lowered the windows to keep the heat from reaching unbearable levels inside the cab, switched off the ignition and adjusted the seat, laying the back as close to horizontal as it would go, closed his eyes, and let his mind drift in the languid channels it most preferred to navigate.

9

"I CAN'T CALL YOU BOTH TOM LATIMER," I announced as we rolled northeast along Interstate 80 from Reno toward Lovelock. "Stephen Giles might not care who the hell you are and never even ask your names, but I do."

"You do what?" asked Tom Latimer the First.

"Care. Who in hell you are. I care. Or should I just call you J. Edgar Hoover?"

The younger agent laughed as he took one hand off the wheel and offered it to me. "Sebastian Walker. You can call me Ian."

I shook his hand, then turned around and stared at the older man, who sat lounging in the backseat with his eyes once again closed. Feeling my scrutiny, he opened one eye and stuck out a long, dry hand. "Theodore. You can call me Ted."

I took his hand and shook it. "Ted who?"

He opened the other eye. "Roosevelt. I think we're cousins, Eleanor dear."

I popped open my seat belt, leaned over the seat back and tried to punch him. Both men roared with laughter.

As their laughter died down, I hung there on the seat back and stared into "Ted's" eyes for a while. He stared back. He was playing a game with me, and I didn't like it one bit. And I wondered why he felt the need to manipulate me like this. I liked playing things straight up and out in the open, doing business cleanly and without the power plays. When I'd worked with him on the dinosaur case, he had been more . . . I thought a while, trying to put my finger on the difference I was encountering in the man. On that case, he had been covert because his work required it, but he had stayed out of my face. He had been more respectful.

Still hanging over the back of the seat, I said, "Your identification, please."

He stared at me blankly.

I took a breath, flaring my nostrils in anger. "Now!"

He pulled a leather wallet out of a pocket and opened it. I found myself looking at a Utah state driver's license. Which belonged to Thomas J. Latimer.

"Oh," I said numbly. "Some days a cigar is just a cigar."

His expression still blank, he returned the wallet to his pocket, re-closed his eyes, and folded his arms across his chest.

I twisted back to face forward, slumped down into my seat, and scowled out at the desert landscape through which we were traveling. I was out in the middle of nowhere, all right, but my problems had come with me, and it seemed I had a new one who was in fact named Tom Latimer.

The desert is a place that usually calms me. To the left of the road were low brown hills with mountains beyond; to the right, a glimpse into the Carson Sink, a bleached white tract of salt pans where the last trickles of the Carson River lay desiccating in the rising heat. The temperature had begun to rise by the time we had left the BLM office, and now was ticking its way into the nineties. I lowered the window and stuck an arm out to feel the hot dry air blast past the palm of my hand, and wished I were alone so I could remember who I was and where I thought I was going.

Five minutes' meditation did nothing to sort out my emotional life, so I decided instead to focus on the so-called job that had been laid before me. I said, "Much as I'm enjoying this sojourn in the Silver State, I am at something of a loss to understand why we're still here. I mean, didn't we fly in here to talk to someone who no longer counts herself among the living?"

"Mmm-hm," the man in the backseat murmured.

"Then case closed. Why aren't we on our way home? That guy Giles sure seemed to think the game was over. Or wanted us to think it was."

J. Edgar Theodore Tom Latimer Roosevelt Hoover stretched and yawned. "We began this investigation at the request of the BLM, yes, but that doesn't mean we end it at their convenience."

"Huh?"

Tom spread out one broad, flat palm and drew an imaginary diagram on it. "It goes like this. The BLM gave us a whistle because, it has been alleged, Patricia Gilmore might be salting the numbers regarding how many of a certain species were present on land Granville Resources wants to develop into a possible mine. Granville has put together a limited partnership and bought up some old claims and filled in with some new ones—"

"The 1872 mining law," I interjected.

With a hint of condescension, Ian said, "Yes, Em, they get to claim the minerals that they as citizens already own." Then he moderated his tone and continued. "Their idea has been to form a district out of some old mining prospects. Some of the claims go back quite a way. There's a lot of history here. Some of the districts were first prospected by men who came across with the wagon trains in 1849 or earlier. Of course, the land itself belongs to the federal government, and must be tended in a way that supports the common good—i.e., Granville can't just go after the minerals like miners used to do. They have to pay rent, and to do anything with the land, they have to get permits—approval for grading roads and exploratory drilling pads—and they have to restore all disused roads and such to their original condition."

"Thank you, Ian," I said, repressing an urge to call him professor. "Now, if this exploratory drilling actually locates mineable gold, do you suppose it will be an underground mine, or open pit? Either would impact the environment, but the open pit will at least initially more strongly impact the flora and fauna. We don't want to shrink the wee critters' habitat so far that we kill them off."

"Some of the newer mines around here are open pit, others are underground," he said vaguely.

I said, "But even underground mining disrupts the habitat. There are roads and culverts leading up to it, and more importantly, stockpiles and ponds. They cover acres, and possibly the same acres the endangered species like. So tell me, is the species in question in fact endangered?" I asked.

Ian said, "Well, there's a save-the-desert organization that's been hassling Granville, and apparently also our pal Giles."

I said, "So Giles wants off the hot seat, right? Citizens arguing? Call out the FBI!"

Tom answered with soft laughter.

A bit defensively, Ian said, "I don't take Giles for the final arbiter of government policy, either, but it's not his job to direct policy, only to enforce it. The save-the-desert guys get all in an uproar, screaming that the mining practices wreak havoc on the environment." He whipped his hands off the wheel in a pantomime of an old lady scared by a mouse.

Ian's attitude was beginning to rankle me. There was a presumption of correctness in his tone, and worse yet, a presumption of entitlement. As a geologist who made her living looking for oil, I was hardly on the side of the angels where pure environmentalism was concerned, but I didn't think that our exploitation of resources went without an impact worth pondering. Challenging the tone of voice that Ian was using, I said, "I'll bet the environmentalists especially distrust the deep open-pit mining, because if they mine below the water table, they have to pump like hell to keep the groundwater from flooding the workings. They pump the deeper underground mines, too. And dropping the water table even locally might change the plant community, which of course is the food supply for the poor little endangered species, whatever it is."

"It's a mouse," Ian said.

"A mouse?" I asked, incredulous. "This is all about *mice*? The people who call themselves environmentalists don't really care about *mice*! If they ever found so much as a wee mouse turd in the silverware drawer of one of their swanky kitchens they'd be setting traps and laying out strychnine cocktails in five tenths of a nanosecond, and you bet they wouldn't file an environmental impact report first."

Ian said, "Or how about the yahoo who burns fossil fuels

to make a special trip to the convenience store in his forty-thousand-dollar car that was made in Japan of iron ores refined in the U.S. to buy a latté made from beans grown on South American slopes that are now eroding like hell because the forest's been stripped off to plant coffee?" He took a breath. "And then drives home and gets on the Internet and sends fifty e-mails to lobby to shut down the 'unecological' mining operations that produced the iron for his car and the gold that makes those mystical little electronic connections in his computer work!"

I was sorry I'd got him started. It wasn't that I didn't agree with him, at least in part; it was the judgmental attitude that bothered me. I'd learned a long time ago that judgment could be a way of avoiding part of the truth. "Temper, temper," I said.

Ian shrugged his shoulders. "That jackass with the latté is really just boo-hooing over the endangered mouse as a tool to obstruct the mining."

"There I agree," I said. "That's using science in the service of politics. A basic distortion of the process. I just wish people would stand up and say, I want to stop this mining. It looks bad to me. I don't trust it. Then we could all come out in the open and compare notes and make an informed decision about which land to mine, and which to leave as a place to go when we need peace and quiet, and which to leave to the blessed little mice."

"We have a system sort of like that, don't we?" Tom said, smiling. "Scrape off a half-ton of pork-barrel politics, and that's what we call Congress."

"You'll have to scrape off the lobbyists, too," I said. "I think 'One Man, One Vote' became 'One Dollar, One Vote' a while ago. I wish I had your faith in government."

As a scientist, I knew how intricately everything in our ecosystem was linked together. Nature has no true islands. A volcano erupts in the South Pacific, dumping ash into the upper atmosphere, and the climate starts to shift. Ten thousand miles away in the Great Basin, it might contribute to a bad season for grass growth and mouse reproduction, and a certain number of coyotes were going to die. That was all just how it was. But here I was, the highest predator the planet had produced, speeding across the desert in an automobile, unlinked from climatic imperatives. Even the lunch I ate this day would have arrived by truck from somewhere else. The impact of my actions would be infinitely harder to define.

"Just tell me about this mouse," I sighed.

Ian shot me a guarded look and said, "Well, mice it is. A kangaroo mouse, to be exact, *Microdipodops megacephalus*. And the only way this mouse is going to get into your silverware drawer is if you carry it out into the Kamma Mountains and leave it there for them. It occurs on the slopes of just a few mountain ranges in northwestern Nevada. In fact, it was not even known to occur *there* until Granville Resources bought up the claims and began to examine their holdings."

I heaved a sigh. "Okay, let me see if I understand all this. Granville wants to develop a mining claim. Certain interests would prefer that they not. The BLM says that to build roads and drill test holes, they have to get permits."

Ian said, "The law further stipulates that in an environmentally sensitive area, they have to file an environmental impact report before they can get those permits."

I said, "And the anti-mining interests have perhaps used the presence of the mice to say that the environmental impact would mean good-bye mice. But Pat Gilmore's preliminary work showed that the mice were multiplying rather than decreasing in numbers, and perhaps even broadening their range. Granville would love it if these rodents were not endangered, and the anti-mining interests might in fact be disappointed."

Ian curled his upper lip in a sneer. "That would depend on whether they were in fact pro-mouse, or just anti-mining."

I turned a palm upward. "So then what's the problem? Can't the BLM just do its job? Or do they think Pat Gilmore sold out to Granville? Or do they have some agenda they're not telling us about?" As Ian's lips began to curl again, I hastened to add, "Forgive my skepticism, but as I think I made clear, my antennae perk up wherever science meets self-interest."

Tom said, "That's exactly why I brought you along, Em."

I turned around in my seat and studied him closely. His eyes were closed, as if he were once again asleep. I said, "Maybe I should be asking this differently: What's all this got to do with the FBI?"

Tom took a moment before answering, his eyes still closed. "That's simple. It has been suggested that, for whatever reason, Pat Gilmore was knowingly presenting incorrect results. That is fraud. On federal land, that means the feds have to step in and settle the squabble."

"But isn't it a little unusual that you would be called in this early? Doesn't the BLM have some internal way of dealing with such matters?"

Tom opened one eye and stared at me, his expression unreadable. "Yes. But the BLM called, and we ride." The eye closed.

We ride. For a moment, I contemplated the thought of Tom Latimer as Cavalry scout. He would have been good: The lone smart guy who rides ahead of the soldiers, scopes out the situation, reports to the general, and then has the brains to scram out of there before the bullets and arrows start flying. The poor man had been born about a hundred and fifty years too late.

And he was still holding back an important part of the story, I could feel it in my bones. I asked, "So what do we do first, Kimosabe?"

He opened that eye again. "We check her story."

"How?"

The eye closed. He resettled himself in his apparent slumber. "Oh, you know the game; you poke around here and there. First you talk to the guy who gave your BLM guy the idea that something was wrong."

"Who? Someone who works for the save-the-desert people?"

"No, there's another certified, bona fide wildlife biologist from the same company who says she kited her figures. He's the man we're about to meet."

10

Virgil Davis shot a hand out to stop the me-
chanical pencil on his drafting table from rattling as a thirty-
ton ore truck rumbled past the corrugated steel building in
which he sat. He sighed, his heavy shoulders slumping with
fatigue. This bit with the permitting did not bode well for the
speedy advancement of the new project, and a speedy advance
was what he needed, now that the price of gold had fallen
even farther into the toilet and cut his operating margin to the
quick. He needed to get a new property on line to provide
the correct economy of scale. To move forward with the job
of creative finesse that was called mining. To stay employed
at all. The new project would be higher grade—more gold
per ton of ore—it just *had* to.

He lifted his eyes to a luridly-colored cross-stitched sampler his third wife had made for him just before she gave up
and filed for a divorce on the grounds that they never saw
each other anyway, so why not make it official? The sampler
read, in Gothic type: FAST, ACCURATE, CHEAP; CHOOSE ANY
TWO. Marilyn had understood him, he thought dolefully. He
shouldn't have let her get away. God knew he could finesse
only two out of three where it came to mining gold.

Mining. The image of Gabby Hayes flooded his mind,
playing the canny, presumptuously optimistic old prospector
with the bullet hole through his hat brim and his sleepy burro
trailing along behind him carrying the gold pan and pickaxe.
The term "prospector" conjured a semi-perjorative image for
some mining professionals: uneducated, limited in his means,
growing older and more grizzled by the minute, foolishly
throwing his life away for a dream of riches. The modern,
university-educated gold-seeker preferred to be called a geologist or engineer, depending on his training and his task.
Or *her* training and task. The world had changed since Vir-

gil's early days in the industry. It took all kinds of people with all kinds of talents to do a job as complex as mining, and some of them these days were female. Here he sat, devoting his life to the quest for gold, doing his own piece of the job in his own way. He was not an optimist. He was a pessimist, but that was a good thing. *I am a pessimist because I understand risk,* he told himself, *and understanding risk means I can keep people as safe as possible while they mine the gold that others have found.* Others. Optimists like Donald Paul MacCallum.

Virgil realigned his mechanical pencil with the edge of his pad of lined yellow paper, savoring the ritual with the defensive satisfaction that went with his refusal to commit his records directly into the state-of-the-art computer which sat behind him on his seldom-used desk. He begrudged computers. He was a staggering analog dinosaur in the land of fleet-footed digital mammals. Two jobs and eight years earlier, when a computer had first appeared on his desk, he had gritted his teeth and learned to work with it, because otherwise, he knew, he would quickly fall by the wayside, old and anachronistic at fifty. But he didn't have to devote himself to the damned machines, or give them his innermost thoughts.

His thoughts flicked painfully back to the subject of the new project, and from there, inevitably to MacCallum, and to the way their confrontation of the day before had gone. The application for Phase I drilling was hopelessly bogged down, and he had to have a map from MacCallum to apply for permitting for Phase II. Any fool could see that. Bile rose again to his throat at the memory of how, when he asked for that map, MacCallum had perched languidly on the drafting stool—the very one on which Virgil now sat—and had cocked his head back in thought, as if schedules and the requirement that they make a goddamn profit were new concepts to him. What in hell's name had Chittenden been thinking of, sticking him with a clown like MacCallum to head up exploration?

Virgil shuddered slightly at the memory of their first meeting two years before, at Granville's corporate headquarters.

Virgil had arrived straight off a plane from South Africa, where he'd been bridging a gap in his personal cash flow with a pick-up consulting job on the exploitation of a buried placer. He'd been jet-lagged and needed a shower and a good night's sleep between clean sheets. But stateside jobs were devilishly hard to come by these days, and the foreigners had all gotten smart and sent their own sons to American schools and taken over the overseas mining industry, and it was only because Granville had an ambitious new president that this job had opened up. So he hadn't dared keep his new employers waiting. Instead, he had pulled a clean shirt, a necktie, and a slightly creased suit jacket out of his luggage during the cab ride in from the airport and had dodged off the elevator and into the men's room a floor below Granville's offices and done his best to freshen up at the sink. It was a nice tie. Gwen, his first wife, had given it to him. Or had it been Ramona, his second wife? Anyway, he'd washed his face and armpits and had put on the clean shirt and stuffed the dirty one down between his passport and the foreign issue of *Time* magazine in his attache. Then he'd plastered down his thinning grey hair with a comb and water, and had forced himself to brace his shoulders and stand up straight. Peering at himself in the mirror, he had worried about the pouchiness of the skin around his eyes, and had tried in vain to condense it with a compress of cold water applied with a paper towel from the dispenser, but had given up, because time was ticking by. All this had been a Herculean effort as tired as he was, but that's what you did if you wanted to stay at the top of this profession, or in it, for that matter. And then he'd gotten back onto the elevator and gone up the one last floor and had cleared his mind as best he could and tried to look cool and purposeful as he strode into the president's office . . . and there next to the president's desk had been Donald Paul Mac-Callum. In field boots, a stained T-shirt, frayed blue jeans, and ten days' growth of beard, lounging on a soft leather chair with one goddamn leg slung over the arm, for crissake. MacCallum had hardly acknowledged his arrival, so busy had he been laughing and telling jokes. Like he was at a fucking barbecue or something, swapping lies with his neighbor over Budweisers. And the president, in his pin-striped three-piece Saville Row suit, had thought MacCallum brilliant. Until his dying day Virgil would think that he had hallucinated that scene.

At length, the president, Roderick James Adrian Chittenden, had turned to him and said, "Ah, Virgil Davis, isn't it? How was your flight? You look beat, man. Why didn't you stop at a hotel and get rested before coming in?"

The room had begun to sway underneath Virgil's exhausted legs. Virgil had tried to focus on MacCallum as a way of shocking himself awake, but what he saw was a man who appeared as relaxed as if God had made his backbone of jelly.

Chittenden had turned back to MacCallum and said, "Don, this is Virgil Davis, the man who's going to scrabble your gold out of the ground."

"Glad to meetcha," MacCallum had said jovially.

His beaming countenance still aimed toward MacCallum, the president had pronounced, "And Virgil, this is Don MacCallum, the man who's going to find even more of that good stuff!"

MacCallum had laughed uproariously, even slapped his knee with merriment.

"And this is Kyle Christie," Chittenden had continued, gesturing toward a tall, blondish man who stood blending in with the curtains to MacCallum's right. "He works with MacCallum."

Kyle had extended a limp hand with all the affect of a dog rolling over to show another its belly, a look of acquiescence rounding his oatmeal-soft face. Virgil's heart had sunk. If this was what Granville had for a project-generation team, he gave his tenure at the company about six months.

But Chittenden had a grand scheme: Having now charged Virgil with the task of transforming MacCallum's discovery into an efficient, state-of-the-art mine, he had formed a limited partnership and bought a bucketful of old lease-hold corporations—faded hopefuls bristling with derelict claims that had

closed down in the 1930's—for pennies on the dollar. Most
such acquisitions involved only producing reserves, but Chittenden had slapped his investors on the back and rubbed his
hands with glee and insisted that, just as he had done at Gloriana, MacCallum would again find reserves just a little bit
deeper than the places where prospectors and miners of the
1930s—the last brief gold rush in the area—had given up and
stopped digging. If MacCallum could do it once, he told them,
he could do it again. Gold which the technology of the 1930's
had missed, that was his target. "It will be another Carlin
trend," Chittenden told his investors, pointing on the map to
the line of immense open-pit operations a hundred miles to
the east. "Except that, unlike the Carlin trend, the ore will be
higher grade, like the Gloriana . . . a line of riches such as
Nevada has never seen!"

Virgil didn't need a geologist like MacCallum or Christie
or anyone else to explain to him that Chittenden had been
talking blue sky to the investors. The Carlin trend was half a
state away, a completely different mineral province. They
might find some kind of trend here, but it would be funda-
mentally different mineralogically, and require as always a
unique system of mining and milling to extract it from the
ground. That was where his years of experience and own
brand of creativity would shine. And he knew that such ventures were risky. He knew that Chittenden's bluster had been
based on his need to loosen dollars from the investors' hands,
but at the same time, he dearly hoped that the plan would
work. It was optimistic, and optimism was the very heart of
exploration.

And MacCallum had found something, he was sure, even
though the bastard was playing it tight on him; something at
least worth taking to the next level, exploratory drilling. But
the permitting process had suddenly grown difficult, with this
damned save-the-desert gang pissing and moaning to the
BLM.

Virgil stared out the window over a line of moveable metal
storage sheds at the view beyond. From his perch here at the
Gloriana Mine, high on the flanks of the Eugene Mountains,

he enjoyed a panoramic view of the Majubas, the Antelope Range, the Jackson Mountains, and the Kamma Mountains beyond them. Or would enjoy the view, if his heart had been capable of feeling joy. Today, he was so exhausted from worry that his eyes dropped from the panorama to one of the metal sheds, to the spot where someone had left the bar that latched the heavy, double-hung doors ten degrees askew. Such untidiness irritated him beyond words. It was the kind of sloth MacCallum would thrive in. Geologists were half crazy, or totally so. He was sure of it.

A few hundred feet beyond the row of metal sheds, outside the eight-foot chain link security fence with razor wire he had erected, stood the trailer in which the biologists from Intermontane Biological Consultants now lurked. This trailer had been Virgil's embryonic field office. Trouble with the save-the-desert crazies had started almost as soon as he had set that trailer on the site. Trouble. And not just the nightmares that had robbed his sleep—ghastly images of the bodies of miners crushed under countless tons of rock, of his own body pinned and dying—but the daytime events that helped fuel them. Like that woman with the ruined face, who had come with those Paiute women who burned bundles of sage. The Paiute had told him, "If you want the nightmares to stop, you'll move."

How had she known about those dreams?

The two women had carried on like that for days, and two women had become ten, and then twenty, as the tree-huggers in Volvos with the long skirts and beauty-shop hair had streamed in from California to help them badger him.

Finally, in desperation, he had stormed out there and said, "Just where in hell do you think I should move *to?*"

The Paiute had taken him aside and said, "About eight hundred feet north. Move your mill and office, and the decline."

"The decline?" he had roared, flabbergasted that this woman even knew this term. "You mean my main tunnel? You been down at the BLM looking at my maps?"

"Yes. Move them north eight hundred feet. It's better rock,

anyway," she had said softly. "It might save you."

So he had filed new plans with the BLM, moving the siting of the offices and mill eight hundred feet north. Then, weirdly, the women had left, and had not come back. But still the dreams came, until one day he had seen the Paiute woman in town. "You said the dreams would stop."

"Did you move the decline?"

"We haven't even started digging yet!" he had said, feeling ashamed and foolish. The fact was that, now that they were gone, he had figured to sink the decline in the original position.

Without blinking, she had said, "You must learn to thank the Spirit for everything She gives you. Thank Her for not throwing Her rocks on top of you. Thank Her for that food in your stomach. Think of every speck of it as the gold you work so hard to get. Then the dreams will stop."

Virgil had recoiled from her words. They had reminded him too much of his Catholic boyhood, of a nun who had twisted his ear as she said, "If you touch a woman in anger or even just take her for granted, you are a rapist."

But, to keep the women from returning, he had moved the buildings and the portal so that the project could move forward. And, being at depth a superstitious man, he had begun to take the Indian's suggestion. Each time, before he stepped down into that portal, he had stopped and said a prayer, touching the rock with kindness and respect, humbling himself before the earth.

The dreams had stopped.

Moving the decline had required a slight deviation in the plan, but in fact the cost had been lower, because she had been right; the rock was better there, and excavation had gone more quickly.

Then that damned mouse had shown up in Pat Gilmore's survey. Now, the sad-faced shithead at the BLM was getting letters threatening lawsuits if the new project proceeded. At least the women had not come back here. And if they did come again, they would now be confronted by a chain link fence and security personnel. Virgil shook his head, still trying to understand what difference eight hundred feet could make. The irony was that he had chosen that original location for the portal because that ground was already disturbed from previous rounds of mining fifty or one hundred years before.

At least the nightmares had ended. The memory of what they had been like now hung about him like the haze of range fire smoke that still assaulted his sinuses. Virgil wondered sourly if MacCallum ever suffered such dreams. He ran his hands feverishly through his stubbly hair. Geologists were definitely insane. *Damn* MacCallum for his insanity.

He stood up to stretch his husky frame and wandered down the hallway into the common area where the employees got their coffee. He stared into MacCallum's mailbox, wincing as if the man might be in there ready to laugh at him again, but there was nothing there but an old newsletter from the Geological Society of Nevada. He pulled it out and read it. It was folded open to a running series of jokes entitled, "The Great Basin Experience."

"You might be a geologist," it began, "if you have worked in more countries than United Airlines flies to." Another said, "You might be a geologist if your spouse mows the lawn." And another, "If you have done a rollover from a 401K to your IRA more than once."

Virgil stuffed the newsletter back into the box with disgust. The damned geologists couldn't even tell themselves from mine superintendants. He wanted to add: "And if you've got so many ex-wives you're paying out in alimony more than you make." He pulled the newsletter back out of the box just to make certain that line wasn't already there. Another read, "If you don't know where you'll be tomorrow." Another, "If you get laid off almost every Christmas."

Virgil threw the newsletter into the trash, grabbed his fifth cup of coffee of the day, stalked back into his office, and slammed the door behind him.

As he settled back onto his drafting stool, another ore truck shook Virgil's table as it trundled by on the haulage road, another truck filled to the brim with his very highest grade ore. At the rate they were blasting here at the mine, they'd strip this site of its high-grade inside of a year, or at most, two. Then, either the price of gold would have to rise high enough to support production of lower grades—an event on the scale of pigs sprouting wings—or he'd have to find some new way of cutting his already excruciatingly tight costs—something like pigs inventing rocket ships. He needed a new hole to be digging or he'd soon find himself back on a plane to another banana republic preparing himself to fight some South African for the honor of absorbing daily doses of humidity, pidgin English, and anti-malarial drugs. Goddamn MacCallum, who would not cough up his assay results for Phase II, and double Goddamn Kyle Christie, who sat around in plain sight doing nothing while his fat salary and motel and car rental bills burned up the company's remaining profit margin. Why couldn't they just get on with it, and cough up another map? The permitting process was slow enough as it was, and the drilling would take months, even years, and perhaps hundreds of holes, if they were going to hope to find whatever was out there. They needed to get on with it!

A gentle tap at the door lifted him from the thin edges of despair back to present time and space. "Come in," he barked, trying to sound busier than he was.

The door opened. A fluff of wheat-blonde hair edged around it, and Laurel Dietz's blue blue eyes and unassuming smile brightened the room.

Virgil's heart constricted with the sudden pain of feeling something other than bewilderment and anger. *God keep me here at home. God spare me from staring into another sea of brown eyes.*

Laurel said, "Hiya, Virgil. I got the new samples all prepped and ready for shipment to the lab. Shall I load them onto the truck?"

Virgil might not ever get used to having women in a mine, but as long as they were here, he wished he had another twelve like her. Bright, able, quick, and *sweet*. "No, get one of those lazy boys out there to do that for you," he ordered.

Laurel's eyes widened, her way of indicating that something was funny. "That's sexist, Virgil. I got muscles." She yanked up one sleeve of her T-shirt and crooked a slender arm into a lampoon of a weight-lifter's pose.

"Aw, Laurel," Virgil murmured. He reached out one thick hand, hesitated a moment, then pulled it back. Her flaxen hair looked so soft and silky. Every time he saw her, he itched to touch it. He told himself it was because she wore it short and kind of messy, like his daughter did. Wendy would be about Laurel's age, wouldn't she? Yes, that was it, of course. He'd have to remember to write to Wendy, if he could find her address. . . .

"And I'm done logging things in, too. Would you like me to drive the stuff on over to Reno?"

"No, Laurel, that's a hell of a drive. I'll get one of the—"

Laurel put her tiny hands together in supplication. "*Please*, Virgil? I'm really bored. I've got all my assay locations input to the computer, and I've updated all the grade maps."

Virgil smiled in spite of his desperate mood. Laurel always cheered him up. "You got some boyfriend over there in the Olinghouse mine or something?" he chided. He wondered how their economics were running. Maybe they could use a new superintendent.

Laurel gave him more of her light-hearted, pop-eyed innocence in the form of polite silence.

Virgil wavered. "Okay, saddle up and take 'em on over there, even though that work's way beneath you." Then without thinking first what it might sound like, he added, "Really, I need you for more important things around here."

Laurel smiled vacantly and started to withdraw through the doorway.

Had that smile been a nervous one? "But first," Virgil added quickly, trying to keep his own nervousness out of his voice, "do you have any idea where MacCallum's got to?" As he said it, he felt a sudden surge of satisfaction, the first that day. It was good to leave a trail of misinformation in the form of such questions, so that no one would link MacCallum's disappearance to the argument they'd had.

Laurel replaced her grin with thoughtful blankness. "No,"

she said simply. She began to recede again, one bright blue eye disappearing behind the door and then the other.

"Or Christie, for that matter?"

"Nope. See ya, Virgil," Laurel caroled, her soft footfalls echoing slightly as she hurried down the vinyl-tiled hallway.

Half a minute later, Virgil heard the engine on a one-ton pickup roar to life, and seconds later saw it race past his office window with Laurel sitting primly at the wheel. As she paused briefly to check for cross-traffic before hurtling through the gate in the chain link fence and down the road that led toward Interstate 80, he noticed that the bed was already filled with the multitude of white sample sacks that she was ferrying to the lab.

He wondered dully why she hadn't told him that they were already loaded.

11

AT LOVELOCK, A RANCHING COMMUNITY NINETY
miles northeast of Reno, we turned off Interstate 80 in search
of the Pershing County courthouse to meet with the other
biologist from Intermontane Biological Consultants, the consulting firm for which Pat Gilmore had worked. We turned
down Lovelock's one short block of half-empty shops (as in
too many little Western towns, commerce had dribbled away
to the big chain stores and fast food restaurants by the highway) and zeroed in on the midget courthouse.

Like the anachronistic storefronts, the courthouse was a
vintage affair. It was round, save for a short Greek revival
pillar and pediment facade stuck on its front, and clad with
pale creamy-beige stucco, so that it looked like a five-gallon
tub of vanilla ice cream decorated with an American flag. I
followed the two FBI agents up the wide front steps, between
two of the six oddly-spaced Ionic columns, and through the
oak entrance doors. I found myself in a central hallway which
ran all the way around the county court's chamber, which
formed the central core of the building.

Tom Latimer nodded genteelly and pantomimed tipping
his hat to me. "This place kind of puts you in a mood for top
hats and floor-length skirts, doesn't it?" he murmured.

Ian stared at me, unsmiling. I was beginning to get the
impression he didn't like me.

I tugged at one blue jeans pant leg, pretending I was lifting
the hem of an imaginary skirt to reveal high-buttoned shoes,
and turned my ankle this way and that in a burlesque of a
turn-of-the-century coquette.

Tom grinned.

Ian jammed his hands into his pockets and indulged himself in looking impatient. Tom as elaborately did not notice
his impatience.

I looked back and forth between the two men, wondering what was getting Ian's undies in such a bundle. "So where's this dude we're supposed to interview?" I asked.

Ian grumbled, "He's waiting for us in the courtroom."

The courtroom itself was splendid, a miniature delight of fine moldings and Greek-revival pediments and pilasters with faux Corinthian capitals painted gleaming white and high-lighted with gold leaf. It was circular in plan, with concentric mahogany railings that separated the small fan of spectator's seats from the dock. The judge's bench, like the courtroom itself, was pleasantly diminutive and framed by United States and Nevada flags surmounted by gilded eagles. Silvery light filtered down from a band of nine-paned windows set in an ornamental frieze high under a domed silver ceiling. Globe-shaped sconces with gilded brackets illuminated the walls, and slender seats like those found in antique theaters curved out to either side of the central aisle. Only one seat was filled. The man in it turned toward us and studied us silently.

Tom stepped toward him and offered him a hand to shake. "You must be Doctor Rodriguez," he said soothingly, show-ing the man his identification.

The man stood up briskly. At full stretch, he did not reach Tom's collarbones, but he shook hands with the presumptive gravity of a five-star general. He turned toward Ian and so-berly shook his hand, too, then turned to me, paused for just an instant, then smiled and bowed from the waist. "*Señorita*," he said, his eyelids lowering seductively.

I was startled. I'd been slimed by a great many men in my day, but never this badly by a man of Hispanic descent. Based on my long friendship with Carlos Ortega of the Denver po-lice, I had expected chivalry from this man, but not entwined with rudeness. Unwilling to go along with rank sexism re-gardless of the circumstances, I stuck out my right hand as insistence that he shake it. Straightening, he took it in his and gave it a lingering squeeze. I moved it up and down like the grip of an antique water pump. He closed his left hand over the top of mine, lowered his eyelids half a notch, and let his smile part his lips.

I had to tug to remove my hand from his grip. Staring angrily into his leer, I entertained an urgent need to wash my hand, and couldn't stop myself from rubbing the palm down across my hip, wiping it off on the rough denim. I glanced at Tom. His expression was almost unreadable, but as he flicked his eyes briefly my way, the glint in them said, This is work. This is not the time for personal issues.

I let a strong glare at Rodriguez suffice to express my feelings.

Blithely ignoring my reaction, Dr. Rodriguez said, "So, gentlemen, you are here to ask me about Patricia Gilmore. A very sad turn of events today." He pronounced "Patricia" with a slight hiss, as if the name created an unpleasant steam in his mouth.

Neither agent said a word. After a moment, Rodriguez's eyes scanned languidly from one man to the other and back again, and then to me, the lines of his face beginning to sag with the slightest hint of disgust. He made a clicking sound in his cheek. "Please sit down," he said.

The agents remained standing.

The silence began to stretch and sag, filling the room with the stickiness of taffy. This gave me time to settle back mentally into my fly-on-the-wall posture and observe Rodriguez closely. I fought to assess him independently of my irritation with him, to free myself of the stink of his egregious salutation. He was at least forty-five years old, and paunchy. I noticed that he wore cheap pants, and his belt was made of faux leather. About when I caught myself looking contemptuously at his haircut, I gave up trying to be impartial and concentrated on trying not to sulk.

I glanced at Ian. He appeared as emotionally flat as a bodyguard, paying strict attention but waiting for someone else to make a move.

I shifted my gaze to Tom. He stood phlegmatically relaxed, hands in pockets, a slight smile on his lips. Did he suspect Rodriguez of something?

Rodriguez narrowed his eyes and spoke. "Gentlemen," he

said acidly, "I am here at your request. You have questions for me. Please ask them."

Tom nodded his head slowly, as if savoring a joke. My stomach tightened.

Ian broke the silence. "Dr. Rodriguez, Mr. Giles at the Bureau of Land Management has told us a little bit about the wildlife survey Ms. Gilmore was engaged in. He has told us, for instance, that Ms. Gilmore's activities were first brought to his attention by yourself."

Rodriguez pulled his head back and knit his brow. "That is not exactly true." He now raised his eyebrows. "But let me tell you the story from the beginning." He sat down on the arm of his chair and raised his hands, a professor lecturing to his class. "Patricia first came to work with us only a few months ago. She was young and inexperienced." He spread his hands palms up. "She made mistakes."

As Rodriguez paused for dramatic impact, I studied Tom's reactions. He had folded his arms across his chest, one hand to his lips. He watched Rodriguez closely, mapping him.

The little man's eyes grew limpid with sadness. "In preparing our Environmental Impact Report for Granville Resources's new project area, Patricia was detailed to take a live-trap survey of the rodent population. Of course, most mining activity in Nevada occurs in the mountain ranges. This is a special habitat, very fragile. It is host to many species which have become isolated by the separation between ranges, an artifact of a change in climate."

My ears pricked up. Now he was talking earth history, and that was my department. I listened carefully, evaluating the extent of the good doctor's knowledge.

Rodriguez began to warm to his topic. "Fourteen thousand years ago, the climate of Nevada was vastly different. This was the time of the great Ice Age. It was so cold that an ice sheet as much as *two miles thick* formed over the northern half of this continent." He paused, letting us absorb this information.

So far he was on target with the facts, but he might have throttled back just a bit on the P. T. Barnum aspects of his lecture. I glanced sideways at Ian and Tom, to see how they were taking this. They were staring at him blankly.

Rodriguez continued. "In the time of the ice, it was not only cooler, but also wetter, with rains such as are not seen here anymore." His hands began to move with the eloquence of a storyteller, evoking the extremity of the storms, the vastness of the terrain. "This area was full of lakes, and the vegetation was much richer. As the ice sheet retreated and the climate warmed, the places of cooler climate did not vanish, but simply moved to higher elevations. What once flourished at four thousand feet found conditions it desired at eight thousand, or ten." He raised a hand slowly, tracing the mountain slopes. "Nevada is a land of mountains and deserts. The mountains are dryer than they once were, but still cooler, and more rich in vegetation, and the desert is most severe between the ranges. Those species which could not adapt to the heat and sparsity of food in the valleys followed their habitat up the slopes. They now live marooned on their little mountain islands, forced to adapt to conditions they find there, or *die*." His hand dropped summarily. He looked knowingly at Tom and Ian, checking to make certain that they were apt pupils. "Subspeciation." He slowly turned his hand palm up, as if proffering them a gift. "Very rare animals."

"Rodents," Ian murmured, his expression still blank.

"Yes, they are rodents," Rodriguez admonished, "each species and subspecies a unique and integral part of the web of life. Not to be trifled with. Certain species are key indicators of the changes in the health of our planet. Take for instance the humble pack rat. It has the habit of nesting, and therefore urinating always in the same place, countless generations of rats, even through many millennia. We call the residue 'amberat.' It entombs the seeds of sometimes extinct species of plants, and imprisons certain isotopes from the atmosphere. . . ."

"Mice," prompted Ian.

Rodriguez let his breath out in irritation. "My attention was drawn in particular by Patricia's population numbers for a subspecies of the dark kangaroo mouse, *Microdipodops me-*

gacephalus kammai. It is in fact a new subspecies. I named it myself." He raised an index finger imperiously. *"She* identified it as a known subspecies found elsewhere, and in fact showed it *expanding its numbers."* He smiled wryly. "At first, I thought she had only made an error. You see, it is difficult to identify subspecies from the live specimen."

I said, "It takes an expert like yourself to properly identify it."

Rodriguez narrowed his eyes, but continued. "Exactly. In live specimen, it is a matter of subtleties in coloration, and small comparisons in length and the thickness of the tail, combined with a close examination of the mammae and of the incisors. It is a marvelous creature. Its skull—"

"An expert like *yourself,*" Latimer emphasized.

Rodriguez sighed with exasperation, as if the FBI agents were, after all, slow students, then plowed on with his tale. "Its skull has auditory bullae which can hear an ant's footsteps at half a mile. Very helpful if your life depends on hearing the approach of a diving owl, whose feathers part the desert air almost soundlessly. Marvelous creature."

I said, "But Pat Gilmore could not identify these subtleties."

Rodriguez lowered his eyelids to bedroom level as he turned his attention from Ian to me. He said, "Exactly, *Señorita.* I began to wonder about Patricia. She is . . . was . . . impulsive. Difficult. She would argue wildly at meetings." His face clouded with grief and regret, and he looked at the floor, as if with shame. "I . . . I began to wonder."

Rodriguez paused for a while, as if overcome, then elaborately recovered himself. "Gentlemen, Intermontane Biological tries to hire only the very best employees, but sometimes . . . a mistake is made. I am afraid that Patricia was just that form of mistake, which . . ." Here he paused, put a hand tenderly over his heart, and closed his eyes. ". . . I assure you I did not personally make. The president of the firm . . . sometimes . . . misjudges." Here he opened his eyes, and looked me over from top to toe, and then halfway back up again. "She did not follow orders. She kept sloppy notes. And . . .

and I fear that her veracity was . . ." He closed his eyes again. ". . . for *sale*."

I might have applauded the drama of his performance if I hadn't been preoccupied with relief at having his gaze removed from the bottom of my fly. But the man did seem to know his natural history. Which was confusing, because his bombast screamed Phoney.

It was clear that Rodriguez believed, or wanted us to believe, that Patricia Gilmore had sold out to the mining interests, that she had kited the figures for a price, helping Granville Resources to push their project through the permitting stage. "So you think someone killed her?" I asked, butting in.

Rodriguez reeled back in horror. "Who would do that?"

"Who indeed?" I murmured.

12

RODRIGUEZ SEEMED PREPARED TO TAKE US OUT TO the project site and catch us a kangaroo mouse just to prove to us how tricky the little guys were to tell from their nearest cousins, and how essential it was to have a fully qualified expert like himself clinch the identification, but the FBI agents appeared to be done with him. On the way down the courthouse steps, Tom glanced at me and asked, "Did he have his Ice Age right?"

"Yeah," I answered. "Glacial Lake Lahontan would have put us forty, fifty feet under water where we're standing now. If I look around these nearest hills, I can probably spot you a relict shoreline, a kind of wave-cut bench in the slope. And he had his dates about right. And I suppose he knows his beans about the critters, too, but I'm no expert on that." When we got to the car, I said, "How about we go on out to the crash site?"

Tom raised an eyebrow at me.

I went quiet, uncertain how to justify my growing itch to be out on the land, away from pavement and government bureaucrats and petty, self-aggrandizing Ph.D.'s.

"Okay," Tom said. "It's probably on our way to the mine, anyway. But out of professional courtesy, we should pay a call on the local fuzz first. Always mind your Ps and Qs, Em."

"We're going to the mine?"

"Of course. Why do you think I brought you along? We won't go in it, of course, but I figured you'd know what to look for around the office of an outfit like that. Maybe they'll have maps and assays. Think you can handle that?"

I rubbed my hands together greedily. "You just leave that to me."

Tom opened the door to the car and stepped aside. "Climb

in, m'lady. Or will you wipe your hands on your jeans again
if I talk to you like that?"

As I clambered past him into the car, I gave him a look
more sour than lemons.

BECAUSE SHERIFF OBERNICK had gone home for lunch, we
were treated to a deputy named Rhett Weebe who kept his
aviator sunglasses on indoors, apparently the better to practice
his intimidating stare. Weebe needed a good intimidating stare
in his repertoire. He was short and shaped like a pear, a fact
exaggerated by the thickness of his lovingly oiled Sam
Browne belt and gun holsters. A pearl-handled Smith and
Wesson .45 perched on each of his chubby hips. Like his
body, his face was also narrower at the top than at the bottom,
suggesting a pinching of the brain, and worse yet he wore a
toupee which adorned his narrow skull about as convincingly
as indoor-outdoor carpeting imitates grass. He had combed
the wiry synthetic hairs down over his hairline to cover the
edge of the matting that held them in place against his greasy
scalp, but had neglected to obscure the tell-tale warp and weft
along his too-straight part. As I took all this in, I wondered
idly how an Indian looking for scalps would feel after taking
his best swipe and winding up with a handful like that, and
decided that such tasteless deceit might just piss off a brave
even worse than having his hunting grounds sacked by Euro-
American squatters. It occurred to me about then that Rodriguez had put me in a pretty bad mood.

Weebe's caterpillar of a mustache wiggled as he spoke.
"I'm glad you boys came by, though a'course the woman's
death is out of your jurisdiction." He cleared his throat and
struck a noble pose, ready to report. "She was found about
two this morning out on the road that runs along the west
side of Rye Patch Reservoir." He turned and stuck a stubby
finger onto the shaded relief wall map behind him. "Rah
chere. Lonely spot, partic'ly at night."

"Who found her?"

"Fellah named Davis, and this other fellah named Steinhoff. They was working late at the mine, comin' home to Lovelock."

"Any sign of foul play?" Latimer asked, giving me a barely perceptible wink.

"Well . . ." Weebe drawled, regarding Latimer's question with suspicion, "not the kind just *anybody* was goin' to notice. Sheriff said it was an accident, pure and simple. Now, I met Pat a time or two, and she was a big ox and about as pleasant to deal with as an angry bee, but that don't necessarily make her careless, does it?" He stared at us one at a time, as if we were the ones who had suggested that the death had been accidental. "No, it don't. So I been asking questions, and there's a lot that don't quite add up about this case."

"Such as," I urged. It was great being along on the FBI's coattails, introduced as a colleague. I could ask anything I wanted and expect an insider's answer.

Weebe stuck his thumbs into his belt just in front of his side arms, which made his elbows stick out over the tops of the pistol butts like a vulture trying to cool his wings. "Such as the fact of what she was doing. Sensitive work. Big money behind them mining companies. And then there's this geologist for the company that's gone missing. Name of Donald MacCallum."

"When'd he go missing?" I asked.

Out of the corner of my eye, I saw Tom's eyes sag almost shut.

Weebe glanced at his watch. "Near's I been able to ascertain, he was last seen yesterday morning."

"Could be anywhere by now," I said conspiratorially.

"Exactly," said the deputy, pointing that pudgy finger at me. "And his guys that work with him are playing dumb." With a flourish, he flipped a pad of paper out of his breast pocket and made a show of checking his notes. "One Kyle Christie said he didn't know where he was, even though I've been given to understand that the two of them work together hand in glove. Neither did one Virgil Davis up there at the mine know where he was; the very same Virgil Davis as found the body. Both of 'em worked with the missing person.

You will note that the mine is in the Eugene Mountains, rah chere." He stabbed a second spot on the map, about an inch above the place where Pat Gilmore's corpse had been found.

I peered at the map. "I heard a news brief over the radio as we were driving up here. It said she was driving home to Winnemucca." I pointed at the network of roads that ran through the desert west of the Interstate. "All those roads out there are graded dirt, right?"

Deputy Weebe nodded. "Yep. The county maintains all of 'em except this one out to the mine, and Granville does that. Real nice road. Amazin' what you can do with *money*."

I was briefly distracted by thoughts of the cheap toupees that underpaid civil employees had to suffer, but shook the cobwebs out of my brain and stepped toward the map to take a closer look. I ran a finger along the road that led from the mine off to the west side of the Eugene Mountains. It dodged around the north sides of two buttes, and then junctioned with the road that ran south toward the spot where the wreck and Pat Gilmore's body had been found. I tried to discern the logic she had used in choosing her route. After leaving the mine entrance road, she had not dodged north and turned east onto a road which ran straight east into Winnemucca, but had instead turned south. She had also foregone the opportunity to turn east onto a second eastbound road which would have put her onto Interstate 80 and likewise aimed her at Winnemucca over a slightly longer route. She had instead continued south, toward Lovelock. "What are these roads like?" I asked. "You think she might have detoured around some bad road? Like washed out, or washboarded?"

Deputy Weebe favored me with a view of his teeth. "Nope. Both these other roads is the better roads. This one she was on ain't nowheres near as smooth."

I nodded. "So she took a poorer road, and one that would have taken her another twenty miles farther south before meeting the next access to Interstate 80. So if she was really going home, she would have traveled about a hundred miles farther than she needed to. Which way was her truck pointed?"

Weebe's moustache stretched into a tight little grin and he took off his aviator sunglasses and narrowed his eyes at me in appraisal. "They say it left the road goin' south," he said, nodding. "You're gettin' it. You're gettin' it. And if she wasn't goin' home, where *was* she goin'? Somewheres else. And then she's *dead*."

I peered into the deputy's pale little eyes, searching for glints of the intelligence he had managed to bury underneath his dim-looking exterior. "And this geologist that's missing, you're going to tell me he's with Granville also," I said.

Weebe pointed that finger at me again and nodded so sharply I feared his toupee might flip off his head. "Just so," he said. "I met him once. . . ." He waved one hand next to his ear in tight circles. "Odd one. Laughing all the time. Made ya wonder. Not sure he was real bright, ya know?" Weebe moved to his desk, pulled open a drawer, and took out a collection of business cards bound sloppily with a doubled-up rubber band. After somewhat clumsily removing the band, he shuffled through the cards until he found the one he was looking for and showed it to me. DONALD PAUL MACCALLUM, GEOLOGIST, it read. It gave a suburban Denver address and phone number.

I said, "What about the other guys who work for Granville?"

Weebe held up Kyle Christie's card. Then he held up Virgil Davis's, which identified him as mine superintendant. "This is the guy who reported the death. And this guy." He held up one that read, JOHN STEINHOFF, METALLURGIST. "Them two brought the body in." He finished his shuffling job by holding up a card that read LAUREL DIETZ, GEOLOGIST. "Nice kid," he said. "She didn't do it."

I said, "We met someone else this morning you might be interested in. You had any dealings with a Stephen Giles from the BLM?"

Weebe thought for a moment. "Seems as I recall that name. Real panty-waist kinda guy, right?"

I said, "Well, I can't imagine him off the pavement."

"Right." Weebe gave me a nod that said, We understand

each other. He stared into space for a moment, then said, "He's new."

"Big turnover in BLM agents?"

Weebe shrugged. "You just get one broken in and they go and replace them."

My mind went wild with the image of Rhett Weebe breaking in Stephen Giles. "What is it you have to get them straight about?"

"Oh, well . . . no offence, but we like to keep the federal intrusion at a minimum in these parts. We got our ways. Folks live here 'cause they like to be able to get up and stretch in the morning without worryin' about punchin' their neighbors in the nose."

"Give me a for instance."

Weebe thought. "Well, they got all these rules and regulations 'fore anyone can even *look* for anything out there."

"You mean drilling permits and so forth," I said.

Weebe quickly warmed to his topic, apparently forgetting that I had arrived with two federal agents. "Yeah. How's we supposed to have our quality of life if we can't have our minerals? You know like they say, 'If it can't be grown, it has to be mined.' Mining's a big industry in these parts, and here the BLM comes in and acts like it's some kind of sin these days to so much as pitch a tent out there. But let there be some tumble-down building or some hole in the ground that's more than forty-five years old, they act like it's a museum piece and you can't touch it."

"You're talking about the ghost towns now."

"Yeah, your mining camps and such. We got some nice old folks live out there in some of 'em without paying any rent, like, so's their Social Security checks can stretch a little bit farther."

"Squatters," I said.

"You could call 'em that. We all pay taxes on that land, can't see as why we can't make good use of it. Anyways, some of these new bucks like your Giles get to throwin' their weight around, stickin' to the letter and all, try to throw the old boys off like they're violating one of Moses' command-

ments. The smart agents just leave 'em be because they know
they're the best caretaker you can ask for. Anything amiss
out there, these old coots'll take care of it for ya. Sure, once
in a while one of 'em loses control of the propane and burns
an old building down, but what's that when you got your
freedoms to consider?"

I glanced at Tom Latimer. He was looking elaborately pa-
tient.

I said, "So but getting back to Patricia Gilmore. What do
you say we all drive out there where they found the truck and
take a look around? We're on our way to the mine where she
worked, anyway."

Weebe answered abruptly, "Can't do that."

"Why not?" I shot an anxious look at Tom, wondering if
I'd just pushed things too far. Tom shrugged, as if to say,
This is your bag of doughnuts, don't look at me.

Weebe sniffed, drawing my eye back to him. "Matter of
public safety," he said officiously. "The fire ain't burned itself
out yet. Matter of fact, you can't get to that mine, either, for
the same reason."

I shot my gaze back at Tom.

He had turned toward the door, his mind already on the
next task weighting his desk back in Salt Lake City. He said,
"Sorry, Em. Guess I brought you out here for nothing."

I chased after him. "No, wait; there's got to be another
way out there. We can come in from the north, or we can—"

"You heard what the man said."

"But—"

"Get in the car, missy. We got one more stop to make,
then we're heading for Winnemucca and our ride home."

13

AT THE SOUND OF A CAR PULLING TO A STOP, SHIR-
ley Cook set down her soup spoon and listened, but did not
rise from her chair at the kitchen table. The door through to
the front room was ajar, and from there the front door stood
open to the day, letting the vagrant breezes in through the
screen door. Sure enough, the air carried the scent of exhaust,
and she heard a car door open and then close. A second door
crunched open. She heard deep voices, too low to make out,
then the footfalls of a person coming up the walk toward her
door, but only one. The second man had waited at the car.
Why? And who was coming? The tension of her alertness
raised her shoulders a quarter inch.

The low iron gate swung open, emitting its customary
squeak, which Shirley had purposefully neglected to oil. It
served her better than a doorbell. Sighted people were not
aware of such incidental noises, and hence did not know that
they were giving themselves away.

Shirley aimed her best ear carefully. A man? Yes, this was
definitely a man coming. He took long, confident strides up
the gravel walk, apparently unconcerned that his approach
was noticed. She heard the porch steps groan as he neared
the door, heard a cheerful *knock-knocka-knock-knock*.

"Who is it?" she called.

"Tom Latimer." The voice was affable, at ease, a bad sign
considering the fact that she had no idea who he was. "I'm
with the Federal Bureau of Investigation." He said this matter-
of-factly, as if they'd just met at some civic event and she
had asked what he did for a living. "Is your name Shirley?"

"Yes . . ."

"Ah, good. I'm sorry, but I wasn't given your last name."
The man waited for a while for Shirley to offer it, but she let
him hang, unadvised, to see what else he would reveal of

himself. He spoke again. "If I may, I'd like to ask you some questions about Patricia Gilmore and the work she was doing. I understand you knew her."

Shirley's right hand closed instinctively around her table knife. She thought quickly. *He said did, not does, past tense; so he knows she's dead. He's with the FBI. The FBI! Did Patsy set something in motion after all*? "Come in," she said, releasing the knife and rising from the table, and added, cagily; "Would you like a cup of coffee?"

"Ah. That would be wonderful," the man said, pushing open the screened door. "And may I invite in my assistants? Or they can wait in the car."

Shirley moved through the doorway into the small living room, walking softly so that she could pick up every nuance of the man's sounds and scent. His voice had come from a fair height; she guessed him to be six foot two or three.

She stopped in the middle of the room and awaited his reaction to her scars. There was always a reaction when someone saw her face for the first time: a moment's hesitancy, an intake of breath, the tiny kissing sound some made when their mouths dropped open in shock. She had learned to use this moment to her advantage, to gauge each newcomer just as surely as if she could see their faces. This one paused. She could hear a soft rustling of fabric, and guessed that he was stuffing his hands into his pockets. A man at ease, or a man in panic looking for something to do with his hands? Now shifting her attention to her inner senses, she gave herself time to evaluate how he felt. Sympathetic, yet reserved. Abstracted. Had he been warned, or was he that unperturbable? "You can invite them in," she said sweetly. It seemed the moment for her witless old lady act.

The man stepped briefly back out the door, and an instant later she heard another car door open and the sounds of his assistants coming up the walk. Shirley waited, unmoving, ready to take in the resonances of these two additional entities. She would assert a slow pattern of proceeding, forcing them off their own rhythms. Unaware of how few limitations her handicap truly put on her, they would treat her like an invalid, giving her plenty of time to read them in fine detail.

Footfalls sounded on her steps, the door opened, and the assistants stepped into the room. One sucked in breath, a low, spasmodic whistle. Male. Young. Tight. Chattery feel to him. An odd scent, too; an unusual lime after-shave laced with the souring pheromones of hours-old uneasiness. He probably deferred, doglike, to this ultra-calm Tom Latimer, who had preceded him. Feared him slightly. It would be easy enough for her to deal with this one. She turned her senses to her third visitor. She had only just decided that it was a female when Tom Latimer said, "This is Ian Walker, also with the FBI."

"Who's the woman?" Shirley asked, expecting her knowledge to throw the first man off his balance.

It did not. "This is Em Hansen," Tom Latimer said calmly.

"Are *you* with the FBI too, Em?" Shirley demanded, realizing angrily that it was she who was getting off her balance.

Tom Latimer answered for the woman. "Em's not with the bureau, ma'am, but she's come with me today at my request. Sometimes I need—"

"What *do* you do then?" Shirley snapped irritably, trying to focus on the woman. She could not. *What a wretched day this is turning out to be*, she thought darkly. *First Patsy's dead, and now this crew shows up.*

Tom Latimer laughed comfortably. "You said something about a cup of coffee," he interjected.

Shirley's attention whipped back to him. Why was he answering for the woman? Was he protecting her? Keeping her down? Or was he in love with her? She couldn't sort out the signals. She shouldn't have let so many new people into the room at once. "I changed my mind," she said abruptly. "State your business. And those two wait outside." She pointed at Ian and Em as accurately as if she could see them. She heard them turn and shuffle out the door.

Tom Latimer exhaled audibly. "We've been asked to investigate allegations regarding the work Patricia Gilmore was doing out by the Kamma Mountains," he said soothingly. "We understand that she was preparing part of a routine En-

vironmental Impact Report for a proposed mineral exploration
project there. We'd made an appointment to interview her
today, but sadly, as you may have heard, she died last night
in a road accident."

Shirley wanted to yell, *That was no accident!* but kept her
mouth tightly shut. Instead, she gave herself a moment to
think and then said, "I heard. What's this got to do with me?"
The second man still felt close. He had stayed on the porch.
The odd chattery quality his space held had increased. She
could hear his breath whistling ever so slightly. *An asth-
matic . . .*

Tom said, "Well, maybe nothing at all, but when Ian telephoned her yesterday to set up our appointment, she suggested that we speak with you, too. She went so far as to tell
us how to find your house. She made quite a point of it,
almost as if she was concerned that she might not keep the
appointment herself."

*Damn! Why didn't she just give them a phone number, if
she had to go and leave a trail of crumbs?* Shirley thought
angrily. Then she remembered that the biologist had only
come there with the Paiute. She realized that Hermione must
never have told the young woman anything more than was
necessary to enlist her assistance. So someone had sicced the
FBI on Patsy, and she'd been worried. *No, outright scared.
. . . As well she should be, messing with the pigs she served.
Hermione had been correct to keep her on the edges of things.
Wait! Had she named Hermione, too?* "Well, I don't know
why she'd do that," Shirley said cagily.

"We don't either, but we assume it had something to do
with her work. The small mammals survey she was complet-
ing. For some reason she thought you'd know about it, too.
Are you also a biologist?"

"Hah!" Shirley barked, now simply displaying the angry
old woman she was, the better to confuse him. "Try making
it through high school with no eyes, then you think about
college and graduate school!"

"I was given to understand Ms. Gilmore herself had only
a bachelor's degree," Tom said affably.

Shirley's mind moved from a slow simmer into a brisk boil, furious with Pat Gilmore for sending these men to her door and even angrier at herself that the conversation had gotten this far. Warbling back into her old lady voice, Shirley said, "Listen, gents, Patsy was a dear girl, and if you'll excuse me, I want to be alone today, you know?" Unable to keep the sarcasm from creeping into her tone, she added, "A friend's death can hit you that way sometimes."

After a pause, Shirley heard Tom Latimer laugh to himself, a brief, comfortable *huh*. "Well, I was going to give you my card so you could call me sometime when you're feeling better, but that makes no sense. What system do you have for recording phone numbers?"

By God, this man is smooth, Shirley thought venomously. She said, "I won't be calling."

"Okay," Tom answered calmly.

Okay? Just okay? I'm off the hook? Bullshit!

"Well, I guess we'll be going," Tom said. "Sorry to trouble you."

Shirley heard the door open. But before Tom Latimer could exit, Shirley caught him by the arm, and hissed, "Don't mess with that young lady, mister."

Tom took Shirley's gnarled hand in both of his, enveloping it in cool, dry flesh. After a moment, he spoke very softly, so that only she could hear him. "I understand what you're saying. And I wish I could say, 'Don't worry.' But the thing is, she's on a path where she could get locked into things that don't suit her, or worse yet, hurt badly. You understand that, don't you? She's too headstrong to protect, so I'm doing the next best thing."

"Which is what?" Shirley demanded, thinking: *You arrogant son of a bitch.*

The man named Tom hesitated a while, thinking over his reply. "Sometimes," he said, almost sighing, "if you want to help a flower unfold as it should, you've got to give it a little tug."

The hands released Shirley's. She heard the door open, and

the soft sounds of the man's slightly less confident footfalls following the others out to the car. She wished she could see him. She wanted to know, from the way he held his head and shoulders, if he really, truly, cared.

14

KYLE CHRISTIE'S GREEN EXPLORER BOUNCED AND wallowed as he maneuvered it up the washed-out dirt track that led up to the ghost town where Sam the squatter lived. The place depressed him. There was little left of Rosebud, just a few tumbled-down shacks and a peppering of adits. It irritated him that MacCallum seemed to see it differently, almost as the fresh, new boom town it had been in 1906. "Just look at this place, Kyle," MacCallum had said to him, the first time they had come up here together. "The remains of a hopeful community of miners, merchants, and real estate developers. They graded streets and erected a hotel, a bank, a post office, and even a fledgling newspaper, *The Rosebud Mining News*. That's enthusiasm. That's great. Above the town site, we have Rosebud Peak topping out at 8,514 feet above sea level, the tallest summit in the Kamma Mountains, and down in the canyon below, we have the ghosts of the rival town of Goldbud."

Goldbud, Rosebud, Kyle now thought as the Explorer lurched sickeningly over a particularly deep washout in the dirt track he was following. *Should have named it Nipped-in-the-Bud.* He glanced left and right, searching for any signs of MacCallum in the vacant expanse of rabbit brush and sage that occupied the hillside. He liked remote places just fine, had in fact been drawn into geology in part for the hope of spending lots of his time outdoors, but he didn't share MacCallum's romance for the old West. In fact, nowadays he liked it only as an antidote to the bad feeling he tended to get in the singles bars in which he kept finding himself.

"What drew the miners, bankers, real estate developers, and journalists here, of all places?" MacCallum had asked him, his face a picture of amusement and delight. "How did they fare in this hopeless isolation? Think of it, Kyle; on this day, we have arrived within two hours' drive from a super-highway, but in 1906, the best access was fifty miles by stage-coach over this dirt road from a stop on the railroad down by the Humboldt River. No farm-bred man could have felt at home here; the soil is rough with grit and starved for organic material, and the only water comes from a few meager springs down the road."

"This town had only one crop," Kyle had said moodily.

"Yes. Gold, or the rumor of it. Think of it, Kyle: In 1907, at the height of the local boom, the combined habitation of the two "Buds" was something over five thousand inhabitants. By 1908, when the cycle of fraud and folly had run its course, most miners had grabbed their picks and single jack drills and had hopped the stage en route to the next great hope."

"So why are we here?" Kyle had asked, feeling as hopeless as those miners.

MacCallum had said, "Ah, Kyle, you have to *look*, man! This place isn't dead, it's only sleeping. Look, there's what's left of the Brown Palace Mine. A man named Leach drifted one thousand six hundred feet of workings under the Golden Jupiter and Ragged Six claims; there, and there. Over there, a man named Quirk worked a claim or two. You got to read the histories to bend time the other way and look into the future."

"They didn't find much," Kyle had observed.

"No, not much," MacCallum had agreed, smiling like a boy on Christmas morning. "But the transit of hope can be traced long after the bones of the hopeful have turned to dust."

Kyle had been so mystified by that remark that he had almost said nothing, but finally asked, "What's that supposed to mean?"

MacCallum had answered, "I can still see every spot some poor sod sank a shovel in this whole valley. I believe I'll get to work."

All Kyle could see now, as he bounced back up the road alone, were the tracks where the occasional four-wheeler had scrubbed away the few stray desert plants that had tried to gain a foothold on the beaten earth. The squatter's monthly run to town in his dilapidated van could alone have caused this much disruption, but he knew that most of the tracks were probably MacCallum's. Kyle stared gloomily at the emptiness that had been Rosebud. Was there more gold here? MacCallum had not said. He had come and gone from the Kamma Mountains for several months, spending two or three weeks in the field and then going home for as long, his typical pattern when he was generating a prospect. Kyle had kept up with him the first week, making sounds like he understood what interested MacCallum in the played-out district, but had gone home with a case of the flu and had not quite gotten around to coming back until MacCallum's last cycle. This time, they had been in Nevada two weeks, and Kyle had walked with MacCallum for the first few hours and then thought of something he needed to do back at the office. The fact was that there was really nothing for him to do until the drilling started except keep MacCallum from wandering off somewhere, and now he had failed at even that.

On the face of it, Kyle knew prospecting as well as MacCallum did: You find something that looks interesting, whack a chunk loose, and send it in for assay. If the assay looks good, you drill. If the drill samples have what you want, you dig. Any fool could do it, and many had. Even in the old days, before the rise of corporate entities with big drilling budgets, the old coots had worked their ways up the creeks, knocking a bit of sand into their gold pans and washing it in a circular swing with a little bit of water. If there was gold in the sand, it quickly lagged into a concentrate, due to its greater density. Following shows of gold up the ravine led to the vein. And if the area didn't "pan out," the prospector moved on. But that was the hit-or-miss school of prospecting. To hit like MacCallum could, you had to know a bit of magic.

"What are you looking for here?" the old squatter had asked MacCallum on one of those first days they had worked this district. He had come out in front of his shack to say hello.

MacCallum's laughter had bubbled like soap. "Gold, Sam. Gold!"

Kyle had asked MacCallum perhaps a dozen times over the years to explain how he looked for gold, and had never gotten an answer he found any more useful than that one, but Sam had reframed the question more simply. "But what *exactly* do you do, Son? Just whack at everything that looks like quartz?"

· MacCallum had taken Sam's question quite seriously, and had pondered for a long while. Then he'd said, "Well, of course; most gold deposits are associated with some degree of silicification." He had scratched at his jaw. "So yes, just looking for silicification and finding it has some significance. But there are numerous types of silicification, aren't there? Like the white, bull quartz of the California Mother Lode district . . . banded chalcedonic vein quartz . . . pervasive silica with no association to normal veins . . . opaline quartz of the hot spring ilk. And there are textures within the quartz, and generations of fracturing or veining. I look at the shape of the fragments if it's a silicified breccia, and at the type of breccia, and its origin."

"But why quartz?" the old man had asked. "You're not mining quartz, are you?"

"Well, gold is a hydrothermal deposit, at least originally, but the clay alteration that's associated with hydrothermal deposits is soft." He pointed at a low spot in the nearest hill. "So that saddle there might represent a fault with hydrothermal alteration. Gold. Lead. Something might be there. A selenium halo around gold. The clay envelope is soft, so it erodes, and the minerals associated with it can easily be removed by weathering. There could be a placer deposit below it, if it feeds a stream; or maybe not. So you might be wise to go and look there, but the clay zone will probably produce no outcrop, or if it does, that outcrop might not have the gold or other elements there at the surface anymore, so you're back to looking for those silicified rocks, because the silica might have come up along structure, and that structure might be the feeder to the mineralization. Or it might be right next to the mineral-bearing vein, like a guide. The quartz is hard—it resists erosion—so you look for a bump. Sometimes they're very large—knobs, ridges—but sometimes they are the size of a filing cabinet or a foot stool, and the bigger one is not necessarily the better, or it might be totally gone, but there is a little float trail or big old boulders out there at the range front. There is no end of ways to interpret it all. But I try not to get caught up in making interpretations. Interpretations make me narrow my focus."

Kyle knew all this, but then again, he didn't. And he couldn't get out of bed in the morning without a focus, even if it was only the need to pee.

Sam had smiled knowingly and asked, "So what do you do *really*?"

MacCallum had leaned back and laughed into the sky. "I just try to keep my eyes open, Sam. That's all."

Kyle had shaken his head. "But that's not all you do, now is it, Don? You find stuff that no one else even knows to look for. I keep thinking there must be little gnomes out here holding up signs for you. And they hide when they see me coming."

MacCallum had patted him on the shoulder and said, "Kyle, old friend, most of the time, there really *isn't* anything there." And then that laugh had erupted again. And then he had wandered off to drink bad coffee with the old squatter, leaving Kyle to wonder why he hadn't gone into used car sales.

Kyle could somehow still feel that pat on his shoulder like it was a big cosmic nudge. Asking himself why he was even looking for MacCallum, he parked his vehicle next to the old brush-painted van which stood near the one shack in Rosebud that still had a full roof on it. The shack in fact had quite an excellent roof, thanks to the squatter, and all four walls were tight against the winds. It had the burned look all wooden structures acquire in the desert after a few cycles under the blazing summer sun and the icy breaths of winter. Pink fiberglass which the squatter had used for chinking hung about like stray whiskers between the aged logs that formed the

structure's walls, and the overflow from a caulking gun
gummed the edges of the panes of the small windows. The
only other obvious touch of modernity was the battered propane tank that rested against the side nearest the portion of
the shack which the squatter called the kitchen. As Kyle
neared the door, the squatter's flea-ravaged hound staggered
up and sniffed at his pant leg.

"Sam?" Kyle called out. "You there?"

An odd descant of whistling that had been drifting from
the shack stopped abruptly and was replaced by the squatter's
sonorous voice. "I was just puttin' some coffee on, come to
think of it. Be glad for the company."

"Oh, I don't need any coffee, Sam, thanks anyway," Kyle
replied, hoping against hope he could get away quickly. "I
was just looking for MacCallum. Wondered if you'd seen
him."

"No, no, no, you don't have to be polite and formal here,
my boy. You just come on in and have a cup of Sam's coffee,
now."

Kyle squeezed his eyes shut in frustration. Acceptance of
this invitation meant an hour lost at least, the man rambled
so. "I just dropped by looking for The Don, really," he insisted, and repeated his inquiry. "I was wondering if you'd
seen him."

"Coffee's good for the soul, son. You got to feed your
soul, remember. You come on in. It won't take me but a
moment to boil this pot." The old man scuffled as he started
dragging his six-gallon Jerry can of water toward the edge of
the shelf.

Kyle sighed in defeat, once again manipulated, once again
pushed into doing something he swore he wouldn't do. "Here,
let me help you," he said disconsolately, as he pulled open
the screen door and let himself into the tight confines of the
shack. Kyle hated being inside of it. Its ancient timbers
sagged too close to his head. "When are you going to get
yourself one of those jobs with a spigot, Sam?" He hoisted
the jug to the counter.

"I'd still have to lift it up here now, wouldn't I?" the old man said cheerfully. "Besides, this one works fine. Waste not, want not. There now, you set yourself down," he added, pushing a stack of *Reader's Digest* magazines away from the less cluttered end of the table. The movement set off a small avalanche of much-thumbed post cards, which slewed into a dish of kibbles he had set out for the several geriatric cats that roamed the room at intervals. One of them stared at Kyle from a narrow, fur-encrusted couch with ruptured upholstery. The animal yawned, managing to pull its kitty lips back so far that they almost met in the back. After considering Kyle abstractedly for a moment, it apparently decided he was no threat, and set to licking its matted fur with a raspy pink tongue.

Sam grunted with the effort of trying to tip the jug. He could not budge it.

He's gone downhill since the last time I stopped by, Kyle decided, and said, "Sam, this just isn't going to work anymore. Why the hell don't you just move to town?"

Sam turned and smiled at Kyle. "And leave my gold? Never." He turned back to his task, and to grunting.

Gold? You have fantasies of gold, old man? Kyle set about rigging a siphon through which Sam could drain the five-gallon jugs without tipping them. He checked the water levels in each. One was still full, but the rest, including the one the man had been struggling with, held only a gallon each. The last time Kyle had visited, he recalled, Sam had easily lifted it. Kyle moved the siphon into the full jug and poured half of each remaining gallon into a large pot which had a lid. Then he hung a ladle off one handle of the pot. "There. That's two gallons right here in this pot for you, Sam. You can just ladle it out a cup at a time." When Sam did not reply, Kyle shook his head and sat down on the bench that bordered the table.

Sam said, "You're a smart one, Kyle. You really undersell yourself." When Kyle didn't answer, he busied himself about the propane burner that held the pan of water, then pulled the sodden paper-towel filter out of his coffee maker, laboriously dumped out a portion of the grounds, and added a tablespoonful from a can of what passed for fresh. He was short, and his bent spine threw his disease-bulged stomach low over stumpy legs and broad hips. As he moved from place to place, the stiffness and forward angle of his torso suggested that he was on a collision course with Mother Earth. Grimy woolen britches hung in sagging festoons from his suspenders, and he wore a faded red union suit, even though the outside temperature was hitting ninety. His hair, which stood out in wisps, was a ghostly white, in stark contrast to his face, which was sunburned to a ruddy mahogany, and the wild growth of white stubble on his cheeks suggested that he was almost due for his monthly clean-up and run into Lovelock for supplies.

"Make mine nice and hot, Sam," Kyle said wanly, hoping that heat might kill a few of the microbes that Sam was now ignorantly applying to his coffee mug with the thumb he was using to wipe it "clean."

"Yep, yep, always nice and hot at Sam's," the old man replied. "Say, I got a few new cards from my daughter since the last time you been out here." He reached up onto a shelf for a shoe box.

Kyle hung his head. Post cards meant an extra half hour. There was no looking at just the new ones. That shoe box had a way of belching forth miscellaneous memories like a cornucopia from hell. Kyle sipped gingerly at the coffee Sam had set before him, and made polite sounds as needed. His mind turned to purée under the enchantment of the old man's sonorous voice. He tracked the course of the sun as the angles of its shadows shifted across the table top, and he occasionally glanced at his watch. The hour passed glacially, and the minutes played little games by stretching out as long and thin as rubber and then shattering into tatters. Finally, when Sam ran out of post cards and began whistling to himself once again, Kyle repeated his question. "So, you seen Don lately?"

"MacCallum?"

"That's the one, Sam."

"Oh, he drops in when he's about; you know him."

"Yeah. What I was wondering is, have you seen him *today*?"

The old man tipped his head back as if trying to remember something as frail as today when there were so many yesterdays. "Nope."

Kyle's heart sank. The old codger would probably forget that Kyle had been here as soon as his vehicle was out of sight down the canyon. "See him yesterday?"

"Nope."

Kyle knew that MacCallum had in fact been here the morning before. He had mentioned it when he had arrived at the mine to answer Virgil Davis's summons.

Exhausted by the waste of an hour, he stood up and lurched toward the door. "Gotta go," he said dully.

"Don't feel you got to hurry on my account."

"See you, Sam."

Sam shook his head kindly. "You got to stop and smell the roses, son. Before you know it, you're gonna be as old and shot to hell as I am."

Kyle pulled the door halfway open.

Sam stared out the fly-spattered window over the propane stove, his eyes bright and a smile on his lips. "Life is what you make of it, my boy."

"Of course."

"I see your pal, I'll tell him you been looking for him."

"Thanks, Sam." Kyle put one foot resolutely in front of the other, moving himself through the doorway.

"Watch your passage on that road, boy; it ain't getting any younger."

"Right," Kyle called over his shoulder.

The old man came to the door and raised his voice to be heard. "And watch you don't drive out east of the range here. There's a fire burning, you know."

"Yes. Good-bye."

Sam began whistling again.

Kyle stumbled to his vehicle as if he had wakened from a deep sleep. His senses were numbed. He no longer felt any sense of where MacCallum was and didn't care. Perhaps this time the little shit had gotten himself bitten by a rattlesnake, or had fallen down an abandoned mine shaft, or worse yet had finally done as he had so many times threatened, and had simply folded his hand and left the damned sorry poker game they called a career. The man was mad. A nuclear warhead could be bearing down on him like a meteor and MacCallum would laugh with delight at the oddity of the experience.

Kyle Christie fired the ignition of his rented Explorer and slammed its automatic shift into gear with a fury he usually reserved for something truly important, like stomping out flaming hundred-dollar bills. MacCallum was gone and had not said good-bye or when he'd be back, and that was Kyle's tough shit. It was his own damned fault for letting MacCallum do so much of the preliminary work. He hadn't even seen his working maps, had no idea what he'd found. There was going to be no new project, so why not just drive back into Love-lock and belly up to an electronic poker machine and get himself drunk? After all, he was more likely to get rich playing a game he *knew* was set against him than banging his head against the quest for gold. MacCallum had taught him that himself.

As he jounced back down the canyon road, the bitterness of Kyle's thoughts ricochetted like a pin ball from Mac-Callum's extraordinary luck to the paltriness of his own existence to the decay of Sam. *Couldn't leave his gold, what a putz. The old fart is just like every other delusionary old sourdough who ever put pick to rock.*

Kyle slammed on his brakes, suddenly putting together a new picture: MacCallum always stopped to see Sam. And Sam thought he had gold.

He slapped the steering wheel with a mixture of frustration and amazement. Here he'd always found something else to be doing while MacCallum piddled around the hills with Sam, and all the time, the old man had been showing MacCallum where the gold was. Maybe that was how the son of a bitch did it!

15

"Shit, that's huge," I gasped, as we came along Interstate 80 around the shoulder of the mountains northeast of Lovelock and the southern edge of the range fire came into view. "It's got to be five miles across."

"Looks like it's spread since we flew past it this morning," said Tom.

"I'll say."

"The wind's come up."

Ian stabbed a finger at the recirculation button on the air conditioning. As subtly as possible, he palmed an arbuterol atomizer out of his pocket, squirted some into his mouth, and inhaled.

I glanced at him, wondering if it was allergies that had brought him to Nevada. Or had it been a libertarian bent? And I wondered at the depth of my own presumptions. I rubbed at my eyes in sudden fatigue. It was barely past noon, but the day was already on a downhill glide.

"My pilot said there were more fires this year than usual," Tom commented to Ian. "What do your sources say?"

Ian stuck out his chest and replied, "There are the usual causative factors—you know, like sloppy campers and lightning strikes—but there have been storms than usual, and the range specialist at BLM told me it's also a change in the fuel."

"How so?" asked Tom.

"As I said earlier," Ian replied, giving me a haughty look, "There's a species out there called cheat grass, an exotic that came in with domesticated herd animals. It's taken over from the native species in a lot of areas because it sprouts earlier and takes up all the moisture, crowding the natives out. Then it dies off, dries out, and . . . then the spark hits." He glanced out at the smoke and made an ineffectual attempt to clear his sinuses. It began to occur to me that Ian was trying very hard to make a positive impression on Tom, and that I was in his way. Instead of working with Tom as a daring duo, he was repeatedly being relegated to the status of walking encyclopedia and chauffeur, while Tom focused his attentions on me.

I stared morosely out across the burning desert. The grass may have started the blaze going, but now it had engulfed the sage brush, and, once ignited, its resinous wood and leaves burned hot as blazes. Little balls of fire leapt hungrily from bush to bush, spalling off a greasy smudge of soot that would blacken the soil itself.

This view of destruction brought back the image of the woman I had just met. I shuddered at the thought of what might have scarred her. Whole patches of her face were ropy with skin grafts, her throat looked like it had been clawed by a bear, and her eyes were so sunken with blindness that I wondered if they were indeed still there. She was missing fingers, too, but I was used to such matters from growing up on a ranch: It's not infrequently that someone loses digits to a combine or some such mechanical necessity, and one does not treat the victims of such incidents as grotesque, because one might be next.

Nevertheless, I had found our meeting with Shirley Cook distressing. She was a tough old girl, but something had her sufficiently scared that she'd put on an act to get rid of us. And she had known Patricia Gilmore, who had been under investigation with the FBI and was now dead. "If we can't get to the crash site, can we at least see Pat Gilmore's office?" I asked.

Tom Latimer had slumped down again in the backseat, folded his arms, and closed his eyes. "No, her office is at the mine, which as the good deputy has pointed out, is on the other side of that fire. Ian will just take us on up to Winnemucca, and I can come back and hit this job another day."

THE TRIP BACK to Salt Lake City was uneventful. I sat up front with Faye, pretending interest in learning to fly a twin, but mostly staring into the distance while I sorted through my thoughts. Tom Latimer was messing with me, and I couldn't figure out why. He had lured me out to Nevada by saying he needed my help. Now he was acting as if his interest in my assistance had ended. That had to be so much manure.

The fact that he was now once again stretched out in the backseat of the plane with his eyes closed was an attempt to try to lure me even further, of that I felt certain. And yes, I was curious, to know what this was all about, but no, I was not foolish. I had enjoyed the day's game of shooting my mouth off about whether Patricia Gilmore had died by accident or by malice, but I did not feel the least bit tempted to carry a dead person's banner into battle solely for the sake of some overheated sense of right and wrong. What was right was to live long and prosper, maybe even have a home that I owned, and . . . perhaps a husband to live in it with me. Besides, I had not even known the lady.

And into what, precisely, was Tom trying to lure me? Surely the Federal Bureau of Investigation wasn't hard up for field operatives, and if they wanted a fourth or fifth forensic geologist to add to their ranks, they could have their pick of fresh recruits straight out of Ph.D. candidacy. The job market was that tight. Why pick ol' Em Hansen, possessor of only a paltry B.A.?

I was damned if I was going to ask Tom any of these questions. That was probably what he was hoping for, and besides, I was not going to go to work as a detective, let alone an FBI agent, so why continue the conversation?

When we got back to Salt Lake City, Tom prepared to load me into his car and take me "home" to Ava's, but I balked. It was only three in the afternoon, and I had told Ava I'd be gone through dinner. Instead, I asked Faye Carter where she was off to.

She shrugged. "No plans. I'm going to put the plane in its hangar and write up my log book, then I thought I'd head home and watch cartoons on TV. Got a better idea?"

"Is home anywhere near the University?"

"Sure. Why?"

I screwed my face around, crimping a cheek and rolling my eyes to indicate surreptitiously that I wanted to shuck

Tom. "Oh, nothing. Just thought I'd hit the library up there."

Faye nodded. "Got ya covered."

I turned to Tom. "Well, thanks for a pleasant outing. I'm sure Ava would love it if you dropped in, even without me for an excuse, but don't ask for coffee."

Tom's eyelids lowered a fraction of an inch. "Ha, ha." He stared at me for a while, frustration clouding his face. "You have a lot of talent, Em, but you're right, it's not my business to try to guide you."

My mouth sagged open with surprise and embarrassment. I said, "Well, I'll let you know if I find out anything that might help your investigation."

"Sure," he said, and headed for his car.

FAYE DROVE A late model Porsche. "Nice wheels," I said, as we bolted into the fast lane and accelerated toward the city.

"Thanks," she answered offhandedly.

Used to money, I decided. *In fact, oblivious.* "I thought all pilots were broke until they made captain for United Airlines."

She shot me a look of appraisal, then fixed her eyes back on the road as she passed a slower vehicle on the right and then wiggled back into the fast lane. "And?"

I decided on the nakedness approach. "I hope that wasn't rude, but, well . . . I'm a geologist, and I'm out of work for the umpteenth time, so naturally I'm looking around to see what else I could do for a living. I love flying, but everyone always tells me it pays less than half what I was making, and that I'd have to cough up untold thousands of dollars just to go from private pilot to commercial-and instrument-rated, let alone get the hours necessary to be hired by a commercial firm. But I look at the evidence before me here, and I get to wondering; here is a woman about my age who flies for a living, wears custom tailored uniforms, and drives a car that costs as much as most peoples' houses. Supposition A—pilots starve—does not match with effect B—you look well-fed. So, using just the teensiest shred of deduction, I wonder if there might be a few angles I have not considered."

Faye blinked. "I'm a trust fund baby," she said succinctly.

"Dang."

"Yeah, but it's not all it's cracked up to be."

I chuckled, not unkindly.

"I know it's ludicrous to ask for sympathy," Faye said, her lips curling with rueful humor, "but I'm serious. Look at it this way: You may hear the wolf scratching at the door, but sometimes the wolf is your friend."

"Sure. Uh-huh. Absolutely. You're nuts."

"You think so? Listen, you have to work to pay the rent and feed yourself, right?"

"Sooo right."

"Well, I don't. Every month, a check comes from my stock broker whether I get out of bed or not. So why get out of bed? Why not just stay there?"

"Sounds like a plan," I said heartily.

Faye downshifted and matter-of-factly left a Toyota in the dust. "No, really. Money is just money. It doesn't keep you warm. It doesn't feed you. I can buy warmth and food—and that's important, I agree—but keeping the creature alive is not everything. What's most important to understand is that money doesn't make you happy. In fact, it can do just the opposite."

"Sure, sure. You look absolutely miserable."

Faye lifted one shoulder and dropped it. "Not miserable, just bored." As she spoke, she lifted her right hand off the steering wheel and flung it open in emphasis.

I stared at Faye's open palm. It was smooth and unmarked, and . . . poignantly empty. I opened my own. It was dry and chapped, and crisscrossed by scars and calluses. Clearly she enjoyed her Porsche, and her flying, and her nice clothes, but as clearly, she longed for something immaterial and beyond her grasp.

As if reading my thoughts, she said: "The Dalai Lama says in *The Art of Happiness* that there's a difference between happiness and pleasure. A Porsche can bring pleasure, but only fleeting happiness. True happiness comes from training the mind."

"Well, sure; I'd like to be as enlightened as the Dalai Lama, too, but let's stick with simple stuff. Like flying and not having to get out of bed."

"It *is* simple: I couldn't learn to meditate, so I had to keep busy."

"Okay . . ."

Faye slapped the gearshift rather more forcibly than was necessary to make her next downshift. "You're right, I'm getting ahead of myself. The thing is, my mind is entirely too highly trained in a different way. It is highly educated, in a Western sense. I've been to the best schools. I've skied the best mountains on three continents and New Zealand. I've sailed from San Francisco to Hawaii, scubaed the biggest reefs, biked to the continental divide, and even tried bungee jumping, God help me. When I'm not being a hopeless jock, I've numbered pot sherds on digs in the Yucatan, volunteered in AIDS clinics in Africa, and taught English as a second language to Indochinese immigrants. I've—"

"And you're *bored*?"

She sighed in exasperation. "I did all these things *because* I was bored. I call it 'High Experience Syndrome.' I've always been able to do anything I want. And I'm so used to *doing* that I don't know how to *be*."

I stared at her in frank amazement. She had just characterized herself down to the last micron, and had done so without a lick of self-pity, only frustration. Looking away, I made an inventory of each joint of each of my fingers, trying to decide what, if anything, to say in reply.

Faye snapped me out of this reverie by rapping me on the shoulder with the back of her hand. "Hey, don't get too excited, you know? Like the wise men say: 'To do is to be,' Descartes; 'To be is to do,' Sartre; 'Do-be-do-be-do,' Sinatra.' "

16

AT THE LIBRARY, I FOUND MY WAY TO THE SCIENCE section, dug out a few texts, pulled up a carrel, and began to turn pages. I wanted to unwind and let the events of the day, and of the week, and in fact of the past year kind of trickle down through my subconscious and settle as best they could. I needed to figure out what to do about Tom, and what to do *with* Ray. I needed to decide what I wanted to be when I grew up. I needed to act like an adult for a change, and force from my mind all thoughts of chasing around Nevada after the riddles of dead biologists and endangered rodents and missing gold geologists, and instead identify a path to follow into a career that would interest me, yes, but also provide a platform from which I might hope to build a more stable life.

So what did I read? Why, a book on the Ice Age, of course, to see if Umberto Rodriguez had had all his facts straight. Actually, as is my habit, I didn't read much of the text of the book, I only perused the illustrations. I am a slow reader, and I pick up information much more quickly from the pictures than from the text. And indeed, it seemed that the vast desert I had flown over that day had not been desert for very long. Less than fourteen thousand years, in fact. Just a blink of an eye, geologically speaking. The book showed pictures of woolly mammoths treadding the shores of wide lakes where dry desert basins now glared white under the searing desert sun. Extinct camels strolled those shores, and giant ground sloths, vanished horse species, dire wolves, and cheetahs.

I turned next to a book on the geologic history of the area. I flipped backward through the section on the Great Basin, so called because it does not drain its surface waters to the sea. I looked at the map. The towering rampart of the Sierra Nevada blocked drainage to the west, and neither was there drainage to the north, the east, or the south. It is in the nature of nature that water responds to the draw of gravity, and flows downhill toward the sea. In any other spot in North America, each drop of rain stands a chance to flow in an orderly fashion downhill following the call of gravity, until, by joining with other drops into rivulets and with other rivulets into streams and thence into rivers, they find the sea. On their way, the drops of rain may tarry awhile as ice, expanding in cracks between boulders, heaving them apart and levering them downhill. The drops thus tumble the massive boulders and pluck up grains of sand and buoy up delicate platelets of clay, prying relentlessly at the surface of the earth until great valleys are formed, valleys which in turn guide the waters to the sea, where the cycle of evaporation, rain, and down-cutting begins again.

But here, in the back of beyond, in the forgotten desert of the Great Basin, no drops find the ocean. To a geologist's eye, such aberrations of nature proclaim the youth of the terrain. Nevada has too recently heaved upward to have developed an orderly system of runoff. And it is still rising, its disorderly rumpus of movement routing all waters to its arid center.

And why was Nevada rising? That morning, I had told Faye the most popular theory, but there on the page were two more. The page began to swim. I was getting tired. It had been a long day.

I looked at the nearest clock. It was barely four; it would be an hour and a half before my truck might be ready at the mechanic's, and even if I got it, I didn't know what I was going to do to fill my evening. I didn't want to see Ray. I speculated that he'd still be annoyed at me over my faux pas with his nephew Teddy. Teddy, the child whose actions had rubbed in the fact that I knew nothing of children.

Did I want any children of my own? When I dug down into my soul, I found not a twinge of interest, but neither did I find disinterest.

I sighed heavily. Not for the first time, I wondered if I was not, in fact, some other species than human, just stuck in a human body as some cosmic joke. *Perhaps I am a martian,*

I told myself. *That would explain why I'm unsure about having children, and feel so out of sync with the human race.*

My mind turned to thoughts of Ray. Handsome Ray of the indigo blue eyes, athletic Ray who spoke with his body instead of words. It would certainly feel good to give him a daughter or a son. He knew all about children, and clearly longed for one . . . or perhaps ten. I shuddered. Of this much I was certain: I was not interested in bearing ten children. Two, max. If indeed my body could produce even one. In all my years of horsing around with sex, I'd never even had so much as a scare of pregnancy, so either I was damned good at prevention or sterile. Or, as I feared, martian.

I rolled my eyes. There was certainly no way to risk pregnancy with Ray short of marrying him. He was celibate outside of wedlock, and I had to respect that. To do so, however, I had to think about other things each time I contemplated the muscular curves at the insides of his wrists, or those smooth, warm spots just below his ears where his throat rose to the firmness of his jaw. His hugs had grown stronger lately, and more lingering, as if to ask a question, but he said nothing and offered nothing. And I waited, my mind and body idling as I tried not to contemplate the enormity of the philosophical stalemate in which we found ourselves. He wanted me to convert to Mormonism and enter his world. I wanted him to step quietly into mine.

Here I sat, holed up in a library, looking for something to distract my busy little mind from the impossibility of budging this exquisitely faithful man from his rock of family, church, and duty. I stood on a razor's edge, hungry for him to toss his way of life over for a less certain one with me, and at the same time certain that if he wavered for an instant from the solidity that his church and family represented, I would run screaming for the Colorado border.

I turned another page in the Great Basin book, and perused an artist's rendering of a giant ground sloth reared up on hind legs, dining on an extinct tree. What did I see in Ray? Was it just the abnormal closeness spawned from the peculiar circumstances under which we'd met? I had been a murder suspect, and he had been The Law sent to watch me, and before the mess had been unraveled, we had together survived terror. But could we survive normalcy?

Ray seldom spoke, and yet I read the speech of his body clearly, and I was happier being quiet with him than talking with anyone else. In the world of dating, he was honorable and brave, having traveled four times over the mountains to Colorado to visit me before I committed to visiting him even once.

I had offered to meet him halfway once, for a camping trip, but he had declined, smiling. "That would be too great a test," he'd told me.

"Of your resolve?"

He'd nodded, even raised his eyebrows impishly while he kept his eyelids bedroom low.

"I'm quite good at fly fishing," I'd replied. "And I know how to cook trout over an open fire so you'd thought you'd died and gone to heaven."

Here he'd grinned, and closed his eyes. I was supposed to take that to mean that it wasn't my cooking that tempted him. Oh, well.

We had been standing beside his vehicle, outside the house where I lived in Boulder, and he had been about to get in that vehicle and drive home to Utah. My landlady's dog, Stanley, had snorted at us and made us laugh.

"Come to Utah," he'd said, and pulled me close and kissed me, a long, searching communication that words cannot approach.

Wrapped in the protection of his arms and scents, I had found courage and said yes, I'd come. Even then, it had taken me two months of loneliness and a job layoff to climb into my truck and head west. Just past Grand Junction, the brakes had begun to fail, forming a metaphor which scared me witless. Was I plunging into something I could not control? As far as my truck went, it was just overheating caused by worn parts on the parking brake, so after letting things cool off a while, I had continued on, telling myself not to set the brake again. But I had next sat by the road just after a stop for corn chips in Green River, and then again after a similarly unnecessary stop in Price. And then I had dawdled for a full week before taking the truck to be fixed. Was I trying to tell myself something?

I dreamed briefly of driving that truck further west, over the road into Nevada, if only to get a close-up view into the gaping maw of the open-pit gold mine I had seen that day from the air. Objects like that both drew and repelled me. It had taken the technological prowess of the most advanced culture in history to dig that hole in the ground, and that made me proud; but at the same time, that technological prowess had, in the name of retrieving just a little more gold, made a scar so deep that it could be seen from space. It was even more disquieting to consider that, of all that volume of rock hauled from the bottom of that colossal pockmark, only one part in ten or twenty thousand was in fact the precious metal the miners sought. Gold reserves were evaluated in ounces per ton of ore. An ounce per ton was considered high grade, in most cases more than enough to warrant the huge cost of mining and refining. Unimaginable tons of rock usually had to be removed before the veins could be addressed. All that for a hard, shiny bit of metal, or vial of dust, which you could not eat or wrap around you to keep you warm. Gold's practical uses were few—electronics and dentistry were all I could recall off the top of my head—and beyond that all it was good for was for stacking in vaults to back currency, or draping about peoples' necks, wrists, fingers, and earlobes to look pretty. And yet people craved it.

I looked at my own rough hands. No rings. No wedding band, and no fussy old settings handed down from grandma. Somehow my iron-clad sense of practicality had always drawn me to prefer land and a winter's supply of bacon over gold, but I didn't have those, either. And now that I thought about it, I really couldn't understand why people put such faith in the value of gold. What good was it, really? If drought and famine came and I exchanged all my water and grain for a lump of gold, what then would I drink and eat? Why was gold considered worth hoarding, and fighting wars to seize,

and for that matter, how was it worth the risk of life and limb
it took to mine it, or the gamble of fortunes in technology
and land rights and stock dollars to find? And how had the
search for just a little bit more of it led to a woman's death
in the empty expanse of the Nevada desert?

My mind sliding into the comfortable groove of investigation, I put the book I'd been holding back on the shelf and
pulled down one that would teach me about the wealth of
kings and the dreams of paupers.

17

SHIRLEY COOK HEARD HERMIONE'S TOYOTA RATTLE
to a stop in front of her house, then heard the door groan
open. As was her custom, Hermione did not approach the
house. Instead, she waited just outside the gate for an invitation.

"Oh, come on in," Shirley growled from the doorway.

The gate squeaked open and clicked shut, but Hermione
made no sound as she came up the gravel walkway. Shirley
wanted to curse at this silence. *The damned woman even
avoids the place where the porch step groans*, she thought.
Presently she felt Hermione's presence crowding in near her—
and finally smelled the barest hint of the woman's exhalations
curling up against her cheek. "Hello, Shirley," Hermione said.

Shirley turned on her heel and led her visitor inside. They
had lost Pat, but another was already arising to replace her,
and to catch her they would need a good plan.

STEPHEN GILES WALKED slowly into the central post office
in downtown Reno, pausing at the standing desk which held
the forms necessary for registering and insuring mail. It was
more than an hour past the time when the service windows
closed, and he was there to receive rather than send an envelope,
but he had chosen this time because there would be
very few people moving about among the long aisles of mailboxes.
He riffled through the forms at the standing desk, giving
the man who was opening a mailbox near his own time
to finish his business and leave. Then he turned toward the
long row of boxes, his hand already rising with anticipation,
but a short woman who was muttering something about cat
food came zipping around the corner, and he pocketed the
key. To cover his aborted motions, he walked ten feet beyond

his box and stared into another one, pretending to be disappointed to find nothing in it.

The woman left.

Stephen hurried to his box—second row from the top, third to the right of the divider—and stabbed in his key. Yes, he could see an envelope in there resting alone in the narrow space, hideously vulnerable to the open back of the mailbox. *What if a postal service worker noticed it?* he wondered anxiously. *Anyone could take it!* He struggled to turn his key, his hand tight and clumsy with anxiety. *This system has to be changed. I will insist. This is not how it should be done; I've told them all along.* He snatched the envelope out of the mailbox, slapped the door shut, and hurried out of the building. *What are they thinking of? Surely this system could implicate them just as much as it does me! If they won't change it, I'll tell them I will not*—Here Stephen's thoughts ended, because he knew what their answer would be. They would simply find someone else. That must not happen. It was disagreeable to do business with them, but, as he had reassured himself many times, a little more filth was sometimes necessary if one expected to reach an ultimate cleansing.

It took all of his remaining composure to maintain an ordinary pace as he turned the corner, transited the three blocks to the street where he had left his pathetic car, checked one more time in the reflection of a storefront's glass to make certain he was not being followed, and climbed in. There he tore the envelope open and hurriedly tugged out the slip of paper inside.

Something was wrong. It wasn't . . . he turned the envelope over, read the name and address. They belonged to the holder of the box next to his.

Stephen thrust the door open, hung his head out the door, and began to vomit.

A car passing on the street skidded to a stop and the driver jumped out. "Jesus, man!" the man yelled. "You all right? Jane!" he called back to his car. "Phone nine-one-one! This man's turning blue!"

Dizzy with fear, Stephen Giles pulled his head back into

his car and slammed the door on his would-be savior's arm. The door bounced open and the man retreated, howling. Stephen slammed the door again, fired the ignition, and accelerated away, clipping the front corner of the Samaritan's car as he went.

The man roared with pain as his wife scrambled to help him, still clutching her cell phone. "Scratch that ambulance!" he moaned, "Call the police!"

"They're coming, dear," the efficient Jane replied. "And don't worry, I got his plate number."

KYLE CHRISTIE SLOUCHED in the doorway to Virgil Davis's office, waiting for the superintendent to look up from his work. "What?" Virgil asked, his eyes still firmly on the papers he had laid out in front of him.

"I can't find him anywhere," Kyle said.

Virgil slammed one hand down on the top of his drafting table, making his mechanical pencils jump. "I haven't got *time* to worry about some asshole who gets his truck stuck out there somewheres! I got things—"

"*You* know his truck isn't stuck somewhere."

Virgil kept his face bowed toward the table, but shifted his eyes ever so slightly to gauge the other man's position. "So?"

"I heard you two yelling last night."

"What are you—"

"I never heard The Don raise his voice before. What'd you say to him to light him up like that?"

Virgil stiffened, at first surprised to find such shrewdness in a man he'd thought devoid of it. But when he turned his face toward Kyle, his eyes had narrowed into slits and his face was hard with rage.

Kyle nodded his head contemptuously. "Nice going. Didn't work out the way you planned, did it? *Now* what the fuck you going to do?"

LEFTY LAMORE POURED her fifth cup of strong, black coffee of the day and set it down on her desk. Before sitting down next to it and starting to work, she stretched, rising onto her toes and raising her arms high over her head, waiting for each

vertebra to click into place. They revolted most days and tried
to stay kinked, but she had learned patience. Besides, this
stretching opened up her lungs and forced her to breathe
deeply and reminded her to accept, for one more day, that
life was fleeting, and to be savored. This mental aspect of her
stretching came with difficulty, because it pulled at her scar
tissue, reminding her once again that one of her fabulous
breasts was gone.

Satisfied that her vertebral column was now fully aligned,
Lefty dropped her arms and sighed, letting out the last great
breath with a mixture of resignation and well-chewed irony.
Such was typically her mood. She scratched at her still cur-
vaceous, if now somewhat more Rubenesque, body, reached
down her shirt front to adjust the prosthesis that filled her left
bra cup, and stared out the window for a while at the wide
sweep of brown Nevada desert that stretched before her. How
she loved this view; empty of all signs of human impact save
for the wind sock that stood at the end of the landing strip
and the adits that pocked the far mountains. There was no
breeze; the wind sock hung limp. Lefty snorted to herself,
thinking that it looked about like the dicks of some of last
night's customers must look about now. The fat cat captains
of industry that had parked that particular biz jet had come
in here last evening looking like a forty-knot wind, but her
girls had taken care of that for them. What a bunch of putzes
this batch of Johns had been. Giggled like school girls. She'd
have to slip the girls a little extra after a gang like this one,
maybe fly in a masseuse with sympathetic hands. She leaned
over the desk to make herself a note.

Lefty's eyes settled to the computer that held the accounting work that awaited her. Business was good here at the
Bronco Betty fly-in brothel, one more fact that said that she
shouldn't service the men herself anymore. Her cancer surgery scar was a turn-off to most of them anyway, and with
those who found it titillating, the accounting work meant that
she was not financially compelled to do business. She had
thus afforded herself the luxury of an early retirement to
madam-only status.

Lefty now sat down and typed her password into the computer. The hard drive hummed and grunted as it did her bidding, bringing up the information for Granville Resources. She sighed again. She had put off reconciling this account, because there was something a little odd about it, and that bothered her. "Okay now, old girl," she told herself firmly, "you've procrastinated as long as you could. You've given it your best time slot—everyone's napping, no one's bugging you—so now crack this little eggy, okay?"

She moved through the database, checking and rechecking the numbers for expenses and payroll at the Gloriana Mine. Next she worked back through the corporate picture, rechecking everything for operations in the conterminous forty-eight of the United States of America. It all checked and tallied, so why was she hesitating to send in her monthly report?

She liked having this account. It was fat and juicy, and Chittenden, the corporate big-wig who had brought it to her, had been a lot of fun. He'd told her he wanted an outside eye on his numbers. A former pilot with the British navy, he had flown in here alone at the controls of the corporate jet and set up the account himself, grabbing a little partying on the side, and it had been a good party, lots of laughs and slap and tickle over the excellent single-malt Scotch he had brought with him from a stopover in Canada. He had tried to take the half-full bottle with him when he left, the cheapskate, but she had closed her hand firmly around its neck. It wasn't smuggling if she didn't declare it, was it? She smiled acerbically to herself, thinking that this wasn't the first time in her career that she had disagreed with the hypocritical crap some men upheld as laws, when they weren't busy breaking them.

Lefty laughed again, remembering the hilarity that had followed when Chittenden had knelt on the bearskin rug in front of the black leather couch here in her office, the better to arrange along her thigh a row of crackers encrusted with caviar and choice cold cuts that he had produced from the refrigerator in his jet. It had been a hot afternoon like this one, and she'd been wearing the same shorts she had on today. He had begun to nibble at those expensive little canapes, working his rather pointy nose like a mouse, and when he got to the fourth one, he had asked, "So tell me, fair maiden, does my contract allow for a little hide-the-salami on the side?"

"No," Lefty had replied, feeling the brashness of her Scotch and damned sick of men who wanted freebies, "but you can hold my breast any time you want."

"Only one?" he had asked.

She had looked down into his mischievous smile and had said, "Yeah, 'cause only one comes off!" and had yanked the prosthesis out and clouted him over the head with it. God bless him, he had shrieked with delight and caught it overhand, then rolled around on the rug cuddling the gelatinous thing and cooing as delightedly as he would if it had been the real item, and had said, "So that's why they call you Lefty!"

You Brits aren't the sissies you seem, she had decided, and had almost given him some anyway, but even though it had been three years since her surgery, she still didn't feel like doing it for recreation.

Lefty shifted her mind from that memory back onto her computer screen, where, with the looseness that comes with humor, she began at last to discern the pattern that had troubled her. She reached instantly for the phone, ready to report it to Chittenden, but then stopped, her hand hovering over the instrument.

She withdrew her hand, thought things through. Even with this irregularity, the numbers did tally, so she had a choice. She could telephone Chittenden, or simply send in her report as usual and let his inside accountants find it themselves. "Yes," she said out loud to herself. "That might be a really good idea, because if I report this directly to Mr. Pommy, then he'll know sooner, but he will also know that I know, and that might just put me in a bad position."

Lefty rose from her desk and walked past the black leather couch to the enormous window that looked out across the fantastic sweep of the northern Nevada landscape. Fighting to quell the small voice inside her that abhorred the kind of mucking around that she had just discovered, she said, "Just remember, Lefty, nobody knows the misery of a bad position like an old whore."

UMBERTO RODRIGUEZ PULLED his metal-flake gold four-by-four up to the pump and set the gas running into the tank. Then he strutted over to the pay phone near the curb, the late afternoon sunlight reflecting smartly off his mirrored sunglasses. When the line connected, he said, "Morgan Shumway, *por favor*."

"Who's calling please?"

"Doctor Umberto Rodriguez." He let his R's roll. He was feeling good.

"One moment." The line clicked as he was put on hold.

"*Sí*, it *will* be only *uno momento, porque* your boss will want to speak with *me*," he told the empty telephone.

The line clicked on again. He heard a man's voice, quick and snappish. "Why are you calling me?"

"Ah, Morgan, good evening. I have good news for you."

"Not now."

"No, of *course*," Umberto cooed, his spirits so high that he bowed deferentially toward the phone, even though his listener could not see him. Then he let his power suffuse his voice with a more martial air. "I am in Wendover; just crossed the state line. I will be in Salt Laky City in about two hours. Where shall we meet?"

"Meet?"

"Yes. I think when you hear what I have to tell you, you will be most pleased that you have come," he said, letting it sound *un poquito* threatening.

There was a pause, then: "No. Later. Be at the Saltair Marina, nine P.M. You know the place?"

"Yes, yes. I am the biologist, *verdad*? I have been to this lake of yours to study your Franklin's gulls."

Morgan again did not answer immediately. When he did, his voice was tight with constrained rage. "Bring your damned binoculars, then!"

Umberto chuckled in spite of the counter-threat that oozed from the other man's voice. "*Hasta nueve*," he crooned, then replaced the phone on its hook. He smiled and caressed the grip of the instrument as he removed his hand and closed his eyes, as if remembering a moment of illicit sex stolen on a warm afternoon. He raised the hand to his cheek and felt the warm plumpness of his own face with admiration. "Umberto, Umberto," he sang to himself, "*Tú estas un hombre ingenioso.*"

LAUREL DIETZ PULLED the pickup truck up by the unloading dock at the assay lab in Reno. Her hands clenched the steering wheel tightly. The hope, the *anticipation* of actually *knowing* something had her wound up so tight that she was almost dizzy.

She had timed her arrival well. There were few cars in the lot. The day shift would have left, and she had guessed correctly that only a small crew would be on during the evenings. Donning her Gloriana Mine ball cap, she hopped out of the cab of the truck and searched for someone to charm into unloading the samples for her.

She quickly found a willing mound of muscle in the person of a young red-haired guy named Zeke, who smiled a special, "how 'bout it?" smile at her. When he was done unloading, he put his thoughts into words: "Got anything goin' for dinner?"

Laurel smiled back her most innocent smile and deflected his question with one of her own. "You got the results of the last shipment yet?"

Zeke stared blankly. "Aw, heck, y'ain't got it yet? It's all uploaded soon as it's done."

"Well, yes of course, but my computer's been down. In fact, if it gets out that I lost them, well . . . Can you give me another set?"

Zeke looked left and right, as if there might be someone else around. "Well, actually I don't have much to do with all that. And, um, I'm the only one here just now, you see, and . . ."

Laurel stepped a little closer to him and lowered her eyelids just a fraction. "You won't rat on me, will you? I was supposed to have those numbers in, and you don't know Virgil Davis, but he has this *awful* temper. . . ."

Zeke gave her a smug look and hooked her ungracefully under the chin with a knuckle. "Well, now, I suppose I can get a diskette out and copy it off for you again—I mean, if you can figure out the code. There's no names anywhere in the system, you know, for security. You got to have the code." He looked back over his shoulder at her for reassurance as he led her into the belly of the building, past glistening machines and antiseptically-clean lab benches.

"Wow, this is neat!" Laurel said. "I've never been in the lab before."

Zeke puffed his chest out with suddenly-assumed pride. "Oh, yeah, it's cool. Totally robotic. The samples come in here with their bar codes and are split there, and through all the equipment there, and the numbers come out here." He showed her into an inner office and closed the door.

Laurel smiled at the array of computers. These, she understood.

"You got the access code for your company, right?" Zeke asked, his doubt again rising. "I mean, shit, if anyone saw me doing this . . ."

Laurel tapped her head. "I have it right in here." *It took me long enough to get it*, she thought. *Damned if I'm going to trust it to a scrap of paper after that hassle.*

Zeke leaned over the keyboard and awoke the machine from its slumbers. After one last hesitation, he typed in the password and initialized the database.

Laurel moved Zeke aside with a flirtatious shove and got to work searching for the right codes. The numbers she was looking for would mean nothing without the index back at the mine, but once she had the assay results imbedded in these codes, she could get the index, she was sure. It was all a matter of matching the right set of numbers and then getting the map out of someone like . . . Kyle. Her hands flew expertly over the keys. *Yes, here they are: last week's assays from the mine. So that means that these other assays under our code are MacCallum's.* She whipped a floppy disk out of her shirt pocket, popped it into the drive, and began to highlight the rows she wanted to copy.

Two minutes later, when she rose from the chair in which she'd perched herself, Zeke put a hopeful hand on her delicate little shoulder. "So how about dinner?" he said, his face growing soupy with lust.

Laurel tipped her head perkily to one side. "I don't have time for that," she said cheerily. *No, much better not to be seen with this guy outside of this building. Keep this interchange just as quiet as it is now. Better something quicker than dinner; something that will seal his silence.* She smirked. *Something no one would believe, even if he opens his bovine mouth and brags.* "But how about a little you-know-what? Right here. Right now." She glanced at the carpet. It was clean enough. "The floor will do nicely."

18

AT QUARTER TO FIVE, I PHONED THE MECHANIC AND
found that my truck was not yet fixed. Something about the
wrong part having been delivered from the supplier. I knew
I could get around Salt Lake City easily by bus or by cab, so
I was not worried about transport, but I still couldn't figure
out what to do with my evening or what I wanted for dinner,
so I stayed at the library and continued to read. It was an
effort, but I began to understand a little about how and where
gold crystallizes in the earth's crust, about the various theories
regarding why the crust had fractured and heaved as it did
across the Great Basin, and about the connections between
the two phenomena. Then I began to read again about gold
as money.

So I was pretty deep in thought when Ray suddenly
touched my shoulder. I about jumped out of my skin. I was
in the middle of the evolution of the gold standard, and had
been concentrating hard to follow the logic, or illogic, of cur-
rencies. "Gol, Ray, you surprised me!" I spun around without
rising from my seat, adrenaline pumping.

Ray's expression was watchful, as if uncertain of his welcome. He settled onto his haunches next to my chair, the
posture pulling his off-duty jeans up nicely around his muscular legs. He also looked a little perturbed. Wasn't this his
town, and didn't he have every right to come looking for me?

I dropped my voice to the whisper appropriate for libraries.
"How'd you find me?" I demanded, embarrassed that he had.

"Took a few calls." His face stiffened. "Why? Are you
hiding?"

In answer, I hung my head.

Ray put a hand to his lips in thought. That was one of the
things I liked about him: He seldom spoke without first thinking through what he had to say. It saved a lot of unnecessary

clarification and rebuttals. His brow slowly knit with sadness, or worry, I was not sure which. At last, he dropped his hand and said, "Dinner?"

"Sure."

He smiled shyly. "There's a pizza place just off campus."

I returned his smile with one of my own. Pizza, the next best thing to total junk food. Ray was learning the simpler, more reliable ways to my heart.

THE PIE PIZZERIA is located just west of the university campus, downhill toward the center of the city. It's the ultimate student hangout, although it seemed to draw young families with hungry children, too. It is accessed from a steep staircase a level down from the sidewalk. Ray and I were shown to a table back by the pinball machines, near an exposed brick wall sporting the obligatory T-shirts offered for sale. The logo emblazoned on them was pretty good, as these things go: the Greek symbol *pi* surmounted by a thick crust and lots of cheese.

When we'd ordered (Canadian bacon and artichoke hearts, oh heaven), we settled in over our soft drinks and waited. Ray took my hand in his and stroked it with his thumb. "How was Nevada?"

So his first call had been to Ava. That meant he was trying to be kind and forgiving, even understanding. A good stunt, considering I didn't really understand why I'd gone to Nevada, myself. "Fine. Kind of interesting." Fishing for something nonvolatile to offer, I said, "I got to sit up front with the pilot. It was a twin-engine Piper, really fast. She let me fly it for a while."

Ray smiled, happy for me. Then he waited for me to say something else.

"Yeah, okay," I began, figuring to throw the whole story out in the open where it could lose some of its bite. "Tom Latimer has this idea I could help him with this case he's working on out there." My best intentions thus offered, I waffled, keeping back those details to which Ray would most likely object. "It's a fraud case. There's this gold mining company that's hired a wildlife biology firm to find out if there are any endangered species on this property they want to develop into a mine, and the field biologist sent in some figures that say the little critters are feeling just great and in fact breeding like . . ." I had almost said hell.

Ray took this in with his usual quiet, then asked, "What's this got to do with you?" His look had become piercing, and coming from Ray's blue eyes, that was somewhat devastating. He had hopes of making detective with the Salt Lake City police, and he had the knack. He had cut right through the fuzzy edges of what I was not saying.

"Well, nothing yet, really." I bit my lip. I didn't want him to know that the biologist had now met her death and that I was already spinning theories about what had caused it. I was supposed to be acting like a girlfriend, and a house guest. "Well, I guess I was supposed to say something about the gold mine. But we didn't see it. There's a big range fire. Lots of smoke. Sage burns so hot you don't want to go driving around out there until it's out."

Ray nodded, his version of saying, "Oh," but he continued to stare. I would have been angry at this scrutiny except that it was half of what had hooked me on him in the first place: Beneath all his fidelity to faith and family, he took absolutely nothing on faith, and, like me, wanted every last bloomin' thing proved to him.

So I dug in my heels and began to stare at the table top.

Ray squeezed my hand. "Em."

I cleared my throat.

"I knew it was going to be hard for you here."

My throat tightened. Tears began to sting my eyes.

We were both silent until the pizza came, and, as we ate, commented only on the succulence of the dish. We drove in silence to his mother's house, and sat in silence in the cab of his pristine four-by-four for many long minutes after he had turned off the engine and set the brake. It was a good thing to do. In this hour of quietude, the weight of the differences between our pasts slipped away, and fears of how the future might evolve melted under the warmth of the moment. Ten-

sion slowly eased into comfort, and it once again became
clear to each of us that we simply liked each other's company.
In silence, we had, as always, found a place for ourselves,
and in silence, outside the ideologies and controversies of
words, we were a couple. He held my hand, I leaned my head
against his shoulder, and Salt Lake City slowly faded from
the rose of alpenglow into the shadows of night. Finally, he
kissed the top of my head, sighed, and said, "Time."

"Yeah."

As he walked me up to his mother's house, he slipped an
arm around my waist, took my near hand in promenade dance
pose, and swung me expertly around. I laughed. He continued
to lead me, now whistling a tune. He released my waist, spun
me, and fetched me back, all the time moving with such exquisite rhythm and physical communication that he was easy
to follow. We wound up on Ava's front steps under the glare
of the porch light, laughing, our arms around each other in
happy embrace. Then, playfully pulling the lapel of his jacket
up to shield me from the neighbors' watchful windows, he
gave me a wonderful, warm, lingering kiss. He followed it
up with a playful peck on each cheek, and said, "Tomorrow,
seven o'clock, same place. You, me. We'll go dancing."

I grabbed his shirt front and pulled him down for another
kiss, the clearest answer I could imagine.

AN HOUR LATER, as I settled into my bed and Ray settled
into his halfway across town, the obvious gaps in our relationship once again rose to plague me. I realized I needed
someone to talk to, and it wasn't going to be Ava. When I
awoke early the next morning and faced the fact that I had a
whole day to kill before I saw Ray again, the need doubled
and tripled. Considering that I knew just about nobody in Salt
Lake City who was not related to Ray, I set aside my usual
shyness and phoned Faye Carter. " 'Lo?" she answered grog-
gily, then, remembering that she was a businesswoman,
added, "Oh. Um, Special Deliveries."

From this greeting, I surmised that she didn't get a whole
lot of calls for her services, or that I had phoned too early.

"This is Em Hansen. You flew me to Nevada yesterday."

"Oh, yes. Em. What's up, Cisco?"

I let out my breath in relief. "Nothing, Pancho. Absolutely nothing. Can you play?"

I heard her laugh. "Sure. Hey, I got to run an errand, but I'll tell you what, you come with me."

"Where are we going?"

"You'll see. Shall I pick you up?"

"*Si*, Cisco, my horse he still lame."

"I'm Pancho; you're Cisco."

"Like I say, real lame."

She laughed again. "Give me an address."

AN HOUR LATER, we were in Faye's Porsche, accelerating into the desert southwest of Great Salt Lake with the CD player blasting Brazilian vocals and exceedingly fine lattes in our hands. It seemed that Faye had a date to deliver something to someone somewhere in downtown Denver, and needed to sharpen a certain skill before attempting it. I had no idea what she was talking about, and I didn't much care. The moment she had arrived at Ava's, I had set aside my confusion over Ray, had remembered that I loved to raise hell, and that was that.

We turned off down a side track that led back east toward the west flank of the Oquirrh Mountains. It was a lonesome place; hot, dry, and beautiful. Faye parked the car near a low hill and popped the hood, pulled out a couple of pistol cases, and set to unlocking them.

"We're going plinking?" I asked.

"Target practice," she said, pulling out a full-sized silhouette target and applying it with duct tape to a rusting, bullet-riddled oil drum that lay up against the nearest rise. "You like revolvers or automatics?"

"Ah, rifles, actually."

"Don't own one."

"Mm."

She said, "Perhaps I am being presumptuous. You of

course don't have to shoot. But I got to bring my aim back up to snuff here before today's run."

"Why?"

"This time I'm not carrying people."

"Oh," I said, not the least bit certain what she meant. And somehow I didn't want to ask, like maybe this was a personal question, or the answer was something I didn't want to know.

She adjusted her aviator sunglasses and tossed me a pair of ear plugs and some safety glasses and popped on a set of shooter's muffs, then set to work loading a six-shot snub-nosed Ruger .357 with a speed loader. She snapped the chamber shut and laid it back down on the open gun case, then applied a clip of bullets to the Colt .45, slipped it into an odd looking holster, and set it back into the other case. About twenty feet from the silhouette target, she unfolded a low camp chair and clipped the .45 holster underneath it. The Ruger she tucked into a holster inside the back of her jeans, and she draped the voluminous blousing of her soft rayon shirt over the protruding butt. A concealed weapon. I began to have suspicions about what she was delivering to Denver. I likewise began to be a little less certain about playing Thelma and Louise.

"You stand between me and the car," she said cheerily, pointing the opposite direction from the target. "No way I'm going to shoot at that."

I backed away, squeezing the little foam plugs into my ears, and sat right down on the front fender of the Porsche. I have perfect respect for firearms.

Faye said, "You wait a moment or two and then yell, 'Now!'" She turned her back to me and waited, shrugging a sudden tension from her shoulders.

"Now!"

Faye whipped the Ruger out of its hidden holster and unloaded it into the target in three two-shot bursts. Then she walked up to the oil drum and had a look. "Dang," she said. "I'm rusty, all right."

She had stitched the target right across the heart, missing

the penultimate ring that circled it with only one shot. "Um, if that's rusty, what's oily look like?"

She laughed. "Oh, when I'm hot I can do a lot better than this. It's a Zen thing."

"Oh."

Faye returned to her position, cranked another speed-loader full of bullets into the Ruger, and let fly with some more premeditated shooting. I quickly saw what she meant. She was a vicious good shot. Needless to say, I began to feel a little intimidated. After emptying a third, fourth and fifth load into the target, she asked, "Are you sure you don't want to have a go?"

I shrugged.

Faye opened the chamber of the gun and shucked the shells, then, leaving it open to show that it was empty, set it on the gun case. She applied a fresh target to the oil drum. I put on the safety glasses and she showed me how to close and open the chamber and work the speed loader, then demonstrated the posture I should use for shooting: feet shoulder-width apart, arms out straight, hands cradling the thick Pachmeyer grip. I eased in the trigger. As the ungodly loud blast of the gun's discharge thumped my chest, I saw the pistol buck high from my planned aim, and a flash of burning gunpowder lit the air around my hands. Even in the brightness of the summer's day, this was brighter. I had missed the target entirely.

"Now that you've felt that, you'll be ready for it the next time," Faye said.

It took more like twenty shots, but I began hitting the target with some regularity.

Faye smiled absently. "Now think of your worst enemy. He's after you. Going to hurt you. Rape you. Your job is to spare your own life. Your only hope to stop him is with this gun." She pointed at the target, her face tightening with alarm. "Here he comes! Now!"

My mind focussed instantly to a point, and I gave him three shots right in the stomach.

Faye pursed her lips and nodded. "Nice work."

I felt kind of sick, right in there next to weirdly proud. I opened the chamber, shucked the shells, set the pistol down on the gun case, took off the safety glasses, and returned to my perch on the hood of the car.

Faye moved the camp chair ten feet closer to the target and adjusted it so that she was facing ninety degrees away. Then she sat down, and, looking at me, said, "You wait a moment or two 'til I look like I'm parking this thing, then yell, 'Now!' like before." She pantomimed driving a car, both hands on the wheel, warming to her play-acting. She put out her right foot to brake and steered to the right, turning to an imaginary curb, then set an invisible hand brake. She began scrabbling around on an unseen second seat, as if picking up a package.

"Now!" I yelled.

In one fluid motion, Faye dropped her imaginary load, yanked the Colt out from under the seat, snapped it to her left shoulder, and pumped off two rounds, tattering the silhouette target in the solar plexus.

"Now!"

Two more, in the heart.

"Now!"

She emptied the magazine into the target's head, dropped the pistol to the floor, whipped the Ruger out of her holster, glanced up to an imaginary rear-view mirror and right towards me. Only then did she relax. "Weak-arm shooting," she said in explanation.

"What if he comes up on my side of the car?" I asked.

"Oh, I think I'll leave that part out of today's practice," she replied. "I don't want to mess up my wax job on the car."

"Thanks," I said drily.

Faye reloaded both pistols using bullets from different boxes, placing hollow points in the Ruger. In the Colt, she racked a hollow-point into the chamber, set the safety, then reloaded the clip with hollow-points, followed by a single fully-jacketed bullet. This, she explained, more fully guaranteed at least two good shots, although it was somewhat dicey to fire at someone with a jacketed bullet, as it would likely go right through and could hit something on the other side. The hollow points were the man-stoppers, designed as they were to flatten on impact and discharge all their kinetic energy into the "target," but they more easily jammed in the automatic's mechanism.

She put the Ruger back into the hidden holster behind her hip rather than locking it away in its gun case. The Colt she slipped into position underneath the front seat of the Porsche.

I began to wonder what in hell I'd gotten myself into this time.

Driving back toward Salt Lake City, Faye said, "You were okay with that Ruger."

"Oh."

She glanced my way. "If you're going to join the FBI, you've got to get used to such things."

I snapped around in my seat and stared at her, eyes narrowed. "Who said I was going to join the FBI?"

Faye pulled her head back in surprise. "Hey, I only work here."

"Tom told you that?"

"He said he was bringing a prospective trainee with him."

"Nice," I said acidly. "Good old Tom. So tell me, are you a trainee, too?"

"Oh, hell no. Too much like working for a living."

"Unlike what you're doing today."

"Today I'm helping out a friend."

I was so angry that my mouth ran away with me. "Oh, great! And what kind of a friend? A Colombian with a kilo of something he needs dropped in somebody's corn field?" I of course instantly wished I hadn't said that. If I was wrong, it was insulting, and if I was right, it was about the last subject I should broach, a good way to wind up dead in a ditch somewhere. *You idiot*, I told myself, *just reckon the price tag on that Porsche, and the hot twin-engined airplane—both nice and fast—and figure the likelihood that her whole story about being a trust fund baby isn't a cover for where she really gets her money.*

Faye began to howl with laughter. "You think I'm running

drugs? Wow, that's a good one!" She thumped the steering wheel with merriment.

Stunned, I measured her laughter. It bubbled and boiled out of her with joy. "Well, shit! You take me out into the desert and trot out a bunch of firearms, and—"

"I'm transporting something to Denver that's very small and valuable, but white powder it is not. Oh, Em, that's a riot!"

"What else is that small and valuable?" I asked stupidly, just before about twenty perfectly legal possibilities began to present themselves in my head. "Or should I say, what else requires someone to fly it in a private plane, for heaven's sake?"

Faye wiped a tear from one eye, and sniffed her laughter into control. "I told you, I get bored. I don't fly for free, but I don't charge my friends much over the price of gas and upkeep, especially when they offer to buy me lunch. And my service is so off the wall and variable that it makes me a good security risk. My friend phoned up last evening and asked me to carry this package today because he needed it in a hurry and because I'm about the last person anyone would expect to see carrying it around." She considered what she'd said for a moment. "Well, actually I'm a rich kid and all that, so I suppose one might expect me to be carrying something valuable, but what I'm trying to say is, I don't look like a delivery boy."

"No . . ." I said, still uncertain.

Picking up on my tone, she said, "The pistol is just protection in case anyone's watching at either end. It just wouldn't be prudent to go without."

"Sure," I said doubtfully.

Now Faye looked at me like I was kind of nuts. "Do you wear a hat when you work in the sun?"

I looked at my hands. "Yes, but—"

"But what? You don't approve of guns?"

"Guns are tools," I said.

"Well, then, these guns are good tools for keeping yourself safe."

"I disagree," I said. "Some people think four wheel drive is there to get them out of a jam if they get stuck. I think it gives false security, and gets you about twice as stuck. Why not just stay out of situations where you might need to defend yourself with lethal force?"

"Make me a list," Faye said, "and I'll tell you where and when I'm ready to be limited by other peoples' behaviors."

"Oh, come on, Faye, the shooting you were doing today was not ordinary shooting. You didn't just learn that yesterday after your friend called up, now *did* you?"

"No."

Faye suddenly looked embarrassed; so much so, in fact, that I almost stopped my questioning there. But this conversation had come this far, and it was time to rip it the rest of the way open. "All right, give: Where and when did you learn to handle a pistol like that?"

Faye's face went through a series of twitches, like she was thinking through not only *what* she was going to tell me, but *if*. "I learned it over the past six months," she said.

"Where?" I insisted, and then, beginning to see the dawn, added, "Or should I say, from whom?"

She gave me a silly, embarrassed display of her teeth. "Okay, so Tom taught me. And, um, right there, where we were."

I leaned back in my seat and appraised Faye from a brand new angle. *Well*, I decided, *I can scratch the nookie motive from the list of Tom's possible agendas. Whatever he's up to, he isn't doing it to get into my pants, because he's already in hers.*

19

IN FOR A PENNY, IN FOR A POUND. ONCE FAYE HAD told me she was taking a small and valuable package to her friend in Denver, I got to asking the obvious questions, and the whole story came out. Her friend was a gem dealer who specialized in resetting antique stones in modern designs, and he needed Faye to run courier for him with a few bits of ice from which an old dame in Salt Lake City had just announced she was ready to part. It was an expensive but relatively secure way of shipping the goods, as Faye was unlikely to lose her way or forget to deliver. She had built up an entertaining little business handling specialty deliveries, and was successful in part because her customers knew she wouldn't be tempted to steal. She did not need the money. And many of them knew her first socially, having met her over foie gras at Grosse Point or over escargot in Paris. "It keeps life from getting boring," she told me, "and it makes a *great* tax write-off. And I *love* to fly, but I'm one of these weird pragmatists who needs a place to fly *to*."

I shook my head in amazement. "But what about the uniform, then? Doesn't that make you stand out like a sore thumb? I mean, it could blow your cover."

"I don't wear the uniform when I'm handling goods, only when I'm carrying passengers. It makes them feel more secure."

"Tom Latimer needs security?" Then I thought through what I was saying. "Well, I know he hates riding in helicopters, but I thought he was okay with fixed-wing craft."

"He is, as you could see yesterday with him falling asleep in the backseat." I was tempted to say something acerbic like, So you're past the uniform stage with Tom, when Faye did her own job of digging herself in deeper by adding, "I only wore the uniform yesterday because you were going to be along, and we had to make it look more legit."

I let the particulars of her relationship with Tom go for the moment, in part because what she'd said opened an even greater can of worms. "Oh, great. So you were in on this scam to get Em to Nevada. So what's the—"

"No, that *was* a legitimate flight."

"You mean the FBI paid you for it? Since when do federal employees get to hire private planes for a trip they could make more cheaply and faster by public carrier?"

Faye bit the side of her lower lip. "Well . . . Tom uses me, well, because of course I'm good, but also because I'm usually available, damn it. Okay, so I don't really charge him. He gives me what it would cost him to fly commercially. It about covers the gas. Hey, I'm building up a résumé, okay? Or I guess you call it a statement of qualifications. I get to say I've flown government agents around on hush-hush stuff. But Tom requires that everything be by the book."

"Sure. That's our Tom," I said, with heavy irony. I was certain that taking me to Nevada with him was anything but according to Hoyle.

"You know what I'm saying!" Faye said with that special note of aggravation women save for defending their choice of men to other women.

"Unfortunately, I do. Oh, lawdy, but I do."

"Tom is a good man," Faye said hotly.

"And that's about all the more I want to know about him, if you'll forgive me."

"Sure." An angry blush began creeping up her throat.

Sticking my foot in farther, I said, "I just want to keep it strictly professional between him and me."

Faye's face reddened further.

"Okay, so I've stuck my toes in past my tonsils," I said. "I am sorry. What I'm trying to say is—"

"No, that's just fine," she said, cutting me off. She took a quick breath and let it out. And focussed purposefully on her driving.

Strict etiquette would have dictated that I let the subject

drop, but this wasn't exactly a moment for manners. "So what *is* his big idea, taking me to Nevada?"

Faye gave me a quick glance, her brows drawn close with confusion. "He's trying to recruit you. What's so hard to understand about—"

"Forget I asked," I said.

Faye braked and downshifted to catch an exit ramp off of Interstate 80, well inside the Salt Lake City limits. "So; why don't you come to Denver with me?"

I had my mouth half opened to say yes when it occurred to me that her invitation seemed a wee bit too pat. Had Tom put her up to it? "No, I'd be in the way. You have to do your delivery, and, well . . ."

She gave me a nudge. "You'll be part of my cover. Just two chicks out to Denver for the day. We can do some shopping, you can fly the plane. . . . "

"Your offer is more than tempting, but really . . ."

Faye made a silly face. "Hey, I don't like to beg, but I'd really enjoy your company. All my friends here are either at work or staying home with half a dozen small children."

Now it was my turn to laugh. "Not a local, *are* you?"

"It's not like this in Michigan."

"I'd have to be back by six."

She held up her near hand in agreement, and I gave her a high-five.

WE SWUNG BY the FedEx station so that Faye could pick up a freshly arrived cashier's cheque that awaited her there from her friend the dealer, which Faye was supposed to present to the seller. The packet included a bill of sale which the seller was supposed to sign, establishing authenticity, and a notarized letter of introduction and identification for Faye, complete with a photograph of her which he had signed across the face. I began to feel even more at ease. Such things can of course be faked, but I figured that even Tom Latimer wouldn't get this exotic in making up a cover to lure me to Denver. Besides, what could he want me to do in Denver?

We then phoned ahead to warn the old lady with the rocks

that two couriers were coming, not just one, and when we arrived at her quaint twenty-room house, we all went through a little charade that we were friends dropping by for tea with dear old "Auntie." Once we were inside and the door was closed, our warbling octogenarian turned into a pleasantly tough old broad who shook us down for identification. After we'd satisfied this protocol, Faye produced a jeweler's loupe and took a look at the stones, which I thought garishly large. The group included a ring with a twenty-two-carat diamond shaped long before the brilliant cut had been developed and a pair of ten-carat teardrop-shaped earrings.

The old dame was very matter-of-fact. "I just don't have anywhere to wear them anymore, and I can support such *important* causes with the money," she told us. And she was nobody's fool. She insisted that both Faye and I submit to fingerprinting. "No offense, girls, but you'd be amazed what people try on us old biddies."

She took us into a study the size of my parents' whole ranch house and worked us over with an old-fashioned stamp pad and a piece of her engraved stationery. Then she did in fact give us tea and cookies, and, ten minutes' worth of chit-chat later, we were on our way back down the walk to the car, about two million dollars richer.

Faye carried the diamonds in a small leather purse stuck deep inside a special pouch in her shoulder bag. She sloped back out to the Porsche just as casually as if carrying only cosmetics and chewing gum. When we were a mile or so from the house, and she had stopped and started and snaked around a bit to make sure no one was following us, she said, "Aw, relax, Em. It's only carbon."

"Sure, diamonds are only carbon. That's why they stick them in pencils to write with. *Graphite* is only carbon! *Diamonds* are carbon atoms which have joined in a tetrahedral pattern with other carbon atoms at great temperatures and pressures!"

"Uh . . ."

"I really am a geologist."

"But it just rolled off your tongue."

"No it didn't. Yesterday at the library I was reading about gold, and I got to flipping through a text on elemental minerals. And *don't* tell Tom I followed up on the Nevada junket with my reading, please," I begged. Me and my big, bragging mouth. Cats outside of bags are gone cats.

"Tom? Tom who? Just tell me more about diamonds and graphite," she said, merging onto the highway that would take us to the airport and her plane.

"Oh. Well, carbon atoms have four electrons in its outer shell, out of a possible eight. So under low temperatures and pressures, carbon atoms will readily form sheets, holding hands with three neighbors. Each atom's fourth electron is free to roam across the surface of the sheet, and these electrons form weak bonds with the next sheet. The weak bonds are easily sheared. That's why graphite is so soft, and such a good lubricant. Diamond is formed when all four electrons form strong covalent bonds. It jams the atoms together into a very rigid tetrahedral lattice, the strongest known. But this takes some persuasion. It's like the atoms become highly organized and cooperative, but they'll only make this agreement under tremendous heat and pressure, like a bunch of congressmen. So diamonds form deep within the earth's crust, in rocks called kimberlites."

Faye laughed. "So diamond mines go deep into the crust?"

"No, the miners wait until the crust gets heaved up and eroded down, bringing an old kimberlite pipe to the surface. In some places, the pipes have eroded away completely—the kimberlite decays into clay at surface conditions—and the diamonds are tumbled away by passing rivers. The diamonds have a higher specific gravity—they're the same size but heavier—than quartz sand, so they get concentrated in pockets in the rock the river flows over. That's called a placer deposit. You can find them lying around on the beach in Namibia."

"Cool! So carbon forms diamonds and graphite. Does it have any other structures?"

"Sure. It can link up into tiny spheres, arranged like little soccer balls. They're called 'bucky-balls' after Buckminster Fuller."

"Learn something new every day."

"Don'cha though."

About then, we pulled up next to the hangar where Faye kept her twin, opened the doors, and parked the car. Faye stowed her goodies and hardware and began her pilot's walk-around, checking the plane for such little problems as chips in the propellors or birds building nests in the air intakes. "So what did you learn about gold?" she asked, when she was about halfway around the plane.

I glanced around to make sure no one was within earshot of our conversation. Even though I didn't fancy working with Tom, it wouldn't be kind to blow his project by blabbing it in front of the world. "Well, like I said yesterday, mostly that it's a hot springs deposit."

Faye popped up from beneath a wing and stared at me. "What?"

"Or let's just call it a hydrothermal deposit, so we don't split hairs."

"We sure wouldn't want to do that," said Faye acerbically, checking the main landing gear.

"What's funny is that all these years I've been drilling for oil and thinking that oil's a shallow deposit, because it's formed from dead critters that rained down from the surface, and that gold must be a very deep deposit, because it comes from downstairs. But I was wrong."

"Imagine that."

I barely heard her chiding. So what if I sounded a bit like a gonzo academic? Knowledge feels good, and an "aha!" can be the mental equivalent of an ... well, you get the idea. "Thing is, gold does come from downstairs, but it only crystallizes out near the surface. Its freezing point is low for a mineral. It crystallizes out at only one thousand sixty-three degrees centigrade."

"A household fact, known to any kindergartner and her pet goldfish."

"You're losing it, Faye. Stay with me now, this is earth-shattering. Think of your hydrothermal fluids—hot rock juice—as a super-heated mineral milkshake squirting through the cracks in the earth. At depth, everything's so hot it's melted, and there are no cracks, just molten mineral molecules forming a pool as big as a county and a mile or more thick. Then as your wad of molten stuff rises closer to the surface, the different minerals crystallize out into igneous rock. The mineral constituents with the highest freezing points crystallize first, as the wad starts to cool. Then the next highest, the next, and so forth. Well, gold has a high freezing point for an element, but it's low for a mineral."

"Now you lost me."

"Most minerals are made up of molecules of more than one kind of atom. Gold is only gold, so it's both an element and a mineral."

"Knock me over with a feather."

"Oh, go number pot shards or something."

Faye was grinning as she checked the ailerons of the Piper, enjoying the bantering. "So gold is one of the last minerals to crystallize out of the hydrothermal fluids," Faye said, checking the port wing tank.

"Yeah, and by that time the main mass of rock has not only crystallized, but also cooled so far that it's begun to shrink and crack, leaving void spaces. Maybe the whole thing crystallized underground, or maybe it flowed out onto the surface. Either way, you get cracks. Or sometimes there's also big crustal movement going on, and the crust cracks and the juices leak out through non-igneous rocks. Sandstones or whatever. But anyway, the gold, along with other low-freezing-point minerals like silver and so forth, crystallize out in those cracks."

"And you call that a vein."

"Exactly. So the neat thing is—"

"I can't wait."

"The neat thing is that, while gold is very rare, it gets concentrated into these cracks, so we can hope to find some. Of course, sometimes it shows up in other types of deposits, like in sedimentary rocks, but that's really rare, and—"

"And you wouldn't want to completely lose me."

"Right."

"And you also get gold placers."

"Bingo. Gold has the second highest specific gravity of any mineral, right between platinum at the highest and silver at next highest. So they drop right to the bottom of the stream bed, and your old prospector can find them with his trusty gold pan."

"Fun in the sun."

"Yeah. But the zinger is that gold's freezing point is so low that gold deposits are only a few hundred, or at most a few thousand feet deep. I've drilled for oil at tens of thousands."

"What about those African gold miners? They always look pretty overheated in the photographs."

"You're thinking of the Witwatersrand. Sedimentary rocks. Fossil placers."

"*Fossil* placers."

"Neat, huh?"

"You didn't tell me this was simple, so . . ."

"But it *is* simple. It's how the earth is made. The earth follows rules. This temperature, that amount of pressure, such-and-such set of minerals, a given set of surface conditions, and you get X. The only thing that's complicated is figuring out what the rules are."

Faye didn't even try to fix a wisecrack on me this time. She just stared at me. Presently, she said, "That's why any idiot can find gold."

I smiled sheepishly. "Any idiot *can* find gold, or at least the more obvious deposits. Persistence and a strong back are great tools. But finding the tougher stuff by figuring out the rules is a lot tougher."

Faye started to climb into the plane.

I climbed up and stood on the wing while she positioned her shoulder bag, flight bag, and firearms. "Somewhere along the line, someone figured out that you could find gold along stream banks. So every idiot went out digging through the stream bank gravels. Then they ran out of stream gravels, and

someone figured out that, all along, the gold had been rotting
out of a certain type of rock. Off they went looking for that
type of rock. When that type was played out, they stumbled
across another producing type, and another. Some geologists
call this a 'search image,' or a model. It's only in the last
hundred and fifty years or so that we've all pooled our knowledge enough to think of new ways of looking for gold, or for
any other mineral, for that matter. Oil, for instance. In Penn-
sylvania, oil was found in seeps in the creek beds, so first
everyone looked only in valleys. Then it was discovered that
the creeks were following easily eroded rocks which were
actually the breached tops of anticlines, which are humped
up layers of rock. So then everyone knew to look at anticlines,
regardless of whether they formed creek beds or hilltops."

Faye was settled in her seat, her eyes wide and pensive.
"Maybe I should study geology," she said sadly. "It sounds
like it keeps you interested, and excited."

I climbed into the copilot's seat, sobered by Faye's longing
for a Holy Grail to chase. I had known a lot of people like
Faye at prep school, and at college; wealthy people who
didn't have to work. So many of them lacked for purpose. "It
can be a formidable pain in the ass to work in this field," I
said, trying to comfort her. "We're so good at finding things
that we keep finding too much, and then there's no scarcity,
and the price of the commodity drops, and we're out of a job
again." I added, "*Much* better to be independently wealthy,"
not sure I meant it.

Faye shrugged.

"And the bosses can be monsters. I can't imagine staying
in some of the jobs I've worked if I didn't have to pay the
rent." There I stopped. I liked Faye, but there were places
where she was softly naive. With lack of purpose, certain
aspects of character do not form. I glanced at the place where
she had stowed her .45. Had Tom Latimer felt moved to protect her, or had she asked for his special training? And was
he enabling her to feel falsely confident, setting her up for
greater dangers than she currently faced? I shuddered. There
were things about their relationship I didn't want to know.

It was perhaps another half a minute before Faye shook herself out of her reverie and put on her headphones. After I had, too, she said, "Leave your door ajar until we're ready for takeoff. It's hotter'n a pistol out there."

"You can say that again," I said, but I wasn't thinking of the temperature of the air.

20

WE SPED ACROSS THE SKY, SKIMMING ACROSS THE eastern deserts of Utah and rising up over the high passes of the Rocky Mountains into Colorado. We saw the steep anticline of white Weber Sandstone at Dinosaur National Park, skimmed over the Flat Tops to Kremmling, and passed over the Continental Divide south of Rocky Mountain National Park. Beyond the divide, Faye bled off her altitude and brought the Piper Cheyenne II down into Jefferson County Airport, my old training grounds, northwest of Denver. While Faye went off to rent a car, I stopped in to visit with Peggy, my crusty old flight instructor. When she saw me wandering into the office, she kept her feet up on the edge of the wastepaper basket, but put down her book and gave me her version of a warm greeting: "Well, look what the cat dragged in."

" 'Lo, Peggy. Keeping the wind underneath your wings?"

"Beats taking baths. What brings you back here so soon? I thought you were over in Utah with loverboy."

"I am."

"So I'm seeing things."

"No, no, just playing hooky. A friend came in for the day, so I rode along to see if I could learn something."

"Must be a hot little set of wings to make it over here for lunch."

"Piper Cheyenne Two. Lotsa horsepower. Love dem flying hosses."

Peggy whistled. "That's a half-million-dollar airplane, *used*."

I think I blushed. I didn't like Peggy thinking I traveled in pricey crowds. It clashed with my cowgirl self-image.

Peggy grinned. "You're gone one week and you're so bored you're already hanging out at the airport?"

I smiled at the irony. Faye and I had something in common

after all. Boredom. "Well, you know how it is. Loverboy used up all his leave coming over to see me, so when I got there all I could do is spend evenings and weekends with him. At least he isn't working graveyards."

"So what's your twin pilot look like?" Peggy wiggled her eyebrows. "Pretty fast work, Em."

I put one hand to my chest in feigned indignation. "He's a she. And I met her yesterday whilst serving our nation."

Peggy brayed with laughter. "Yeah, make this good."

"No shit. I was working. Well, not for pay, but my old FBI contact, Tom Latimer, asked me to fly out to Nevada and look into some case about an endangered kangaroo mouse."

Peggy tipped her head back and guffawed.

"What's so funny?" I demanded.

She pulled herself together and picked up the book she'd been reading when I came in. "Oh, it's nothing. I just been reading *Seven Arrows*."

"Sure," I said, rather sarcastically. "You read cereal boxes, Peggy."

"Come on, get some culture. I read bodice rippers and murder mysteries, like the rest of the educated world. Finished the new Sharon McCone mystery an hour ago and this was all I could find to read while I wait for my next student. Someone left it here. It's a book about the Cheyenne medicine wheel."

"Oh." I knew very little about Native American religions. I had seen a medicine wheel on the side of the Big Horn Mountains in Wyoming. It was very ancient, and was made of stones laid out like spokes radiating from a hub, with an outer ring of stones connecting the spokes.

"It's pretty interesting, actually. All about the symbolism of the medicine wheel and an Indian's-eye-view of the coming of the white man."

"And that cracks you up," I said drily. Peggy and I know each other well enough to give each other shit.

Peggy inelegantly flipped me off and said, "No, dear heart, I'm just laughing because . . . well, let me explain." She opened the book and flipped pages until she found the illustration she was looking for, a diagram of the wheel. "The cardinal compass points have symbolic meanings, see. The Four Great Powers, or medicines. East is Illumination, the eagle. 'The place of Illumination, where we see things clearly far and wide.' Like when we're up flying, right? The big perspective, just like the eagle. It's part of why we fly."

"You're getting lofty on me, Peggy." But I knew what she meant. Much as I loved the earth, and in fact spent my professional life studying it, I felt more at ease high above it, where I could see a long way. "So fine, I'm an eagle. But what got you going was the mouse. I suppose that's another spoke on the wheel."

Peggy pursed her lips. "Right. South, which is Innocence, or Trust. Symbolized by guess what?"

"A mouse."

"Yeah, exactly. 'The South is the place of Innocence and Trust, and of perceiving closely our nature of heart. And there's a whole story in here about this *jumping* mouse." She flipped the pages of the book again. "And also a nice one about the eagle. Damned thing eats too many mice and it weighs too much and can't take off again."

"Nice symbolism, indeed," I said acerbically.

Peggy put a hand to her breast and gave me a supercilious smile. "You flew east today to see me. In a Cheyenne, no less. Illumination, just as I said."

"Sure, sure. But yesterday I flew west. What's that?"

She read, " 'West is Looks-Within place, which speaks of the Introspective nature of man.' It's symbolized by the bear." She looked at me and began to laugh again. "Yeah, that fits, too. You are the master of introspection; you think entirely too much, and it makes you as cranky as a bear."

"Thanks a lot," I said. "It's nice to be so accurately perceived. So tell me in what way I'm an idiot when I'm facing north."

Peggy opened the book again. "Let's see. North is Wisdom. The buffalo. Aw, hell, we already killed all of them critters. No wonder we're in such a world of hurt!"

I shook my head, beginning to feel annoyed. "Speak for

yourself, Peggy. You've been sitting on the ground too long."

Peggy's laughter dribbled down to a small chuckle. "Yeah, you're right." She flipped the book back and forth. "But still, it's kind of interesting. The whole idea is that the symbolism of your actions and perceptions forms a mirror to your soul. Kind of a nice thought." She looked me straight in the eye, her expression now totally sober. "You might want to give a careful read to this story about the jumping mouse. Make sure you got all the spokes to your wheel."

Peggy always was a good teacher.

WE CRUISED DOWN the highway toward downtown Denver, a cluster of spires sticking out of a bowl full of smog. We turned off at Speer Boulevard and found our way up Lawrence Street to a spiffy new brick building. We parked the car and got on the elevator. When the doors opened on the fifth floor, we stepped out into a small, tastefully decorated waiting room. Aside from a nicely framed antique watercolor of a Colorado mountainscape, which immediately drew my eye, there was very little in the room other than a pair of understated, but choicely comfy-looking waiting chairs. The floor was covered with deliciously soft carpeting, and the recessed lighting delicately reflected off walls covered with raw silk in a subdued shade of gold. I felt as if I'd been gift-wrapped. The room had a rich, yet peaceful feeling to it, as if waiting was a God-like thing to do.

There was a second door, emblazoned with an elaborate letter R in red-gold leaf. Beside the door was a buzzer button. Faye pressed it.

"Hi, love," said a deep, sonorous voice.

I spun around, trying to figure out where the voice had sounded from.

"The speaker's recessed, up there with the lighting and the security system," Faye said softly. "Smile nice for the camera." Then, much louder, she said, "Buzz us in, asshole."

The door lock clicked. Faye pulled it open. We stepped into a second softly decorated room, this one with a small Louis XIV writing table and three chairs.

A tall, globular man with Santa Claus cheeks and lascivious eyes emerged from a side room, setting a jeweler's loupe and a box of glittering stones on the table as he did so. The door clicked shut behind him. He said, "Faye, sweetie. You got the rocks?" He began tugging at her shoulder bag even as he gave her a peck and a squeeze hello.

Faye swatted him across one cheek with the back of her hand. "Back off, Atilla. Em, this is Rudolf. Rudolf, unhand me."

Rudolf gave me a playful wink and swept his hand across Faye's waist. Detecting her hidden pistol, he let go of snatching her bag for a moment and groped at her back, fascinated, his eyes rolling erotically. "Oh, I just love women who pack iron. Where'd you get this, sweet cheeks? That bang-bang boyfriend of yours?"

She swung her shoulder bag at him. "Here's your ice, tiger, now cool off."

Rudolf grinned at me. "I just love to get it on with girls like Faye. It makes me feel real masc."

Faye glanced over her shoulder at me. "Watch out for him. He's more omnivorous than he likes you to think."

Rudolf let out a rich giggle. "The old ladies like to think that big bad Rudy only bites the boys."

"So you're more wolf than reindeer," I said. "I'm Em Hansen." I offered him a hand. "Shake that please, but don't eat it," I added, figuring that outrageous is a game that any number can play.

Rudolf enclosed my hand in one gigantic mitt, turned it over, and kissed the inside of my wrist. "Emmmmmm. Nice of you to keep Faye-Faye company. Welcome to my little kingdom."

"You reset diamonds *here*?" I asked, retrieving my hand.

"No, no, no, no. Back there. Come." He removed a card key from his pocket and put it in a slot by the inner door. It opened into a slightly larger room in which sat two men and a woman, each of whom were bent over jeweler's workbenches, hard at work. They sat on high stools, and wore special visors with magnification loupes. The woman turned around and said, "Oh, the shipment? Let me see!"

Faye pulled the leather wallet out of her shoulder bag and presented it to Rudolf, who closed his eyes and sniffed at it as if it were food. Eyes still closed, he unzipped the wallet and dug in greedily with his fingers. He quickly extracted the ring and put it to his cheek. "I love that old lady. She gets me some of my best pieces."

"So you've seen these before," I said.

"Oh yes, my dear. I never buy without seeing. I visit dear 'Auntie' every chance I get. She has a weakness for lavender roses, and I never go without at least a dozen of them." He popped open his eyes. "In exchange, she calls me first each time she decides she's ready to part with one of her little gumdrops."

"She said she gives the money to worthy causes," I said.

"Oh yes, she loves her little environmental groups. She's particularly fond of anti-mining causes. Don't you just *love* the irony? I mean, where does she think her little baubles came from?"

"But it makes sense," Faye countered. "It's good karma to give back from that which takes away."

My antennae were up and alert. I asked Rudolf, "Is she connected locally, or does she go on the road with her environmental activism?" I was of course instantly thinking about the save-the-desert group that Tom and Ian had talked about in Nevada the day before, the group which was slowing down progress at Granville Resources.

Ignoring my question in his excitement over the ring, Rudolf turned to his woman jeweler. "Linda," he said. "Hold out your hanny."

Linda closed her eyes and stuck out a hand. Rudolf dropped the ring into it. "Ooooh," she said. "I like the weight."

I said, "Do you think 'Auntie' would talk to me about this anti-mine stuff?"

"Oh, I'm certain she would. Twenty-two carats," Rudolf crooned to the stone. "I first met this ring six years ago. I have been in lust for it. God bless 'Auntie' for having no heirs." His eyes danced my way again. "Each time one of her pet environmental charities comes begging, she gives me a call and says, 'The Russian white is ready to go,' or, 'Are you ready for the teardrop earrings, Rudie?' "

"That old tartar calls you *Rudie*?" I asked, aghast.

"Lavender," he purred. "Roses. They work on her like liquor."

There was another round of frivolity when Rudolf pulled the teardrop earrings out, but then he slung the earrings into a safe, spun the dial, and handed the ring to one of the men.

I said, "So do 'Auntie' and her friends want to close down any gold mines?"

Rudolf patted the man's shoulder cozily, then turned back to me. "Enough of business. I am starving. There's some great ahi to be had at a joint not far from here. I ordered in. Come." He led us back into a fourth room, which was an unglamorous kitchenette with a bare Formica table. "Please excuse the informality, Em, but I can get so much more dirt out of Faye here, where there's nobody listening."

Linda walked through and grabbed a cup of coffee. "Don't listen to a word of this. He's just a tightwad. Ahi's just a fancy term for tuna salad."

"Get back to work, or I'll have you lashed!" Rudolf roared, opening the refrigerator and pulling out three takeout lunches with what looked like a Chinese sesame salad done up with fresh fish instead of chicken. His hands moved quickly and with great finesse as he removed them from their Styrofoam containers to plain white china plates and served us up some bubbly apple juice in glasses. We sat down at the table and prepared to dive in.

Rudolf lifted his fork. "So tell me, Emmy dear, why are you so interested in environmental groups that want to shut down gold mines?"

"Well," I said, "I'm a geologist. Just yesterday I was out running around looking for a gold mine, but—" I stopped short. Rudolf's eyes suddenly riveted on me, and his expression drew up from silly fat guy to a reflection of the sharp mind that had to be in there to develop a business like this.

He put down his fork and set his elbows on the table and folded his hands in front of his lips. "Tell me."

"There's not much to tell," I said. "I didn't get to the mine."

Rudolf leaned across the table towards me, giving me a look that Ray would have saved for his wedding night, and groaned. "What a tease you are. Diamonds are fun. But gold . . . is serious shit."

I swallowed a bite of the tuna without tasting it. "Is it? Then maybe you can help me understand a few things about it. Like, what makes it like it is? I mean, central to its value is its nice yellow color and its luster, of course, and—"

Rudolf leaned even closer across the table, his lunch and gossip forgotten, and took my hand. "It is not just yellow, dear Emily, it is *gold*. It is *brilliant*. It is *warm*." He took a deep breath. "Its chemical symbol, A-U, is an abbreviation of the Latin *aurum*, which has the same root as *aurora*, the radiant dawn. It brings us the very essence of the sun."

I swallowed again, a bit harder. "And, well, its malleability is important, because you can work it. Make jewelry and so forth."

Now stroking my hand, Rudolf said, "Malleable is too small a word to describe this metal. It can be shaped into fabulous objects, or drawn out into wire, or hammered into incredibly thin sheets—an ounce can be hammered into a sheet three *hundred* feet square. A wafer five millionths of an inch thick."

"Yes. Well, and it can be plated onto microswitches," I said.

Rudolf brought my hand up to his chest. "Yes. Highly conductive to electricity. The perfect plating for microelectrical contacts, because it does not corrode or tarnish in air."

I yanked my hand back. "Uh, yes. But why doesn't it corrode or tarnish? I mean, it's right below silver on the periodic chart, so the atom has the same number of electrons in its outer shell, and yet silver oxidizes like mad. Why doesn't gold?"

Rudolf leaned back and opened his left hand and stroked the insides of his rings with the fingertips of his right. It was a gentle, yet impassioned gesture, the kind of touch one saves for the forehead of a sleeping child. He said, "Gold is a very large, very contented atom. It is at peace, at rest."

"What makes gold so special?" I asked desperately.

He laughed. "It's the relativity effect."

"The what?"

"Atoms are such tricksters," he said. "Why is one perceived as green and another yellow? I don't know. They're all made up of the same few parts—protons, neutrons, gluons, quarks, with electrons spinning around them—and the mass of all those bits exerts a pull on those electrons. The bigger the pull, the tighter in the nucleus pulls the electrons. And think of the figure skater: She starts twirling, and as she draws her arms in, she spins faster and faster. At the atomic weight of gold—precisely at the number of neutrons and protons and so forth that make it gold and not the next atom smaller— the electrons approach the speed of light. You're in Einstein land. Things go around corners and laugh at you." And like an atom of gold himself, Rudolf drew himself in and hummed.

"All that, right down inside the fillings in your teeth," I said.

He rose suddenly from his chair. "Wait," he said, and hurried back into the workroom, where he knelt down and worked the combination on his safe and reopened it. From it, he extracted something wrapped in a velvet sack and a pair of long, shallow wooden boxes, which he brought to the table. Pushing my lunch aside, he set them down in front of me and opened the velvet sack.

Inside was a lump of white quartz. It was a nice specimen, full of tiny crystals, but it didn't knock me out. But then Rudolf handed me a jeweler's loupe, which is a large hand lens, and directed my attention to a concavity at the center of the specimen. "Handle it carefully, dear. Do not place your fingers near the center."

I adjusted the lens near my eye and angled the specimen

so that light struck it squarely at the center, a task I had performed a great many times in my years as a student and as a working geologist. There is always a delicious moment of anticipation as the range is sought and the focus found, and then the object jumps into view, a revelation of the earth's magnificence at miniature scale. This time my wait was fabulously rewarded. Wire gold burst into my field of observation, brilliant and glowing. As always when I examined hand samples through a lens, I felt a sense of privilege at seeing something so intimate and tiny brought up to the scale of my existence. I said, "Nice!"

"Gimme see," said Faye.

To Rudolf, I said, "That was a lovely specimen. But I'm trying to understand something about gold mining. And the price of gold. And something about how mining and gold prices connect with the world we live in."

"Can you be more specific?" Rudolf asked.

I thought. "Well, that's the problem. There's something about all this that I don't quite grasp. I mean, I've worked in a commodities-based industry ever since I graduated from college. Oil and gas. The price of a barrel of oil is set by the demand for it, except of course that every sheik and his brother are trying to control that price. But oil and gas are different from gold. Oil and gas as energy. Fuel. Gold is—"

"Money," Rudolf said. He passed the sample and hand lens on to Faye, and with a small, reverent flourish, opened the lid of the first box to reveal a series of antique coins encased in plastic jackets. He pointed to one marked with the pouting profile of a long-haired man. "George the Third," he said. "This is a Guinea, so-called because the gold was mined in Guinea in West Africa. Minted in 1789." He pointed to another. "A Sovereign. See the queen? Elizabeth the First, seated on her throne, grasping her orb. Beautiful work. It dates from the late fifteenth century, and was nominally worth one British pound. And this, the Centenario, fifty pesos. The Venetian Ducat, thirteenth century. The French Napoleon, twenty francs, this one 1815. These are numismatic coins—collector's items. They are very interesting, and pretty to look at, but their value is as much in their age as in their gold content. They were usually alloys of gold and silver. Electrum."

The second box contained an array of new, and much brighter, gold coins, each about an inch and a half in diameter. They lay uncovered, and their brilliance dazzled my eyes.

Rudolf leaned very close to me, and spoke directly into my ear. "These, my dear, are *bullion*," he uttered, the word taking on extra richness with the depth and sonorosity of his voice. "You are looking at the right of the individual to own gold. Our government has not always granted us this right. Dear 'Auntie' doesn't fully understand this. She has been allowed to have her jewelry, and the caps on her lovely old teeth, but it is only in the past two decades of her lifetime that her government has granted her the right to own gold outright."

I could feel the heat of his breath on my ear, and the urgency carried in the vibrations of his words made my pulse quicken.

"These coins are not money in the sense of having an assigned value," he continued, "such as a five-dollar, or a ten-dollar piece, although a few have a stamped nominal value. No, with these, you understand their value is in the weight. Each contains precisely an ounce of gold. Then, whatever an ounce of gold is worth, so goes the value of your bullion coin." He pointed at them one at a time, lingering over the fine ornament minted into each in bas-relief. "The South African Krugerrand. The British Britannia. The Canadian Maple Leaf. The Chinese Panda. The Australian Nugget. The Belgian Ecu. And the American Eagle." He traced a delicate antelope; a helmeted, trident-brandishing Britannia; an exquisite five-pointed leaf; a bear swaying from a frond of bamboo; a radiant kangaroo; a circlet of stars; and the proud symbol of American pride and vision. This last he lifted reverently from its velvet cushion and turned over into my hand. I felt its density sink into my palm, and I bent to examine the coin more closely. On the back strode a powerful woman dressed in flowing Grecian robes, her hair lifted by the wind.

In her raised right hand, she brandished a torch, and in her left, she held a branch of olive leaves. She seemed to rise from the fan of radiance that surrounded her, as if leaping through the ring of tiny stars that edged the coin. Rudolf ran the tip of his smallest finger over the word that was inscribed in an arch above her head. LIBERTY.

The eagle on the coin's face had put me in mind of Peggy's story about the Cheyenne medicine wheel, about flying East, the province of Eagle, and of Illumination. I wondered if this woman on the reverse side then symbolized the West, the Looks-Within place, or Introspection. Was that the domain of freedom? And how did freedom and liberty relate to gold, and money, and for that matter, mining? I had always been proud to be a daughter of the west, the land where an individual could rise or fall on his or her own merits. I had gone into the oil business partly because it had seemed an elemental exercise of my freedoms to look for commodities, but my environmental friends questioned that. And I questioned the shortfall between their lifestyles and the ideals which they espoused. They denigrated oil drilling but drove cars. Some ate meat but hated hunting and slaughtering. The old "I use it but don't condone it" conundrum. I sighed. It seemed that, no matter how much I learned, there was always just a bit more to be understood before ambiguity would untangle itself into a greater truth.

I heard Rudolf's voice just inches from my ear and snapped out of my reverie. "Liberty," he whispered. "This is the lady of my heart."

Faye spoke. "Is she your key to freedom?"

Rudolf plucked the coin from my hand. "No," he said. "This is for the small investor. They are *beautiful*," he said worshipfully, "but not so beautiful as *this* . . ." He whisked the two boxes away to the safe and produced a third, larger one. This, as the others, he set carefully in front of me, and lifted the lid. Inside lay a brick of solid gold.

My breath caught in my throat. The bar seemed to gather all light in the room and to propel it ravishingly, and with near sexual heat, into my eyes. I had never seen gold so pure;

had not known the depth and splendor of its luster. I wanted to fall into it. "This is gold," I whispered.

"Yes," Rudolf sighed in return. "*This* is gold."

Faye shook her head. "You just keep that lying around, Rudolf? Is that for the business?"

"No," he said impatiently. "The jewelry we fabricate here is alloyed, as I explained. Four nines—twenty-four carat gold—is pure, but it's too soft to wear on your body. You don't see fabricated jewelry that's more than twenty-two carat. Eighteen is common; three-quarters gold. We use that for the prongs that hold the gems to the piece, because you need the strength. Good gold chain is eighteen-carat. You see fourteen at the cheap shops, or as little as nine or even eight. Or it's plate. No, *this* I keep around for its beauty. And for its *value*."

"You mean, as your hedge against inflation?" Faye asked saucily.

"Heavens yes, dear, but I keep a great deal more of it where *you'll* never see it."

Interrupting their discussion of material wealth, I said, "If eighteen carat is only three-quarters gold, what makes up the other quarter?"

"That depends on what color you desire," Rudolf said, his voice unconsciously modulating to the tones I suppose he used on his richest customers. "To set diamonds, you might want a very white gold. You'd use silver, or nickel or palladium. A red gold wants copper or a touch of zinc. Green tints are achieved by using varying proportions of copper and silver, nickel or palladium. Here, look into my last little treasure." He opened a box which contained a smooth, black stone and a set of metal wands with flattened ends. The brightest and yellowest was stamped "24," and each other descended to lesser and lesser carat purities, all the way down to a dull, tinny-looking "6." "This is a touchstone," Rudolf murmured. "You rub an object across the stone and compare marks with the wands. It was the first method used for assaying the purity of gold, back in five hundred BC."

"This set is twenty-five hundred years old?" I asked, incredulous.

"No, no, my dear. This set is modern. I bought it in a bazaar in India just two years ago. Not every last pocket of the world is as technologically advanced as we are. Your gold mines in Nevada are light years ahead of what they're doing today in, say, parts of Brazil. The men dig ore out with their hands if they can't find shovels, and they carry it to the assayer in baskets, on their shoulders."

Rudolf closed the fourth box and straightened. He raised his eyes pensively toward the ceiling. "So many terms we use in everyday life arise from the search for and handling of gold. For instance, 'acid test': another early method of assaying, as you'll recall that only aqua regia dissolves it—the water of kings. 'Didn't pan out': our efforts went unrewarded. This refers to the sourdough prospector's primitive method of testing for gold, which is of course still in use. 'Good as gold.' 'Worth its weight in gold.' 'A king's ransom.' They're talking about gold, the province of kings. The list is endless. Even your term 'malleable' derives from the Latin *malleus*, a hammer, referring to the hammer originally used to form metal foil. The term is defined by the most malleable metal of all: gold."

I stared at my uneaten ahi. The sight of Rudolf's brilliant, shining specimens was alluring, and on some level deeply stimulating, almost titillating. I felt confused, and deep inside, repelled. "Sure, gold keeps our cell phones and computers humming, so maybe it has a new importance to our culture, but it seems an anachronism. We're not on a gold standard anymore, and the few kings still around are mostly figureheads. And with the speed of communication that those microcircuits provide, the world has become a smaller place. National boundaries are softening with the rise of the power of multinational corporations. Perhaps they're the new monarchs."

Rudolf lowered his large body back into his chair with a thud, his face clouding with anger.

I glanced at Faye. She was shaking her head at me. Clearly I had blown some test.

"Transportable wealth," Rudolf muttered, staring into his tuna. He began forking it rapidly into his mouth, and when he spoke again, I was no longer certain that it was to me he was speaking. "You clearly don't get that, but that's no matter, as it's more for me. Other metals may come and others may go, but come the crunch, gold is the only one that is universally recognized as money."

21

BACK OUT IN THE RENTAL CAR, FAYE WAS STILL shaking her head in amazement. "You sure got him going," she said, stabbing the key into the ignition, started the engine, and pulled out into the stream of traffic.

"What do you mean?" I said defensively. "I stuck my foot in my mouth, clearly, but what did I say that was so insulting?"

"You should feel complimented, Em. You had him rolling like I've never seen him roll before. He set his whole line of jeweler-boy nonsense aside for you, and trotted out what really mattered to him. All I've ever rated was a show of his pretty stones. Shit, Em, who knows what else he would have pulled out of that safe if you hadn't opened your big yap."

I stared straight forward, still flummoxed.

Faye stopped for a traffic light and laughed. "I suppose he had to find his polar opposite one of these days. Rudolf of the understated elegance meets the renegade Boston Brahmin's spawn, cowgirl Em, who values land over all things."

"How do you know that about me?" I snapped. She was right, of course; my mother had been raised with wealth and social standing back East and had run away to Wyoming, and land made lots more sense to me than gold.

Pulling forward again with the stream of traffic, she said, "I'm sorry, that's rude, you're right. But Tom's been telling me about you for months. Hey, I was jealous at first, but—"

"Jesus Christ, Faye, this is scaring me!"

Faye glanced at me with a look that suggested that she found me both sweet and naive. "Okay. I'm sorry. But tell the truth: If you hadn't seen where the diamonds came from, you'd have thought they were costume jewelry, not because you've never seen wealth before, but because that kind of wealth—gaudy and ostentatious—seems foolish to you, and extreme."

I opened my mouth to reply, but closed it again. She was right; I had found the diamonds howlingly impractical, what my grandmother called costume jewelry. But the ending to our visit with Rudolf hadn't seemed the least bit funny to me. I felt embarrassed, and still wasn't sure why.

"It's a cultural thing," Faye said. "I read it in a course I took on the Puritan settlers. Wealth is okay, as long as it's understated, but luxury is something that is . . . distrusted."

I bit my lip. If I'd thought for a moment that Faye was doing anything but expressing intellectual curiosity about my cultural heritage, I would have jumped out of the car at the next light and found my own way back to Salt Lake City.

A soft warbling saved me from having to comment. Faye pushed her shoulder bag my way and said, "Dig my cell phone out of here and answer it, will you?"

I did so, and struggled to open the thing and figure out how to speak into it. "Faye's phone," I said, for want of a better opener.

There was silence, and then a man's voice, familiar but distorted. "Em. That you?"

"Yeah. Who's this?"

"Tom Latimer. Say, while you're there in Denver with Faye, would you do me a favor?"

I felt like Alice down the rabbit hole. First a woman I'd just met was reading my mental tea leaves to me, and now I was getting calls on her cell phone. And I was so stunned to hear that Tom wasn't surprised to find me answering that phone that I just said, "Sure," even as my brain spun into high speed to try to understand how he'd known where I was.

He said, "Go and visit a woman named Gretchen Mac-Callum. She's the wife of the guy everyone was looking for there in Nevada yesterday. She lives there in Denver. She works nights and turns in at about seven or eight, but she might be awake by now. Either way, go visit her, will you? I need your take on something."

I stared into the phone for a moment, as if it held the last shred of reason in the universe and I just couldn't figure out how to pluck it out from between the funny little keys.

He said, "Em?"

I groaned, "Am I dreaming this?"

"Just talk to her a for a while, try to find out what she thinks might be going on out there."

I continued to stare. Said nothing.

He said, "Give me to Faye. I'll give her the address, then I'll call Ms. MacCallum to tell her you're coming, and advise her of her rights pursuant to the Privacy Act and so forth."

I handed the phone to Faye and returned my gaze to the high walk of the Rockies.

FAYE PULLED THE rental car up in front of a sleepy-looking home on the west side of Denver. It seemed a comfortably affluent, residential neighborhood: ranch-style houses, mature landscaping, a late-model sedan in every driveway, a sport utility vehicle gleaming untouched in the garages of most. The houses across the street brandished wide picture windows at a glorious view of the Front Range of the Colorado Rockies, which rose abruptly from the plains not many miles distant. As I glanced down the row of houses, I noticed that one homemaker was in the process of closing her blinds against the hot reach of the afternoon sun.

The picture window on Gretchen MacCallum's house, a gray brick job, was eclipsed by heavy drapes, the mark of a day sleeper. A ten-year-old station wagon sat in the driveway.

I knocked. After a chorus of dog barks, the door clicked open and a petite woman about fifty years of age answered the door. Her hair was rich and wavy. She smiled pleasantly. "Em Hansen?"

"Yes. I'm sorry about the interruption of your sleep."

She stepped aside to let a black and white mutt step out beside her and sniff me. She clipped his collar onto a long chain and shooed him out into the yard. "Oh, that's okay. The kids will be home soon, anyway, and I try to be up by then. I'm just having breakfast. You want a cup of coffee? Come on in. And doesn't your friend want to come, too? Or should

I say, your associate." She lifted her chin toward Faye, who had stayed in the car.

"No, she's working on her flight plan. She's a pilot, and she's about to fly back to Salt Lake. She has to have her paperwork ready. Coffee would be great."

"What's she sticking to the window?"

Alert and observant, I decided. I turned to see what Gretchen was looking at. Faye was sticking a black rod to the inside of the windshield with a suction cup. "I think that's her GPS," I said. "Global Positioning System. It's a—"

"I know what a GPS is," Gretchen said, laughing. "My husband is a geologist, remember?" She led the way into her kitchen. "So what's this the FBI needs to ask me about? This all sounds very mysterious." Her laughter faded comfortably into a light titter as she set to pouring coffee into two celadon-green mugs. The room, which was both kitchen and breakfast room, enjoyed a wide glass door overlooking a semi-neglected garden. Several days' worth of newspaper lay askew on the table, and three half-chewed dog rawhides were catching dust kitties underneath. The upper surface of the low bookshelf which lay beyond it held countless weeks of ejecta from kids' school packs. The overall effect was one of peaceful disarray. Dust motes danced in the afternoon sunlight. I wanted to take my nasty errand and run.

But it was too late. Gretchen now sat on one of the chairs at her kitchen table, her bare feet up on another. She sat leaning back, with her coffee mug resting against her chest as if it were a portable iron lung that was helping her to breathe. Caffeine addiction is something I understand in all its permutations.

She was observing me calmly. Clearly, no one had told her that her husband was missing. Or so I thought. "I hope you haven't come all this way to ask me where my husband is," she offered conversationally. "Because I don't know."

I sat down and poured some milk into my coffee, figuring I needed the protein for the work ahead. I picked up the mug, which I could see was handmade, subtly different from

Gretchen's. It was a nice shape, and fit my hands comfortably. "So you know he's missing?"

"Missing? Don? No, he's not missing. Everyone else on earth might not know where he is, but *he* does."

"Oh. So he's done this before?"

Gretchen took a sip of her coffee and returned it to cuddling position. "Perhaps you should be a little more specific about what 'this' is."

I tensed. What had Tom told her? Nothing? And had anyone from Granville Resources yet phoned her? "Well, I take it he hasn't exactly told anyone where he was going. Or that he was planning to be gone."

Gretchen raised one shoulder in dismissal. "That's no big deal."

"So he does this kind of thing often?"

"Well, not every day of the week. But Don has his moments when he likes his privacy. He hasn't always worked for Granville. When he was independent, he sometimes went off the map and I wouldn't hear from him for a week or more. Maybe two."

"And that was okay with you?" I set my mug down. "I'm sorry. That was a rude thing to ask." Gretchen's response had opened new doors of possibility, and suddenly I wanted to know: Could a husband and wife have this comfortable a relationship? Could one wander off as needed, and be allowed such privacy? Such freedom? Such trust?

Gretchen tipped her head to one side and observed me as if I had some kind of problem she was being too polite to point out to me. "You're not married, I take it."

"No. Never have been," I answered, embarrassed.

"Well, Don and I have been married for who knows how long. We met in college. He used to come visit a lot. Then one day I realized that he didn't go home anymore. About then, my roommate decided it was time to find a little more privacy, and so there you have it, we were together. It was a long time after that that we got married. I think we needed paper to prove to some company he was working for that they should move my stuff along with his when he was shipped overseas for a couple years. Then we had the kids, and came back to the States. He quit the company he was working for and went out on his own as a consultant, and he'd sometimes be gone overseas a couple months at a time. He particularly liked Australia, because the Aboriginals there have this habit called 'walkabout.' When they get to feeling that special itch, they just wander off until they feel like being home again."

"And you're okay with him going walkabout?"

Gretchen considered my question. "He's very considerate. He'll always get in touch before it would occur to me to worry, albeit that's a long time. But you see, I know him well. You just have to understand the man you're living with. Don's not just like everybody else, but if he was, he couldn't do what he does. Finding gold, and other things people want found."

"It amazes me that you can understand that," I said, thinking of how little Ray seemed to understand that I had other things on my mind than fitting in with his crowd.

"Well, sometimes it's kind of a hassle. The kids go through these stages where they're really a handful. But I don't know, sometimes it's easier to deal with that kind of situation with the guy gone than if he's always here. And then other times he's home for months at a time just working out of the house, and then he does most of the kid care. It works out."

"How long has he been working in Nevada?"

"You mean for Granville? He's been with them . . . oh, five, six years, I guess. No, wait." She glanced at the ceiling. "Yeah, Benny was in fifth grade. Six years. But not always in Nevada. They had him down in Chile awhile before Mettler—he was president and CEO of Granville—retired and was replaced by Roderick Chittenden."

"Chittenden changed the program?"

"Well, he actually started a second company. A limited partnership. That's because what he's doing is risky, and this way he doesn't risk the investments of the general stockholders of Granville Resources. The limited partnership uses Granville's infrastructure—rents its employees, if you will—

to get a second project going that would use the same offices and mill. Then the limited partnership will come in as a joint venture with Granville. You see, Chittenden started this new thing of buying up old claims and trying to put together bigger projects. It's kind of high-risk."

"Is he getting anywhere with it?"

Gretchen laughed. "Well, Don told him he was nuts."

"In so many words?"

"Yes. I was sitting right across the table from them. This table, in fact. Chittenden had flown in to pitch the whole idea to him. He pointed out that Don had just found something just like it. The Gloriana project was put together from old claims that hadn't been mined far enough to hit the main vein. And Chittenden pointed to the Carlin trend and then at the Gloriana and a couple of other mines that seemed to line up and said, 'Why not a Gloriana trend?' Well, Don about laughed his head off. He said, 'Nice idea, but the Carlin mines are at least all in the same kind of rock and were generated by the same episode of mineralization. Your so-called Gloriana trend is so many apples and oranges.' Chittenden came back with, 'So I'll open a fruit stand.' Anyway, a job's a job, and Chittenden treats him very well, as I've said. So Don still goes over to Nevada a couple, three weeks at a time, then like I say, he's home for a couple of months."

"He doesn't go into an office?" This sounded great to me. I began to think that this guy MacCallum must glow in the dark to enjoy such freedom on the job.

"He has a desk here in the house. A lot of the more established guys do that. Don couldn't stand it if he had to go into an office."

"And that works?" I asked wryly. I was beginning to feel like MacCallum was just me with a Y chromosome and a hardrock mineral hammer, and I wished I could find a job like his.

Gretchen chuckled. "Yeah, he gets bored. Starts having too many beers. Puts on weight. Goes back to Nevada. Comes home rested and fit. He's like a dog that needs a bone to chew on." She laughed. "I sometimes think that if he *was* a dog, he'd be the type that constantly jumps the fence and gets into trouble."

I watched the dance of the dust motes in the bright slash of sunlight immediately over my coffee mug and wondered if Gretchen might be interested in adopting a slightly over-aged child. Or maybe she'd just let me hang out under her kitchen table and chew on one of the abandoned rawhides. "So you don't think there's anything special about this particular absence," I asked, trying to focus for a moment on Tom Latimer's question.

"No. Well, yes, I did wonder why he wasn't there when I called him on his birthday. But that was only yesterday, and I'd spoken to him the morning before." She stared at me for a long moment over her cup, as if slowly reasoning something through, but still she was not alarmed, only perplexed. "Why are you guys worried about this, anyway?" She laughed again. "And why the FBI? Has Donny got himself messed up in something interesting this time?"

"What do you mean, 'This time'?"

"Oh, you know, geologists are always out there snooping around. They find things they aren't looking for sometimes."

I nodded. This I knew only too well. "Yeah, I've had my moments. But what's Don found?"

"Oh, once he was hired to work on a prospect that was really just a cover-up for a drug operation. He had a nice lunch with the *patron* and found his own way home. Another time, he found a corpse in a mine. But the guy'd been dead a while, and Don was able to show from his passport that he'd only been in the country a few days. That and a few *pesos* in the right pocket, and he was out of there again. That time was in Mexico. Mexicans are pretty nice to innocents like Don."

My own identification with him aside, I was beginning to get an interesting image of what Donald Paul MacCallum must be like. Smart and capable, if he'd stayed employed this easily in the waning job market of minerals, or so-called "economic," geology. Easy going, a free agent in a world others found gummed by emotional stickum; yet faithfully settled into a family, or his wife would not be sitting with her feet up, so comfortably telling me all about him. I hoped he truly was okay, so I could hope to meet him. So I could ask for a few pointers on making a living while being the kind of dog who jumped fences.

Gretchen smiled pleasantly, but cocked one eyebrow in question. "You haven't told me why the FBI is interested in him."

I dodged the question. "Well, I don't know for certain. I'm not exactly with the FBI. I'm a geologist, actually, but I'm consulting to the FBI on a case that involves the area where your husband's been working. Something about an endangered rodent."

Gretchen put her coffee mug on the table and stretched. "Oh, yeah, that mouse. Did that biologist blow the whistle like she said she was going to?"

My hands tensed on my mug. "She was going to blow the whistle? On whom?"

"Ohhhhh, now I get it. Yeah, this wildlife biologist— what's her name, Pat somebody?—she was doing a study on this little mouse out there, and she told Don that this other guy at her company said it was rare and endangered, but she said they were all over the place. She cried all over Don's shoulder about it one day when they happened onto each other out there in the field, because they were working the same area or something."

"What did she tell him?"

"Oh, that the other biologist was making a big fuss about it and trying to make her look bad in the company. She said he was taking advantage of the fact that she's this big, horsy kind of girl, by putting lesbian magazines in her desk drawers for other guys to find. You know how conservative business can be; if they think she's an 'out' lesbian, she's as good as cooked for trying to have any credibility around the workplace."

"So she was going to blow the whistle, you say. On the other biologist?" I asked, with a mixture of repugnance and thrill of the chase.

"I guess so."

"Was his name Umberto Rodriguez?"

"Don didn't say."

"So she was probably gathering evidence to show that the other biologist was the one who was falsifying data."

"Yeah, something like that. Don said she was going nuts doing catch-and-release for some kind of study, getting bitten staring into their little mouths. You can get sick doing that. Hanta virus, as a for instance." She made a face to show her nursely disapproval. "So she must have gotten the numbers she was looking for, huh? And she blew the whistle, and in ride the Mounties, right?"

I thought carefully how to answer her question. The last thing I wanted was to get jammed into the position of having to tell this woman that a death had occurred on her husband's job site. It would then occur to her that his disappearance might be a bit more out of the ordinary than a casual stroll off the map. That he might be involved in Pat Gilmore's death, or dead himself, his body not yet found. "Yeah, something like that, I guess. I don't know much about who's accusing whom of what. Did he mention a BLM agent named Stephen Giles?"

Gretchen searched her memory. "Stephen . . . Oh yes, I remember that name. Don was really upset about him for some reason."

"Was he slowing the project down or something?"

"No, that wasn't the impression I got. I'm not sure he said. Just that he didn't like him. Don said he was going down to Reno to meet with him, because he didn't want him coming out to the field."

I smiled ruefully. "I can see him feeling that way." I fitted this bit of information in with my previous understanding of MacCallum. "I hear your husband's a fairly jolly sort."

"Jolly?"

"You know, laughs a lot."

"Oh yes. Anything ironical will crack him up."

"BLM agents don't strike him as ironical?"

She made a swatting gesture with one hand. "What's so ironical about working for a living?"

I shrugged. She hadn't met Stephen Giles.

"So your husband has an office here in the house," I said. "Mind if I take a squint?" I knew from long exposure to men in the workplace that seeing the office was often seeing the man. Tidy ones often went with pinched minds, and messy ones meant anything from depressive sloth to creative genius, depending on the type of mess.

Gretchen thought for a moment. "Well, I guess that would be okay. His work is proprietary, of course, so let me first take a pass through there and make sure he didn't leave out anything critical. I mean, as an FBI consultant, you can of course get a search warrant and all that if you have to, but being a geologist you understand about proprietary interests."

"Sure." Her calm was unshakable. That meant she was either trusting to a fault or absolutely certain that she and her husband had nothing to hide from anyone, anytime, anywhere, except of course the company's secrets.

She rose and moved to the far corner of the kitchen, opened a door, and stepped through it. "Yeah, come ahead. Looks like he locked up his files and took his current stuff with him, anyway."

I followed her into the garage, a deep two-bay unit which had been insulated with pink fiberglass and lined with book shelves. Having only one small window facing out onto the garden, it was dark, but Gretchen switched on a boom lamp over a drafting table that stood under that window, and the room warmed with light reflected from the table's surface.

I looked around the space. Loosely organized clutter radiated out from the drafting table, spilling onto the tops of oak file cabinets and into oak bookcases. The space felt very cozy and nestlike for a converted garage; the man had raised the floor across the back half of the area, setting heavy plywood sheets up on two-by-four stringers, and had covered the floor closest to his drafting table with a large oriental rug. It was beautiful. I bent and touched it. The knotting was exceedingly fine, and if I could believe the eye I had developed at my grandmother's knee, it was silk. Putting the expense of such an artifact out of my mind momentarily as the anomaly it was, I rose and concentrated instead on the surface of the table, my eye drawn by its disordered sense of productivity. As was typical of a great number of geologists, he had eschewed a desk for this larger surface, which had a narrow rail across the front to prevent him from leaning onto an unrolled map and creasing it. It was a warm space, a contemplative space. Two large stereo speakers were stuffed into the adjacent bookcases, and the jewel cases to a number of CD's were scattered among the pencils and abandoned scraps of paper. I took a squint at the CD's. The man liked the blues.

Over the table, against the wall, hung a sepia-toned photograph of a bunch of Wild West saloon gamblers eyeing each other suspiciously over a roulette wheel. I stared into it, trying to understand its significance.

Seeing what had caught my eye, Gretchen spoke. "He likes to keep things in perspective," she said.

I cocked my head her way in question.

" 'Life's a crap-shoot,' " she said. " 'Never count your winnings 'til you've left the table.' That sort of stuff."

I smiled uncomfortably, wondering if the man who had stared into that picture had already cashed in his chips. His friend and colleague Pat Gilmore was dead, gone the same night he had disappeared. There had to be a connection.

Avoiding Gretchen's eyes, I peered into the next framed picture that hung over the table. It was a black and white flash photograph of two men standing in a cavern. They were dressed in what looked like oil skins, and were wearing boots, hard hats, and head lamps.

"That's Don touring a mine in Australia," Gretchen said. "Don loves to run around in holes in the ground. It's not for me. That's him on the left."

"Who's the other guy?"

"That's Kyle Christie. They've worked together for years. Don does the lion's share of working up the targets, but Kyle has better staying power where it comes to exploratory drilling. That can take months or years. Hundreds of holes. They have a kind of nasty joke about it: Don generates, Kyle penetrates."

"Must be a guy thing." I leaned closer to get a look at MacCallum. He wore safety glasses which had caught the glare of the flash. With the hat and bulky suit, I could only surmise that he had a rather long nose. His companion was tall and rangy.

"That picture doesn't look much like him," Gretchen said. "It must be over twenty years old. He's gained some weight." She was silent for a moment, and then said, in a tone of voice that sounded ever so subtly impatient, "But Kyle hasn't changed."

"What do you mean?"

"Oh, don't mind me. They're good friends. It's just that Kyle leans on Don so. If it weren't for Don—"

"He'd be out of a job?" I asked. It was an easy deduction. Unless I missed my guess, Gretchen was feeling impatience on her husband's behalf. "Kind of like yin and yang, are they?"

I turned and looked at Gretchen. She looked slightly sad. "Don's very protective of his friends," she said, and left it at that.

"It isn't just anyone who feels comfortable in mines," I commented, getting back to the photograph.

"Oh, Don loves them. He says he likes to be down inside the Earth and see something nobody else has seen. I always told him he's just jealous of women, who get to create babies in their dark places."

I forced this concept out of my mind. I did not want to think about growing babies in my dark cavern. At the same time, hearing a woman speak of this most inward capacity with such directness and strength thrilled me.

I continued around the office space, reading book titles at random, trying to take the essence of the man from the cocoon he had spun around himself. Books on mining history rested next to texts on mineralogy. Mineral specimens winked from sample bags stored in cardboard boxes along the bottoms of the bookcases. Another box stood full to overflowing with wine bottles. "Nice taste your husband has," I said, noticing the labels.

Gretchen laughed again. "Yeah, that's Don's little splurge. He's always taken his bonuses in stock instead of cash. When Chittenden came on, he made those bonuses fat, giving him a part of the new limited partnership. When the stock went up he loosened up and bought himself some of his favorite grape juice. That and good Scotch. Like I say . . ."

"So Granville's been kind to him?" I inquired, trying to make my question sound neutral and ho-hum, as if I were only making a polite reply to her statement.

"He's done pretty damned well. At least, on paper. But that's why that picture over the drafting table is there. To keep things in perspective."

"How so?"

"Well, you see, when Don went to work for Granville, they were a penny stock on the Vancouver exchange. Then Don—well, Don and Kyle, technically—discovered the deposit that's now the Gloriana Mine, and Chittenden came in and did a big promotion, and the stock went way up. Now the mine has even proven out, so you'd think they'd be doing marvelously, but in fact the stock is down. Why? Some foreign country or another came off the gold standard and started selling off their bullion. Don said that even though the price of gold is now up again a bit, the stocks have stayed down. When the price went down, a lot of people shifted their speculation from gold stocks to Internet stocks instead. He said the action's moved on to another table."

I shook my head. "One day gold is money, the big hedge against inflation. The next day it's just jewelry again."

"You got it. Two years ago, his stock was worth over a couple million dollars. Today, half that. You can't take that kind of thing seriously."

My jaw plummeted into my shirt front. "A couple *million*? And you lose half that and it's not a *big deal*?"

Gretchen shook her head. "Men like Don believe in the rewards that come from what they create or find with their talents, not in their skill at using capital to make capital. He tried selling a little bit of the stock and diversifying, but it made him terribly nervous. He couldn't do it. So instead, he just stays in the game. Besides, if he didn't work, he'd be bored, like I said. I know what you're thinking, but he thinks of that stock like a pat on the back. That's why I still work. I want to make sure our kids go to college."

My head was spinning. I peered more closely at Gretchen, wondering if she'd been eating some of the sedatives she must handle at work. "But—"

Gretchen was leaning against one of the bookcases. "I know it must sound nuts, but like I say, we've been together for a long time, and you just don't take short-term changes seriously, if you're smart. Sure, even on what Granville pays Don in salary, we could buy a bigger house and new cars, but if everything crashed again, then what? We'd be out on the street. Geology is a boom and bust business. He's always telling me that whatever gets valuable, a geologist can find so much of it that it's worth nothing next week."

"Don't I know it," I said glumly. "We geologists are always working ourselves out of a job. I work in oil and gas. Or should I say, I *did* work in oil and gas until recently."

"Perfect example. You find so much oil we're swimming in it, and the price drops. Or some Arab chieftain with fifteen Cadillacs starts a cartel and knocks the Americans out of the saddle one more time."

"Yeah," I said, "and some CEO with an MBA in bean counting comes in and gets paid big bucks for merging with some other company and firing three-quarters of the talent. Makes you wonder. But gold is supposed to be different," I said. "It's not just a commodity, it's considered money, even if countries are going off the gold standard."

"Right, the big hedge against inflation. But what drives inflation? Don told me that the price of gold reflects how secure people are feeling in the capacities of their governments to maintain order and protect them from chaos. The record high came within months of when the Iranians took American hostages. It was a whole new world in which someone else suddenly held a wild card. The price crested eight hundred dollars an ounce."

I shook my head. "Isn't there a little more to it than that?"

"There must be. The government set the price at thirty-five from 1933 until 1968. The hundred years before that, they kept it at twenty. So you have to consider at least two factors; how secure people feel, and whether or not their government controls the price."

"Yes," I said. "And where there are two variables you know about, there are at least two more you don't."

"Right. But don't ask me what they are. I'm just a nurse. I just do bed pans." She laughed again, this time an ironical, so-what chuckle. "Right now, gold is down and its price is not controlled, so I'll be an optimist and take it to mean that we're in good times."

"Are we?" I realized that I didn't know. Like MacCallum, I lived on the strength of my talents, and believed in them above anything a big, seemingly insensitive government might do for me. I abhorred fences, and saw them as things that needed to be jumped.

Gretchen yawned. "This house is paid for. Our cars are paid for. The wine is his big splurge." She followed my eye to the floor. "Yeah, and that rug. All else fails, it'll pay for a year of our kids' college."

"Where'd you get it?"

"Don won it in a card game with an Arab at a fly-in brothel called the Bronco Betty. It's out in the desert north of Winnemucca. No, don't get any ideas; men don't just go to whore houses for the sex. The Bronco Betty has a bar a little like a night club, except that the girls will do a little more than show it to you, if you want. Don stops in at the Bronco Betty now and then because the madam, Lefty, is a friend of his. She does a little speculating in mining properties. She used to own one of the mining claims that Chittenden's limited partnership bought up."

"Did Don act as the go-between in that transaction?"

"No, but he coached Chittenden. You see, Lefty has a taste

for single malt Scotches, and Don got Chittenden to take her an especially nice one."

"What kind was that?" I asked, keeping the conversation going.

"A twenty-five-year-old MacCallum, of course. Smooth as they come. I think he told her he owned the distillery."

"She believe that?" I asked, suddenly wondering if Gretchen was the one who was being fed a line. What if MacCallum was not on walkabout, but simply lying low somewhere because he'd just killed a wildlife biologist?

"If she did, I don't know how she can stay in business. But anyway, we're getting off the story of the rug. Don was out there one night too drunk to drive back to town, and Lefty staked him to enough cash to get into a card game with some high rollers. A sort of left-handed thank you. He could have lost his shirt, but when he woke up in the morning, he was sleeping in the back of his vehicle with that rug folded up underneath him. He had a devil of a time getting it home on the plane. He told me it was a good thing he passed out when he did, as the next hand would have brought the stakes up to me versus the Arab's jet. So no, I don't worry about Don. Heaven and left-handed madams look after the Don Mac-Callums of the world."

"But this time—" I stopped myself.

"Don't worry about Don," Gretchen said, easily reading the anxiety in my face. "That old sourdough hasn't gotten up from the big poker table yet. And he's still got a wild card up one sleeve or another."

Avoiding Gretchen's eyes, I turned and stared at Don MacCallum's drafting table, and studied the way the bright light from his boom lamp glared off its pale beige surface. It reminded me of the sun striking the desert floor. I had, for an instant, the notion that I was, as Peggy had suggested, an eagle, afraid to land. I was flying high over the parched landscape, witness to the stark leavings of a man's disappearance, and now my vision filled with the smoke from the fires of his restless plunder of nature's rare and fragile resources. And with this change in vision, I imagined his notes burning like so much sage brush, ignited to hide the evidence of a crime.

22

I SAID VERY LITTLE TO FAYE DURING THE FLIGHT back to Salt Lake City. I had her drop me at the garage where my truck was being repaired rather than at Ava's, and waited until I saw her drive well out of sight before storming across to the pay phone near the sidewalk to place a call.

Tom Latimer answered on the second ring.

My voice boiling with anger, I said, "Okay, *Tom*, I've got your information. But first, you are going to come clean with me. How in *hell* did you know where I was today?" Words spilled out of me, and I didn't wait for an answer. "Was getting me to Denver some big game you and Faye cooked up so I could do some of your leg work for you? That was a nice woman you had me interrogate, and she loves her husband. Or is this hazing part of your recruitment crap? Or is that just some bullshit you're dumping on Faye? She's a nice person, you know, and she doesn't need some old—" I stopped myself. Angry as I was, I did not want to throw dignity to the wind by taking shots at his age. "Have you thought of *asking* me if I want the damned job, or is it more fun to *mess* with me?"

There was a brief silence on the other end of the line, then Tom spoke in a very polite, very matter-of-fact tone of voice. "Em, I am sorry to have upset you. You are a very private person, but we do live in an open society. On a typical day, it does not take an operative of the Federal Bureau of Investigation to figure out where you are. Since you ask, I knew where you were because I dropped by to see you this morning, and Ava informed me that you had left some time earlier with a tall young woman in a Porsche. Simple deduction suggested to me that you were with Faye. And, since I was privileged to know what she had planned for the day, I hoped you might assist me by talking to Ms. MacCallum. How did it go?"

"No way, Tom. First you tell me about this recruitment shit."

"Then you're interested?"

"I am *not* interested!"

"Damn."

"Tom, you cut this out! You've been playing me like a prize trout. I thought we were . . . that we had an *understanding*. I am a geologist. I am not a—"

"*Fine*, Em. I'm sorry to—like you say—mess with you." He sounded contrite, but now also angry.

I stared into the phone, deflated. "That's it?"

"If you say so."

"I do."

"Then that's that. But would you mind telling me what Gretchen MacCallum said?"

"God damn it, I—"

"Sorry."

"Of *course* I'll tell you. I just—"

Tom fell silent.

After a moment—in which I reminded myself that I was standing at a pay phone in a public place, surrounded by normal citizens on foot and in cars who were enjoying the sunshine like nothing was totally wrong and confusing—I said, "Listen, it's not that I'm disinterested in this case, it's that I don't like being manipulated into pursuing it. If you'll be direct with me, I'll help you where I can. But I am not looking for a job with the FBI, and that's final."

Tom said nothing for a moment, then, "That's reasonable. What do you need to know in order to help?"

"Tom," I said, my voice rising again, "you're still hiding behind words. Cut the shit!"

He sighed with exasperation. "I repeat my question. What do you need to know?"

Now that he seemed willing to talk, I had no idea what to ask him. That gave me a nasty sense of *déjà vu*, like I was back in that restaurant where he had first launched this whole business on me and I was wondering what was hitting me. Which brought to mind the couple that had sat at the next table, and all Tom's nonsense about asking what the relationship was between them. Intent on throwing that pie back into his face, I said, "So tell me who the people at the next table were, and how they bear on the case."

Tom didn't say anything for quite a while. Then he said, "I'm not sure. The father, Morgan Shumway, is a lawyer. The daughter is dating Roderick Chittenden."

Now I was silent for a moment. "What kind of lawyer?" "Environmental."

"Nice way to piss Daddy off. Date a land raper."

"One would think."

I let all this sink in, but it didn't form a picture for me. Finally, I said, "Gretchen MacCallum said she's not worried about her husband because he wanders off with fair frequency. She says he told her that Pat Gilmore confided in him that Rodriguez—or I have to presume it was him, Gretchen didn't know—was trying to smear her, and she was gathering data so she could expose him. 'Blow the whistle' is the phrase Gretchen used. Pat Gilmore referred to him as 'another guy on the team.' And she says MacCallum didn't like Stephen Giles any more than I did.

"Gretchen also said that a couple years ago MacCallum's Granville stock position was worth two million, but today half that, but that it was no big deal. She's a nice lady. Smart. Self-assured. MacCallum seems nice, too, judging from his workspace and from the woman who loves him, but—" I paused, trying to decide whether I should share my suspicions. "—he likes expensive wines, and drinks too much when he hasn't got anything happening. They live modestly. They have two kids and a dog. I like her coffee mugs. That's about it."

"So she doesn't sound concerned."

"No, not at all."

"And you read her for a straight arrow."

"Unusual, yes. Bent, no."

"Can you think of anything else?"

"No," I said, still uncertain of what I thought of Don MacCallum.

"Nice work. Thanks."

"You're welcome."

"Okay. Give me a call if you think of anything you forgot."

I stared into the phone a while longer, as if it were supposed to cough out some kind of token of the effort I had just made, but I couldn't figure out what button to push, or for that matter how I'd wound up in a token booth. "Okay."

"Bye."

"Bye."

The line went dead. I hung it up, and only then realized that I had begun to tremble with excitement.

As LUCK WOULD finally have it, my truck was waiting for me, its brakes once again roadworthy. I paid for the repair, but before I drove to Ava's house to get cleaned up for my dancing date with Ray, I sat a while and thought. It felt good to be back behind the wheel of my old friend, and at that moment, I needed all the good feelings I could get. That truck was suddenly my oasis of familiarity in a world that was not quite making sense. I had told Tom off, just as I had been planning all the way back from Denver, and yet wanted to phone him back immediately and ask him what the situation in Nevada was all about. Similarly, I was looking forward to my date with Ray, and yet had a sickening feeling that the evening would end with a fight. It was safest to just stay in that truck, and I knew it.

Presently, I switched on the ignition and began the drive to Ava's house, already stiffening against any comments she might make which would be designed to pry out of me where I'd been that day and with whom. She was for the most part a very reasonable person who did not stick her nose in where it was not wanted, but I was, after all, a guest in her home, and a non-Mormon in whom her devoutly Mormon son was interested. I was sure I gave her the willies.

Further luck was with me, and Ava was not home. I let

myself in with the key she had lent me and headed upstairs
to take a shower. I scrubbed my hair and did my best at blow-
drying it into some semblance of a style, then reached into
the closet for the one item of clothing I had brought along
which might be described as a dress. It was in fact a blouse
and skirt, made of rayon, so it hung pretty nicely around my
so-so figure. I brushed my hair up to a high gloss, and was
even thinking of digging the one tube of lipstick I owned out
of the bottom of my toilet kit when I got to looking at the
framed photographs of Ava's daughters which graced the
walls of the room. Every girl over fifteen was wearing lipstick. They were gorgeous, each one of them, to the bone,
but the cosmetics made them look not just pretty, but also . . .
I struggled for a word, and then it struck me. They looked
compliant. Or at least, that was how they looked to good ol'
Em, the dog peeking in from outside the fence.

I left the war paint where it lay and went downstairs to
wait for Ray, wondering what I thought I was doing in a skirt.

IT WAS THE first time I had been entirely alone in Ava's
house, so I indulged in a little wandering around and looking
at things. I won't call it snooping—I opened no closed drawers or doors, and I lifted no papers to look underneath—but
it was definitely an inspection. Everywhere, I found photographs and other mementos of happy family events. Sadness
began to well up inside of me. I had no such events to remember.

I let myself into the backyard and sat down on a bench
and had a small, quiet cry. As I was growing up on my parents' ranch in Wyoming, I had dreamt of being part of a
bigger, happier family, but now that I was being included in
one, I felt isolated and alone. The feeling made little sense to
me. Certainly, I took issue with the price of being part of that
family—giving up my beliefs, at least nominally, and giving
up my status as an independent, solo entity—but that wasn't
all of it. As the tears flowed, I realized that, at the pit of my
being, I feared that I could not receive the bounty of belong-

ing and togetherness they offered, and I could not understand why.

As the minutes ticked by, I watched the sun dip toward the western horizon, toward Nevada and all of its open loneliness. I wondered why I felt so much more at home in the emptiness of an arid landscape than chin deep in the comforts of a true family. I liked some of Ray's relatives more than others, but that was to be expected. And they seemed willing to receive me simply because I was important to Ray. But I was not one of them, and would never be. I began to berate myself, telling myself that I was only putting off the split that had to come between myself and Ray and his big, close family. I decided that I had to be pretty callous to take a sip of their happiness, knowing that I was almost certain to walk away. I asked myself, *What business do I have visiting here, soaking up their kindness, when I know I can't be one of them?* I hung my head, contemplating my selfishness. I felt a pervasive sense of shame.

I heard Ray let himself in through the front door and move through the house, his rhythmic, catlike stride clicking off the front hall tiles, then muffled on the carpeting, and finally sounding on the concrete walkway outside the sliding door I had left ajar. When he saw me, he moved quickly to my side, put a hand on my shoulder, and asked softly, "What?"

I rubbed the tears from my eyes. "Oh, nothing. Just trying to sort myself out."

Ray came around in front of me and took my hands and guided me up into his arms and kissed me, long and gently, then tucked my face into the warm place beside his throat and held me.

In spite of my guilt, I felt safe. "I'm sorry," I said. "This was supposed to be a happy evening."

"Tears first, then dancing," he murmured. "No hurry. You look wonderful."

I tightened my arms around him and drank up his kindness. It was perhaps five minutes before I came back to the surface of the world and began to feel uncomfortable that at any moment Ava might return and see us embracing in her garden.

"I'm ready," I said, giving him another kiss on the neck. "Let's go."

RAY TOOK ME to a place called the Manhattan Club and taught me some of the finer points of swing dancing. Gliding across the floor with him was a delight, or as close to being totally delighted as I've ever experienced while dancing. Much as I like dancing, I've always thought myself a no-talent. But Ray was a strong and dependable lead, and he quickly taught me to balance myself better and move more smoothly through a number of steps. For the first time, I really understood how to place my feet so that he could guide and spin me, and when to brace myself so that he could pivot around me. I must say also that it was a feast to spend that much time touching him, woman to man, seduction being one of many things that dancing was invented to communicate. During the slow dances, I moved right up close to him, and let him feel my hips move against him, and was pleased to feel him respond with even more sensual movements. He was strong enough and had such exquisite balance that he could lift me and roll me across one thigh like I'd seen professional ballroom dancers on TV do. It was really fun, and the whole experience had me in something of a lather by the time he gave my hand a tug and led me toward the door, the parking lot, and what I presumed would be the drive straight home to Mama's.

But Ray did not drive me back to his mother's house. Instead, he took me up the hill to the mouth of Emigration Canyon, from which we could enjoy a view of the city lights. "Donner Park?" I asked, noticing a sign. "You mean, as in the ill-fated Donner party, of what's-eating-you fame?"

Ray gave me a dour look and kept on driving to the opposite side of the canyon, to the This Is the Place State Park, the place where Brigham Young first viewed the Salt Lake valley with his emigrant Mormon faithful. He parked the car and came around and opened my door and took my hand, silently inviting me to take a walk.

We ambled along for a while, his arm tightly around my

shoulders, until we came to a flat rock that formed a rustic bench. He settled me on it. Then he went down on one knee, looked deep into my eyes, and said, "Emily Hansen, will you be my wife?"

My jaw about hit my knees.

He waited.

I gasped for air.

He began to look a bit frantic. "Well, will you *think* about it?"

"Oh. Ah. Sure, I'll . . . think about it."

"What did you think I had in mind?" he asked heatedly, but then he put a hand out to indicate that he wanted to take that question back, and said, "I'm sorry," and hung his head.

I took his chin in my hand and lifted it. "Don't be." For once, I was the one who was short on words.

He stared up into my eyes, his own filled with hope and worry and unasked questions.

I wanted to kiss him, but couldn't. I was too scared. Finally, I found my voice, and blurted, "I'm supposing that being your wife means the whole bit, doesn't it?"

"Bit?"

Now we were back on familiar ground, where I prattled away like I had verbal diarrhea and he answered in monosyllables. "Well, I mean, you bring me up to this park. It's like you want the whole thing: wife, children, church. And probably not in that order. Like I'd have to give up birth control, for heaven's sake, and have a dozen kids, and this is coming out all wrong."

"Yes."

"Yes, the church? Or yes, it's coming out all wrong?"

He opened his palms upward. "*Yes. Church.*" As in, what were you thinking?

"No."

"*No?*"

"No . . . I mean, I'm not sure. I mean, Ray, I know so little about—I mean, *damn* it! Ray! So that's the deal? I give up my world, my profession, my . . . life as I know it for yours, right?"

Ray's eyes had grown dark with anger. This was the fight I had been avoiding, and the look in his eyes was why. But then suddenly he closed them, and I felt alone and scared in a different way. I wasn't sure I could breathe.

A long while afterward, his lips moved again, and he said, "Please consider it," and fell silent. Only then did I realize that he held a ring of gold in his strong, elegant fingers, ready to slip it into place on my hand, the better to anchor his life to mine.

23

AFTER A FEW FRACTURED HOURS OF SLEEP, I GAVE up on lying with my eyes closed and got up to pace around the thick, sumptuous carpeting in Ava's guest room. At about four A.M., I dressed and drove out across the sleeping city in search of a cup of coffee and a place to walk, or even run. Some time after daybreak I found myself well north of Salt Lake City on the causeway that leads out to Antelope Island.

Antelope Island is a state park and nature preserve formed by a bald, rocky mountain range that rises from Great Salt Lake. It had just the brand of loneliness I needed: just me, a few thousand shore birds, and a long view to the west. The six-mile-long causeway cuts out across the lake about a half-hour's drive north of Salt Lake City, and leads past rafts of grebes and bobbing gulls. When the kiosk opened, I paid my admission fee, parked the truck, clambered over a crude trail that led to the northern tip of the island, and stared out across the early-morning stillness of the lake, which is famous for its high salinity. There is no outlet; all waters that flow in from the surrounding highlands stay put until they evaporate in the desert heat, leaving behind salts in concentrations far exceeding that of sea water.

I looked out across the emptiness toward the west. The Great Basin. Salt Lake City crouched at the eastern edge, and Reno waited at the west. What had Peggy said about the western spoke of the medicine wheel? That it represented the bear, or Introspection? She was right, I seemed to have the temperament of a bear. Perhaps the Great Basin was a place where there was ample room for me to wander until the wheel brought me around again to my senses.

From the point, I found my way south along the western edge of the island, from which I could look out across thirty miles of hypersaline water to the far edge of the lake. I walked along the shore to a thin meadow in the desert scrub. The wide trail that had been formed by the tramplings of human feet was cross-cut every few feet by much subtler pathways formed by much smaller animals, mostly rodents. Here, a very narrow one led to a burrow; there, several small ones coalesced into a rodent super-highway that was still a faint trace next to the one obvious enough for humans to follow.

I sipped the last dregs of the coffee I had bought, stuffed the cardboard cup into my back pocket, and stepped down onto a sandy beach. I would have taken off my shoes and enjoyed the feeling of the sand between my toes, but there was a haze of flies dining on a paste of dead critters along the strand. Wondering what they were, I crouched down and picked up a handful, and fished into my jacket pocket for my hand lens.

Ten-power magnification told me I was looking at two very lovely things. The first was oolitic sand, which is composed of tiny crystals of aragonite rolled up into minute balls. The chemical is precipitated from the hypersaline waters of the lake, and the waves roll it into concentric shells, like so many pale seeds. I had seen oolite samples in my freshman Geology lab at college. Geology students find them cosmic, because they're so nearly perfectly spherical.

The other thing I saw was the remains of a few thousand tiny brine shrimp. I pulled the U.S. Geological Survey flyer I had gotten at the entrance booth out of my other pocket and fell peacefully into several long, semiconscious minutes of self-education. The flier informed me that the lake is too salty for larger organisms, such as fish, but that the ghostly brine shrimp, bacteria, and algae make up a rich ecosystem. The shrimp population overwinters as eggs and dormant embryos. As warming waters bring a late-winter algal bloom, the little critters hatch out and begin to meet, greet, lay eggs, and crank out a series of short-lived generations of the minute swimmies. By late May, the shrimp have grazed the algae to a nub, and they gradually die off until December, when water temperatures drop below the point that will sustain the adults.

They then die, leaving just eggs and cystose embryos until the water warms again in March.

Hence, the paste of dead shrimp carpeting the beach. Just another example of the balance of nature: Times are good, you live; times aren't favorable, you die.

I thought ruefully that there were hundreds of thousands of very successfully breeding humans living on the shores of this lake, and I couldn't seem to join their numbers. Mixing my metaphors, I wondered if it was because I couldn't stand to roll around under the pressure of the currents and become perfectly round and smooth with all the other little grains.

I lifted my gaze to the far shore again, longing for the emptiness and privacy I had seen two days earlier in Nevada.

I PHONED RAY from Ava's house, catching him on his lunch break. Ava stood in the doorway listening, so I kept it brief. "Ray. I'm going to Nevada for a few days, so I can think things over. I'll be back." It was the best I could do, balancing forthrightness with an overwhelming need to protect myself from the loss I already felt.

On the other end of the line, Ray said merely, "Oh."

"I'll, um, call," I said, feeling guiltily that I should add something. Like perhaps an explanation or an apology for my chicken-heartedness.

"Please."

"I will. And . . ."

Ava was now watching me with the eyes of an eagle.

I turned my back to her. I had placed the call in front of her because I wanted her to hear, but not be able to directly question my plans, but I did not want her to hear what I wanted to say next. I whispered into the phone. "I . . ."

"I do too," Ray answered, his voice tight with pain.

I hung up the phone, sat down, and tried to eat the breakfast Ava had left out for me. She came the rest of the way into the kitchen and leaned against the edge of the counter, her arms folded across her chest. And stared at me.

I forced food into my mouth and chewed. "Well," I said, keeping my eyes on my cereal, "it worked for Jesus."

"*What* worked for Jesus?" Her tone was classic Ava: even-tempered, excruciatingly polite, and not to be avoided.

I flushed with embarrassment, uncertain of the sketchy training in matters biblical I had received from my paternal grandmother, and even hazier on where exactly Christ fit within Mormon theology. "Well, didn't he go into the desert once to reason things out?"

Ava snorted, as far as she went towards expressing contempt. "Yes. Just don't let it go forty days and forty nights," she said, and left the room.

AN HOUR LATER, I was packed up and giving Ava a civil apology for my abrupt departure when the phone rang. She answered it. "It's for you, Em," she said, giving me a probing look.

I stood in her front hallway, feeling conspicuous. "Hello?"

"Em, it's Faye."

"Oh. Hi."

"I wanted to say how sorry I am for getting crosswise with you about Tom. About this recruitment, and everything."

"Oh." I wasn't used to people apologizing to me, least of all for being haplessly sucked into a third party's manipulation games. "So he told you I reamed him a new . . . ah . . ."

"Asshole? You did? Well, he probably deserved it. No, I just got to thinking about it, and um, yes, I spoke with him about you a little bit last night, and we had words—trust me on this—and it just really dawned on me that I was being . . . well, he's a good guy, but he has his moments when he plays Svengali, and he ought to be spanked."

I savored an image of what that might look like, and laughed.

"So; forgive me, please?"

"I really don't think you have much to apologize for."

"Oh, yes I do. Hey, I don't need to build up karma over this, see? So please, accept my apology. Besides, I want us to be friends, and if you're anything like me, you'd be thinking what a presumptuous shithead I am about now, getting in your face and telling you your business yesterday like I did. I really am sorry."

"It's nothing." I felt Ava's eyes on my back.

"So let's have lunch again some day soon."

The phone was cordless, so I wandered down the hall a bit, trying to give Ava the hint that I wanted a little privacy. "Look, I'd love to, Faye, but I had a . . ." I couldn't tell her about Ray's proposal and the ensuing fight with Ava listening. "I'm on my way to Nevada."

"Oh, so Tom got hold of you after all?"

"What do you mean, 'after all'?"

"Well, there was that Indian shaman who was trying to reach you."

"No, he didn't call me."

"Oh, good, then. For once, he kept his word. I told him to stay out of your business, and he said he would."

Faye had a way of staying out of my business that didn't stay out of my business. I wanted to scream, but I said, "Well, you can pat him on the head. He's being a good boy."

She laughed. "Well, you have a good trip. And hey, take my phone numbers with you, so if that truck of yours breaks down again, you give me a call, okay? You know I always need an excuse to fly somewhere."

"That's absurd. You don't go flying all the way out to Nevada in a half-million-dollar airplane to fetch some yuk like me whose twenty-five-year-old beater of a truck breaks down."

"Em, you've forgotten."

"Oh, yeah. You get bored."

"Call me. Humor the poor little rich girl." She gave me her home number and cell number.

I said, "There is one thing you can do for me."

"Name it."

"You read a lot of esoteric stuff. You got a book called *Seven Arrows*?"

"Great book. I highly recommend it. But I lent my copy out already."

"Oh."

"You can get it at any good bookstore. Try Sam Weller's. They have a great Western Americana section. Or try The King's English. Lovely little bookstore."

"Thanks."

"Anything else?"

There was one other thing. "Yes. You can go back and visit 'Auntie,' and ask her if she knows anything about the environmental group that's trying to block the development of Granville Resource's new project in the Kamma Mountains."

"Okay."

I said good-bye to Ava and headed out to Sam Weller's, where I found a used copy of *Seven Arrows*, as well as some interesting-looking books on the history of Nevada, both natural and human. Then I got back into my truck and headed west into the Great Basin and whatever capital-I Introspection I might gather there.

I MADE IT clear to Wendover, where Interstate 80 meets the Nevada border and a phalanx of slot machines, before curiosity got the better of me and I phoned Tom Latimer.

"I'm just heading out of town," I lied. "My truck's all fixed, so I'm going west for a few days to kind of take a break. Just thought I'd say good-bye."

"Thank you." He sounded genuinely pleased that I would call.

Embarrassment tightened my throat, and I presented the excuse for calling that I had rehearsed over those long miles of salt flat that stretch between the western shore of Great Salt Lake and the border. "And, um, I had some more thoughts about my conversation with Gretchen MacCallum. Thought I'd pass them on to you."

"Oh, great. Let me get a notepad ready. Okay, shoot."

"Well . . ." I drawled, because I didn't really have anything specific to report. "I mean, I have a feeling about MacCallum. He's kind of an interesting sort. I don't know if that has any bearing on things, but . . ."

"Interesting how?"

"Well, just the fact that he's still employed catches my attention. If you think it's hard to stay employed in oil and gas these days, you should try mining geology. They call it economic geology, for some reason."

"I see. Anything strike you as unusual about Granville Resources, or about the way MacCallum does business with them?"

"No. Well, it's very unusual that he managed to accrue two million dollars' worth of stock. He must be something kind of special, or unusual, to get much stock at all, even as bonuses. I mean, nowadays companies don't have to offer that much in employee incentive plans. So I got to wondering if he's got some special deal going."

"Such as?"

"Well, I don't know." I pulled my punch, not ready to suggest that Gretchen MacCallum's husband might have a motive for murder. Something in me wanted dearly for MacCallum to be that lone wolf she loved, because then he just might have some answers to my quandaries. "Dirty doings would be your department."

"And what falls in Em's department?" Tom inquired.

"Well, if he's just Joe Geologist, then maybe the higherups in the company think he's a golden goose that they have to hold on to."

"Tell me more."

"It's less common these days, what with layoffs and so forth, but you used to see this in the commodities exploration business. It's called the golden handcuffs. If someone's really hot at exploration, you make it too expensive for anyone else to hire them away. You make him too cozy to leave. You give him stock options, or a piece of the action; some special reason to stick around. Maybe if he leaves, he isn't vested in the stock, and he loses it. Who knows? The irony would be that MacCallum doesn't have to work anymore, not with seven figures in stock, so why's he still there?"

"I'll bet you have a guess."

"Yes. Maybe it's really because he feels loyal to Granville, or to the whole industry. Or maybe he just needs something to do. Or maybe he's just still working to keep his exploration partner employed."

"How do you figure that?"

"It's just a hunch." But then I thought about the photograph of the gamblers that MacCallum had hung over his drafting table. "It's something I'm trying to sort out, I guess. Explorationists are a funny bunch. They're optimists. In order to go exploring, you have to believe some goody might be out there. I always worked on the exploi*ta*tion side, not explo*ra*tion. That's where you maximize the production of a goody someone else has already found. Someone like MacCallum. A true explorationist is half wizard."

"Like yourself," he chuckled.

I paused a moment, wondering if he was beginning to butter me up again, or truly paying me a compliment. "No, I make a lousy explorationist. I'm too much of a pessimist."

Tom said, "Ah, but that's what makes you a detective. You may not have visions of goodies that aren't likely to be there, but you're spot-on about the nasty things that *are*. Not many people can stand to look at things that make them uncomfortable. You stare right into them."

"I am *not* a detective," I said.

"Okay."

Silence filled the telephone. I imagined him writing the numbers one through ten on his notepad so he would not ask me why, if I was not a detective, I was on my way to Nevada.

I said, "Well, I'd better be going," wishing he'd come out with the information about the shaman who'd tried to phone me. I began to think that Faye must have misunderstood him. We had met no Indian peoples during our brief tour of northwestern Nevada, let alone a shaman, so why would one know to call the Salt Lake City FBI looking for me?

Tom said, "Have a good trip. Oh, and one more thing . . . no, forget it."

"What?"

"No, you'd accuse me of messing with you."

"Right." It was my turn to count to ten. "Okay, you got

my curiosity up," I said, trying not to sound eager. "But if you mess with me, forget it."

"Then I'm not going to say, because this is too far out there."

After another ten counts, I said, "You're good, Tom."

He laughed. "I have to be. But scout's honor, this is legit, no mess."

"Alllll right."

He chuckled some more, just a relaxed laugh between friends. "Someone called here yesterday afternoon asking to speak with you."

"Who?"

"A woman from Nevada."

"Someone I know?"

"I don't think so. You know a Paiute shaman named Hermione?"

I snorted, pretending surprise. "You're right, that's pretty far out there."

"Yeah, it is. I told her you didn't work here, but she said she wanted to know how to reach you. I asked her what her inquiry related to, but she wouldn't tell me."

"So naturally, because you're working on a wee *potential* fraud case in her neck of the woods, you followed up and did a search on her in your Big Brother database. And?"

"She lives over on the Pyramid Lake reservation, at a place called Sutcliffe."

" 'Sutcliffe' sounds Paiute as all hell. So does 'Hermione.' "

"Us white folks have imposed a few things on the Paiutes, Em. For all I know, Sutcliffe was a federal agent who pocketed the Indians' government dole and charged them for the exotic grain seeds they were supposed to magically know how to farm, now that they could no longer pursue their hunter-gatherer lifestyle. Heaven knows what her Indian name is."

"Native American name."

"Or whatever appellation does not offend her or her tribe. Or band. Word has it Paiutes consider themselves more an association of bands than a tribe."

"Whatever, Tom. But you were about to tell me how she's connected to Granville Resources, or to the biology of endangered rodents."

"Like I say, Em, you have an excellent nose for shit."

"It has such a distinctive odor."

"Well, here's your answer: She last attracted the attention of federal authorities when she protested the placement of the mill, offices, and mine portal of the Gloriana Mine, which is the mine your friend MacCallum found, and where our friend Patricia Gilmore had her office. Granville complained to the BLM, and the BLM tossed it over to us. That time, the controversy went away on its own."

I whistled. "And she wants to speak to me."

"She does."

"What became of her protest?"

"They moved the whole works."

"How far?"

"Eight hundred feet."

"Sacred ground?"

"That's a good guess, Em. I hadn't thought of that. But she never said."

I thought a while. Shamanism sounded fascinating, even alluring, but also way over my head and downright scary. I took a deep breath and said, "Don't give me her phone number. I'm on my way to Nevada to do some thinking, not to get into trouble, and if my sniffer is worth anything, she smells like forty miles of bad road. I am going to Nevada because it's close by, and it's big, and it's open, and because there's hardly anyone else there. I am going to Nevada to be by myself and figure out what I want to be when I grow up, and if she calls again, please tell her I went the opposite direction and I won't be back."

Tom chuckled appreciatively. "Okay. But what if she's waiting for you at the border?"

I glanced nervously around the phone booth, paranoid that he might be right. No one was in sight but a few passing motorists whizzing by on the highway. "What are you raving about, Tom?"

"She's a shaman, remember."

"Sure. And I'm the reincarnation of Cleopatra. See ya, Tom."

"I thought you were Eleanor Roosevelt. Write when you get work."

"Will do," I said, suddenly happier than I'd felt in months. "But right now, I gotta run." I stared westward toward the rampart of the first mountain range beyond the state border. It was brown and dry, and it danced in the heat. "The desert calls."

24

OVER THE NEXT TWO DAYS, I FOLLOWED LAZILY along the path followed by the 1849 emigrants, indulging my love of Western history. I stopped to examine the Humboldt River near Wells, where the main trace of the emigrant trail swept south from the northeast corner of Nevada. I had, until then, been following the approximate route of a southerly spur that a few hapless emigrants—such as the ill-fated Donner party—had taken across the salt flats of Utah. The main route of the trail, which began at Independence, Missouri, wound westward through a corner of Kansas, and all of Nebraska and Wyoming into Idaho, where it forked, at a southerly swing of the Snake River, into the Oregon Trail and the California Trail. The California Trail descended into northeastern Nevada, then followed the westward-flowing waters of the Humboldt until that river sank into the desert south of present-day Lovelock. There, as I've mentioned before, the emigrants staggered, already exhausted from months of travel, illness, and fouled water, across forty waterless miles. If they made it across the Forty Mile Desert, they caught the easterly-flowing Truckee River or Carson River and headed over the Sierra Nevada Mountains into California. Others turned north-west before Lovelock and instead crossed the Black Rock Desert, which took them into California near Mount Lassen.

I stood on the bank of the Humboldt River, listening to my truck ping as its engine cooled, and thought how different it must have been to pass this way in an ox-drawn wagon. The first emigrants had not even had a trail to follow, only the river and the reports that good farm lands lay farther west. Nevada had not been a state yet, nor had Wyoming, Utah, Idaho, Oregon, or California. Until 1848, California, Nevada, Idaho, and Utah had not, in fact, even been United States territory.

I tried to imagine the terrain as it had been then, without telephone poles, or pavement, or the distant burger stands and gas stations that marked the edge of Wells, and wished I'd seen it then. I had not forgotten the argument I'd had with Ian Walker over the mining versus environment debacle, and neither had I fully sorted out exactly where I stood on it. I was a geologist and had made a good living finding resources that other people took from the ground, but I didn't always approve of how that taking was accomplished. And, as Ian said, I drove a vehicle made entirely of mined materials and powered it with fossil fuels, and did not know exactly where those resources came from or if a system of environmental safeguards or employee safety governed their extraction. For all I knew, I was burning fuel purchased from some Middle Eastern male who thought I should be kept ignorant and behind walls or covered by heavy veils.

Perhaps in an effort to rub my nose in my own unintegrated value system, I stopped again near Elko to take a tour of one of the open-pit mines in the Carlin Trend, perhaps the one I'd seen from the air. I will say again that the mine was huge, and that I was both aghast and impressed; aghast that such a scar had been made on my planet, and impressed that my species had figured out how to do it. There seemed to be a lesson encoded in this dissonance, something about limits, both economic and technological. Certainly the fact that we could, as a species, accomplish certain technological feats did not dictate that we should necessarily carry every one of them out. I was fond of trout and could catch one or two with a fly rod, but even though I would have loved to eat trout more often, I wouldn't bring in a huge net and haul in every one in the lake. At the same time, I knew I was mixing my metaphors again. Trout are, if properly managed, a renewable resource. Gold is finite and rare.

I stopped in Battle Mountain to restock my larder and refill my five-gallon water jugs and to purchase an atlas of the back roads of Nevada. And I stopped just about every other place it occurred to me to stop, most of which were just lonesome summits along the highway, where I'd leave the truck and walk out into the desert to kick pebbles around for a while. When I passed through a town large enough to have a good grocery store, I bought a trout or a couple of links of sausage, a potato, and a fresh vegetable, and wrapped them in aluminum foil and put them underneath the hood on the engine block of my truck, and drove until they were cooked, then sat beside the Humboldt River and pretended I was eating something I'd pulled out of an oak barrel on the back of my wagon. I tried to imagine that, like the emigrants of one hundred and fifty years earlier, I was headed for a better life.

I had picked up a book before leaving Salt Lake City that gave the date of the arrival, in what is now northern Nevada, of the first people of European descent: 1826. The grizzled men of the competing Hudson's Bay and Rocky Mountain Fur Companies had trudged over the mountains into this empty country looking for beaver. The book informed me that they had blithely set about emptying the region of its fur-bearing bounty, each killing every beaver he could find quickly before his rivals could find them. I wondered, with no small sense of shame, if the compulsion to strip a territory of its resources was a dominant gene found in most peoples of European descent or if, worse yet, it was simply part of being human.

The Great Basin had been the last territory in North America explored by peoples of European descent except for, perhaps, some parts of the Arctic. Prior to the appearance of the fur trappers, miners, ranchers, and emigrants en route to California, wandering bands of Indians had lived there for at least twelve thousand years. I remembered classmates in college rhapsodizing on the subject of Indians living in harmony with nature, as if it had been a lifestyle choice. I reckoned that the Indians had made a damned fine accommodation of the limitations the environment imposed upon them. They had not enjoyed the luxury of imports like my truck and its gasoline and the box of canned food that rode in its bed. With no pleasure, I read *Seven Arrows* and found a description of just how long most Cheyennes stayed in harmony with nature or even each other once the white man dangled trade goods under their noses.

The fact was that the environment of the Great Basin was so harsh that pre-White Indian culture had not developed past the humble scratchings of a hunter-gatherer society. And yet current theories suggested that the first Indians in the area hunted and gathered so effectively that they triggered the demise of the Ice-Age animals already stressed by the changing climate. The cheetah, the dire wolf, the camels, the horses, and the mammoths could not compete with the efficiency of the tool-wielding humans. And what, precisely, constituted harmony with nature?

I lay in my bedroll at night pondering this conundrum. If living in harmony with what nature provided was a good thing, then why was it so hard to contemplate giving up the comforts and convenience of modern houses, microchips, blue jeans, and foreign-grown coffee? Could it be defined as not using any resources I couldn't carry on my back? Or should I set an arbitrary limit of not using anything that had been grown or mined more than a day's walk away? Monarch butterflies migrated thousands of miles each year. Were they in harmony with nature? And should humans seek harmony at the expense of using vaccines and vitamin pills, and shrink their average life expectancies back down to the age I currently enjoyed? What then? Would I have been happier living in a roaming tribe, pregnant at my first menses and dead of infection by my mid-thirties? *At least then*, I thought sadly, *I would have known where I fit in.* As I thought these thoughts, it occurred to me to wonder why I was having them. Were they inspired by my foolish interest in the Granville Resources case? No, it was something deeper. Somehow, the whole story reminded me of the impasse in which I found myself with Ray.

Each day, I telephoned Ray, or tried to. I left terse, embarrassed messages on his answering machine, saying that I was all right, that the weather was fine, and that I loved him. I figured that might be about what MacCallum would say to Gretchen, if all he got was the machine. I wondered if he had yet called her. I wondered where he was. I wondered what he was doing. Was he, like me, just driving around somewhere in the Great Basin trying to sort himself out?

I would have tried to call Ray again at night, but I slept miles off the highway, out of sight of through traffic and away even from my pickup truck, so that the only scavengers I'd have to worry about were those that might come on four legs. As I lay underneath the stars, he bloomed in my thoughts. I tried to put him out of my mind. I had learned about myself, over the long, lonely years that had been my life until then, that, when things just seemed too complicated for solutions, it was best to let go for a while and ruminate. Let go and give myself this kind of time, and this kind of space.

In turn, the desert received me, stripping away my confusion layer by layer.

I SUPPOSE I always knew, on some level, that I would eventually find my way all the way back to Lovelock. As I drew closer, I told myself that I wanted only to explore the open country with which Tom and Ian had teased me by driving through it so quickly. But I also rationalized that it would be a consideration to stop in and see the nice sheriff's deputy—what had his name been? Weebe?—and ask him what he had discovered during his investigation into the death of Patricia Gilmore. He had been the odd man out, disagreeing with the sheriff, so it seemed the neighborly thing to do. And Tom needed my help, so what was the harm?

By the time I had swung northward around the Sonoma Range, past Golconda and Winnemucca, and had come back southwestward, past the scorched remnants of what had been a high desert scrub where Patricia Gilmore's body had been found, and on towards Lovelock, I was intent on paying the man a visit. And so, on the fifth day after first meeting Deputy Weebe and hearing about the death of Patricia Gilmore, I pulled up once again in front of the Pershing County Sheriff's Office.

Weebe was there, greasing up his stubby fingers as he munched his way through a liverwurst sandwich and a bag of rippled potato chips. "Ah, Em Hansen, right? One of the FBI guys. I remember you. Have a chip?" He seemed quite elated to see me.

"Don't mind if I do. Just passing through. Thought I'd stop in and see how things are going. Learn anything more about Patricia Gilmore's death?"

Weebe's hand closed spasmodically around the potato chip bag, reducing the contents to small flakes with a sickening crunch. He looked left and right, to make certain we were not being overheard. "Come with me," he said, and led me into an inner office. There, he closed the door behind us before opening a drawer in his desk with the care one might take if it were rigged with motion-sensitive explosives. "I keep this clear in the back, with the wrong label on it," he said, producing a manilla file. "Sheriff Obernick told me to keep my nose out of this. Hah. He filed his report already sayin' it was accidental death, so you bet he don't want me finding otherwise. But look what I got."

I realized about then that I had not explained to Weebe that I was not actually *with* the FBI, and that my visit was therefore totally unofficial, but rationalizing that it made no difference if I listened to what he had to say, I leaned forward attentively and smiled.

Weebe selected a sheet of paper filled with pencilled notes written in a looping, schoolboy hand. It was a list of names, with thumbnail comments about where each person had been the night Pat Gilmore died, and what their motive might have been to kill her. "I got a list here of everyone as stands to gain from her death. Looky here. These all are miners, but that's just for bein' thorough, 'cause they're all local boys. I know 'um. So they're not really on the list. Now these—" he pointed at a second grouping "—these ones is more interesting to me. I got Virgil Davis, big guy runs the mine. She stops his action? He's gonna hurt bad. Gotta close the mine in, maybe, and go somewheres else. Mebbe no work for an old geezer like that nowheres."

"Wait a minute. How could she close the mine? The endangered species she was studying is in a different place altogether." *And I remembered, she found that mouse to be just like everybody else's mouse, and increasing its numbers and range, not diminishing.*

"Well, see, they need her to okay the places where they want to drill for another ore body. I been talkin' to folks." Weebe squinted at me, tapping the side of his head.

"But how does shutting down new exploration close the existing mine?"

"Runnin' outta ore. Like I say, I know some miners. The grade's holding, but the price is dropped."

"Oh." I took it to mean that they were finding the number of ounces of gold per ton of ore they had expected, but that the price per ounce of gold was lower than projections at the outset of mining. "So Virgil Davis has no alibi, and may have had a motive."

"He lives up by the mine. Very suspicious. He'd of known when Gilmore left that night, could of chased her down and done something to her. *And* he's the one as found her. Makes ya wonder, don't it? Not a whole lot of witnesses out in that country. Well, he had John Steinhoff, the mill manager, with him and they vouch for each other, but then, maybe they was in cahoots."

My spine felt momentarily cold at the thought of death in the kind of country in which I'd just been camping. Alone. I pressed onward, shrugging off the chill. "Hmm. I see you've got MacCallum, the exploration geologist."

"Right. Still missing. Kinda makes you wonder."

"Oh, yeah. And who's this?"

"Kyle Christie. Worked with MacCallum. He *claims* he don't know where his partner is. Verrry suspicious. And he looks purty nervous. If *he* ain't done nothing he shouldn't, I'll eat my hat."

Ignoring the fact that his double negative cancelled out his assertion, I said, "Okay. And these guys. Joe Enciso. Nelson Jobes. Laurel Dietz."

"Other geologists at the mine. I checked 'em all out. Enciso and Jobes got alibis, they were on shift underground when it happened. Dietz is this little blonde girl. She couldn't of done it."

I glanced at him. "You're sure?" I wanted to watch his face, and see whether his supposition was based solely on her gender. "She was underground, too?"

He shrugged his rounded shoulders. "No, I don't know. But she said she'd gone home a long time before Gilmore left the site. She has no eyewitnesses to prove she did, but I talked to her a good little bit, and she don't got it in her. Nice kid." He nodded and scrunched up his face knowingly.

"Hmm. And who's this?" I asked, seeing another name I recognized.

"Rodriguez. Little beaner as squealed on her to her boss. He didn't like her, see? Hated her, near as I can figger. It bears watching."

"But you don't know where he was the night of the crime," I said, noticing that the space beneath his name was blank. I noticed also that I was rather shamelessly encouraging Weebe to continue to presume that Patricia's death was, in fact, a case of murder, and not a bad luck road accident as his boss had surmised.

"Nope. Didn't get to him before he disappeared."

"Rodriguez is gone, too?"

"Yep. Suspicious, huh?"

"Yeah, like you say, makes you wonder. So did anyone do an autopsy?"

"Sure, the coroner took a squint at her. 'Accidental death,' just like Obernick. Old drinking buddies, them two."

"And who found her?"

Weebe tapped his finger on the page. "Virgil Davis and John Steinhoff." He tapped the page again. "Motive. And no alibi. What's to say they didn't wait out there and get her themselves? Then all's they's got to do is drive on into town and go boo-hoo, we found us a dead lady."

"Can you show me on this map where the wreck was found?" I pushed my road atlas his way.

Weebe ran his finger up and down the map, but couldn't put a fix on the spot. "Well, it's somewheres where the road goes into a curve, and it's south of the crossroads here."

Very gingerly, I turned to a pithier topic. "So how you reckon she was got?"

Weebe scrunched his face again. "Shot out her tire."

"You're kidding me! You got a tire with a bullet hole in it?". The scene instantly appeared in my mind in lurid detail: Lone woman in pickup truck barreling along a deserted road, nearly floating over the washboarding as she hurries home. A bullet hits her front tire, exploding it on impact. The truck swerves, bucks, flips end for end, crushing the cab and killing the occupant. I thought briefly about phoning Gretchen MacCallum and asking if her husband was a particularly good shot, but decided against it.

"No. But one front tire was differ'nt from the others, and there weren't no spare. The whole hulk was burned from that range fire, see, but I took a good, long look at it after they brought it in on the flatbed."

My mind raced. If Weebe was right, someone had hidden in the sagebrush, waiting for her to pass, and that person had hurried to the overturned truck, made certain his victim was dead, and then coolly changed the tire and disposed of the other. To pull this off, he—or she; it wouldn't require great strength, only accuracy—would have left tracks in the swelling clays of the desert floor, or might alternatively have left telltale signs of having erased them. "You got tracks?" I asked, excitement mounting.

"No," he said, his face crumpling into a pout.

"So you haven't actually seen the site of the crash."

"No."

"Oh. Why not?"

Weebe sucked in a long breath and adjusted his Sam Browne belt. "Well, first there was that fire. Then when that burned itself out, I did go out there, see, but I wasn't ezzackly sure where the wreck had been. And I've had to be careful how I ask people . . ." His voice trailed off, and he ran a finger across the desk top, unconsciously hanging his head like a little boy who's been caught rustling cookies.

"Because Sheriff Obernick has other *ideas*," I said diplomatically.

Weebe's lower lip had pushed up into a full-blown pout. "Ezzackly."

I DROVE OVER to the yard where Weebe told me I would find Pat Gilmore's truck, or what was left of it. It was a full-sized, high-sprung, four-wheel-drive Ford pickup with a big engine. She must have been going pretty damned fast, because the roof had been slammed down halfway to the dashboard, like a safe had been dropped on it. She would have had to have been a dwarf to survive that kind of compaction. I winced with empathy.

The truck had been roasted stem to stern in the range fire. The inside of the cab had been gutted by the flames; just a melted residue of plastic on metal springs, not much evidence that I could glean there. The glove compartment door was open, although that didn't indicate much. Mine flopped open every time I hit a bump.

I walked around to the tire which Weebe had thought suspicious. The fire had cooked it, too, but sure enough, the gummy mess around the rim brandished the remnants of a different belting pattern than did the other three, and there was no spare on the bed or bolted up underneath it. I straightened up and thought this through. Pat Gilmore had been a wildlife biologist, a professional who worked in remote areas, probably by herself. To run a trap line survey around old mining claims, she would have had to drive up some pretty sketchy old two-rut roads. I couldn't imagine her being stupid enough to try that without a spare tire.

I walked all the way around the truck, still pondering Weebe's hypothesis. *If I had just shot out someone's tire and caused them to crash*, I decided, *I would check the tire and rim to make certain I'd left no ballistic evidence. If I found, for instance, an impact mark from the bullet, I would remove that rim and dispose of it far, far away.*

Then another, even more sickening thought occurred to me: *And if I was the least bit concerned about leaving evi-*

dence, I'd set fire to the whole desert to conceal it.

I staggered over to my truck, half ready to vomit. I climbed in and shut the door, and even with the heat of the day, considered closing the windows. I felt unsafe, exposed, suddenly unable to forget and filter out the hideous impact of the callous disregard so many members of my race held for natural resources such as deserts, and the thousand million animals and plants who lived there. Somehow, I could better cope with the thought of a human killing one other human than a human setting fire to a whole ecosystem just to cover the already vicious and dishonest act of murder.

I turned the key in the ignition and drove away, turning left and right at random, until I found myself driving down a residential side street near the edge of town. The houses seemed spare and restful, blandly innocent, but still I shook with fear and sadness, and wondered if the killer lived behind one of these doors.

But I had no real evidence that Pat Gilmore had been killed, and had not just messed up and crashed all on her own. I chastised myself for my overactive sense of drama, hoping I could stuff the genie back into the bottle and just drive away.

I saw a house that looked familiar, and I realized that I was approaching the place where I'd met the woman with the ruined face. I stopped the truck about a half block away from Shirley Cook's house and let it idle in the middle of the lane, trying to figure out what to do next.

Then a strange thing happened. I was just noticing that an old white Toyota sedan was parked in front of Shirley's house, and deciding that she must have a visitor, when that visitor came out of her front door, came down the walkway to the front gate, and stood looking at me, as if she had been waiting for me to arrive. She was broadly built and had long dark hair parted in the middle and the wide, flat facial planes of a Native American.

Tom Latimer's words rang in my ear: *What if she's waiting*

for you at the border? The hair stood up on the back of my neck.

I jammed the truck into reverse, backed it into a driveway, and pulled quickly away in the opposite direction.

25

I DECIDED THAT I MUST BE LOSING MY MIND. I HAD come out here to think and relax, and here I was seeing freak-ish portents in the actions of total strangers. It was time to leave the world of humans altogether, at least for a while, and head out into the heart of the arid lands, those busily inhabited realms in which all is revealed and nothing is covered. Hu-mans are more secretive and deceptive in their thinking and in their behavior than the creatures of the desert. Certainly, the horned toad tries to look like a stack of sharp pebbles so he can hide from his enemies and lay in ambush for his prey, and tiny mice that feed on sparse grasses hide from the heat and predators during the bright hours of day, but the trails of their passage lie open for the eye to see, and there is no crowding canopy of leaves to obscure the far horizon.

But, like a food junkie trying to give up chocolate, I de-cided to leave civilization by way of the road on which Pat Gilmore had died. I told myself that, like Weebe, I probably wouldn't spot the place where she had crashed, and that I was only going there so that I could see what was left of the desert after the intense burn that had roared over it like a blackening storm. So off I went, taking the interstate back east eight or ten miles and then turning off on the dirt road in question.

The landscape was indeed black. I had expected to see burned vegetation, but was not prepared to find that even the earth was burned. The silty clay soils laid down as Ice Age lake beds and dried hard through the millennia were black-ened, scorched by the heat and coated with what I presumed to be burned resins from the sage brush. The brush itself was reduced to bare nubs sticking up from the ground, and the grasses were gone entirely. Not a creature stirred; no bird flew overhead, no insect scraped across the barren ground. I felt nauseated. I may as well have been on the moon.

And I had no trouble finding the spot where Pat Gilmore had hit the bank. It was a long road, but there weren't many curves, and there were fewer with sufficiently high banks to flip a truck. As typically happens with such dirt roads that are heavily maintained by graders, the blade had, over time, cut farther and farther down into the soil and kicked up a higher and higher bank beyond a wide, shallow ditch. The road was washboarded and not lacking in chuck holes, the very problem the grader repeatedly tried to solve. The place was wide open and lonesome. Standing in the bed of my truck, I could see a hundred miles, and the only other vehicles I saw moving were ten or fifteen miles east on the interstate. I could see how easily Pat might have lost control of her truck and hit the bank. And, judging by the curve of the bank and the length of the gouge inscribed by the edge of the front bumper, I determined that the bank had caught the front end of the truck and guided it up and over into a flip.

I got out and wandered along the ditch and around through the remnants of sage that stood above the bank. I found no footprints. The men who had come to retrieve the burned-out truck had not left the road. I moved farther and farther out from the impact site, cutting wider and wider arcs through the baked ground. And found the missing spare tire.

I knelt down and inspected the remnants of steel belting that emanated from the roasted hulk. They matched the other three on Pat's truck, and the rim looked right, too. I felt all the way around it, and found no bullet dings. Weebe's theory, like nothing else in sight, was all wet.

I sat back on my haunches and had a good laugh at myself. Pat Gilmore had not been murdered, she had simply hit the bank, like Sheriff Obernick had said. The force of impact had launched the spare tire out of the bed of the truck. I had carried spares loose like that myself. Perhaps the truck had even struck a bit of flint, and sparked the fire. I had simply drawn the wrong conclusion from fragmental evidence. I laughed so hard I cried. I stood up and danced, I whooped, I howled. If I could be so wrong, then all things were possible in my world.

*   *   *

THE DESERT LAY before me. I picked another dirt road at random and drove around the south end of the Majuba Mountains through Poker Brown Gap. My goal was the mountains and valleys that lay to the northwest, and the spur of the emigrant trail which had been blazed to avoid the dreaded Forty Mile Desert. I had read more on the Forty Mile Desert the evening before as the sun sank toward the western horizon, turning the pages of one of the local history books I had purchased in Battle Mountain.

The book contained an excerpt from a diary kept by a woman named Sarah Royce, who with her husband and two-year-old child had joined a wagon train which traveled over the Emigrant Trail late in the summer of 1849, the year the California Gold Rush fanned the sparks of emigration into a raging fire. Her party missed the turn to the meadows just southwest of Lovelock where emigrants fed and rested their oxen before attempting the Forty Mile Desert. They found not restful meadows, but instead a broad, lifeless pan of salt where the great rivers had died under the fire of the desert sun, a place of mirages, abandoned wagons, dead cattle, and lost dreams. She described the horror of having to retrace fifteen precious miles to gain the meadow. Fearful that they might be trapped like the Donner party if they didn't make the high passes of the Sierra before the snows fell, they waited only two days before again setting forth. A few miles onward, as she lay in the bed of her wagon to shelter her child, she heard her husband bid farewell to one of their two oxen as it fell dead in its harness. She stepped out of that wagon and proceeded to walk, ranging miles out in front of her party, leading them toward their goal through sheer will and prayer.

With Ian and Tom, I had crossed the Forty Mile Desert along Interstate 80 from Reno to Lovelock in just over half an hour, but now that I'd read Sarah Royce's diary I felt that slicing through it again on a high-speed highway might somehow denigrate her experience of crossing it on foot. I decided that a visit to the alternate route, blazed by those who had hoped to bypass that desert but had instead found another and had annoyed Indians as well, might better fit my current mood. Sarah Royce's experience had seemed uncannily familiar. Perhaps through her eyes and words, I had begun to perceive my own terror that, if I walked the metaphorical trail that lay before me, I might in some way perish. Ray had made his offer only three days earlier, but already his well-charted life felt lost somewhere behind me, like a missed meadow. I wondered if, even now, I could turn back and find him waiting, hard to find, but still there. Yet the thirsts of my spirit moved me onward toward . . . I was not sure what. I preferred the unknown to the uncertain. Perhaps I was searching for Liberty, the woman of the West, who strode fiercely from a sunburst of gold.

As I crested a rise that opened out into a flat valley between two lines of brown hills, I wondered if such hungers of the soul had lain at the center of the dreams that had moved children of the eastern forests and prairies to venture west along this trail. A century and a half earlier, the frontier had called men and women outward. I was traveling inward. I laughed dryly, trying to pretend for just one more day that my journey followed a physical trail where, having grown up in the arid lands, I stood a better than average chance of survival. I did not wish to contemplate the fear that Sarah Royce's story had touched in me. Like her, I faced my desert with inadequate tools and knowledge. Little had lain between her frail success and the failures of countless others. At the Frontier, there are no guarantees.

26

LAUREL DIETZ PULLED HER RED CHEVY BLAZER to
a stop just below the adit that had caught her attention. She
set the parking brake with quick efficiency, picked up her day
pack and rock hammer, got out, and hurried up the slope to
the breach in its dry curves formed by the gaping hole and
the mound of spoils just below it. She scanned the low shrubs
of rabbit brush and the scraggly sage for the telltale tags she
had learned would mean that MacCallum had sampled this
position during his exploration. She was getting good at retracing his steps. This was a time-consuming and tedious pain
in the neck, but it was necessary if she was going to reconstruct his database. With detached admiration, she thought
again how crafty he had been in scrambling his records to
prevent anyone else from interpreting them.

As she neared the adit, Laurel saw what she was looking
for: a metallic tag hanging from a clump of sage, Mac-
Callum's mark. It was right at the brink of the hole some old
prospector had bashed into the hillside. Just as with about
every second sample she had relocated, he had re-sampled an
existing adit.

She admired that. It was a deceptively simple plan. Do
what everyone else has done, but do it better, with broader
knowledge and superior vision. And do it with a bigger exploration budget, so you can assay a hundred times as many
locations in a fraction of the time, and then you can see the
really big picture, a new picture, one no one else has had a
chance to see.

Laurel glanced over her shoulder to the east, down the
flank of the mountain, toward the graded road that ran up the
valley. Kyle Christie's vehicle sat by the side of that road,
right where it had been for the last hour. She could just make

out the lazy hulk that was Kyle himself, lolling in the slim shade his vehicle afforded. What a joke that he still came out here, pretending to be working. The whole field office knew what a goof-off he was. But in fact, it was convenient that he was lazy. It made her plan easier.

Kyle had either not noticed her or had decided not to follow her. That was good. It would be hard to explain why she was spending her time off running around the Kamma Mountains. She did not want anyone asking such questions until she was ready.

When she reached the metallic tag, Laurel pulled out her notebook, jotted down its number, then marked its location on her map.

She had to hand it to MacCallum. Retracing his steps was a great education. Until now, she had thought him simply lucky, or at best an idiot savant. He certainly laughed like an idiot. But no, he was smart, very smart. She would use his tricks herself again in the future, once she had finished supplanting him as company wizard.

STEPHEN GILES SAT at his desk at the BLM office in Reno, his eyes glazed. The phone on that desk was ringing, but he did not answer it. He did not hear it. He did not notice the room around him.

For each of the last four evenings, he had gone to the downtown post office in search of the letter he had expected to receive, but there had been nothing in his box each time. No envelope. No check.

Without that check, no trip with wonderful new luggage and clothes. No precious moment of release into the world he knew was his, if he could only get there.

And after everything he had done to earn that money. He thought briefly of lifting the receiver of the telephone that sat before him and exposing the double-crossing sadists for the crimes they were committing, but knew that no one would suffer more than he if he did so.

Instead, he bent his head and wept.

*   *   *

KYLE CHRISTIE SAT in the shade of his vehicle, sipping at a bottle of Gatorade. It was the sixth day now since The Don had disappeared without a trace. He had now called the rental car agency in Reno, to see if MacCallum had turned in his vehicle in preparation for flying somewhere—who knew? Tahiti? Afghanistan?—but no dice. His account was still active. No one at the mine had heard from him, and he'd gotten the same story at the head office. He was almost ready to phone Gretchen.

Kyle surveyed the range of mountains that stretched before him. He could still feel the presence of MacCallum, just as if he'd seen him an instant before, laughing as he loaded up the day's samples. It was not the first time he had known MacCallum to wander off on his own, but this time, he wondered grimly if his old partner was just trying to get rid of him.

Kyle glanced to the west, up into the south end of the Kamma Mountains. He could see a red four-by-four moving around up there. He knew that it belonged to Laurel Dietz. He scratched absentmindedly at his balls. Laurel was kind of cute, but she didn't quite do it for him. Nothing. Zero. No fizz in the beer. That was too bad, because she was handy, and it had been a long time since Kyle had gotten any.

Laurel had, for some reason Kyle could not quite discern, taken to doing field work. She was supposed to work only in the mine, marking the working faces of the stopes for assay and tracking the results through the computer. Suddenly, he began to worry. Was there something Chittenden had not told him?

He turned his gaze back to the south, the better to forget, for another minute or two, that the years were dribbling by, and that he didn't have much to show for them, and that, if MacCallum did not return, his professional goose was as good as cooked.

He swatted at a grasshopper that had found its way onto his knee.

Far away the first faint vibrations of an approaching engine caught his attention. He looked again to the south, down past the point where the faint traces of the Applegate-Lassen Spur of the Emigrant Trail crossed the wider, graded Seven Troughs Road next to which he sat. Yes, it was a pickup truck, he could see it now, coming his way. He watched it, thankful for something to watch. It rolled along at a healthy, yet conservative clip, kicking up a plume of silt that hung in the quiet air. The truck grew and grew, rumbling up the road toward him, until it was now only a half mile distant, now a quarter mile. As it hove even closer, he saw that the truck was very old, and noticed that it had out-of-state plates.

27

IN THE MIDDLE OF A BROAD, DRY VALLEY, I PULLED
over to ask directions of a man who was, for some reason,
sitting beside his vehicle doing nothing. I leaned out the window. "Was that the Applegate-Lassen Spur back there?" I
asked, pointing to a faint crossroads a half mile back.

"Yeah," he said. "There's a sign there made out of a chunk
of old railroad track."

"Thanks. Can I get over to Rabbithole Springs over that
route in a truck like this? I don't have four-wheel drive."

"Maybe. There's a washed-out bit down around the south
end of the Kamma Mountains there." He stood up, sauntered
over to the truck, and leaned on it, giving me a witless smile.
"You an experienced off-road driver?" he asked. He was tall
and had fading blonde hair and deep sun-creases in his face.
He looked about Tom Latimer's vintage.

"Yeah."

"Out joy riding?" he asked, making conversation.

"Just driving."

"Where ya headed?"

I shrugged my shoulders. "Not sure. Just goin'." I pulled
in my elbow and reached for the ignition.

The man said quickly, "I'm doing some minerals exploration around there. I was about to head that way, if you'd
like to follow along." He shrugged, kind of a "I'm just a goof,
don't take me seriously" gesture. "Then if you get stuck, I
can give you a hand. If you want."

"Okay," I said, starting to laugh.

"What's so funny?" He looked a little annoyed.

"I'm sorry," I said. "It's just that it figures: I'm a geologist.
I drive out into a place where there's probably only one biped
per hundred square miles, and what do I find? Another geologist."

The man grinned sloppily. "Hey, cool. I'm Kyle Christie," he said, offering me a hand to shake.

A nervous tightness whipped through my body. *Not only do I find another geologist, but he's Don MacCallum's exploration partner.* "Glad to meet you, Kyle," I said, shaking his hand. I almost asked after MacCallum, but decided that surely by now he had shown up again. Maybe he was right down the road at Rabbithole Springs, and I might meet him. The idea really bouyed me up.

Kyle's grin spread. "Yeah, there's one for the GSN newsletter," he said. "If you're in the back of beyond and you meet another human being, you might *both* be geologists."

I narrowed my eyes in confusion.

"Oh," he said. "Maybe you don't get that newsletter."

"No, I don't. GSN?"

"Geological Society of Nevada. You got a name?" he asked cheekily.

"Sure," I said. "Sorry; forgot to say. I'm Em Hansen."

OKAY, I KNEW that Kyle Christie wasn't just doing me a favor in showing me the road, but he looked harmless enough. He looked like your typical field geologist, all faded blue jeans and tattered Filson mapping vest, and like his Geological Society of Nevada newsletters would suggest, "You might be a geologist if at parties you admire your friends' gold chains around their necks, and they quietly observe your hand lens rope," and, "If your baseball cap has the logo of a company that's no longer in business," and, "If people comment on your sagebrush cologne."

At any rate, we would be traveling in separate vehicles, and I figured that somewhere along the line I could pump a little information out of him and report it back to Tom. So Kyle led the way back down the road toward the pair of faint tracks that turned off, and bounced and wiggled and teetered over the miles that led toward the Rabbithole, which was a fairly large spring a few miles away. It turned out to be something of a gathering place, or as much as one might expect to find in the middle of the desert. Two young men in a tarted-up Jeep Wagoneer were just loading up as we arrived, having apparently finished a picnic that featured beer and deli sandwiches. "And I thought *my* vehicle was dusty," I commented to them, pointing to the fine tawny silt that was caked all along the sides and wheel wells of the beetle-black Jeep.

"Just came across the Black Rock," one of them said, in a voice that told me that he thought he was an incredibly cool dude. He pointed over his shoulder to the west, where the valley we were in appeared to open up downhill into another one of the broad basins that lay between Nevada's ranges. His companion finished his beer, belched, crumpled the can against his forehead, and pitched it into the rabbit brush.

Now, that pissed me off. I was out here to find enough emptiness that I could fill myself with solitude, and these guys had to go and throw a beer can into it. "Well, have a nice day," I said cheerily, and even waved, doing my most subtle impression of a dork. "But, um, you forgot this," I said, and, stooping primly, picked up the beer can and handed it back to them. I would not have dared do that if a tall man who was obviously trying to make an impression on me had not been standing right next to me. In sudden afterthought, I glanced toward Kyle, making certain that I had not just signed my own death warrant. His mouth had sagged open. My heart sank.

The man at the wheel of the Jeep said, "Fuck you," slapped it in gear, and scrubbed out onto the road. A hundred yards up, his companion once again threw the beer can out into the brush.

Kyle exhaled and stared at the ground.

"Jerks," I muttered under my breath, and strolled away from him, setting out to walk around the spring so I could hope to put the insolence of the men in the Jeep and Kyle's pathetic reaction to them out of my mind. I was mad at the men for littering, I was mad at Kyle for being a coward, and I was mad at myself for being reckless. As I moved briskly along, I asked myself where I'd gone wrong in my estimation of him. I hoped silently that he would be gone by the time I came all the way around to my truck.

Steep banks led down toward a pool of warm water that trickled in from a narrow seep. Bullrushes grew from the waters, their lush, impossibly thick stalks standing in stark contrast to the sparseness of the vegetation that grew only inches away from the spring. A few mud hens scooted away, squawking at me. About halfway around the pool, I heard footsteps right behind me. Kyle had put on some speed with his long legs and managed to catch up with me without seeming to hurry. He wouldn't stand up to a couple of yawps throwing beer cans, but he sure could stretch his legs when he wanted to chase a woman.

When we got to the uphill end of the springs, I came across the crumbling remnants of a fieldstone building. "What's this?" I asked.

Kyle shrugged his shoulders and said, "Well, I don't know. My partner says there was once a small placer mining camp here."

"So as part of your exploration, you're going back over the known mining districts?"

He considered my question for a moment, head hanging, lips twisting this way and that. "Well, they say the best place to find gold sometimes is where it's already known to occur."

"Oh. You go after what was missed."

Kyle's head jerked slightly, as if a twenty-watt bulb had just gone on inside his head.

Time to change the subject, I decided, wondering if he was being proprietary or just couldn't discuss the subject intellectually. He was hard to figure. The man had to be bright to have a job in this tough market, but like a loaf of bread baked without quite enough leavening, he seemed oddly dense, and flat in places. He reminded me of certain geologists and engineers I had known in the oil business; dutiful types who had gone to college and even graduate school and had been well trained to scrupulously carry out standardized tasks, but who lacked the spark necessary for original or independent thought. The duller ones fell incrementally by the wayside and suffered layoff after layoff while the more ambitious ones went into management and sometimes grew vicious.

I have learned more about the natural history of the canids from working with men than I ever did from having one as a pet. There are your alpha wolves, who rule with or without wisdom; your beta through omega pack dogs, who rank from top to bottom in the great game of power consciousness and there are your few lone wolves, who go off and do something unusual. Kyle so far just struck me as a good doggie, but like Deputy Weebe had said, he bore watching.

I put him back to work as a tour guide. "So this was a placer mining camp. I saw some other ghost towns in the map atlas. Were those mining camps too?"

"Sure, like Gilby's Camp," Kyle said. "There was a whole little town there back in the late twenties. Guy dug a mile-long tunnel that was supposed to intercept the workings of the district further north there, which had shut down because of drainage and haulage problems. Built a hundred-ton cyanide mill, the works. The polite histories will tell you that he ran into the same flooding problems, but it's more likely that he knew he wouldn't make it. That the whole thing was a scam from the beginning." He chuckled appreciatively.

"A mile?" I said. "That's a lot of scam."

"Oh, you'd be amazed," he said. "You whip your investors into a frenzy, show them nice surface workings, big mill, take them for a ride down your tunnel into the bowels of the earth, and the fools will fall all over themselves to invest."

"But still you're doing the work. All that digging, I mean."

He took off his sunglasses and looked at me, his smile withered down to a smirk. "Maybe he thought he'd get lucky. Anyway," he said, now waxing sardonic, "you know the definition of a mine?"

"No. Tell me."

"A hole in the ground with a liar standing over it."

"Ah."

I gazed at him for what I hoped was a polite moment, then began to walk back to my truck in preparation for parting company with him. But before I got there, a plump, granny-looking woman of about sixty-five or so rode up on a three-wheeler. "Ah, good, someone's here," she said. "Couldn't get those creeps in the Jeep to stop. Can you two spare a few minutes? I found this old man up the road needs help. He's taken a fall and hit his head, and I can't lift him."

I glanced sideways at Kyle just in time to see his facial muscles tense. "Old guy in a brush-painted van?" he asked.

"Yes," she said. "You know him?"

"That's Sam," Kyle said. He heaved a deep sigh. "Okay, let's go get him."

I said, "I'm Em Hansen. This is Kyle."

"Pleased to meet you, dear," the woman replied. "I'm Sally Dancer. We'd better get going. The poor old boy looks pretty weak."

Kyle and I each got in our own vehicle and made a small parade as Sally Dancer led us a couple of miles up the road toward a place where it passed through a narrows between two prominences in the Kamma Mountains. I saw the brush-painted van a short way up a side road that spurred to the north. Beside the van, lying in its shade, I saw an old man with white hair. We hurried to the spot but, by the time we got close, I was glancing overhead to see if there were vultures circling yet. The old man did not look good—ashen, weak, and panting—but he was alive and conscious. Sally had propped him up on his side with his head on a rolled-up jacket. The back of his head was bruised and bloody.

Kyle approached him hesitantly. When Sam saw him, he smiled brightly and said, "Why, hello there, Kyle. . . ." He stopped to pant. "You find MacCallum?"

My ears pricked up. Was MacCallum still missing?

Kyle bent over the old man, bracing his hands on his knees. When he spoke, his voice was heavy with resignation. "No, Sam, Don's still gone off somewhere." He sighed with exasperation. Then, his tone growing brittle with something close to annoyance, he said, "You seen him since I came by your shack the other day?"

The old man smiled, and let his bright little eyes widen vacantly. "Seems I've got myself in a bit of a . . . a pickle here, son. Was on my way . . . back from town last night when a . . . a tire blew . . . guess I took a fall."

"Looks like you didn't get very far changing that flat," Kyle said sardonically.

Sam closed his eyes and panted. "Got winded. Heard a car coming . . . walked down . . . stood in the road to . . . flag 'em down. Get some help, you know? . . . They just honked . . . get out of the way . . . damnedest thing."

"They just drove on by?" I asked, appalled. "Was it two jerks in a black Jeep?"

Sam looked confused. "White Stetson . . ." He closed his eyes and concentrated on trying to take a breath.

"You must have dreamt it, Sam," Kyle said. Giving me a knowing look, Kyle made a circling gesture around one ear, so I'd know the old coot was daft.

"Well, I'm glad you got out of the road, Sam," I said. "Those idiots in the Jeep might have finished you off if the white hat didn't."

"Must have stumbled . . . don't know . . ."

"Let's get you into town, Grandpa," I said.

Sam's eyes flew wide with panic. "No! No, missy . . . take me home . . . I'll make coffee . . . it's . . . it's . . ."

"Good for the soul," Kyle said, finishing Sam's sentence dejectedly. He moved from his bent position into a full squat. "Well, let's just see if we can get you up."

The old man coughed. "Don't know . . ."

I said, "I really think we should take you into Lovelock."

"Yes," said Sally.

"No!" Sam wheezed. His eyes glittered. "No, no, don't you be worryin' over me, now . . . just been there . . ."

Kyle said, "What Sam wants, Sam gets. Let me tell you, ladies, I've known Sam for a while now. He only goes to town for his mail and more grub. You try to take him by force, and you'll find out how strong he really is."

"Don't have no use for doctors. . . ." said Sam.

"Okay," said Sally. "I'm a retired nurse. I'll sit with him until he's stable, then I'll go to town and see what I can do to bring him some help."

Sam stretched his mouth into a grin, pulling back his whiskery cheeks to reveal a gap where several teeth were missing to one side of his upper middle two, which were stained yellow. It made him look like a little mouse. I tried not to feel total horror at his state of decay. We locked eyes, and I saw deep inside them a mixture of trust, innocence, and a tattered, yet still strong, force of will. "Just take me up the hill," he said, now wheezing slightly. "Got to get back to my gold."

"We could lay him in the bed of my truck," I said. "I've got a sleeping bag . . ." I let the words trail off. Kindly as I felt toward the old guy, I wasn't sure there would be a way to wash his effluvia off my precious bed roll.

"Let's get him into the van," said Sally, giving me a wink. "Kyle here can have that flat fixed in a jiffy."

Kyle set his face like concrete and got to work. I helped him while Sally fussed over Sam. When we were ready, Sally said, "On the count of three. One, two . . ."

We lifted him. He was as light as a sparrow. As we settled him onto the backseat of his van, I connected with his breath, and almost gagged on the fusty, rotting air that rose from his decaying interior. It smelled like my grandmother's had only days before she died.

Kyle closed the side door of the van and handed me the keys to his vehicle. "Will you follow me, please, and I'll drive you back down later? That way I can say I can't stay, because I have to bring you out. Otherwise, he'll have us up there for hours."

I squinted at Kyle, appalled at his insensitivity. "Don't you think he could stand a little company?"

Kyle's face stiffened in anger. "Oh, certainly. He'll keep us there feeding us watered-down coffee, showing us his postcards, and . . . this guy MacCallum I work with thinks he's great company, you know? Spends hours with him . . ." His voice trailed off, and he looked away.

I thought, *You sound like a pissed-off kid whose ailing dad has just taken advantage, and your petulance does not become you,* but I said, "You keep talking about this guy MacCallum. Maybe we should find him and tell him that his friend is sick."

Kyle let out a deep sigh. "I've been looking for him for days. He's . . . gone off somewhere."

I wondered more than ever where that somewhere was.

We headed on up the track, and a mile or so up, we came across the sketchy remains of another mining camp. I could see the remnants of the head frame that had once lowered men and equipment down a shaft, and the crumbling concrete foundations of several buildings were still evident. Only one structure still had a roof, and I presumed that to be Sam's habitation. Kyle parked his van outside of it, and we helped Sam in, and got him into what he called a bed. I turned around to get him something to eat and drink, and was immediately fearful of touching anything. The place was a mess, and inches deep in uncleaned dishes, mouldering cans of pet food, and lounging cats. The stench was nearly overwhelming. It was obvious that Sam had been ill for a while, and that he knew he was dying. He had just one instinct, and that was to come home to die. He seemed at peace.

Sally bustled her way to the stove and set a kettle to heating. Kyle retreated to the door, his hands jammed into his pockets and his shoulders hunched. He looked like a caricature of a sulking vulture.

I moved to Sam's bedside and put a hand on his shoulder. He was fading in and out, but suddenly he looked up at me, his eyes clear and sharp. He smiled, and grasped my hand. "It's a good life," he said, for the moment not even panting. "Remember that. It's a gift that we're on this earth, and every moment is pure gold."

I stared down into his eyes, drinking in his words. In that instant, he was no longer old and decrepit, but timeless and overflowing with joy. I felt honored to be near him. And I thought, *Did MacCallum see this in him? Or did he take advantage?*

Sam's eyes closed, then opened again. "Thank you for bringing me back up to my gold," he said. "It's important to be where you're supposed to be." A moment later, his eyes glazed again, then closed.

I moved over to where Kyle stood by the door and said,

"He's asleep, Kyle. I think Sally and I can take care of this."

Kyle backed out the door, motioning for me to follow. Outside, he said, "Uh, I was hoping we could continue our tour."

I thought this over briefly. Gathering information for Tom Latimer was all fun and games, but if it meant bouncing around looking at crumbling buildings with this guy, then it was no deal. Besides, he might know absolutely nothing that would bear on the case. And he didn't know where Mac-Callum was.

I looked up into Kyle's hang-dog face. "This MacCallum guy you're looking for," I said, "where do you think he's gone?"

"I don't know," Kyle said morosely. "He just took off, and didn't even tell me he was going. He and I have been together for years." He put a hand on my shoulder. "So what do you say?"

I shook my head. "I think I'd better help with Sam. Thanks for the help getting over to the Rabbithole."

"Well, uh, I got to get back to work, yeah." He began to move toward his vehicle, then stopped. "Um, if Sam says anything more about MacCallum, would you . . ."

"Sure," I said. I began to turn back toward the door.

"I'll just be out taking samples, you know. I could kind of wait for you."

"This might take awhile."

"But your truck's way down the road. I should at least take you to it."

I shook my head again, wishing he would just leave. "Sally can take me on the back of her three-wheeler."

"Oh. Yeah." He started to move toward his vehicle, but then turned back yet again. "Well, I work out of a mine over east of here, but . . ." His face brightened again. "Of course, you could meet me down in Lovelock, where I'm staying. I'll buy dinner."

"I won't be going back that way."

"Or I could show you the mine," he said, hanging on like a tick. "It's not far at all."

Now he had my attention. "Is it open-pit or underground?" I asked.

"Underground. Very modern. Rubber tire," Kyle said, watching me like a tiger inching up on its prey. "In fact, my plans aren't carved in stone. I could take you there now."

My busy little mind got the better of me, spinning out rationalizations. I thought, *The mine. Wasn't that where Pat Gilmore's office was? Yes, when I'm done here, I could drive over there, just take a look, and give Tom a call. Before of course continuing onward to the back of beyond. Nice spicy little side trip. The key is to not let anyone know that I know about the rodent thing, or Pat Gilmore's death, or that I've ever heard of Granville Resources before. . . .*

Just then, Sally came over to the door. "He's resting comfortably now," she said. "Thanks for the help. I'll just stay with him a while and make sure he's okay. You two scamper along."

I turned back to Kyle, and, shrugging my shoulders, said, "Why don't I just follow you on over there?"

28

AS SALLY DANCER CLIMBED BACK ONTO HER THREE-wheeler, she made a decision. Sam was definitely failing, and she would honor his wish by phoning a friend of his rather than the local authorities. But she figured that he wouldn't go anytime today, or even tomorrow, so there was time for another hour or two of buzzing around on her three-wheeler before she headed back to the camp she had set up over by the ghost town of Scossa. There, she would get on the ham radio and make that call.

Sally headed down Rosebud Canyon to the road that led toward Winnemucca. Once outside of the narrows, she found a faint track that led along the flank of the Kamma Mountains that she hadn't driven over before, so she decided to follow it.

She noticed it partly because two other vehicles had just been over the route, leaving fresh tire tracks. She paused for a moment and looked at the tracks more closely. Yes, they still had delicate crumbles of soil associated with them, so they had definitely been made since the last rain. A wandering thunderstorm could erase these crumbles with a few violent drops on this parched earth, but the last rain might have been months ago. But the last strong wind would also have destroyed this fine a tracing, and there had been a good one about two days back. She liked examining tracks. They were like little histories.

A quarter mile farther up, the fresh tire tracks stopped. She paused to examine them. One vehicle had turned around, making a messy job of it and taking a sagebrush out by the roots in the process, and the other had left the faint road and headed uphill into the stiff, short grasses.

This pissed Sally off. She loved off-road motoring, but only so far as it followed existing trails. She believed firmly in making no new tracks, as this hastened erosion and killed delicate plants and crushed the burrows of animals.

Sally got off her three-wheeler and stomped up the hill. The tracks led around a shoulder in the mountainside, out of sight. And they led only one way, just four tire tracks mashing the soft clay soil, compacting it into uselessness. Perhaps if the trail was truly fresh, and the jackass who had done this had not simply ground his way over the crest and down into the valley where the old squatter named Sam lived, she would find the culprit and give him a piece of her mind.

A short way up the hill, she spotted a human foot print pointed the other way, coming toward her. It was not the print of a boot. Boots left the marks of raised treads, but this print was flat and featureless, like a leather-soled dress shoe would make. A skid mark led downhill toward it, as if the fool had been having trouble with his footing. She put her own foot next to the print. It was not much larger than her boot, perhaps a man's size nine, like her husband's.

Sally straightened up, thinking. Something about finding the print of a street shoe up here seemed more than a little odd to her. She stopped, hesitating. Had some horse's ass gotten his vehicle stuck and then abandoned it? Hell, it was thirty miles to the nearest phone booth to call AAA. What had this moron been thinking?

Sally started moving again, but now followed the tracks more slowly, looking for more footprints. Yes, here was another. Funny that the footprints appeared only intermittently, as if the hiker had been stepping mostly on stones, trying to leave as few tracks as possible. Here there was another skid, and even a handprint, as if he had been hurrying along, but stumbling. In a hurry. At least the jackass had had the sense to wear gloves—here was an impression of the seams—otherwise he'd have torn his hands up for sure.

As she came around the shoulder of the mountain, Sally saw that the tire tracks led straight toward some old mine workings. But she saw no vehicle. Where had it gone?

She headed toward the workings, hurrying now. She saw

the remains of an old head frame off to one side, and the twisted remnants of some much newer fencing around an excavation, bent down at the front. As she neared the adit, she could see that it was not a simple exploratory scraping, as so many of them were. Nor was it the mouth of a tunnel, which would have traveled horizontally into the mountain, but a shaft, which went straight down. The mouth of the shaft had been surrounded by fencing, as was required by law to protect passersby such as herself from falling in, but something or someone had crashed through it.

Sally stepped to the hole in the fencing, saw that the tire tracks did indeed travel right over the brink and into the hole. She stepped closer, carefully positioning herself against the bent remnants of the old head frame. She peered deeper into the hole. At the bottom of the shaft, perhaps twenty feet down, she could see the faint gleam of chrome. She knew immediately that it was the reflective strip on the back bumper of a four-wheel-drive vehicle.

How lazy, she thought disparagingly, figuring the owner had gone through this game to avoid paying a dump fee. But then she rethought her deduction. *It looks like a fairly new vehicle, a pretty nice one. . . .*

Sally reached into her fanny pack and extracted a small signal mirror which she always carried in case she became stranded. She tipped it this way and that, working out the angle of the sun and of the shaft, lining things up so that she could get some light down the hole. By the insignia, she could see that it was a late-model Ford Explorer.

Sally's roaming splinter of light picked up the driver's side door. The window was open, and something appeared to be hanging out of it.

It was a human arm.

Sally straightened up, angry and horrified. "Son of a bitch," she said aloud, swearing for the first time since her days in the navy. "Guess I'm going to be making more than one call."

*   *   *

VIRGIL DAVIS FELT his hand rising towards Laurel Dietz's
hair before he had even consciously considered the act. It
shone like the precious wire gold he could see on the prize
mineral samples the men had brought out of the mine, and
seemed twice as rare. Another inch, and his fingers would
touch it.

She spun around in her swivel chair. As always, her blue
eyes were large and bright and marvelously free of contempt.
Their purity amazed him so. "What's up, Virgil?" she asked.

"Just wondering what you were doing," he answered, shyly
hiding his hand behind his back. He leaned over her to stare
into the computer screen which had so strongly held her attention while he approached. He saw lines and columns of
numbers. They meant nothing to him. Then he turned to the
desktop next to the computer. There he saw one panel of a
tightly folded map. "Where's that?" he asked, noticing the
sample locations peppered over the contour intervals. Then
he saw letters: K-A-M . . . "Oh, is that one of MacCallum's
maps of the Kammas?"

For once, Laurel's eyes expressed alarm.

"Sorry," he said, silently cursing himself for upsetting her.
"Didn't mean to—"

"That's okay, Virgil," she said, reflexively lifting one delicate hand to the bandana that circled her neck. "Maybe it's
time to show this to you, anyway."

She unfolded the paper.

Virgil's pulse quickened. It was indeed a map of the
Kamma Mountains. He could see that the map had started as
one of the maps out of the ill-fated Phase I permitting application, but someone had added to it, working off to the north
where Phase II lay! "Laurel," he cried, "you're marvelous!
I've been looking all over for MacCallum's map!"

"Well, this isn't it," she said. "I made it. I know the new
project is way behind schedule, so in my free time, I've been
out recompiling Don's locations. And adding his assay results."

"But how did you find them?" Virgil said, astonished. "I dug all through his papers!"

"Oh, I know. Even Kyle didn't know where MacCallum kept his map, and without that, his assays meant nothing," she said, smoothly diverting his attention back to the map. She tipped her head to one side and looked at him from under her eyelashes, the picture of innocence. "I knew you'd be worried, because the project would be falling behind, so I've been reconstructing things." She ran a finger up the middle of the Kamma Mountains, right through the old shafts that had been the Brown Palace Mine in the ghost town of Rosebud. "And you can see he's got a nice vein mapped right through here. He's smart. He went after the halo of accessory minerals, just like he did when he found the veins we're mining here at the Gloriana."

Virgil snatched up the map and began to roar with delight. "Laurel, you're an angel! You've done it! Now I can go for Phase Two permits and get Kyle drilling! Oh, God, Laurel, you've saved my bacon!" Then he looked guiltily at her. "I'll of course give you full credit. I tell you, this project has been the limit, with first that Indian making us move the mill, and then Pat Gilmore screaming about the mice, and then, hell, even Rodriguez disappearing when he promised those Phase One permits."

"Oh," said Laurel. "Yes." She blinked at him.

Virgil blushed with embarrassment. "Sorry. But you understand, don't you?"

"Oh, yes, Virgil." She blinked again.

"Well," Virgil said, his spirits again rising, "I'll get that Christie bastard—" He stopped himself again, his face growing dark with consternation. "Laurel, he does nothing around here. Nothing."

Laurel smiled primly.

"The day after MacCallum . . . went away, I told Christie to cough up a map, and you know what he said? He said to pull it out of . . . but I can't repeat that in front of you."

Laurel reached out one delicate, shell-pink hand and placed it on Virgil's. "I understand," she said. "You work so hard.

No one could have gotten this project up and running as fast
or as well as you did. Everybody with half a brain knows
that. And you've had so little help."

Virgil had to stop and reign himself in from an almost
overwhelming urge to bend down to her, take her angelic
head in his coarse, rough hands and pull it to his heart. But
that would be unspeakable. Instead, he gave her what he
hoped was a winning smile, and said, "I'm going straight to
my office and call Chittenden and tell him what you've accomplished!"

Virgil turned and hurried off, but allowed himself one
longing backward look.

Laurel was still sitting in her swivel chair, her waifish figure resting on its upholstery with all the gravity of a feather.
He wasn't certain, but there seemed to be an increased pink-
ness on her perfect throat.

29

KYLE CHRISTIE LED THE WAY TO THE MINE. ONCE again, I turned onto the road on which Pat Gilmore had crashed, but I followed Kyle to the north instead of going south to the crash site. After five or six miles, we turned east again onto a road that led up the slopes of the Eugene Mountains. As we ascended the slope, I looked south and could see black fingers of burned earth left by the range fire reaching across the valley floor.

The entrance road to the mine was the best-kept dirt road I had been on so far in Nevada, and we approached a gleamingly modern mining complex. Sheet metal buildings rose bleak against the dry landscape, and crisp new chain-link fencing rose like castle walls around it. The layout had the air of a military depot; no frills, but clean and solid. It had clearly been designed and built by someone who knew his business.

After signing several forms at the security station declaring that I held Granville Resources harmless for any injuries I might sustain while on site, I passed through a metal detector and met the man who had laid out the complex. Virgil Davis was a thick-set guy in his sixties with the gruff, harried look of a man who had no patience for bullshit but met it daily. "Who's your friend, Christie?" he barked at Kyle.

Kyle put his hands on his hips and tried to look unfazed, but managed only to look petulant. I stuck out my hand. "I'm Em Hansen. I'm a geologist. I'm just visiting the area, and Kyle was kind enough to invite me up to see your wonderful facilities. I generally work in oil and gas, so it's a real treat to see a mining operation," I said.

Blushing, Virgil Davis ignored my hand. His brusqueness softened. "Glad to meet you," he grumbled. "You safety trained?"

"Yes, sir. Like I say, I've worked on drill rigs, and for many years. I have perfect respect for heavy machinery."

"Well, let's get you a refresher anyway. We're not OSHA here, we're MSHA, Mine Safety and Health Administration." He turned back to Kyle, his demeanor once again turning dark with annoyance. He grabbed him by the arm, and hauled him down the hall a distance no doubt designed to intimidate him and exclude me from the conversation. Still, I had no trouble understanding what he said. "Get her down the hall to the safety officer and get her the fifteen-minute refresher. You aren't taking her underground. You lack the skills, and I don't have any tour guides sitting around just waiting for you to run your girlfriends down there."

"Fine. I'll just show her the surface workings," Kyle said sulkily.

"You can show her the mill if it's okay with John, but get her trained. I don't like anyone on this site who doesn't know the drills." Having said this, he turned and stormed down the narrow hallway, turned a corner, and disappeared from sight.

Kyle grinned sheepishly. "Guess he likes you."

I almost said, Guess he doesn't like you, but thought better of it.

Kyle motioned for me to follow him to the safety officer's room. As we stepped down the hallway, he leaned closer and lowered his voice. "For him, this is actually a good mood. Something must be up. He usually ignores me entirely. Of course, he's still pissed at me for getting on his case a few days ago. My partner, MacCallum, like I said, he's gone, see? And the afternoon before he turned up missing, I overheard the two of them arguing. Big show down. Virgil was telling MacCallum he was dragging his feet about the new project. He threatened to turn MacCallum in to Chittenden if he didn't cough up a map, and MacCallum's telling him where he can find it, if you know what I mean. MacCallum called him a son of a bitch and left. So I went up to Virgil and gave him what for, right? And he tells me to piss up a rope. Then he demands that I give him a map, but I wouldn't do that. No way." He made a horizontal slicing motion with one hand to show me how firm he had been about this.

I nodded. The nod meant "You're a hopeless putz," but I let Kyle think it meant "I admire your fidelity." Kyle was beginning to get on my nerves. I had known more than a few like him in the oil business. I had come to see that there were three levels at which a person could ply the trade of geology. First, one could, through hard work and study, learn to describe the geology—be it an ore sample, or a drilling log, whatever—with competence. Second, one could, through experience and with reasonable intelligence, learn to make interpretations based on the observations described. This, I equated to the journeyman level of function as a geologist, and I was sure that Kyle filled this bill when he stood over a drilling rig. But thirdly, and this was not common, one could—if one really "got" it—make predictions, some almost uncanny, based on those observations and interpretations. This third category was what I thought of as the master level, where the practitioner breathed in the geology and became one with it. This was MacCallum, the man Kyle believed could really "see" the gold. But there was also a fourth—accidental—category of practicioner, populated by those who just got lucky. And a fifth category: the huckster.

Kyle's no wizard, and he knows it, I decided. *He's just marking time, waiting for MacCallum to return from his mystical wanderings*. That and the disappearance of Donald Paul MacCallum would explain why he had been sitting by the road goofing off when I first met him. I smiled to myself. Another word for goofing off was gold-bricking.

The refresher course was largely a homily about not touching anything unless told I could do so, except for the bit about the use of a self-rescuer. A self-rescuer, it turned out, is a hand-sized chemical factory that all miners are required to carry on their persons whenever they go underground, a piece of equipment considered every bit as essential as their boots, their hard hats and the headlights mounted on them, and the battery packs that are clipped to their heavy webbed belts. In case of emergency, the self-rescuer can generate oxygen through a reaction between chemicals contained inside it. This reaction creates heat, a lot of it. The safety officer told me, "If told to do so, put this mouthpiece in your mouth and bite down, like a snorkel bit. It will grow hot. It will blister your lips and burn your throat. Do not take it out until and unless you are told to do so."

I smiled bleakly. The array of required safety equipment suggested three things about going underground: something heavy might fall on me, it might get very dark, and, if these two things happened, I might find it hard to breathe. I began to feel less disappointed that Virgil Davis had said I couldn't go there.

After the refresher, Kyle rustled up John Steinhoff, the metallurgist who ran the mill. John was another big man, and he had bushy black eyebrows. He was just getting a cup of coffee from the kitchen facility when we found him. "Sure," he said. "We're about to pour a doré. You two can tag along, and I'll show you the system. Put on your hard hats."

"The system" turned out to fill two big metal buildings several stories tall. Flying conveyor belts on steel superstructures, metal staircases, railings, and catwalks ranged everywhere, and the air vibrated with the thunder of the workings of the machinery.

John pointed first to a big metal grating over the dumping portal. A thirty-ton ore truck from the mine was just backing toward it. "That's the grizzly. Anything too big to fall through the grating goes over there in the yard for further crushing. Below the grizzly, the ore goes through a bunch of screens. Anything over three-eighths of an inch goes into a secondary crusher like a big mortar and pestle, called a cone crusher."

John led us up along catwalks and out onto a soaring one that jutted upwards from the outside of the first building. It followed a conveyor up into the air toward a dumping chute that led toward the second building. The ground sloped down and away. I was sixty or seventy feet in the air with nothing under me but a steel grid and a pair of railings, and the air thrummed with sound around me. I made myself think about something else, and I was glad when we returned to the building. We followed staircases back down to the downhill side into the second building, and followed the moving belts of one through to an inside room. There, a rig that looked like a giant Rube Goldberg device led through a set of hoppers and into a ten-foot-long steel cylinder that lay rotating in a huge cradle.

"Ball mill," John hollered over the din. "It has a rubber liner, that's why it's so quiet."

If that was quiet, I didn't think my ears could handle noisy.

John pointed to the hoppers. "Trash catcher," he said, regarding the first one. "A lot of shredded plastic comes out of the mine. All the blasting materials and such come packaged in it." He pointed to the second one. "This one's a gravity dropout. It catches any gold that makes it through this far as nuggets. We don't get much at this mine. We're dealing with two-hundred-mesh stuff tops. Microscopic, most of it. Beyond here, you've got rock flour. During the process, it gets mixed with water." He took us outside the building toward a series of enormous tanks. "This first one is a settling tank. We decant some of the water, so the solids are fifty-fifty with the remaining water. Then we adjust the pH, and on to the big tanks."

John led Kyle and me back inside and around a series of catwalks to raise us two stories higher, then out through a door onto a catwalk that led out over a battery of gigantic tanks. Each was thirty feet tall and about twenty feet in diameter. We moved out directly over them, following walkways forged of the steel mesh. I looked down into a thick, roiling, gray liquid, like the boiling mud pots at Yellowstone National Park. "What's in those tanks?" I shouted, beginning to go hoarse.

"Cyanide," John roared back. "Like I said, we adjust the pH with lime, then add cyanide and shoot air through it. There are big blades under there that keep the solution stirred up so the solids don't settle. Then—"

Not wanting to think about the blades, I asked "How much cyanide do you use?"

"We consume about a pound of cyanide per ton of ore,"

John answered, casually leaning on a railing. "You have to be careful with it. All kinds of regulations here in the States. The settling pond below the mill is lined with plastic to keep it from leaking into the groundwater, and it has netting over it to keep the birds out."

I found myself gripping both railings rather tightly. "Exactly what does the cyanide do?" I asked.

"It leaches the gold. Cyanization is a process developed in 1898. Before that, all you had was gravity separation and smelting; you know, like your prospector with his gold pan, only on a larger scale. We'd run the ore through a mill to break it up, then run it over a shaking table. An improvement was made when we learned to put mercury into the transverse riffles in the table to amalgamate the gold particles, but then you had to retort off the mercury, and that could be messy."

"I suppose so," I said dryly, certain that I did not want to be around while something as toxic as mercury was being distilled through the process of boiling it in a cauldron.

Kyle caught my sarcasm and gave me a come-hither wink.

"And a lot of gold was left behind in the tailings," John said, deep into his art now. "Sometimes ten or twenty percent, and you couldn't even have gone after a microscopic deposit like we're mining here. But then like I said, in the last hundred years cyanization was developed. It's revolutionized gold milling. There are operations out there that just buy up historic mines and all they do is heap-leach the tailings. No excavation at all. Hell, I knew a guy in college who did a one-man miniature heap-leach one summer. He laid out a couple tons of tailings on a sheet of plastic and set a lawn sprinkler going over it, spraying it with cyanide solution. He caught the runoff downhill in a fifty-five-gallon drum of carbon, and at the end of the summer, he picked up the drum and had it processed. Made himself a tidy profit."

I shuddered at the thought of a cyanide sprinkler left going unattended, and wondered if I'd quite heard him right over the noise. "Where does the process go next?" I asked, urging John and Kyle to move back toward the building. I had had enough of hanging over the tanks.

John led us back along the catwalk, striding comfortably, king of his realm. He led us along a trail of piping marked with yellow labels with black letters and arrows showing flow directions. They said things like PREGNANT SOLUTION and BARREN SOLUTION. It brought back to mind Gretchen MacCallum's suggestion that men who worked in mining envied the creative powers of women. I decided that the incessant ear-blasting rumbling of the mill was beginning to purée my mind. Or maybe it was the ammonia-like odor that pervaded the air around us. "By the way, what's that chemical smell?" I asked.

John turned, surprised. "You shouldn't be smelling anything," he said. "I don't smell anything." He looked at Kyle.

Kyle shrugged his shoulders. "It's a gal thing," he said. "They have noses like bloodhounds."

John shrugged his shoulders, too, then pointed out one more stack of equipment, this one a tangle of pipes running in and out. "We pull the oxygen back out in this vacuum tower," he said. "Then it goes on through here, and we kill the cyanide."

"Kill it?" I asked. "What's that mean in terms of chemistry?" John had erected a magnificent mill, and clearly ran it with an iron hand towards efficiency, but it was beginning to occur to me that there were differences between metallurgists and chemists.

John looked at me and blinked. "We add zinc."

"So the gold combines with the cyanide, and then the zinc replaces the gold," I said.

John shrugged his shoulders. "Yeah. You need the oxygen to get the gold to grab onto the cyanide, and when you add the zinc . . ." He was beginning to look annoyed at my ignorance. This was as simple as pie to him, just a big metallurgy set to be set up well, kept clean, and run efficiently. "Then the gold solution goes on to the filter room." He pointed up through the ceiling to a place where the pipes disappeared again. "But you can't go there."

John led Kyle and me back up through a series of hallways to a control room in which sat a fat man in a white suit who

was watching an array of computer and closed-circuit TV
screens. "This is where we track everything. In this monitor,
you can see into the filter presses, those long cylinders.
They're filled with diatomaceous earth. We shoot in the pregnant solution. The gold and silver come out in the filter, and
the barren solution returns to the tanks. Then we take the filter
pack down to the furnaces." He led us down one more level
and into a small room that was presided over by uniformed
guards with side arms.

John stepped up to a thick glass window and pointed
through into the inner room. I stepped up next to him, grateful
that at least in this room, the thundering rumble of the machinery was muffled down to a dull roar, and I could hear
myself think.

The glass was at least an inch thick and shot through with
woven steel wire. Through it, I could see a blast furnace and
a row of thick iron cauldrons in the shape of split logs about
two feet long, and a couple of larger ones in the shape of an
inverted Hershey's kiss.

The blast furnace was running. A pool of liquid inside it
glowed with unimaginable heat. "We're just in time," John
said, smiling into the glass.

We watched the white-hot pool with fascination, and even
the guards stepped up to the glass, a row of kids watching
the candy maker mix the wondrous goody. Presently, men in
padded heat-reflective suits stepped forward and tipped the
furnace, pouring first into the Hershey's-kiss-shaped cauldrons.

"That's the slag from the diatomaceous earth," said John,
with satisfaction. "When it cools, we ship it off to a refinery,
as there's some gold and silver in it. Not much, but enough
that the refinery will pay to have it."

The men in the suits now moved the heavy half log cauldrons into place and again poured, filling them one at a time.
An incandescent liquid rolled into each of them, and immediately began to cool.

"That's the gold?" I asked.

"Yes, those are the doré. Gold and silver, mixed," he said, his voice rich with satisfaction.

"How do you ship them?" asked Kyle, speaking for the first time in half an hour.

John eyed Kyle. "Don't get any ideas, smart guy."

Kyle laughed weakly, the omega dog once again showing his belly. I was getting kind of sick of his act. Here he was trying to impress me, a kid his daughter's age, if he had one. For the first time, it occurred to me to look at the third finger of Kyle's left hand, to see just how brazen he was being. No ring. Which of course proved nothing, but I was willing to bet that if he'd been married, he wasn't anymore.

John drew my attention back. "From here, the dorés go to a refinery, where the gold is extracted through chlorination. Chlorine is bubbled through the molten gold. That converts the silver and any base metals to the chlorides, which float to the surface. Then they do electrolysis, using the crude gold as the anode. The cathode is pure gold. They take it to four nines—ninety-nine-point-nine-nine percent pure—unless it's going to the electronics business. Then, they take it to five."

"Why is it so useful in the electronics industry?" I asked.

"Because it is the most noble metal," he answered, still talking more like a medieval alchemist in a robe than a chemist. He smiled, and spread his hands, palms up. "It's gold."

BACK IN THE office building, I asked to use the rest room, and was shown to a door that led into a large, tiled room full of lockers, showers, toilets, and sinks. I presumed this was where any women miners changed to go underground and where they showered when they came off shift. I marveled that there were any women going underground at this mine: Historically, miners had considered women bad luck.

As I busied myself in the toilet booth, I heard the outer door open and footsteps patter across the tiles. When I stepped out, I craned my neck around the row of lockers to see what a female miner looked like, expecting to see someone who looked pretty tough. What I saw was a petite, delicate-looking blonde with enormous blue eyes. She looked

pretty clean to me, and wore blue jeans and a nice blouse,
not a miner's coverall. She was emptying things out of her
locker and stuffing them into a day pack. She glanced briefly
at me, but offered me no glint of personal connection. She
turned her attention back to her work.

"Are you a miner?" I asked.

She glanced up at me again, as if to make sure a person
really stood near her talking to her. "No," she said.

"Geologist? Engineer?"

She withdrew a hard hat and a mineral hammer, and
stuffed them into her pack, beginning to hum to herself, ignoring me.

"You work underground here?"

Again, she did not reply. She did not make further eye
contact. I did not exist. I got a really cold feeling about her.
I left.

Down the hall, I found Kyle talking to another man whom
I guessed to be another geologist. "No shit," the man was
saying, as I came up behind Kyle. "Virgil called Chittenden
and told him what Laurel had been doing and *wham,* he said
to send her right away, and bring that map and don't forget
the data. If I heard right, she's not just going to Reno, she's
on her way to corporate headquarters!"

Kyle's usual Who me? tone of voice had drawn taut. "You
say she has a *map*? I mean shit, where'd she get MacCallum's
map? *I* couldn't even find it!"

"She *made* it," the man said. "Went back out there and
found enough of MacCallum's tags that she could reconstruct
his pattern. And somehow she cracked his code and got the
assays and made her own map. That's one neat piece of computer hacking. I tell you, I knew she was smart, but that's
downright scary."

Kyle's agitation hardened into rage. "The wheedling little
twat! What she think she's doing?"

"Hey, calm down, man!" the other man said, holding up
his hands in surpise. "She's a nice kid."

Kyle's voice kept rising. "A map and a bunch of exploration assays aren't going to tell you anything!"

The other man gave Kyle a derisive laugh. "Maybe she's got the eye MacCallum has."

Kyle turned then and saw me. His eyes were huge and hot with anger. The transformation from the floppy puppy he had been showing me was startling. He looked at me like I was part of the wall, then turned back to the other man. "Nobody has his eye for gold," he barked. "Nobody!"

An eye for gold. On any other day, the allusion would have struck me as romantic, but I had just gone through a mill with a metallurgist who talked like the lineal descendant of a Medieval alchemist, so it sounded almost normal. But Kyle's public discharge of anger was even stranger. It was as if the omega dog had gotten rabies. But was his anger borne of loyalty to MacCallum or fear for his own position? The whole metaphor of the wolf pack ran quickly away with me, and I wondered if this omega realized that he'd been following not the alpha wolf, but a lone wolf who needed to be by himself. And I had to admonish myself that I did not know what being a lone wolf meant to MacCallum. *It might mean something very different than it does to me. . . .*

The women's room door opened behind me and I heard a pattering of feet moving down the hall away from us. Kyle turned and watched over my shoulders, the veins beginning to stand out in his face. He pushed past me, and I turned, too, and saw him hurry after the petite woman I had seen emptying her locker. *So this is Laurel Dietz,* I decided. *She's going to see Chittenden, the jovial Englishman who presented himself to Tom Latimer at the Reno airport the day we first arrived.* As I watched Kyle storm after her and slam a door behind them, I decided it might be about time to leave.

30

LAUREL DIETZ BENT TO PULL THE ZIP DRIVE FROM her computer and shoved it unceremoniously into her pack. Her notes followed, and then personal items: a mechanical pencil a college professor had given her, the inscribed map weight she had received as an award. She did not know exactly what Chittenden had in mind by hurrying her off to corporate headquarters, but she was confident that it was forward progress in her overall plan. In fact, it was a forward leap. Perhaps she would vault right over the stint as chief project geologist she had envisioned and go straight to exploration manager. But she would be coy when she got to corporate headquarters, bide her time, play it cool, as always.

Kyle burst through the door and crashed it shut behind him. "What the fuck you selling?" he demanded, his voice low but hot with anger.

Laurel kept her mind on her task. She heard Kyle's words, but they were as unimportant to her as static coming over a radio. The Kyles that rattled around the universe were so simple for her to deal with that she barely noticed them. Her computer was up now, so she leaned over the mouse pad, highlighted half a dozen files, and moved the mouse across the screen to the trash can icon and clicked on it. When the screen asked her if she was sure she wanted to delete the files, she clicked yes, and they began to fly across the screen.

"What the fuck you erasing?" Kyle spat.

Laurel continued to behave as if Kyle were not there. After a lifetime of dealing with men like him, she had learned that presenting no response to their aggressions usually confused them into quieting down. She began to stick more personal materials into her pack. Unfortunately, a few of them were right under Kyle's nose.

"Listen, sister," Kyle hissed, "you selling something to

management, you got to let me in on it! *I* went out there and got that data with MacCallum. *Me*! You don't just go grabbing it!"

"Those data," Laurel said, keeping her voice soft and chirpy, like a bird's. He was a wimp trying to be a bully, and bullies were in fact noisy cowards. He was not letting go as quickly as she had thought, but she knew that if she pushed him up against his own stupidity, he would show everybody within earshot what a total jackass he was, everyone would sympathize with her, and he would be one more minor obstacle out of her way.

Kyle blustered, "*What*?"

Tighten further, Laurel thought automatically. " 'Data' is plural. The singular is 'datum.' So it's 'those data,' not 'that data.' " She straightened up, came around the corner of the desk toward the last few items which she had stored on a nearby shelf, walking right past Kyle.

Kyle stepped in front of her. She saw his hands rise, and in the next instant felt his hands close around her throat, felt her feet leave the floor as he yanked her viciously upwards. For a split second, she closed her eyes, and when she opened them again, she had once again reached to the very bottom of her soul and found the coldness that had always waited there to serve her at moments like this. *Don't look into his eyes*, she reminded herself, as the first symptoms of oxygen starvation began to thin her brain. *Don't let him confuse you*. Forcing herself to forget what was happening to her neck and head, she reached her hands down to Kyle's crotch, took hold of his testicles, and squeezed with everything she had, then gave them the formidable and satisfying twist she had learned so long ago.

Kyle dropped her and staggered back against the wall, holding his crotch. His face went pale and he began to emit the most absurd gurgling sound. *So he was just like the rest after all*, Laurel decided, as the ringing in her ears diminished and her sight returned. *And like the others, the stupid bastard will blame it all on me*.

And that meant that it was time to go.

Laurel adjusted the bandana that was knotted about her neck, covering the red marks she knew would be forming. It was a thin armor, but in one way or another, always seemed to serve. With increased speed, she grabbed the Brunton compass and mineral hammer off the shelf and stowed them in the side pouches of her pack. Then, without another thought toward Kyle, she walked out the door.

31

I WAS STILL CONSIDERING THE IDEA OF MOVING down the hallway toward the room Kyle had followed Laurel Dietz into, so I could perhaps make out what he was shouting, when the door opened and she came back out. Her face seemed oddly mottled. She pattered down the hall to the back door that led off toward the mill and passed through it. I could hear a vehicle start up and the gravel crunch as she drove away.

I knew better than to be there when Kyle came out. I turned and hurried in the opposite direction. I took a jog to the left down the catacombs of hallways that led through the building, hoping I was nearing the guard's station and the door that would lead out to my truck.

I heard Virgil Davis's voice and followed it, my confidence growing. His office had been close to the guard station. His door was ajar. I heard him roar, "*Dead*, you say? Oh, shit!"

I threw on the brakes and stopped just outside his door, glancing over my shoulder to make certain that Kyle wasn't behind me.

No voice answered Virgil's. That meant he was on the phone. He squeaked nervously this way and that in his swivel chair as he listened to the caller, then said, "Well, yeah, I was wondering where in the hell Rodriguez was, but no, I haven't seen him since . . . let me think . . . it was days ago. The morning after Pat Gilmore wrecked her truck, we had a meeting at The Griddle in Winnemucca. I saw him there, I'm sure of it. You don't think—" He listened again, then roared, "You found him *where*? Drove it into a mineshaft? Are you kidding? That asshole never drove that pretty-boy piece of shit an inch off the road. Sheriff, this is not good. Someone's fucking with us, you hear me? I mean, when John and I found

Pat, there was no reason to think it was anything but an accident, but now—" He listened. "No, like we told you before, her truck had flipped and she was hanging out the door. Yes, it was open, which is damned lucky or we'd have had a devil of a time getting her out of there. The whole cab was crushed! No, like I said, the brush just next to the truck had caught fire, and you know how fast that stuff can get going! Did I. . . . How the hell do *I* know how the fire started? You come across a crash, you see fire, you *act*, man!"

By this time, I had eased up closer so I could see in through the gap left between the half-opened door and the jamb. Virgil had his back to me and did not see me.

Laurel's red Chevy Blazer rounded the building and came past Virgil's window. Virgil leaned forward and waved. She waved back, a cheery smile fixed to her lips. His head turned, following her motion, and I could see him now in profile. His eyes filled with sudden longing.

He spoke again into the phone. "What? No, like I told you, we did not see anyone else on the road. It was just at dusk, remember? And I would have seen the headlights if anyone else had been out there. . . . Running *without* headlights? I suppose so, but what kind of an idiot—" He stopped short, listened for a while. "Of course. Yes, I see what you're saying. No, I'll keep everyone here. You come ahead."

The sheriff was coming? *Oh, hell*, I thought, and, taking care not to make a sound, I hustled past Virgil's office, waved brightly to the guards as I hurried out through the metal detector, burst out into the full glare of daylight, and raced to my truck. Rodriguez had been found dead. I did not want to become part of a sheriff's investigation. I would highball it out to Winnemucca, phone Tom Latimer from the first phone I came upon, give him the dope I had on Kyle and Laurel and whomever else seemed stuck to this case, and have him call Sheriff Obernick and Deputy Weebe to keep me the hell out of it.

As I fired up my truck and pulled away, following the cloud of dust that billowed out behind Laurel's red Chevy

Blazer, it occurred to me that Virgil had not reported her departure to the sheriff.

BY THE TIME I pulled into the outskirts of Winnemucca, I had begun to calm down. The sun was almost kissing the mountains in the western sky, and I was beginning to realize how hungry I was. And yet I felt jarred, and longed deeply to report my findings to Tom and be done with them. I decided that a public phone booth was not the place, and instead found an inexpensive motel in which to spend the night. I turned off the main drag and drove parallel to the railroad, searching for something less upscale than the Red Lion, which was already flashing neon into the evening, advertising its slot machines and casino delights.

I found a nice old place called Scott's Shady Court Motel and checked into a tiny room that was tucked into a back driveway. The room was one of a funny little row of conjoined cabins with individual high-peaked roofs. Across the front of each, above the door, was painted the name of a female saint. I held the key to Santa Susana.

Inside, I dumped my duffel on the bed, grabbed the phone, and dialed Tom Latimer's number. He did not answer. He had left for the day.

Taking a deep breath, I dialed Faye Carter's number next. When she answered, she sounded surprised and jubilant to hear my voice, but when I told her what was going on, she sobered up fast and put Tom on the phone.

"Tom," I said. "I'm in Winnemucca. Can you take down the number at this motel?" I dictated it to him, then continued. "Listen, today I found out a bunch of things, and you need to know them, whether you think this is a murder case or not." Then I stopped, because I knew that, whatever I said next, I was going to sound like the idiot I now knew I was.

"Go on, Em," Tom said, his voice gentle. "It always goes like this when you're starting out."

I ignored the assertion he was making and continued. "The sheriff just found another body. The other biologist, that guy Rodriguez."

"No shit."

"No shit whatsoever. I was up at the Gloriana Mine when the call came through. I . . . well, I have to back up." I told Tom about meeting up with Kyle Christie, about the mill tour, and the woman named Laurel. I added my speculation about the condition of Kyle's career, and tossed in the obvious enmity between Kyle and Virgil Davis. That led me back to Davis's fond farewell to Laurel.

"You *have* been busy," Tom said approvingly.

"Tom, I am out of my depth. The fun and games are over. Okay, I've walked into my share of murder cases in my day, but that was then and this is now. I was a dumb kid with my eyes stuck shut. I'm a big girl now, and I want to live to grow up into some kind of an adult."

Tom cleared his throat. "Sounds reasonable."

"So what do you think I ought to do? I heard Virgil say he'd keep everybody there, and I took off like a jackrabbit. Sheriff Obernick's going to wonder. He doesn't know who I am, and—"

"I'll take care of that."

I let out a breath. "Thanks, Tom."

"You going to be at this number all night?"

"Yes. I've got to clean up and get something to eat. But yes, then I'll be here, with the door locked. No more silly games. I'll be a good girl and stay put."

Tom chuckled. "Sure you will. I'll call you back when I have something. This may take a while. You go on out to dinner, but try to stay out of any place that might have anyone from that mine in it, you hear? Or just send out for a pizza."

"I hear," I said, but knew that in a town like this, that wasn't going to be easy. Tourism was probably the biggest industry in Nevada, but mining was a close second.

I hung up the phone and lay down on the bed and thought about things for a while, then realized what a total ass I'd just made of myself. As I began to calm down, I began to realize also exactly how hungry I was, but even more so, how dirty and dry I felt. I had been camping for three days in the desert without a bath.

I dug into my duffel bag. Fortunately, I had thought to pack a swimming suit. I shucked off my clothes, put on the suit, grabbed a towel, and headed around the end of the buildings toward the swimming pool I had noticed on the way in. It was enclosed in a skeletal building. It was by then past eight in the evening, and the pool building was a sea of shadows, so I felt around for a light switch. An eery blue light suffused the room as underwater floodlights came to life. I stepped inside and stood at the edge of the water, which stretched at least forty feet before me. I stared into the blue depths, marveling at this anomaly of cool, clear water in the middle of the desert.

I was alone. I dropped my towel on a chair, tucked my room key down inside my suit, and dove in, letting the cool waters rush past my face. The sensation was bizarre. I felt drier inside than out.

I turned face up and swam, looking upward through the alien liquid, trying to make sense of what my body was experiencing. I was in bliss and total confusion simultaneously. I wished I did not have to rise to breathe.

BACK IN MY room, I tried once more to telephone Ray. When I got his terse, "This is Ray, leave a message," message, I hung up and sighed. There are no atheists in fox holes, and there are no tough girls who can do without their cop boyfriends when they're sitting in motels with local sheriffs looking for them. Just then, I would have walked across broken glass to feel him hug me.

I had plenty of canned food with me, but had a hankering for a steak and some fresh vegetables. So I went first to a large chain supermarket near the main route through town, but just inside the door, I was confronted by a line of electronic slot machines. A man was sitting at the nearest machine, on a thickly padded stool attached to the machine, feeding in quarters. He looked like he had been there a long time. I turned tail and ran back to my truck.

Eventually, I found something that looked more like my speed on a side street called Malarkey, at the intersection of

Railroad Avenue. It was a restaurant and bar in an old residential hotel called the Martin, a white stucco job across from the railroad depot. I let myself in through the bar, which was a large, fairly well-lit room full of locals who were visiting at side tables over beers and whiskeys. A few men were playing electronic poker through machines that were set flush into the top of the bar. A woman came out and asked me if I was there for dinner. "Yes, please," I answered.

She smiled. "Well, there's no tables just now. Do you want to wait, or is it okay to sit with someone else?" When I looked surprised, she explained. "This is a Basque restaurant. We serve family style. You can have a table to yourself or go like the locals."

Forgetting Tom's warning to avoid miners, I smiled, welcoming the thought of sitting with someone who was truly from there, unlike the crowd of migratory imports I had just met at the mine. "I'm starved. Find me a seat."

"Let me check." The woman went inside the adjacent dining room and spoke with two men who were seated at a table for four. They nodded, and she came back for me. "You can sit with Larry and Joe. They's good guys. Don't mind them, they's had a little wine. Celebrating. Larry's made some extra money."

After I had sat down and the waitress had taken my order for entrée and imbibition, I said to the men, "Hi. I'm Em Hansen. Just visiting here in Nevada. Thanks for having me at your table."

The two men smiled and nodded. One was dark and broad-cheeked and had coal black hair and eyes. I took him for an Indian. The other's ethnicity was harder to place: He was also dark-haired, but in a more European sort of way, though he looked like he didn't see the sun very much. "I'm Joe Anchordoughy," he said. "This is Larry Scarface."

"Anchordoughy," I said. "What country does that name come from?"

"I'm Basque," Joe said. "My friend here's Paiute." He grinned at him. "Give a war whoop for the lady, Lar."

Larry laughed and took a sip of his beer. "Paiutes are not warlike, Joe, you know that."

"You had your moments."

"Let's not get into that."

I changed the subject. "What do you do for a living around here? Ranch?"

"No," said Joe. "We're both hardrock miners."

I about gagged on the glass of red wine the waitress had just slipped in front of me, and I covered my reaction by helping myself from the communal bowls of salad and garlicky soup that stood in the middle of the table. "Where?"

"The Gloriana, west of here."

"That's an underground mine?" I asked politely, resigning myself to making pleasant conversation for the duration of the meal.

"Yeah, like I said, hard rock."

"I'm not sure I know the distinctions," I said.

Joe took a bite of his steak and chewed, mulling my question. "Well, you got your open-pit mines, and then your hardrock, which is underground. Then of course you got your coal, which is something else again, either underground or open-pit or drag-line."

"You worked them all?" I asked.

"No. A hardrock miner don't like open-pit. Don't like coal, neither. The back's too low. A'course, a coal miner don't like hardrock. The back's too high."

Larry laughed appreciatively.

"What's the back?" I asked.

"What you'd call the ceiling," Joe answered. "The rock you're working at is called the face."

"Oh." I wondered where the terms came from, but didn't ask. I didn't want to know if they referred to what the world was like if you were working lying on your belly with about two feet of clearance, as in some coal mines. "So tell me; it's dark down there, right? How do you stand that?"

Both men laughed with delight. "A'course it is," Joe answered. "You're a mile down inside the earth. No lights in there!"

"Well, then, you wear a headlight, right? But don't you ... um ..."

"Get claustrophobic?" Joe asked.

"Yeah."

"Nah! We like it, don't we, Larry?"

"Yeah." He nodded with enthusiasm and took another crusty roll and smeared butter on it. Both men were eating with hearty appetites.

"No, really," I persisted. "You say you're a mile down there. You're inside the earth, in a tight space, working with explosives. Doesn't that worry you?"

"No. We know the risks. We avoid them."

"But don't you miss the sunlight?"

Joe thought on this awhile, munching at another mouthful of steak. "No, I like it. It's always the same temperature, the same humidity. I'm all alone, no one's bothering me ..."

"You're *alone*?" I said, appalled. "But you come out for lunch, and—"

"Nope. Stay under all day. Ten-hour shift. Takes too long to come up for lunch. Besides, like I say ..."

Larry spoke. "It kind of grows on you. It's like coming home."

Joe laughed again, and shoveled more salad onto his plate. "Strange way to serve the Lord ..."

I EXCUSED MYSELF before dessert and headed back to my motel to see if Tom had called. There was a message that he had, and that I was supposed to call Faye's number. She answered on the first ring. "Good. It's you. Here's Tom."

"Em," he said. "There's going to be a postmortem. I want you there."

I flopped back on my bed and said, "*What*?"

"They're calling in a medical examiner from Reno. The body is there in Winnemucca. I want you to get a look at it before they carve him up."

"Now, really, Tom!"

"You wanted to get cleared of this, right? I told them you were working with me. You want to make that stick, or do you want to run for it and take your chances? You left the scene today, darling. It's your choice. And I need that evidence."

The ceiling seemed to be spinning a lot faster than one glass of wine should have made it go. "Okay," I said, my voice faint. "Give me directions."

He did so. "You'll have to hurry; the man's almost there. After you make your observations, report to both sheriffs—the body was found right on the line between Pershing and Humboldt Counties, you lucky dog—and tell them what tests you want run."

"Tests?" Panic began to rise in my chest. "I don't know anything about—"

"Yes, tests. I told them you are a forensic geologist. You going to make a liar out of me?"

I closed my eyes. "No. But Tom—"

"No buts. I just stuck my neck out for you, and you are going to perform. Make something up if you have to. When you're done, go back to your motel and stay put. Ian—you remember him, the agent from Reno—will be there in about two hours. I'll be out first thing in the morning."

THE BODY STANK. It had begun to putrefy, and I was glad that most of it was draped with a sheet. I wadded up my jacket and held it to my face as I lifted that sheet from the feet, trying to look like I had the barest clue what I was doing.

"What chew looking for?" asked Sheriff Obernick, a beefy guy in a Stetson.

Deputy Weebe leaned toward me, chewing a toothpick like he was at a barbecue. "Forensics guys allus look at the shoes first," he said knowingly.

I exhaled quietly. At least I'd started at the right end. I bent and looked closely at the shoes, and just to make it look like I was really on the ball, I pulled my hand lens out of my jacket pocket and got in really close. What I saw made me forget all about the stench.

"What is it?" asked Deputy Miller, of the Humboldt County Sheriff's Office.

"Sand," I said. "Very round sand. You got any hydrochloric acid here?"

"No," said the medical examiner. "Why?"

"I think these are oolites," I said, my mind swimming with wonder. "I wonder how he got—"

"You see what?" asked Sheriff Obernick.

"It's in the welts of his shoes," I said. "Oolitic sand forms by the shores of lakes. You get it by Great Salt Lake, in Utah." I straightened up for a moment and thought. "But of course, there were lakes here, just a few thousand years ago. Ten at the most. But—" I bent again, and stared at another portion of the shoe. "Ah. He *has* been to Great Salt Lake."

"How do you know that?" asked the medical examiner skeptically.

I pointed at what I had been looking at and handed him the lens. "*That* is a brine shrimp," I said cheerfully.

The medical examiner made hmm-hmm noises, appreciating what I had noted. "Yes, well, we have lakes around here, too. Pyramid, Walker. Perhaps he had been over there just before he—"

I said, "No, brine shrimp require hypersaline conditions in a perennial lake. *Those* you do not have here. I was just at Great Salt Lake a few days ago, and read a brochure." I realized that this sounded weak, so I added, "But of course, the thing to do is to take some samples and send them to the lab back at Quantico." I smiled smugly. I was getting away with it.

"Hmm, yes," said the medical examiner. "Of course. What other tests would you like run?"

I thought fast. "Well, why don't we just place one whole shoe in a sample container and send it in?" I said. "That way our folks can look at all the clays that might be there, and . . . well, like that." Then, to take the spotlight off myself, I asked, "What's your take from your initial examination of the body?"

The medical examiner spoke. "Dead several days, at least. Head wound. The sheriffs here tell me that the body was found belted into the driver's seat of a vehicle up in the

Kamma Mountains, down in an abandoned mine shaft, but it's clear to me that he was dead before he got there."

"Lividity?" I asked.

"Yes. The body had rested on its back as the blood settled, not in the front of his body, as would be the case if he'd died face downward hanging from the seat belts."

"Had the rigor mortis been broken, too?" I asked, playing my last card of knowledge of dead bodies.

"Hard to say. First guess? The rigor formed and passed before he was placed in the seat."

Sheriff Obernick said, "There were footprints on top of the tire tracks coming back downhill from the shaft. We're working on that."

"Good," I said. "Make sure you get photographs before you try to make a cast. That soil would be crumbly. And get a soil sample for Quantico, too. We can type the clays."

Obernick nodded. I tried to remember to breathe.

Outside in the parking lot a few minutes later, I asked Deputy Weebe a question. "Do you remember questioning Kyle Christie the morning after Pat Gilmore was killed?"

He nodded. "Like it was yesterday."

"Do you remember precisely what he said?"

Weebe half-closed his eyes in concentration. "Sure. I asked him what he knew about Pat Gilmore's death, and he said, 'It was an accident, right?' "

"That's pretty good recall," I said, encouraging him.

He pulled a small notebook out of his pocket. "No it ain't. I allus write things down."

"What else did he say?"

"Well, I asked him where this guy MacCallum was, and he said, 'Why do you guys want to talk to him?' Now, that sounded real cagey to me, so I put a little heat to him. Told him I wasn't no fool as to think that Pat's murder was no accident."

"And what did he say? Exactly," I asked, leaning over his shoulder to look into the book.

Weebe read the entry. "He said, 'Good thing she was in Pershing County when she flipped that pickup, or you wouldn't be investigating her death, Deputy Weebe, sir.' "

I straightened up and peered at Weebe in the dim light of the street lamps. His toothpick went round and round and round. "You never actually went out there, did you?" I asked. "I mean, you never saw Pat's truck before it was hauled into the yard, and that was days later, after the fire was put out, right?"

"Yeah," he said. "Why?"

"Well, I was just wondering. At the time you spoke to Kyle, did you yet know that the truck had flipped?"

The toothpick stopped turning as Deputy Weebe's jaw went slack. Then it rose again as his lips formed a little circle and he said, "No."

"Of course, Virgil Davis and John Steinhoff saw it. They could have told him."

Weebe stuck his thumbs into his gun belt. "No, I don't think so," he said. " 'Cause I remember the sheriff telling them to keep their lips zipped 'til he'd had a chance to investigate."

IAN WAS WAITING at the motel when I returned. He had checked into Santa Paula, a few doors down from my room. He did not look glad to see me. "Tell me about the autopsy," he said abruptly. He remained standing in the middle of the room, even though I had sat down.

I put my feet up on the midget table that inevitably shows up in motels. "Body probably killed in Utah. Someone went to a lot of trouble to bring him back to Nevada." I told him about the oolites and brine shrimp in the shoes, and about the footprints leading down from the shaft.

Ian didn't seem to like my analysis of the evidence. "Couldn't he have driven back out here, gotten unlucky, and—"

"No, the lividity was wrong, too. Blood settles to the lowest parts of a body shortly after death. It leaves a dark bruise. He'd been moved."

Ian crossed his arms and said nothing.

"You getting anywhere with that guy in the BLM office in Reno?" I asked.

"The mysterious Stephen Giles? A few things," he said. "I thought you wanted to stay out of this."

"Just passing the time."

"Well, he threw up and then slammed a tourist's arm in his car door," he said derisively, "but that just suggests that he has a weak stomach."

I said, "Yeah, weak stomach. Where was he?"

"Downtown. I've been looking into him, though. I put a tail on him. He's an odd one. Keeps a storage locker at the edge of town. Near as I can tell, there's nothing in it but a leather suitcase wrapped up in plastic wrap and a cardboard box."

"What's in them?"

"I don't have cause for a search warrant."

"And you have nothing on Don MacCallum."

He looked bored, but the fact that he kept talking let me know that he wanted me to be impressed with him, for all the most resentful reasons. He said, "MacCallum's still AWOL. No one knows anything, or at least, no one's saying if they do."

"And Laurel?"

"Laurel Dietz? The one who high-tailed it away from the mine?"

"Yes."

"Gone. She went south toward Lovelock, like you said. Obernick saw a red Blazer with a blonde in it as he was coming north along that road, but he didn't have any reason to stop her. By the time the highway patrol knew to look for her, she was gone. Kyle took great pains to let the sheriff know that she'd been there and just left—he went so far as to say he'd seen her messing about in the hills not far from where Rodriguez's body was found—and we of course had your report shortly after. Could have made it over the Sierra into California. We're looking."

"They said she was going to corporate HQ."

"If so, she didn't get there on a commercial flight. Yet. They're watching the Reno airport."

At the mention of that location, an idea came to me. "Chittenden has a company jet. What if it was waiting at the general aviation terminal? She could be—"

Ian whipped a notebook out of his breast pocket and scribbled a note. "I can see why Tom wanted you," he muttered.

I sighed in exasperation, sick of the heaviness of his contempt.

Ian shook his head at me. "It's a real compliment, you know. Tom's legendary. Most rookies would give their eye teeth to work with him."

I snapped my head forward, astonished. "*Legendary*? What do you mean? I thought he was some wise guy who got crosswise with some higher-up and got stuck in the boonies."

Ian laughed at my ignorance. "Tom Latimer? No, he had his pick of places to be. Don't you get it? He's got this incredible success ratio, and years and years in the Bureau. They wanted him in management back at Quantico, but he turned it down. Wanted to stay in the field. Said he could see the world more clearly from the edge of it. They call him 'the Zen master.' "

I snorted with disbelief. "He's a smart shit, but—"

Ian threw aside all artifice of acting cool. "I can't *believe* you! You've been handed the chance of a lifetime. Tom Latimer asks you in on a case—*Tom Latimer*—shit, he's trying to *recruit* you! And you think he's some sad sack also-ran put out to pasture, and you give him the air! That's wild!"

I stared at the floor, hoping it would open up and let me fall through it.

32

IAN WOKE ME WITH A KNOCK AT MY DOOR AT FIVE. I'd say it was bright and early, but it was in fact so early that it was not yet bright. "I'm on my way to the airport to pick up Tom," he said.

"Airport?" I asked, yawning. I was standing there in an oversized T-shirt that read CHEYENNE FRONTIER DAYS, kind of squinting at him through a four-inch gap between the door and the jamb.

"Yeah, the one right here in Winnemucca. He wants you to report. I'll be back in half an hour. I think you'd better shower and dress and get your head together."

"Thanks," I said, not the least bit sure I felt thankful.

He disappeared. I heard him start up his car and roll out of the lot. Only then did it begin to occur to me that, if I was expected to get up and receive Tom, I was not yet off the hook. That did not bode well. I had had quite a bit of trouble getting to sleep after everything I had seen the day before. On a normal day, a crashed, roasted pickup truck would have left me feeling a little blue, but add to that an unknown Native American staring at me from a blind woman's dooryard like she's expecting me, Kyle Christie, an old man found dying by the road, a rumbling gold mill, a stinking corpse, and the conversation I'd had with Ian, and I may as well have mainlined caffeine.

I think I got to sleep at two-thirty or three. As I showered off and dressed, I thought with some irritation that going short on sleep when up past my eye sockets in a murder investigation was beginning to be an all-too-familiar experience. Least of all did I like admitting to myself that I was once again just that: up past my eye sockets in a murder investigation. I vowed to do the bare minimum required to get untangled from this mess and get back on the road.

But to where?

I sat on the edge of my tumbled bed, hair still wet, duffel packed. I stared at my hands. I still had no idea what I was doing, except perhaps running away, and that was not acceptable.

I heard a car pull up outside, then Ian's knock. Hefting my duffel to my shoulder, I stood up, put one foot in front of the other, and headed toward the door.

TOM CHOSE THE dining room at the Red Lion Inn for our meeting because at that early hour it was virtually empty. There were a few chain-smoking diehards still up from the evening before jamming money into the electronic slots in the lounge outside the cafe door, and there was one early-rising mother scrambling to order pancakes and juice for her children, but aside from that, the place was empty. We sat in a booth under the windows that looked out across the parking lot. I faced the glass, wanting to keep an eye on my truck, to remind myself that I had a means of escape.

"The highway patrol found Laurel Dietz's Blazer," Ian reported. With Tom listening, his voice had returned to more civil tones.

"Where?" asked Tom, as he perused the menu.

"Lovelock airport. We checked Flight Following to see if anyone filed a flight plan out of there yesterday afternoon or evening, but no luck. Several people did, however, see a jet land there. That would have caught my attention, too. It was in fact such a rare sighting there that no one knew what kind it was. We're looking for more witnesses and circulating photographs of likely small carriers."

"Why not just find out what kind of jet Granville flies?" I asked.

Ian fell into a brooding silence.

I said, "It was a clear night, and there's no law against flying around without a flight plan, but somewhere along the line, it would have eventually linked up with Flight Following, unless Chittenden's a total cowboy."

Tom put down his menu and looked at me. "Why would

Chittenden send his jet, and where would he take her?"

I shrugged my shoulders. "He didn't send his jet, he flew it himself."

Tom narrowed his eyes. "How do you know that?"

I narrowed mine right back at him. "Dinner in Salt Lake City. A man named Tom Latimer is putting the munch on a woman named Em Hansen to help him with a case. At the next table are a man named Morgan Shumway and his daughter. The daughter is telling Mr. Shumway that her new boyfriend flies a jet. Flies it himself. You're still holding out on me. You know something about her you haven't told me. And you want me to go look at dead men's shoes. You little—"

Tom held up a hand. "No. Wait. Until now, I hadn't made that connection myself." His face hardened. "That's why I wanted you trained and in the Bureau, Em. You pick up things others miss. And don't get paranoid on me. I have to keep things under wraps for the very best reasons, as well as the worst. I ran a security check on you before I made you that offer, but that doesn't mean you've promised to keep your mouth shut. You—"

I cut him off. "What I overheard was that Chittenden wanted Laurel Dietz double quick *with* her maps and data. Your guess is as good as mine why he yanked her out of Nevada."

"No," Tom said. "In this case, my guess is not as good as yours. You know what those maps and data were intended to be used for. I do not."

I closed my eyes and let out my breath, giving myself a moment to think. I was tired; no, exhausted. And just like Tom had implied, I was shooting my mouth off. "Well, on the face of it, maps are exploration tools. MacCallum had been out taking mineral samples at locations all over the Kamma Mountains."

"What controls the locations of the gold?" Tom asked. "Why doesn't he look in the valleys?"

"There may be gold in the valleys, but it would be buried under thousands of feet of sediment. It's hard enough to locate a vein when you've got an outcrop to lead you in to it."

"So Laurel Dietz was reconstructing a discovery that MacCallum had made," Tom said.

I leaned back and folded my hands. "I thought a lot about that last night," I said. "And there's something wrong. Maybe she did. But the thing is, it's not that easy to find gold, or it would all already have been found. The initial prospecting just defines a drilling target. And even the drilling takes a lot of luck, and—" I thought of what Kyle and the other male geologist he had spoken with in the hallway at the mine offices had said. "It takes an eye for gold. Not everybody has it. It's that unquantifiable knack, that ability to see something that isn't showing itself yet. It's a special thing about the really good geologists. They take a bunch of data, discontinuous, incomplete data, and fill in the gaps. The fossil record is incomplete. Most of the rocks ever formed have been buried, torn apart, or outright destroyed. Evidence gone. So they make an interpretation."

"But that's not science," Ian challenged.

I leaned toward him and put an index finger on the table. "Some people call that shoddy science, because an interpretation is not a fact. They call it more of an art, in the sense that historians practice an art, or should I say, a liberal art. Well, the thing is, interpreting history is how *this* science has to be done. We can't directly observe things that happened millions or billions of years ago, so we look at what's happening now, see what pattern that leaves on the face of the earth, and interpret the past by matching patterns. We collect all the evidence we can, pull together our interpretations, and build an hypothesis. We test the hypothesis as best we can, and if it stands, it becomes a theory."

I closed my eyes and took a deep breath. At the core of my being, I really didn't care what Ian thought about my science, but I wanted Tom to understand. I wanted him to understand that I was not shooting from the hip except as a way to scare up enough data to get my process started. "Tom, a good theory predicts things that have not happened yet, or things that are not yet discovered. And if it doesn't, we amend it and test it again. That's why I like science. It does not fight the facts, it bows to them, even woos them. And geology is in my view the most romantic science of the bunch. At its best, the practice of geology looks not only into the past, but also in so doing helps train its practicioners to make a best possible, best educated interpretation of what we're going to observe in the future." I sat back, my words spent.

Ian was looking blank.

Tom was smiling with his whole face.

The waitress brought our breakfasts.

I picked up a stick of bacon and stabbed it into the yolk of one of my basted eggs, dipped, and munched. It's a disgusting habit, I suppose, but it tastes wonderful. "Well, anyway, the point is that I don't think that Laurel Dietz can take someone else's raw data and necessarily figure out what they were thinking, let alone direct an exploratory drilling project from it."

"The mystical MacCallum is needed for that," Ian said.

I shot him daggers with a glance. His comments were beginning to get under my skin, and I felt like telling him that he could do with a little more original thought and passion and a little less boot licking if he wanted to get anywhere with Tom.

I took a few forkfuls of hashbrown potatoes and washed it down with some orange juice, then raised my glass to the waitress to order more. As long as this breakfast was on the FBI, I was going to eat my fill. "So I don't know what the gag is with Laurel. I don't know what was said to Chittenden over the phone. I don't know what Chittenden wants. He seemed like a loose cannon to me when we met him at the Reno airport."

"So you remember him," Tom said.

"Yes, of course. All bright eyes and ain't-I-something, with a sly something underneath. I wouldn't accept a ride with him if I was stranded in a blizzard."

"No?" said Tom. "But you're right, he does fly his own jet. Used to fly for the British navy. Harrier jump jets."

I put a hand over my face. Jumping mice, now jumping jets. It was a bit much. I uncovered my eyes and looked at

Tom. "So maybe he flies the way they do business on the Vancouver Exchange," I said.

Tom smiled with satisfaction. "Give the lady a cigar."

Ian cut in, somewhat pettishly. "What are you talking about?"

Tom answered, "There is a contrast between the way stocks are traded on the American exchanges and in Canada. We have a Securities and Exchange Commission expressly to impose rules on how business is done, to keep things kosher."

"And Granville Resources is traded on the Vancouver Exchange," Ian continued, looking at me more than at Tom.

"Yes," said Tom. "Granville Resources is what's called a junior company, a small upstart next to some of the big mining corporations. More volatile. Somewhat less easy to—as you say, Em . . . *predict*."

"Tom," I asked, "What are the environmental regulations regarding foreign-traded companies doing mining business in the United States?"

Tom put down his fork. "Therein lies a rub. We have had a few problems with all this in recent years. Like the Summitville project in Colorado. Canadian company came in and started a heap-leaching operation, then left, leaving a huge mess for the American taxpayer to clean up. Foreign companies are required to post a bond for clean-up, but this regulation is in conflict with our desire to stimulate commerce, so the bond is often pitifully undersized, as in the Summitville case. We tried to sue for payment in Canadian courts, but there is no reciprocity between the two countries."

"Shit."

"Exactly."

"But Granville seems different," I said. "Here they have a whole project hung up while they wait for an environmental permit."

"Yes," Tom said, leaning back and taking a sip of his coffee. "That part confuses me. That's where I need you again."

"*What?*" I slammed down my fork. "Listen, Tom, it's all fun and games to get me looking at a dead man's boots so I can get off a leaving the scene of a crime charge, but I've had enough now! I'm going to be a good girl. I'm—"

Tom was staring at me over his coffee cup. He took another long sip.

I curled my fingers into fists and shook them over my plate. "*Tom . . .*"

Tom said, "Ian, will you excuse us for a moment?"

Ian got up, dropped his napkin onto his seat with more force than was necessary, and headed out of the restaurant.

Tom leaned back in his seat. He took one more sip of his coffee and set it down, staring at the cup. "Sure. Just chuck it all, give up this career business, and go make some babies with Ray," he said.

I raised my shoulders to my ears like he was a bad wind I was trying to deflect.

He said, "You're what, thirty-three? You don't want to wait any longer. Nice baby on your lap, just the thing, then you'll feel fulfilled."

"Shut up!" I began to shake.

His voice grew quieter. "No, you're right. I shouldn't push you into a job or a career or anything else you don't want. A woman your age should be knee-deep in Little League and diapers. Hang over that washing machine. Worry about stains."

"You bastard!" I hissed.

The agent slapped a hand over his heart. "Ouch. Truth's arrow pierces me at last." Suddenly he looked over toward the table where the young mother sat with her three children. "Here's the test right here," he said.

The woman was struggling to tie her little boy's shoes while she held the baby in her arms. A third, intermediate-aged child chose that moment to knock her juice off the table and begin to squall like she was dying. The woman's eyes went round with desperation.

Tom rose from our table and moved quickly to her aid. "Here," he said soothingly, "Let me help you. I'll hold the little one while you get the bigger ones straightened out." She looked uncertain for a moment, but then melted, gratefully

gave up her baby, and bent to wrestle with the chaos her other
two were inflicting on the universe.

"Coo, coo, coo, coo," Tom said to the baby, smiling
sweetly into its pudding face. "Coo, coo, coo, coo."

The baby curled its lips with delight, astonished to find
itself the object of anyone's undivided attention.

To me, Tom said, "C'mon over here, Emmy-girl. You
gotta see this little sweetums. Come on, girl!"

The harried mother glanced up anxiously at Tom, but he
reassured her with a smile.

I felt a similar brush of anxiety, but the difference between
me and this woman was that I didn't just suspect that he was
putting us on, I was certain. I wanted to kick him for using
her to get at me. At the same time, I'd known Tom just long
enough to know that he never acted a part he didn't at some
depth live. The look of love he focussed on that little
pudding-faced child was both tender and honest.

I dragged myself to my feet, resigning myself to finding
out what he had up his sleeve this time. Hornswaggling me
out to the back of nowhere to check out a little murder and
corruption was one thing, but this particular side excursion
had the look of raw manipulation, and if I smelled something
sour, it probably wasn't day-old diapers.

Holding babies has never been my territory. Stuffing my
hands in my pockets, I led with my nose and examined the
infant like a museum visitor staring through a glass case.
"Very nice," I muttered.

"Hands out of your pockets, girl," Tom said boisterously,
"you got a baby to hold! Come on, don't be shy, this one's
a zinger." Again the mother looked up, this time more confused than anxious. Tom gave her a conspiratorial wink. "An-
gling for a grandchild," he told her.

I shot him a look that said, You should be ashamed of
yourself, and grudgingly readied my hands for the load.

He passed me the kid. "Like this," he instructed, rearrang-
ing my arms so that the child was more firmly against me.
"Lean back a bit. Let gravity help you out. And here, get her
head a bit higher. You got it. That's it." To the woman, he

said, "Em's my only child. Never had much practice at this."

Aromas of loaded, synthetic diaper and sticky baby suffused my nostrils, and I fought to suppress my gag reflex. Then, gathering my courage, I looked down into the gelatinous little face that now stared into my own. To my not very great surprise, I saw, staring back, just another human, small size, concerned yet curious. I might as well have picked up the waitress, or anyone else in the room, for all the maternal instinct I was feeling. As I continued to stare, the baby's face began to mirror my own, its expression shifting slowly from uncertainty to worry and then outright horror. It began to wail. "Here," I said, stuffing it back into Tom's arms. "Your hot idea, you hold it." To the woman, who was probably a good six or seven years younger than I was, I said awkwardly, "Beg pardon, ma'am." Then I stormed out through the lounge and lobby and out the door, ran across the parking lot, and climbed into my truck. Hoping to escape. Hoping to outrun my own feelings. I didn't even get my keys out of my pocket before I started crying.

I crumpled onto the steering wheel, my head in my hands, wailing. My lips swelled, and my head grew thick as wool. My heart felt both heavy and empty, like an abandoned cast-iron pot.

Moments passed. Out of the corner of my eye, I saw the door at the front of the Red Lion open again, and after a while heard the soft, slow concussions of Tom's shoes as he came across the warming pavement toward me. He stopped beside my door, not far off but not too close, being what I suppose for him was respectful. He knocked on the window.

I rolled it down.

"I'm a real shit," he commented.

"Grade A."

"I like to excel at what I do."

"You outdid yourself this time."

"Wonderful. You're not crying, are you?"

"No." My lips began to tremble again. I said, "Girls who don't love babies never cry," and began to sob. Tom said nothing, so I added, "I'm not really a woman, or even human, and worse yet, I'm the last one to figure it out."

He said nothing for quite a while, and then, "Let's go for a walk."

I got out of the truck. We headed south toward the older buildings in town, and soon came to the railroad tracks, a sufficiently lonely place to say what we needed to say, and stopped. I straightened up and regarded the distant hills, all bald and dry in the lavender air of morning. "I didn't feel a damned thing for that kid," I said.

"Of course you didn't," he replied.

I wheeled around toward him. "Oh, so now you're my psychotherapist," I spat. "Why don't you just spell it out? I'm a weirdo with a talent, and you've got the perfect sheltered workshop for me to curl up into. Is that what you do? Go around recruiting cripples? Do they perform better than *normal* people who get distracted by little things like childbearing and love lives? Huh? You want to see if my heart is dead, so you know I'll make a *fine* field agent, all malleable and faithful as a dog, at least till I drive off the road some evening when some asshole plays something crooning on the radio and I finally just plain *lose* it?"

He said nothing. He just stood there and took it. I found myself looking into the eyes of a man who was not guarding his soul, a man standing at the edge of a half-forgotten town, naked right down to his sorry little heart. He cleared his throat uncomfortably.

"Make it good," I said bitterly.

"My wife used to talk like that," he said.

"You're *married*?" I said, appalled.

Ignoring my question, he said, "We met in college, and married as soon as we graduated, and I went to work. She used to keep me up late asking me if I wanted kids."

"What did you tell her?"

"That I was too selfish. Yeah, too busy climbing the ladder at the Bureau, too busy doing what I liked to do in my free time, too busy thinking about a hundred other things. Then one day I realized something was missing, and I said, 'How 'bout it?' and she said she'd get back to me."

"Real executive like."

"Yeah."

I expected next to hear the same enraging story I'd heard from half a dozen women friends in the oil business: She gives up baby-making for the guy, then, when she's too old, he feels his own mortality coming and leaves her for a younger dish with a fertile womb. Perhaps that was where Faye was scheduled to come in. I said acidly, "But she was past menopause then, and—"

"No," he said. "It didn't take me that long."

"Okay," I said. "So what happened?"

He said, "Then everything was different. Thing was, she wasn't a woman who wanted kids just to have kids. She wanted a relationship. People were people to her, not categories. She went to bed and had a dream that there was a little girl out there that needed her to find her, and she went to it like a woman possessed."

"So you have a daughter," I said, my voice rocky. I added this information to the meager store of personal facts I knew about him.

"No."

"No?" I felt like I was on a conveyor belt, being drawn somewhere I didn't want to go. "Why not?"

"Because my wife is dead," he answered.

I stared at my feet. "I'm sorry."

"So aren't we all," he said softly. "She was a good woman."

I took a breath and looked away. I didn't want to care about him just then.

"She was killed by a sniper," he said. "Standing at the kitchen window, three months pregnant, cooking me dinner."

My body suddenly felt like lead. "You don't think—"

"That that bullet was meant for me? Oh, yes. And whoever did that would have been kinder to kill me directly. Instead, he killed the best part of my life and left me alive to remember it."

We were standing side by side, both staring out at the mountains. There was nothing I could say, except that it was clear to me now why he felt that he had to help women like me and Faye get to a place where we were less vulnerable; but at that moment, that was not the thing to say at all. I put a hand over my face and rubbed it hard.

Tom said, "I like my work. And I still like to do what I like to do in my free time."

I let things hang in the air for a while, then, as gently as I could, said, "Please come to your point. How does all this involve me?"

"Make room for everything you are."

"Sure." A train approached, the ground rumbling as its titanic weight concussed each grain of clinker between us.

Tom stood with his hands in his pockets, once again the Tom I'd first gotten to know. He was taking a moment to do the thing he liked to do, and that was just to be.

"You've been a shit to me," I said.

"You're right," he said. "I am sorry. I got you wrong."

"Oh?"

"Your pal Carlos Ortega there in Denver said you were contrary as hell; I took that to mean that if I wanted you to do something, I'd have to trick you into it. But you're smarter than that."

"No, I'm not."

"Whatever. I am sorry. I just thought you'd be good. And even if you don't want to be a detective, investigations keep finding you. You should at least be trained, so you don't eventually get yourself killed." He rubbed the back of his neck. "And I'm arrogant. I wanted the annoyance of training you all to myself."

I smiled. "Thanks anyway."

"De nada."

"Think you'll marry Faye?" I asked, wiggling my eyebrows at him.

He laughed. "No. She'll probably get sick of me."

I laughed, too, in spite of myself.

Tom reached out and tousled my hair.

"So what do you need me to do?" I asked. "I'm heading out into the Black Rock Desert first chance I get and stay out of the line of fire, but I guess I can run a few more errands for you before I leave."

"And when you get back to Salt Lake City, we'll talk some more?"

"Do I get a choice?"

"Great," Tom said. "First, I want your ideas on forensic tests for anyone who might have walked away from that mine shaft where they found Umberto Rodriguez. Geological traces you might expect to find in the shoes, that sort of thing."

I said. "That would be clays and such. That's volcanic rock up there. A rhyolite, I think, by the look of it. Volcanics rot out to certain clays pretty fast, and it's the clays that a person wouldn't think to clean off of his shoes. At least not someone so ignorant as to have left oolitic sand and brine shrimp on Rodriguez's shoes."

Tom grinned appreciatively.

I shook my head, more at myself than at him. He had his ways of giving me strokes, and I had to admit that I liked getting them.

We walked back to the parking lot at the Red Lion Inn and I pulled out my map atlas and spread it on the hood of my truck. "Near as I can figure from what the sheriffs were saying last night, this is where Rodriguez's body was found. It's not far off my route to the Black Rock. I'll grab you some rock and soil samples if you like."

"No, I'll have the boys out of Reno do it. It has to be done with proper chain-of-custody documentation to be admissable as evidence," he said. "But I do need you to make one more stop on your way, if you would."

"All right. What is it?"

"I need you to go see Shirley, that blind woman back in Lovelock. I had a few more questions for her, but it was clear she wasn't going to talk to me. But I have a feeling she *will* talk to you."

33

BEFORE I HEADED OUT TOWARD LOVELOCK, TOM offered me the use of a cell phone.

"No way," I said. "I don't want you jingling me up any old time you want. Besides, where I'm going, there are no cell phone repeaters, or if there are, I'm going to keep on going until there aren't any."

Tom smiled. "I envy that. Well then, my little mouse, if you won't let me give you a jingle, then let's put a bell on the cat. Here's my cell phone number." He got out a pen and wrote it down on one of his business cards. "Call me on this number as soon as you've spoken with the lady. If you don't get through to me, try Faye's cell number. I'll write that here, too."

"Sure thing, kitty."

"Jing-a-ling." He waved good-bye.

I aimed the truck toward Lovelock, and started off. I was short on sleep, but aside from that, things were looking up. I figured to stop in at the blind woman's house, chat her up, phone in my report to Tom, and move on. I could still be in the Black Rock Desert by noon. By nightfall, I would put Kyle Christie, Virgil Davis, John Steinhoff, Laurel Dietz, Donald MacCallum, and all the rest of the gang at Granville Resources out of my mind.

But of course, that mind of mine got to drifting over the details of the case. As I rolled over the miles of asphalt ribbon, I did not meditate on Ray and his perhaps desperate proposal—it was beginning to occur to me that his timing had reflected outright fear that I would do what I had now done (leave)—but instead pondered the meetings with Stephen Giles, Umberto Rodriguez, "Auntie" the diamond lady, and even Rudolf the gold fanatic. My thoughts touched on Gretchen MacCallum and her peacefully chaotic kitchen, and

I wondered if she was still as calm as on the day I had spoken with her.

As I passed from the area of burned sage and desert soils into the untouched sweep of gray-green desert slopes, I decided that the case was a hopelessly snarled mess, and yet oddly miscellaneous. On the face of it, a mining company had set up a new mining facility and had bought up some old claims, hoping to find a second ore body so that they could achieve an economy of scale and continue production. The price of gold was declining, so continued operation required that the cost of production not exceed the value per ounce of the shining metal. Snags in permitting had occurred when it was discovered that a possibly endangered rodent lived in the new project area. The biologist tasked to survey the mice had reported them hale and hearty and identical to untold millions of mice over a ten-county area, and was found dead the night before the posse was due to haul her in for questioning. The BLM agent who had reported her to the FBI seemed weird and nervous, and had crashed his car and puked; hardly actionable offences, but, as Deputy Weebe might say, he bore watching. Beyond this, the geologist who had been prospecting for the new project had gone AWOL, and things seemed to be flying about a bit up at the Gloriana Mine. But all these events might mean very little and in fact be coincidental.

These events had added up to a great big ignorable nothing, in fact, until Rodriguez was found obviously murdered. That had been one coincidence too many. It seemed odd that anyone would go to the trouble of bringing his corpse all the way back from Utah, but it made sense if it was done to cover the fact that Rodriguez had been in Utah, because that knowledge of that fact would point to his murderer. *And what was he doing in Utah?* Naturally, I got to wondering if Rodriguez knew Morgan Shumway. *Could there be a connection there?*

There were more than a few moving parts to this case that I did not understand. I was in fact so unsure about the whole thing that I didn't even know what questions to ask. And now that I thought about it, Tom had once again sent me to question a woman without giving me any specific guidance re-

garding what to ask her. That realization quickly collided with
an important question: How had Tom gotten involved with
the case in the first place? Why not just Ian, the local operative? Was it standard operating procedure for the likes of
Tom Latimer to fly clear across the Great Basin to investigate
the neuralgic worries of a BLM agent?

At Lovelock, I followed the first ramp off the highway and
headed back to the blind woman's house, half furious with
Tom for having once again played me so expertly, and half
downright impressed. He wasn't just a Zen master, he was a
master at sleight of hand. But I had reason to hope that Shirley knew something that would at least tell me in which hand
he was hiding the missing piece, and I knew just how to use
my irritation at Tom to get her to talk.

"WHO'S THERE?" ASKED the blind woman. She stood just
inside her screened door tipping her head this way and that,
as if picking up a radio transmission that would tell her what
I looked like.

"My name is Em Hansen. I was here a few days ago with
a couple of guys from the FBI," I replied. "Um, they don't
know your last name, so I don't know what to call you."

"Call me Shirley," she said. "Come on in, Em."

She led me in into her kitchen and touched a chair on
which she wanted me to sit.

"Coffee?" she inquired. "You seem a black, no sugar type
to me."

"You are clairvoyant." I was in fact suprised by her welcome, after the way she had hurried us out of her house the
time before.

"A big cup," she said. "You seem tired."

"Thank you. And yes, I am tired." I sat down and patted
the long-haired cat that lay on the next chair. It narrowed its
eyes at me, a cat's way of saying it liked me.

"I had a feeling you'd be back," she said, cutting to the
chase. "All on my own. I didn't need Hermione to foretell
this one."

Hermione. So that *had* been the Paiute shaman standing by Shirley's gate the day before.

Shirley said, "She said you were here yesterday, but didn't come in."

"I drove by. But I wasn't trying to find you, really," I said, taking care to keep my tone calm and matter-of-fact. I already disliked the way this conversation was going. I began to wonder if I should leave.

Shirley laughed. "Hell no. *We* were trying to find *you*." She cackled slightly and set a cup down in front of me. "And don't be so frightened. We mean you no harm. Quite the contrary."

How did she know I was frightened? I peered hard at Shirley to make certain that she did not in fact have functioning eyes behind her ruined eyelids. She did not. I cleared my throat. "Well, we'll get back to that, I'm sure," I said, trying to hang onto my last shred of control over the conversation. "But first, you should know right up front that Tom Latimer sent me. He's that guy I came with before. And I will report to him. And you have the right not to answer any and all questions."

"Okay then, Miss Hansen, why do *you* think you're back?" She tipped back her head and brayed with laughter.

"I'm back because things have heated up around the Patricia Gilmore case. Understand, the FBI was here not to investigate her death, but to look into her work. The thing is, now this other guy she worked with—Umberto Rodriguez—has also been found dead." I waited to gauge Shirley's response to this news.

She pursed her scarred lips a moment, then smiled and said, "Good riddance."

"I had a feeling you might think that. I found him offensive, myself. I didn't know Pat Gilmore, but I'm willing to bet she would have loved to watch him shoot out of this universe like a watermelon seed."

Shirley roared with laughter at this image. She said, "You have some anger there."

I brought myself up short. She had me off balance and

talking too much, and was reading my feelings entirely too
accurately. I decided to walk right into her attack, the best
defense being a surprise offense of pure candor. "You're
right. I've worked with too many annoying men for too many
years. I'm always on their playing field, and I don't find that
to be a level place. And you know, for years I thought it was
just sexual discrimination, but then I realized that men crap
on each other, too. It's how they do business. Everything's a
big pecking order thing, a big paranoid job of who's got
power over whom, and when I met Rodriguez he one-upped
me by making a big show of recognizing my gender. So am
I angry? Yes. Because now I see that he couldn't just do that
alone; he needed the passive cultural complicity of the two
men who were standing right next to me, and they can fuck
themselves, too."

Shirley Cook thumped a hand on the table in her laughter,
her ravaged face drawn back into a rictus grin. "Oh, that's
rich," she howled. "Passive cultural complicity, that's glorious."

I began to see why Tom thought she would talk to me and
not him, but so far, I had done all the talking, and there was
something about this woman that was bringing out every
ounce of malice I held toward the male of the species. I did
not like it one bit. She had me seeing only black in a full-
color world.

"Exactly," she said. "If your friends weren't playing the
same game, Rodriguez's behavior would mean nothing."

I forced myself to take several long, deep breaths. I said,
"Something like that. But the thing is, Rodriguez was murdered. So perhaps I *should* tell you why I'm really here."

With abundant sarcasm, she replied, "That *would* be helpful."

"I am not sure why I'm here."

She let out guffaw.

I said, "Tom Latimer asked me to come talk to you, but
he didn't give me any direction. I could analyze that to death,
but I won't. I'm just going to tell you that he's been keeping
me in the dark about certain aspects of this case, and that

annoys me. Tom's the only one that knows what the case is really about. But it serves a purpose: it keeps old Emmy snapping at the bait."

Shirley continued to laugh. I was clearly making her day.

I took a long suck at my coffee. "So what do you think? Is there something you know about Pat Gilmore, or about her work, or about her death, that I should know? You see? I don't even know what questions to ask."

The cat had moved from my lap onto Shirley's. She stroked it for a while, making me wait for an answer. "Patsy Gilmore had a hot temper. She made me look cool, and that's a trick."

"Even hotter'n me?" I asked ironically.

"Oh, yes. Patsy was a volcano. But she was good at her work. She knew her species and subspecies, no matter what Rodriguez might suggest. And she knew how to go about a survey. She knew, for instance, to talk up the old-timers in the area, like an old squatter named Sam. He sent her around to talk to me."

"Do you mean the guy who lives up in Rosebud?"

"Lived. Sam was a smart old weasel," she said bitterly.

"*Was*? Then he *died*?"

"Yes, last night."

A wave of remorse washed over me. "I just met him yesterday. He'd taken a fall. I should have—"

"Don't be sorry," Shirley said forcefully. "He had a mess of cancer. He'd been hanging by a thread for months. He knew his time was coming, and about the last thing he wanted was to die in a bed all done up in funny pajamas with tubes coming in and out of him. It was *quality* of life that appealed to Sam, not *quantity*."

"Did a woman named Sally call to tell you? I mean, he wasn't alone, was he?"

"Nah. Folks like Sam are never alone. He was on a first-name basis with half the critters out there. And Hermione was with him."

"Oh, so Sally called *her*?"

Shirley let out a cackle. "No one has to call Hermione.

She smells things in the wind, if you know what I mean, but yeah, some woman called her and she went out there and did her bit with the smoke and eagle feathers and phoned me this morning to say that his 'passage into the spirit world' was a good one. Injun stuff. You understand?"

"I suppose so. . . ."

"Well, I don't," she said sourly. "But don't you go sending your FBI guys out there looking for his body. You won't find it."

"Why not?"

Shirley laughed sardonically. "Hermione gave him a Paiute send-off."

"What exactly does that entail? Do they hide their dead?"

That brought Shirley up short. After a moment, she said softly. "They take them out into the desert and hide them so that grave robbers won't dig them up for their belongings."

Something struck me. "Is *that* why Hermione wanted the mine moved? Does she have kin buried in an old adit up there?"

Shirley shook her head, impressed with my guesses. "You're quick, just like Hermione said."

"I've never met Hermione!" I squealed.

"No, you haven't met her in the sense you mean. But she knows about *you*."

"How long had Sam lived out there?" I asked, desperately trying to deflect the subject.

"Ten, twelve years."

"And you say he was on a first-name basis with the animals, and that Pat Gilmore used to talk to him?"

"He was a good observer. He saw a lot of things."

"What did he see?" I asked, staring into her empty sockets.

Shirley aimed those sockets at me as if they had eyes, lending drama to her next words. "Well, to answer that question, I need to back up here a bit, and tell you a story."

She leaned back in her chair, preparing herself to tell her tale, working her audience by making it wait. "A long time ago, there was a girl, and she had a brother. This girl and this brother went hiking in the hills and found an old adit. They decided to play. Now, this brother, he was a bit impulsive, and when he found a stick of dynamite in that adit, he decided to wave it around a bit and tease his sister with it. It was very old dynamite, you see, and extremely unstable, and it went off just from the shaking."

My breath hissed as it came in through my teeth.

"Yes. That brother was killed. That girl was me. You might divine from this that I am not particularly fond of mines."

I shook my head, oblivious that Shirley could not see me shake it.

"Just so. Well, the years have gone by, and folks have pitied me, and I have lived in this community. I am an irascible old bitch. Don't much care for company. I cannot truly live alone, and I know that, or I'd probably be out there in Rosebud or Scossa like the Sams of this world."

She paused to take a sip at her coffee, then continued. "So I must be practical. I must keep in mind that mining is the major economic support of this district, and so I do not bite the hand that feeds me. But I do have my opinions. I can remember what this place looked like, when I could see it. It was big, and wide open, and brown in high daylight, and shades of grayish green and lavender when the sun touched low to the horizon. Yes, I can remember all that. And I remember what the animals were like who lived amongst the little bushes, all running around out there in the dark to avoid the birds of daytime, with their little trails that wind between the gray-green sagebrush, and the yellow rabbit brush, and the red paintbrush, and the tiny white phlox, and all the rest. And I remember the gray coyotes, and the flittering birds, and the tawny antelope, and all the insects that sprang up and went splat against my father's windshield. And the clouds, oh how I loved the shapes of the clouds. The mare's tails that foretell a storm, and the big thunderheads of summertime, and the heat dancing above the ground that feeds them. I listen to them still, listen to their thunder, and the shock of silence when you're all alone out there, not listening to this old refrigerator hum."

Her voice dropped down to a whisper. "I *love* this country. And if I can't live out there like I'd like to, then I want to save it for the little animals."

I sat completely still, afraid to break her reverie.

She took a deep breath and continued, her voice back at a normal level. "So I started me a little consciousness-raising group, and gathered together a few folks who feel like I do, but there aren't that many. Had to link up with a few Indians over there at Pyramid Lake, and with folks from out of state. You have to be careful, but they can do you some good. You're listening carefully now, I can tell."

"Yes."

"That's good. You see, the whole idea is to pay attention. Listen to the Earth, Hermione would say. Well, along comes Patsy Gilmore like a rogue buffalo, all stamping and snorting, but she's a good girl and she's willing to call things as she sees them. And she comes to me, and I tell her a few things, and she does herself a good job. Pat Gilmore was assigned by her company to study the little rodents that live out by the Kammas. She was supposed to add that to the EIR she was filing."

Was she about to tell me that Pat Gilmore had found the animals to be increasing their numbers, as Giles and Rodriguez had said? Or had she found something else, which they had not reported? I leaned toward her. "I was told that she found the mouse in question alive and well and increasing its range. Was that true?"

"Oh, yes. That statement is true. As far as it goes."

"What are you saying?"

"It's too bad you can't go out there and talk to Sam. He'd have told you that three years ago, some bounty hunter went out there and shot all the coyotes in and around the Kammas. Now, if you snatch out the top predator from your food chain, what exactly do you think is going to happen?"

"The rodents are going to breed until they run out of food."

"Exactly. *Boom*, mice by the millions. But that doesn't mean the ecosystem is healthy. Too many mice in one small space with no one eating the sick ones, and disease runs right through them. And some of those diseases can get us humans, too. Hanta virus, for instance. Then you add the range fires we've been having, with all this cheat grass brought in by the cattle that shouldn't have ever been here, and not only do the mice die because they don't have anything to eat, but the coyotes can't come back even if someone stops killing them. There's nothing for the antelope, either. Or the birds. Seen many of them out there?"

"Come to think of it, no. But I'm from Wyoming, where it's less arid. I thought—"

"You thought there were no seed-eaters because it's a desert. That's crap. The Paiutes lived on rabbits and birds out here, and on seeds. They harvested pine nuts until we cut down all their trees for fire wood, and they had a festival each year for marsh birds down on the lake that used to seasonally fill the Carson Sink before we diverted that water for irrigation. And what are we growing? Cantaloupes. Great use of the resource. We dried up Lake Winnemucca there next to Pyramid Lake—nothing there but a dry valley now—and we had Pyramid Lake itself half gone before the Indians finally learned how to make us stop."

"I think I begin to get the picture."

"Twelve thousand years the Indians lived here before white man came. We called them primitive. Hell, I'd like to see any one of *us* go out there and last a day without a cooler full of food from the supermarket. And those Indians weren't perfect, but they got along without lying and cheating and shooting each other, either. And it's amazing they're still here, after they got their first dose of cholera. Some accounts will tell you that nine out of ten of the Paiutes died the first big emigrant year."

"But wait," I said. "I can play devil's advocate here. I read about the animals that lived here before the Indians came. Camels, cheetahs, mammoths. One theory says that they died not just from the change in climate, but also because the first humans killed the few that were left."

Shirley took a noisy suck at her coffee. "That is as it may be. Over there on the California coast, you can go through the shell middens left by the coastal tribes, see what they were eating. They'd move into an area and hunt out all the abalone first, then the next favorite, then the next, and eventually they'd end up with nothing but nasty little snails and move on. And while I don't think for a minute that any mammoth could still make a go of it in modern-day Nevada, the first red men may have hastened their demise. Sure. But let's look at what they were doing right. They had no guns, no metals, no wheels, no domesticated animals, and yet they got along. The Paiutes here were one of the least warlike of all the tribes. They lived humbly."

"Hunter-gatherers," I said.

"Right, they did not farm. When the cycles in nature supported it, they ate well. When cycles of cold or dryness came, they suffered. It was a simple justice. They had no need for digging holes in the ground," she said, her lips drawn into an ugly sneer, "except to bury their dead."

"What is a Paiute burial like?" I asked softly, thinking of Sam.

"Paiutes believe that you have to get rid of the body so the ghost won't haunt you. So you take it away with all its belongings and put it where it can't be found. They don't want anyone digging it up for its goods, or the ghost will get loose again and there comes trouble." She laughed. "I wonder if Hermione buried that filthy couch he had."

We were getting pretty far afield. "You were telling me about how Pat Gilmore understood the ecology," I prompted. "And about what she was putting in her EIR."

"Yes. Patsy." Her face fell.

I waited in tense silence, hoping I had not cut off her garrulousness.

At length, she cleared her throat and continued. "You were wondering what Patsy found out there, and I told you. And she was getting ready to write her report. She had all her documentation ready. Well, on the night she died, she phoned me."

I stayed quiet as a mouse. Here it was, the answer to the question I did not know to ask.

"Yes, she phoned me from her office out by the mine. She said all hell was breaking loose. She said Rodriguez had been harassing her by trying to make her look like a lesbo, and he'd been calling her on the carpet with her superiors at Intermontane Biological. All that I knew; it had been going on for a while. But what I didn't know was all the rest. About what was going on at Granville Resources, and at the Gloriana Mine."

I said, "You have my undivided attention."

"Well, now, maybe I shouldn't be telling you all this. I kept my silence for a reason, and—"

"You can't stop there!"

"Until I heard about that guy Rodriguez being murdered, I thought it best to keep my silence, but now . . ."

"*Now*, Shirley!"

Shirley cleared her throat and continued.

"A thing you may not know is that such environmental posturing is all a bunch of crap the BLM puts on so citizens like you think they're doing their job."

"What?"

"This is true. Some of us call the BLM the 'Bureau of Logging and Mining.' Out here, their express purpose in life—their policy—is to promote mining. There has never, in the history of their governance, been a mining project turned down for environmental reasons."

"You're telling me that environmental concerns are not, in fact, holding up Granville's project?"

"Exactly. Something funny is going on out there at Granville Resources."

"What?" I demanded to know.

Shirley said, "Rodriguez was on the take."

This didn't make sense. "Surely holding up the project wouldn't earn him anything from Granville."

"Maybe I should say Rodriguez was on the *make*. He wanted that mouse listed as endangered, *and* he wanted to be the only one who could identify it. *The* expert. So's folks would have to call him in if anyone in a three-state area had even the tiniest notion of digging a culvert, or blading a road, or any construction—a house, a school—that might impact the natural habitat of his pet subspecies."

"So if Pat—"

"He wanted her out of that job. *He* wanted in. It was a slick little scheme he had."

I said, "But wait a minute, isn't that a—"

"A conflict of interest?" Shirley leaned back in her chair and sighed heavily. "Heavens, yes. But on the other hand, it did not run counter to my own interests, so . . ." her voice lost its volume. "I kept my mouth shut. And I told Pat to do the same."

"Because her population numbers would have made the permitting possible?"

"Yes, and because there was no way she should trust those men." She laughed bitterly. "Seems I was right about that, wasn't I?"

"But the new mine at the Kammas was possibly going to be an open pit mine, like the big ones at the Carlin trend," I said. "I should think you'd move heaven and earth to stop one of those from getting permitted."

"Oh, don't get me started on those!" She whipped one hand back and forth in front of her face, as if fending off an annoying insect. "They mine eight hundred feet below the water table, did you know that? To do that, they have to run pumps around the clock, a ring of them, pumping two hundred and fifty thousand gallons a day. There's *water* in that ground, water like you wouldn't believe, and the only people beyond a few citizens like me and the poor witless ranchers—all ought to be shot anyway—who are objecting are the assholes down in Las Vegas, who want the water to spray up into the air in their gaudy big fountains. And they want it for their motels, for when the idiots from New Jersey fly in and want to take long, hot baths and flush the toilet for each ounce they piss!"

I said, "I've heard that—"

"Those mines up by Carlin are a mile across! And they're a thousand feet deep, and like I told you, eight hundred feet of that is below the water table! And do you know what their remediation program is, for after they're done ripping that out of there, for a half ounce of gold per ton? They turn off the pumps and let it fill up into a lake!" She slammed her hand onto the table top, scaring the cat.

I said, "And let me guess—"

"You don't have to guess!" Shirley bellowed. "That water will not be potable, like they claim, because they don't know and they don't care. They don't *live* here!"

As silence fell in the small kitchen, I noticed that the cat had found a safe corner of the floor and was washing itself. I kind of wanted to take a bath, myself. I understood her rage, but it seemed to be the kind that goes looking for a target more than a solution. After what seemed like a respectful interval, I said, "You wouldn't tell the FBI all of this, so why tell me? Is there something you want from me, Shirley?"

"Isn't that obvious? I want the damned mines closed!"

"And you think I'm going to help you?"

Shirley's ravaged face stiffened.

I said, "And Hermione. Is she out to end mining, too?"

Shirley exploded. "Hell, no. She'll give you some claptrap about harmony and balance. There is no balance in mines. It's just greed and take, take, take, and to hell with anyone who gets hurt in the process!"

I took a moment to breathe. I had no interest in pointing out to her how thoroughly her life had been supported by mining, from the asphalt shingles that kept the storms out, to the nails and stucco that held her house together, to the clay in the kitchen and bathroom porcelain than made it possible to use chemicals to keep her living space sanitary enough so that she could live to be an old woman. That was all basic stuff. She had said it herself: She wouldn't last long if she had to gather grasses and build herself a hut like the Paiutes had a scant hundred and fifty years earlier. And it was split- ting hairs to suggest that she was going after gold mining in particular, a commodity she felt she could do without. Cer- tainly, gold was an abstraction to her, and she would argue that she could live without gold crowns in her teeth or the marvels of high-speed computing and communications. She had lived most of her life before their impact had even been felt. But there was something sadder, and more frightening in her tirade. I sensed beneath everything, beneath even her anger, a deep and abiding self-loathing which said, *I am a human. Humans destroy things. We have no right to walk upon this earth.*

I stared into my coffee, pondering her outburst. Oddly, it reminded me of Ian's tirade in support of the pro-mining end of the spectrum. Where she was self-loathing, he had been as self-indulgent. Where did the balance lie?

I decided to ask the few last questions I could muster and get back on the road. "A woman named Gretchen MacCallum said that Pat had told her husband that she was about to blow the whistle. Did she tell you about that when she called that night?"

"You mean Don's wife."

"Yes. You know him?"

"Funny little gopher. He had the gall to come pick my brains about the old mine properties out there in the Kammas."

"Why do you call him a gopher?"

"They're all alike. Busy little scrabblers, digging their little holes in the ground."

"Let's get back to Pat Gilmore," I said, avoiding further doses of her bitterness.

She was silent for quite a while, but then said, "Yeah. Pat was on her way to Reno to give her data to a guy on the radio there."

That all tucked together, as far as it went, but it didn't explain why someone might take the trouble to kill her, and it didn't explain who had killed Rodriguez, or why. "So she was going to expose Rodriguez."

Shirley's head snapped my way, as if she were looking at me. "Oh, hell no. She said he was small potatoes. She was after someone I never heard of. Some grifter named Morgan Shumway."

34

I STOPPED AT THE LOCAL SUPERMARKET TO GET A snack, and then drove around looking for a relatively private pay phone from which to raise Faye Carter, who, it seemed, was still waiting for Tom at the Winnemucca airport. "Oh. Em," she said. "What's the haps?"

"Tom told me to report in on some stuff. Can you jot down a few notes?"

"Sure, but he'll be here any minute. You can tell him yourself."

"Nope. Sorry. Kind of in a hurry." *In a hurry to go where he can't find me.*

"Okay. Shoot."

"Thanks. But first, did you ever get hold of 'Auntie'?"

"Oh. Yes," said Faye. "She said she's unaware of any environmental group trying to block the expansion of Granville Resources' mines in Nevada, or anywhere else for that matter. Not them specifically, anyway. She knows that there was a dust-up over the Gloriana Mine when it first started up, but thought that it just involved the Paiute nation."

That tallied with Shirley's story. "Did you tell Tom all this?"

"No. Was I supposed to?"

I smiled into the phone. The woman had the makings of a good friend. "No, but please tell him now. Ready for the notes?"

"Ready and waiting."

I began by telling her the story of Shirley Cook, her agenda, and her unfortunate brother. She made me pause periodically so that she could scribble down notes, and began to hum a tune. It was familiar. Eventually, she equally absentmindedly began to add words to the melody, but although the tune was so familiar I could almost name it, I couldn't understand a word of it. "What's that you're singing?" I asked.

" 'Clementine.' In Latin."

"You intellectuals are all alike. No, you're making this up. But let's get on with the notes, okay?"

She raised her voice and enunciated clearly. "*In caverna, in montanus, excāverant prō aurum, habītāverant metallicus, et fīlīa, Clementia.*"

"You're raving."

"*Mea cara, mea cara, mea car', Clementia, perdita et istī semper, misereō, Clementia.*"

"Okay, okay, I don't want to know how 'ruby lips' comes out in Latin."

"I only know the first verse."

I needed to get on with it and get gone. "What luck. Now, back to business. Tell Tom that Pat Gilmore was on her way to Reno the night she was killed. She was going there to blow the whistle on Morgan Shumway."

"Shumway . . . okay, got it. Anything else?"

I told her about Rodriguez's scam. "What do you think Shumway's up to? This must be what Tom came out to Nevada for. He—"

"Hold on a sec," Faye said. I heard her voice go muffled as she moved the receiver away from her mouth. When she came back on the line, she said, "Tom just drove up. He said to meet us at the airport there in Lovelock, and he'll take your report himself."

"But—"

"I'm fueled up and ready, and I don't need a flight plan for this short a hop. Race ya," she said, and clicked off the line.

I held the phone for a while listening to the dial tone. Finally, I had to concede that the line was dead, and that Tom had me where he wanted me one more time, so I slammed the phone back into its cradle. Then I picked it back up and tried to call Tom again at his number. He didn't answer. Neither did Faye. I paced a tight circle for a half a minute, cussing under my breath. I waited again, tried a second and a third time. Finally, I gave up, got in my truck, and headed for the Lovelock airport.

As Faye's airplane taxied up to the low building where I was waiting, the door popped open and Tom stuck an arm out and waved me toward the plane. I hurried toward it and, as soon as the propellors stopped moving, climbed in, figuring that Tom was using it as a private place to talk. Instead, he said, "Buckle up. Faye, take off when ready."

"Whoa!" I hollered. "Just where d'you think you're taking me this time?"

Tom grinned. "To a nunnery. Come on, buckle up, we can't take off with you rattling around loose like that."

Ian, who was sitting in a back seat, rolled his eyes.

Faye leaned over and gave me a puckery smile. "Our destination is the Bronco Betty Ranch," she said. "I understand it's a fly-in brothel. It's not far. Maybe twenty minutes."

I popped on my headphones as Faye started the engines again, and switched to intercom so I could talk to Tom. "Speak."

"What did you find out?" he asked. "Something about Pat Gilmore's destination the evening she died?"

"This is kidnapping!" I wailed.

Tom looked gleeful. "We are in fact going to a brothel. But don't worry, I am not selling you into white slavery; the madam is a bookkeeper."

I said, "And . . ."

"And she keeps the second set of books for Granville Resources. It took a little footwork to dig up this little fact, but we have our ways. Ian here figured it out." Tom backhanded Ian's shoulder, a friendly cuff. "Everything is uploaded via satellite from Granville's Reno office, and from the mine. Did I tell you Ian's a whiz with a computer?"

"Telemetry," Ian said, looking smug. "And I cracked their code. Some stupid shit was sending to the madam naughty notes."

Tom patted Ian on the knee. "When they have satellite dishes, you have to ask why," he said. "It took him a little while to figure out where the signal was going. Now tell me about your talk with Shirley."

"I could have given that to you over the phone."

"Yes, but on the phone you can't look over my shoulder into Granville's books. This is where your knowledge of geology-based industries is going to come in very helpful, I'll wager."

"You have a search warrant?" I asked.

"Yes," he answered. "I had to stick my neck out a little to get it, but at the FBI, we're each allowed at least one hunch per decade, and I think something about Granville stinks."

As we skimmed over the summits of the Eugene Mountains and continued north beyond Winnemucca, I pondered the fact that a search warrant cannot be gotten in the blink of an eye. This meant that Tom had been looking for those books for a while, and had discovered their location long enough ago that they had been able to get that warrant. And what significance could Granville's accounting books have to an endangered species fraud? Once again, Tom had been holding out on me.

WE TOUCHED DOWN on the private landing strip at the Bronco Betty Ranch and parked by the satellite dish. It was a nice looking spread: big, sprawling rustic ranch house, several "guest" cottages, and a dolled-up stable with just a few horses. Aside from the animals, the place looked deserted, but I surmised that that was because the human residents were all still asleep, having worked the night shift, as it were.

Faye propped the door open and stuffed her quilted sunshades into the windows so she could wait in the plane while I followed the men to the ranch house. Ian followed a step behind Tom, carrying a notebook computer. We knocked and were admitted by a husky man who wasn't prone to smiling. As he scrutinized Tom's identification, I looked around the room. It was a large common room with open beams that had been converted into a sumptuous party pad with a long carved rosewood bar. There was a big stone fireplace even though the nearest source of firewood had to be a hundred miles west.

At the back of the room, a long hallway led down to rooms with closed doors. To the left, I could see a gleaming kitchen, and just to the right of the bar, there was a closed door with a sign that read OFFICE. Our glum greeter said he'd go find Lefty.

Lefty, who took her time putting in an appearance, strolled in from one of the outer cottages. She turned out to be a pleasantly zaftig woman dressed in shorts and a tank top. She had plenty of curves and an easy manner which included laying a friendly hand on Ian's wrist and calling him love names. Ian blushed exquisitely. She said, "So you want to see some books, do you honey? You have anything that looks like a search warrant? I don't mean to seem unfriendly, but I got to maintain my ethics for my clientele." Having thus de-fanged Ian, she let go of him and gave Tom a voluptuous, ironical smile, having clearly marked him as the alpha wolf in the pack.

This apparently fell well within Tom's sense of funny, because he gave her a grin that showed plenty of teeth. "In fact I do," he answered. He got out his paperwork and showed it to her. "We're specifically interested in a client called Granville Resources, and we will confine our search to their records. Now, mind you, if we don't find anything of interest, no one need ever know we've been here."

Lefty gave him an equally toothy grin, her heavy eyelashes sagging lower, and I was glad for Faye's sake that she had stayed in the plane, although I was certain that, as the day was growing hot, she was going to start to heat up out there pretty damned quickly even without watching her boyfriend getting vamped.

"I like the way you think," Lefty told Tom, "but just to be on the safe side, I'm going to sit with you and let you know when you've wandered out of the places that warrant allows you to go." She unlocked her office and let us in. There, she sat down at a large desktop computer and typed in a password and then navigated until she found what she was looking for. Then she hopped out of her swivel chair and said, "There it is. Have at it."

Tom signalled Ian to take a seat. He inserted a zip drive into the appropriate port. With Lefty's direction, he copied Granville's files onto it, then retrieved the zip drive and said, "I'll just set up my computer, make sure I've got everything."

Tom said, "Why not put it on the coffee table, so I can sit down here and take a little cruise through the numbers with Ms. Lamore."

Lefty shifted her spine coquettishly at Ian, working another blush out of him. "It's your party, cowboy, but why not just step back through that door and use the bar? You can spread out more and sit nice and *upright*." She smeared this last word on him like Vaseline, grabbing him by the wrist again as she said it.

Tom fought to suppress a chuckle. Ian grabbed his case and stormed out the door and into the bar.

Tom sat down, donned a pair of half-glasses that made him look almost professorial, and started scrolling through the records on the screen. "Do you keep a hard copy of this?" he asked.

"No. Client's request," Lefty answered.

"And who set up the account?"

"One Roderick James Adrian Chittenden, in the flesh. I take it he's the big cheese."

"President and CEO," said Tom. "You mind speculating why he came to you instead of using a firm in Reno?"

Lefty laughed. "He probably *does* use a fancy firm somewhere. I usually get the second set of books, if you know what I mean."

Tom arched an eyebrow at her.

She said, "And I keep them straight as an arrow. But you know how it goes, garbage in, garbage out. Sometimes I can smell it."

"And what perfume did our Mr. Chittenden wear?" Tom inquired.

"No smellier than most," Lefty replied. "Flew himself in here in a cute little biz jet. A bit 'king and country' for my tastes, but I kind of liked him. Better tan than most Brits."

"You took him for a royalist?" Tom asked sharply.

"Classic limey," she replied. "Right down to the imperious swagger."

Tom smiled to himself. "Always look to the Crown to have an interest in metals mining," he said.

I asked, "What do you mean?"

Tom shifted about in the seat, stretching what had to be a tired spine. "In days of old, when knights were bold," he began, "gold and metal mines would have been the property of the king. Think it through: In a feudal system, the farmlands and hunting grounds belonged to a handful of overlords who maintained an army to protect their serfs from bandits and local skirmishes. The serfs worked the soil and paid in grain. The overlords organized themselves one way or another beneath a monarch, who was in charge of the big fights, such as fending off neighboring kingdoms who wanted to grab the farmlands. To finance these little skirmishes, the monarch needed money. Gold is universally recognized as cash. But as important sometimes would be the other metals, for making arms and armor and strategic tools. No way our clever monarch wants these resources under the control of anyone but himself."

"But that was the Bronze and Iron Ages," I said. "We've had a little thing called the Industrial Revolution since then."

"Which made the empire even more splendid," said Tom. "With increased efficiency in gun manufacture and shipping, you can expand your network."

Lefty settled her splendid buttocks on the edge of the desk. It was clear that she liked Tom. But I wondered at how casually she had opened these books.

"The days of empire are over now," I observed.

"Old-fashioned empire, yes. But now our revolutions are coming closer and closer together. We're in the technological revolution, in which tricks like communications through satellite dishes are possible. One no longer needs a physical, land-based stronghold in order to hold power. Now, one can rule by forming strong corporate structures that resemble the mythic hydra. You cut off its head in America, and it laughs at you through the mouth it keeps in South Africa, or the one in Canada, or Panama. And then they organize, collectivize."

"But—"

"Look at OPEC if you don't believe me, Em, or NAFTA. Their days of power wax and wane like any other kingdom, but their influence over the way we govern, over our daily lives, is extreme, and their effects are felt instantaneously. We are passing out of the days when land and army based superpowers ruled the globe. With the invention of the microchip, and global communications, we have catapulted ourselves into an age when we must once again fight like dogs for what we think right. If you don't believe me, then you haven't been paying attention to what the World Trade Organization has done to our environmental legislation." He turned his face back to the computer screen. He was no longer smiling. "These organizations do not exist for the betterment of human rights or for environmental conservation, nor do they necessarily give a shit about our bill of rights, our constitution, or our system of governance. America is the last great superpower, and, while certain corporate wise guys have been busy taking advantage of the openness of our society, the best among us have been leading the world out of oppressive systems of government. So let's not let the multinational corporations drag us into a new form of feudalism."

"What do you think is going to happen from here?" I asked, trying to take in everything he'd just said.

"I don't know," he said. "And that, my dear, is what has caught my attention."

Well, that was all a bit beyond my grasp, so I turned my attention to Lefty, hoping to understand her better than I could decipher Tom. "You seem oddly jolly about having this account busted," I said.

Without turning his head, Tom shifted his eyes to Lefty, awaiting her reply.

"You may draw your own conclusions," she said, not denying my observation.

I moved over and stood behind Tom as he shifted through the records. To Ian, Tom called, "Let me know when you find something interesting." Not if, when.

I asked, "What do you expect to find?"

"Payoffs."

Lefty pulled herself up and reached toward the keyboard, leaning against Tom's other shoulder. She began moving the cursor through the records. "Try over here," she said, bringing up a ledger and resorting the list of checks by payee. "Perhaps you're looking for little ornaments like this." She moved back to the couch, sat down, and put her feet up on the coffee table.

I looked over Tom's shoulder again. She had highlighted a miscellaneous series of checks that were by name only, no company. One of them was drawn to a certain civil servant.

"Ian," Tom called. "Search on Stephen Giles."

From the other room, Ian answered, "Got it."

To me, Tom said acidly, "Not even six figures. Don't you hate it when public servants sell themselves so cheaply? Now, the question is, what exactly did he have to sell?" He tapped the screen. "I want to know who was signing those checks. Do you get the originals?" he asked Lefty.

"No. But the bank would at least microfilm them before destroying them. Or if the customer asks for them, they send the originals. But I don't get them. I just get the statement, and that only electronically."

To Ian, Tom called, "Phone Reno. Get onto this account. Seize all checks at the bank." To himself, Tom murmured, "What I wouldn't give to see one of those checks in its original envelope."

"Why?" I asked.

"Because I want this gang on mail fraud, just in case I can't make anything else stick."

"Ian!" I called.

"What?"

"That bit with Stephen Giles slamming his car door on some guy's arm. Didn't you tell me he dropped an envelope on the pavement?" The fever of the chase was upon me. My mind was humming. The experience of working this close to Tom was exhilarating.

Ian stepped into the doorway, already dialing his cell

phone. "Yes. But it was addressed to someone else."

I said, "Well, maybe he keeps a box under his name. Was he anywhere near a post office when he dropped it?"

Ian paused to think, then answered, "Yes. The downtown Reno office is a few blocks away."

"Get a warrant," Tom said. "We now have cause. And get after that storage locker of his, too. Get on the phone. Now."

"You got it."

Tom leaned back in the swivel chair and closed his eyes in meditation. I moved around beside him and watched him a moment, trying to reconcile Ian's revelation that he was a man of some standing within the Bureau with my previous assumption that he was a political has-been who had been ditched at a remote office. Tom the Zen master would not chase clear across the Great Basin to investigate a wildlife biologist accused of faking species population numbers, and neither would he show such great interest in a bottom-ranked BLM agent who was taking bribes, or even in a junior mining company that was paying them. There had to be something bigger that had caught his interest. Something much bigger, and more centrally repugnant to him. I said, "You're still holding out on me. *Damn* it, Tom. Why?"

His eyes flicked open. They were hard as flint. "It's my job," he said. "You want in?"

I leaned very close, lowering my lips towards his ear. Almost at a whisper, I said, "I like my freedom."

Tom stared into the computer screen. He did not reply.

I was just opening my mouth to say something spiteful, when Ian stepped back in from the bar. "Reno is going after those warrants," he announced. "But it may do us no good. Giles has split."

Tom swiveled quickly around to face him. "Gone? Where?"

"No report yet. I just had someone call him, and he didn't show up to work this morning, and didn't call in to say why. No answer at his house. I'm talking right now to someone who's on his way to that storage locker where he was keeping that suitcase." He stopped talking for a moment, shielding his other ear to listen more closely. Then he looked up. "Locker's empty."

Tom said, "Get someone to that post office. Ask if he's been seen there. Then cover the airports."

"I'm on it." Ian disappeared back into the bar.

To Lefty, I said, "Are there any really big drains on this account?"

She moved in again and went at it with the keys, moving down the debits list to a string of extremely large drafts, no name, only a number. "That'll be an account in the Caymans," she said.

"Chittenden's siphoning off funds," Tom said, and very drily, added, "The stockholders won't like that."

I said, "Not stockholders, limited partners."

"Right," said Lefty. "The stockholders would demand oversight. But if you want a big infusion of cash that's harder to trace, you set up a limited partnership for a specific phase of development, and the cash can go straight into a separate war chest."

Tom nodded to her. "If your other talents are anything like your accounting skills, then I hope they don't go wasted."

Lefty gave his shoulder a squeeze.

Tom said, "But still there's something wrong with this picture. Granville has to drill eventually, and it costs big money to drill. If he keeps draining the war chest at this rate, there will be no money to pay for it. And then Chittenden's little hustle will be plain as day." He rubbed his eyes. "This one goes to the Securities and Exchange Commission anyway," he muttered. He looked annoyed. "Except that a limited partnership is too cute. Granville can make up some story about where the funds went. Investors bite on this kind of cookie every day of the week."

I said, "But this isn't even what you were looking for."

He looked at me, his eyes steady. I realized that he was waiting for me to say something else.

"It wasn't Chittenden you were after," I said.

His eyes gleamed even more brightly.

"So this is where Morgan Shumway fits in."

Tom's eyelids lowered and lifted again, a slow blink. "Yes, Morgan Shumway," he said, satisfied with my progress.

I wanted to scream.

The intensity of Tom's gaze reeled me toward him, riveting my attention on him and him only. I felt like I was falling into his eyes. It was an electric moment, an instant on the brink between go and stay, heaven and hell. I began to lose track of which way was up. I whispered, "Morgan Shumway is a lawyer. What kind of law did you say?"

"His firm works exclusively in support of environmental interests."

My brain jammed in place. It did not fit that Rodriguez should phone an environmental lawyer and then turn up murdered. Unless . . .

"Think it through," Tom said.

I blinked. Moments ticked past. "An endangered species case. What exactly does Morgan Shumway do with environmental interests?"

Tom nodded slowly, rewarding his student. "He has made a specialty out of suing the U.S. Fish and Wildlife Service."

So this was what had drawn Tom Latimer across the Great Basin. He had not been interested in Pat Gilmore, or Stephen Giles, or even Granville Resources, except as doors in toward Morgan Shumway. "But the Fish and Wildlife Service is the agency that lists species as endangered," I said.

"Precisely," Tom replied. "But the Fish and Wildlife Service has suffered budgetary cutbacks, just like everybody else, which has resulted in such an enormous case backlog that they seldom even start the process toward listing a given species until someone sues them to do so."

"And you're about to tell me that Shumway's suing to list the newly identified subspecies of jumping mouse," I said. All the little parts of the puzzle were beginning to click together.

"Yes."

"But if it is in fact endangered, then the Fish and Wildlife Service will list it. I don't see how that would benefit—"

Tom's face had grown tight with anger. "Oh, it absolutely

benefits the Morgan Shumways of the world. Because if they list it, then he has won his suit. And if he wins, he recovers court costs and legal fees."

"And those fees add up to a fat income, right out of the taxpayers' pockets," I said. "What a parasite! And then the Rodriguezes of the world move in and charge you five thousand dollars a pop to tell you whether you can put in a temporary road. He didn't care whether it was really a distinct sub-species or not, or even if it was truly endangered. He was just a blood-sucker who had found a red corpuscle to dine on!"

Tom nodded. "Ticks. I spend my life chasing ticks and leeches."

Lefty had lowered a hand to the keyboard and was scrolling through the data to another payee entry. "Looks like threatening to sue can pay handsomely." She pointed to the screen. There was a nice, fat check drawn to Morgan Shumway.

Tom jerked forward in his chair.

I whistled. "I'll bet you won't see that declared on his Form Ten-forty."

Tom said, "In my dreams I hope it to be true. Then I have him on income tax evasion. And he's disbarred. So we want to leave this little bomb just ticking away in place, and see if he fails to declare it."

"But why would Chittenden bribe Shumway?" I asked.

"To drop the case, of course."

"But has he?"

Tom hesitated. "Not yet."

"Then I repeat my question."

Tom leaned back in his chair with his eyes shut and said nothing.

While Tom cogitated, I watched Faye through the picture window. The heat had gotten to her. She was strolling back and forth on the tarmac, looking longingly at the building in which we sat in air-conditioned comfort. She tugged at her shirt front, working it like a bellows. Finally, she headed toward us, striding along on her long legs. I heard the front door open beyond the bar where Ian was sitting, then heard her voice: "Ian! God damn! I been sitting out there all morning in that hot station wagon with those kids and that dog! Now, are you coming home with me, or *what*?"

Like a stuck rabbit, Ian squealed, "That's not funny!"

Tom rolled his head back and roared with laughter.

Faye whooped with embarrassment. "Sorry, Tom! I thought Ian was alone out here."

Faye's jest loosened my brain. Scenes from the previous day raced through my mind. Suddenly, Kyle Christie's tale about Gilbey's Camp floated through my head, of corporate officers setting up beautiful surface operations to thrill the investors while pocketing the cash. I said, "Tom, what if Chittenden was paying Giles to *delay* the permits. And paying Shumway to sue."

Tom opened his eyes and stared at me. "But Giles was holding up the permits because of the mouse," he said.

"Exactly," I said. "You and I are so used to seeing environmental protection laws slow jobs down that we didn't think much of it when Giles held up the permits. But when I talked to Shirley Cook this morning, she asserted that the BLM's first priority is not to protect the environmental resources under their care, but to promote mining. So Giles maybe would have to be paid to *delay* them, not *hurry* them."

Tom said, "Why would Chittenden want to delay permitting?"

"The price of gold is down," I answered. "Granville might be hanging right at the edge of profitability."

"But if that's their problem, they'd want to hurry a new project. Or they could just batten down the hatches and wait for the price to rise. Nobody's forcing them to drill."

I said, "But look at everything that's happened. So far, Granville has only applied for permits on the first phase of drilling, right smack in the area where Pat Gilmore was doing the mouse study. According to Giles, that area is being held up pending the outcome of that survey. So where's Phase Two? Kyle Christie said that Virgil Davis had a big argument with MacCallum, agitating for another area to drill. He gets on MacCallum, and MacCallum disappears. Try connecting those dots."

Tom looked at me like he thought I was nuts. "You think Virgil Davis killed Pat Gilmore, mistakenly thinking she was holding up the project, then killed MacCallum, because he wouldn't cough up a map for Phase Two?"

"No," I said. "But he pissed MacCallum off. From other descriptions I've had of MacCallum, that seems out of character. He sounded easygoing and philosophical. He laughed a lot. So where is he, after this argument? Maybe Chittenden said, 'Don, you're looking kind of tense. Let me just fly you down to the Caymans. I'm in no hurry for that new phase of drilling. I have a wildlife biologist to kill, quick before she busts my permitting holdup, and I have to be back in Reno in the morning to look bright eyed and bushy-tailed when the FBI show up, but I have a jet right here, no sweat.' "

"Or maybe MacCallum is dead."

"Maybe. But one way or another, they don't have his information from which to apply for a second area. Yesterday, Virgil tells Chittenden that Laurel Dietz has a new analysis of MacCallum's data, covering a second area. So what's Chittenden do? He skyhooks her right out of Nevada."

Tom closed his eyes, meditating on my ideas. "Go on."

"Well, that could mean either of two things. First, the obvious guess, he does not want those data made public. And that would mean that she had found nothing, which news he might wish to keep from investors."

"And your less obvious guess?"

"Perhaps even just having a plan presents Chittenden with a problem."

"Explain."

Almost breathless, I said, "*Think* on it, Tom! Pat Gilmore is on her way to go public, showing that on the surface, there's no reason to hold the first permit up. Wham, she's dead. MacCallum could make it possible to file for a second permit, but he has conveniently disappeared. Kyle Christie is sitting on his rump in plain sight, just as if he knows there's nothing he needs to be doing. Rodriguez—" There I stopped.

I had no idea why anyone would kill Umberto Rodriguez. He represented the other side, which would want the permitting at a dead stop. So why kill him? "Okay, maybe Rodriguez got carried away and decided to blackmail Shumway."

Tom asked, "What are you saying?"

"What if Chittenden sees the price of gold dropping, sees the mine about to shut in, and knows damned well that he's got a snowball's chance in hell of getting a new project that's going to make money. Why not pretend he's got a project, but it's just being delayed? Environmentalists use laws and regulations to delay projects until they're unprofitable. It's a standard operating procedure: Tie things up in court. Outlast the developer. Bleed him of all his investment capital. So why couldn't Chittenden buy it done on himself, so he can pocket the money and say, 'So sorry, old chappies, but it's bum luck this time, eh, what?' He tells the investors not to worry, this is just a delay, but in fact he's bought a *delay* from Giles— not a hurry-up—because otherwise the BLM might have rubber-stamped the permitting process. Giles had his bag all packed, ready to go. He got his payment, and he's history."

Faye stood in the doorway with her cell phone in her hand. "I just spoke to 'Auntie' again. She confirmed that no group in Nevada she knows about is protesting Granville's project. But Shumway is. She looked at her desk diary. He phoned her trying to get her group involved with it." She gave the date.

Tom peered into the computer screen. "That's the day after this check from Chittenden was drawn. He must have gotten it FedEx." I'm beginning to like this. I'm beginning to like it a lot. "If you're correct, the payment to Shumway is so he *will* sue to list the mouse. Chittenden says, 'Get that mouse listed, maybe rile up a bunch of environmentalists for me.' Yes, I like this. This way, Shumway is almost certain to hide the funds from the IRS, because he'll be hiding them from everybody else. We wouldn't want the world to know that Shumway the great environmentalist is actually in bed with a mining concern."

I said, "Yes, and it would explain something else. What if

Rodriguez connected the dots and took himself a trip to Salt Lake City to shake down Morgan Shumway? If you're the great environmental lawyer, you wouldn't like that, would you? No, you'd whack the guy on the shores of Great Salt Lake, drive him over to Nevada in his own vehicle, sit him up in the driver's seat, and steer it into a mine shaft. You tell yourself he won't be found for months, if ever, and if he is found, the sheriff will think the fellow just screwed up and found himself a hole to drive into. Meanwhile, your buddy Chittenden knows just where to dump him. He sends the guy out to pick you up and drive you back to Reno, and flies you home to Salt Lake City in his private jet. You're gone less than twelve hours."

Tom was smiling. "You have a devious mind, Em Hansen. Who's our man on the ground?"

It was all beginning to come together. But my heart sank. "Someone who's been over that country looking for gold would know each and every shaft big enough to sink an automobile into." I gritted my teeth. "And here he comes at night, bringing Morgan Shumway over the back road through the Black Rock Desert into Reno, and there's an old squatter named Sam standing by the road trying to flag him down."

Tom said, "Wait, what are you talking about?"

"Sam's an old squatter who lived out there. He was changing a flat on the road the other night. He tried to flag down a passing car, but they wouldn't stop. Next thing he knew, he was waking up seeing stars."

"Where did you say this Sam lives?"

I shook my head. "I said lived. He had badly progressed cancer, and that blow to the head eventually finished him. I helped take him home yesterday. He died last night."

Tom ran his hands through his salt-and-pepper hair. "Do you remember anything else that Sam told you?"

I let my mind idle, so his words could float up. "Something about a white hat. Hey, that could be Shumway's Stetson! Remember the one he set down on the table in that restaurant? Looked like a real cherished item. It had a grosgrain ribbon around the brim. They don't make them like that anymore, do they? It was cream-colored, but in the dark . . . He'd send his clothes to the laundry, but he'd never wash that hat."

Tom showed his teeth. "I've got you now, you so-and-so," he muttered. "Just as soon as I get back to Salt Lake I'll get a warrant."

"I guess it just goes to show you," I said.

"What?"

"The bad guys don't always wear black hats."

Tom nodded. "And what color hat is MacCallum wearing today? Sounds like you suspect him of murder."

I shook my head. "He'd have to be pretty cold to kill an old man like Sam. Besides, he's missing."

Tom said, "But, what if Chittenden's known where he is all along, and has him help Shumway out with a little biologist disposal? But then Sam sees him, so he parks the car down the road and runs back and sneaks up behind him and gives him a tap on the head."

We sat quietly together for a moment, staring at the floor. Then I said, "The only flaw in all this is, how would Chittenden know that Shumway was approachable in the first place? The two of them wouldn't exactly travel in the same circles, and he wouldn't risk approaching just *any* environmental lawyer." But even as I spoke, I remembered Shumway's companion at the restaurant, the young blonde who had flogged her daddy with stories of her wine-bibbing boyfriend, the guy who flew his own jet. "Oh, yeah. The daughter."

"Yes," said Tom. "The daughter. She seemed to address daddy with a certain disregard. That had to come from somewhere."

I said, "That was quite a big diamond she was wearing. Is our boy Chittenden engaged?"

Lefty chimed in. "Nah, ol' Roderick's the type who'd keep himself quite a string of girlfriends. Give 'em shiny baubles and they go down like ten pins. And if you're talking about a rock the size of your thumbnail set in a wad of gold, it's a zircon. He showed it to me last time he stopped in, said he'd won it in a crap game over in Reno. Kind of fits, doesn't it?

Lots of show, but he keeps all the real goodies to himself. Nevada is one big playground for boys like Roddy. Some places are called the land of opportunity. Nevada is the land of opportunists."

Nobody laughed. I shook my head in disgust, thinking of all the soon-to-be-worthless stock Gretchen MacCallum held. When the limited partnership went down, the rest of Granville would probably go with it. And unless we could pin something on Chittenden, he would be sipping rum punches in the Caribbean and laughing over the whole episode like it had been just another jolly good sortie he'd flown in his jump jet.

Tom said, "We still don't know where MacCallum is."

I said, "No, and we still don't know who killed Pat. It's possible we can tie her to Shumway. How about this: He's suing to list the creature even though she says it isn't a sub-species or endangered. She doesn't like the way Shumway stinks, and threatens to expose him. He says he's going to call her back but doesn't, so she takes off. And *bam*, she's dead. While she was waiting for that phone call, he's moved into position out on that road."

"That won't stick," Tom said. "Because when Pat dies, Shumway's sitting at the next table from us in Salt Lake City."

He was right. "Okay, how about Chittenden? We saw him in Reno the next morning, so he was there."

"He was not there," Tom said. "I checked. He had just flown in from cooperate headquarters, where the evening before he was front and center at a big dinner for board members."

"But he could have taken calls there. And made calls. He maybe had someone there at the mine, and told him to go out there and wait for Pat where there weren't any witnesses and put a scare into her. She was not easy to scare. Things might have gotten out of hand."

"But who would that be?" Tom asked.

"Exactly," I said. "Who? Because whoever it is, he's still out there, hiding in plain sight."

* * *

LEFTY FOLLOWED US out to Faye's plane as we loaded up.
Tom turned to her and shook her hand. "Thank you, Ms.
Lamore," he said.

"Oh, think nothing of it," she said. "I may be a whore, but
that doesn't mean I like people screwing with commerce."

Tom gave her an appreciative grin.

"Come back any time," she said.

"Thanks." He turned and climbed into the airplane.

Faye gave Lefty a long, heavy-lidded look that said, Give
up, he's mine.

Lefty replied with a throaty laugh.

On our way back to Lovelock, I watched the miles of
desert sweep away beneath us. We passed back over the Eugene Mountains, where a mine and a mill and all its workers
waited in ignorance as their employer sucked the life fluids
out of their operation. They would be shut down soon, and
all would scatter in frantic search of increasingly scarce jobs.
Many would never work in their chosen professions again.

We passed next over the great, black burn that had jumped
up around Pat Gilmore's crash, and I found myself wondering
how she would have felt to know that in screwing up and
crashing her truck, she had obliterated many of the animals
she had gone to school and trained so hard to defend. Then
my brain bumped over a mental speed bump, and I remembered that I had, only half an hour before, once again included
her in the tally of persons killed to keep Chittenden's scam
going. Which had it been, murder or accident? As we
skimmed lower and lower on our approach back into Lovelock, I turned around and looked at Tom. "I need to talk," I
said.

He nodded. "Wait till we land."

On the ground, Ian busied himself with his cell phone
while Tom led me aside into the shade of the nearest building.
"Speak," he said.

"Pat Gilmore," I said. "First, I decided that she had been
murdered by Stephen Giles or someone else in order to keep

her mouse data under wraps. I based that deduction in part on the timing. That was a beautiful example of drawing the wrong conclusion from the wrong evidence, and Deputy Weebe pulled the same stunt with different evidence. He thought someone had shot out her tire, because there was no spare with the truck when it was hauled into Lovelock.

"Next, I drew the wrong conclusion from the right evidence. I found the spare, and decided that she hadn't been murdered, that she had just had an unfortunate accident. But now, I'm looking at this again. If someone did rig that crash, her spare tire might still fly out into the sagebrush."

Tom cut me off. "You think someone killed her. Who?"

"I don't know. Because now that I know more, I think it was pretty stupid to kill her. Why not just fire her and let Rodriguez and Shumway run their scam?" Besides, I heard Virgil Davis say that he and John Steinhoff found her body, so either they were both in on it, which I doubt—"

"Why?"

"Because Virgil has a soft spot for women. He let me in yesterday, and he let Laurel Dietz go. I had just two quick moments to take her measure, but she's . . ."

"What?"

I chose my words carefully, and adjusted my tone so it would not sound like sour grapes. "Well, she's one of those women whom men think are cute little cupcakes, all sweet and fluffy and wouldn't say shit for a bucketful, but I had a different take. I think she's a taker. I think she's tough as nails."

Tom said, "And you don't think Virgil and John could be tough?"

"My take is that their story is true, that they came on the scene very soon after the crash. For one thing, Virgil said the sage *adjacent* to the truck was already burning, so they hauled Pat's body out and ran for it. You see, it doesn't work that the brush should be burning before the truck, and I don't think that two men who are capable enough to set up that whole mining facility would be so lame that they couldn't make up a better story than that."

"You'd think."

"So then, someone rigged the accident and lit the sage to cover it. Can you get a forensics team on that truck?"

He smiled patiently. "They've been on it since last night. I got a crew out of Reno, a little leg-up to the local authorities."

"Tom!"

"I was going to tell you. There's been so much going on—"

"*Tom!*"

He put a hand on my shoulder. "Hold on. Let me tell you. So far, they have found that the percussion marks on the inside of the truck do not match the photographs which fortunately the medical examiner took of Pat Gilmore's wounds. The killing blow was at the top of her forehead."

"What shape was that wound?" I asked.

"Small. Squarish. They couldn't find anything inside the truck quite that size and shape. And—and you'll like this— they have found a charred bit of sage wood jammed inside the accelerator of her truck."

I blinked, playing the movie in my head. "So someone killed her, stuck her in the truck, jammed the accelerator open, and popped it in gear, aimed at that curve. He—or she— could do that easily. The truck was an automatic, so all he'd have to do is set the brake, jam open the accelerator, then reach in and release the brake. But the truck flipped, so he couldn't get his twig back out of the accelerator."

"There are marks on the hood consistent with failed attempts to jack the vehicle back over onto its wheels."

"And he saw someone coming—Virgil and John, it was dusk, so they had their headlights on, and he would have seen them miles off—so he lit a fire and ran for it."

"That would be my theory," Tom replied. "And I would think that, this time, you were drawing the right conclusion from the right evidence."

Was I correct? I reminded myself how recently I had made all the wrong presumptions regarding that death, and had then done it again. I didn't really know these people, didn't know what made them tick. For all I knew, Virgil and John had rigged the whole thing and played their game of poker with perfectly straight faces. Surely they had more to lose than most anyone else out at the mine if the project shut in. They had built a whole kingdom out there.

Tom shook his head in sympathy. "It may be a crime you cannot solve, Em. You've got to be willing to let those ones go, and pass them on to someone who can at least apply heat in the right places. And sometimes, folks do get away with murder."

I jammed my hands in my pockets, thinking bitterly of all that charred desert, and of Pat Gilmore dying so wrongly out there on her way to do what she thought was right. "Okay," I said, but it wasn't. "Where do we go from here?"

"I've sent someone out to grab those soil samples from the Kammas," Tom answered.

"So you think Shumway killed Rodriguez," I said.

"It's my first guess," he replied. "And this time it *is* the province of the FBI. Federal lands, crossing state boundaries, defrauding the government." He stretched. "Well, that'll be it, then. Thank you, Em."

The case was beginning to unravel right through my fingers. I should have been glad to let it go, and to be rid of Tom and the risk such jobs bring, but I wasn't. I said, "But all this still doesn't tell us where MacCallum is. If he's alive." Even in the desert's heat, I fought off a chill as the image of those thirty-foot-tall vats of cyanide came suddenly to mind.

Tom folded his arms across his chest, watching me.

I stared back. "Well," I said, "I suppose I'm holding you up. You got to get going. Go catch yourself a crook."

He smiled. "I've ordered up a search warrant for the Gloriana Mine complex. It's just into Humboldt County, so we have to go back to Winnemucca to pick it up."

"Well, have fun."

"It's been nice working with you," he said.

I looked away. Neither of us moved.

Tom's smile spread slowly into a grin. "Admit it, Em, this is the work you like to do."

I looked up into his eyes in total misery. "I can't *decide,* Tom."

Tom reached out and touched the top of my head in much the same way my father once did. "Want to just come along for the fun at the mine?" he asked. "You'd be useful up there. You know your way around the facilities. I could use your help. And no bullshit. Everything straight up and out in the open."

The sudden kindness in his touch tingled down through me, and I thought of Ray. I could not decide between the two paths. I wanted to cry. "Sure," I answered. "Why not? I can do that and still head out to the Black Rock afterwards, right? The day is still young."

"Climb in," said Tom.

I squinted at him. "Huh? No, I'll meet you there. I've got my truck here, remember?" I forced a smile, and said, "You think I'm going to let you hijack me again?"

"Fair enough," he said, giving me a pat on the cheek. As he headed back toward the airplane, he turned and called, "But give me a good lead. Phone me. That warrant may not be ready when I get to Winnemucca, and I still have to get my ass up that mountain."

I GOT MYSELF some lunch in Lovelock, then dawdled a while at a little pioneer's museum by the highway. After the first hour, I called Tom's cell phone number every fifteen minutes to see if he had gotten the warrant and started out, but I got no answer. I wished I had Ian's number, as he seemed more inclined to answer it. I reached Faye, who was again waiting at the Winnemucca airport, but she had not heard from Tom, either. She said, "Tom's phone is on a different service provider from mine. That could mean he isn't receiving your calls, or perhaps his battery's just weak."

I finally got restless and headed out, figuring it was better to be a little ahead of him than way behind. I didn't want to miss the party.

As it was, I arrived and found no other cars in the visitor's parking lot in front of the mine offices. It was hot as blazes, so I wasn't about to wait inside my truck. Instead, I got out and sat in its shade.

After about ten minutes, one of the security guards came out to see what I was doing there. "You lost?" he inquired, making a joke of things.

I looked up and smiled. I recognized him from the day before. "No, just waiting for a friend," I said.

"You can wait inside if you want," he replied. "I remember you. You're the one who went through the metal detector yesterday like your pants was on fire."

"Yeah, that was me," I said, smiling sheepishly.

"Come on in," he said. "We've got cold water in a cooler in there."

"That's mighty kind of you," I answered, and got to my feet.

Inside, he had me sign the necessary forms again and showed me back through the metal detector and into a small waiting area just beyond it. "I'll tell Virgil you're here," he said, in a fatherly tone.

"Oh, that won't be necessary," I said hurriedly. "I'm just waiting for, ah—"

"Company policy," he said, and dialed a phone.

A moment later, Virgil appeared from around the corner in the hallway. "Em Hansen, right? Won't you come with me, please?" His expression was stern, rather like a school master who was taking a child into his office for a chat. I followed him, and sat in the side chair he indicated. He sat on a stool at a drafting table instead of at his desk. "So," he said, "You're with the FBI."

I smiled apologetically. It didn't seem the moment to try explaining the peculiarities of my non-relationship with the FBI.

"I suppose you aren't going to tell me anything of what you were doing here yesterday, or why you're back again today."

I thought of telling him the truth, that I had arrived the day before as an honest-to-gosh tourist, but figured he wouldn't believe me. Instead, I just shook my head.

Virgil folded his arms across his chest. "They told me you're a geologist, too," he said.

"Yes, that's true."

"If you were an exploration geologist and you wanted to disappear for a while, where would you go?" His tone was sad, and full of longing.

I knew immediately, of course, that he was speaking of Donald MacCallum. "So he's still not shown up?"

"Correct."

"Has anyone checked with his wife lately?"

"No. I hate to call her again. I think she's begun to worry."

I pondered this. "Let me try," I said. "Can I use your phone?" I glanced at the clock on Virgil's drafting table. It was almost mid-afternoon. She would be awake now, and greeting her children home from school.

Virgil dialed the number and handed the receiver to me. The line rang twice, then Gretchen answered. "Hello?"

"Hi, Gretchen? This is Em Hansen. You'll recall I stopped by and talked with you a few days ago."

"Yes." Her voice didn't sound quite as easy as the day before, but she was hardly a blubbering mess.

"I'm sorry, is this call an imposition?" I asked carefully.

"Well, people keep calling me," she said irritably.

"Who's been calling?"

"Virgil Davis, he's the mine superintendent, and Kyle Christie."

"What have they wanted?" I asked. "Are they looking for Don?"

"Hah."

"What *are* they looking for, then?"

"I don't have to answer you."

"That's right."

She hesitated. "Oh, they just want his maps. They're always just pushing him. If they only understood . . ."

She was still not worried about him, only annoyed that people were pestering him. "So you haven't heard from your husband since I visited you," I asked.

Gretchen pulled the conversation up short. "I . . . hey, I'm sorry, but I got to go."

"Gretchen—"

"Gotta *go*." She clicked off the line.

I set down the phone and stared straight at Virgil Davis. Gretchen had still not been worried about her husband, and when I asked her directly if she'd heard from him, she would not answer. I suddenly connected that dot with the conversation I'd had with the two miners in the Basque restaurant. "I know where he is," I said, so amazed that I hardly realized I had spoken the words aloud.

"Where?" Virgil demanded to know.

I looked left and right, sorry I had opened my mouth. "My associates will be here soon," I said hastily. "Then we'll find him."

He was on his feet. "*Where?*"

"I—I spoke too soon. I don't really know. I just have a suspicion."

Virgil held out his hands in supplication. "*Please.*"

"Well, I—" I stared out the windows toward the metal storage units that were lined up out there. "Are those locked?"

"Some of them. They're just for core samples."

My mind raced. I knew I should wait for Tom and for the search warrant, but just peeking in the door couldn't hurt, could it? And if I was right, I could—

Virgil had figured out what I was thinking. He headed out the door, moving fast. I chased after him, following at a gallop. He charged through the maze of hallways and burst into the outside heat through a door I had not previously seen. It led straight out to the storage units, which stood safely inside the electronically-controlled gate and chain-link fencing. Virgil strode right up to the only one that was not padlocked, grabbed the iron handle, and wrenched it open. The door groaned, shuddered, and shifted on its hinges, slowly opening.

Inside, I could see the back end of a beige Ford Explorer.

35

VIRGIL STRUGGLED PAST THE SIDE OF THE VEHICLE and stared in through the glass. At once, I saw his shoulders drop as tension ran off him like water. "Jesus God," he said, "For a moment there, I thought he was in it."

I squeezed past the door and scraped my way around the back bumper to the other side of the vehicle. He was right, there was no telltale odor that would foretell the presence of a corpse, but I had not expected one. I simply wanted to see the vehicle and know for certain that it was MacCallum's. I pressed my face to the glass by the driver's side window. I saw the happy jumble of field gear I would expect in any field geologist's vehicle: a beaten-up file box, a rock hammer, his Brunton compass, empty Gatorade bottles on the floor, and in the cup holders, rocks. A big cardboard box full of white cotton sample bags had come open in the back of the vehicle and spilled all over it. But there was no Donald Paul MacCallum in there.

"Well, hell," roared Virgil, "then where is he?" He had his hands up to his temples, and gripped his head like it was about to burst.

I could see where his mind was going. Two bodies had been discovered already, but neither one here. He himself had had the misfortune of finding one of them. Now the vehicle rented by a third person who had been missing for a week had been found right here on the ground for which he was responsible, a facility in which huge weights of rock were routinely dumped through immense grinding machinery, and where gigantic vats of acid boiled over rotating blades. "Virgil, stop!" I said, moving around the vehicle to stand next to him. "He's not dead!"

"But his vehicle's here, and—"

"Don't worry," I said, putting a hand on his arm to calm him. "He's in the mine. He's just hiding."

Virgil burst out of the storage shed and strode furiously toward the door back into the building.

I hurried after him, begging him to stop. I tried every kind of logic I could, even hung on his arm and dug my heels into the gravel to keep him from going underground before Tom arrived, but I had no authority to stop him. Virgil moved steadily and forcefully back into the building, heading straight for the equipment room. There, he buckled on his gear belt and reached for his hard hat. He was a man possessed, and he was going under.

Virgil yanked a battery out of the recharger, muttering angrily all the while. "You FBI are deceitful, you know that? I thought you were what you said, a geologist. Why, I—"

"I *am* a geologist. But I'm also a detective. Is that so hard to understand?" I could hardly believe I'd heard myself say that.

"*Well*, detective," Virgil said angrily, "If you're right, I've got a man hiding in my facility that shouldn't be there. I'm not harboring a killer. I found a woman dead out there with fire burning all around her, and if you think that was a barrel of laughs, think again!"

"It's possible he didn't do it. Let's wait for the others."

"Wait? As far as I know, he killed her, and if he thinks hiding in my mine is going to save him, he's insane!"

With that, he threw his body back into high gear and headed toward the door.

As he came past me, I grabbed his arm. "Virgil, wait. Let me come with you." It was a crazy thing to suggest, but I had blown it, totally screwed the surprise of Tom's imminent arrival, and I could at least atone by offering witness to what happened before he got there.

Virgil stared at me, wild-eyed, his mouth open. Only then did I remember that he still thought I was a federal agent. He turned and headed back to the equipment rack, and began to harvest a second rig. "Here's a hard hat," he said, "Adjust it there. And here's a belt and a self-rescuer. Remember your instructions? This is your headlamp battery. The switch is here. Take these boots, those running shoes aren't to code." When he had me trussed up, he took a stern look at me and said, "Here's a pair of safety glasses. You should have a Tyvek suit to keep the dirt off you, but—"

"Jeans wash fine."

"Here's a tag. Put it in your pocket."

I held out my hand to receive the small brass circle. It had a number stamped into it. I shoved it deep into my front jeans pocket. "Will I need a jacket?" I was wearing a thin T-shirt, having planned to fend off the heat of the open desert.

"No," he said, staring deep into my eyes. "Where we're going the sun won't shine, but you'll be warmed by Satan's breath."

36

KYLE CHRISTIE LISTENED TO VIRGIL'S AND EM'S receding footsteps from the floor of the storage closet just off the equipment room, where he had been hiding while he caught a nap. *Just my fucking luck to hit on a federal agent*, he thought, as panic seized his brain for the third time in a week.

He stood up, already sweating, and listened to make certain that they had not returned for any missed equipment. Too late, he was beginning to put two and two together, and anger spurred his panic into action. *Hell, she was out there looking for me, not Rabbithole Springs! And I bought her whole fucking story!*

He stepped carefully out of the closet. His breath came shallowly.

He made a hurried mental list of those persons who had seen him arrive this morning. The security guard, yes, but he had told him that he had come to use the computer. And the guard would confirm that he had arrived before the Hansen bitch, so no one would suppose he had been following her. Could he plead the truth, that he had only wanted to scare Pat Gilmore, so she'd back off on her threats? The lesbian stuff hadn't even phased her, and then, when Chittenden had told him to just plain steal her data, she'd caught him! He'd gotten the stuff off the hard drive on her computer, but he knew that it was her original field notes that would convince a jury, anyway. Hand-scribbled notes, made over weeks and months, in different colors of pen and pencil, all wind-blown and gritted with dirt. He had been picking through her desk looking for her notebooks when she came in. What followed was horrifying, even worse than that Dietz bitch twisting his balls. Pat had charged at him, demanding that he explain himself, and he had backed down and told her to call Chittenden

if she wanted to know. The humiliation of that moment still
burned like acid. His bosses might intimidate him, and little
weasels like Deputy Weebe might keep him at bay, but to be
cowed by a woman was more than a man should stand. And
she had said that this tore it, and if Chittenden didn't have a
good explanation, she was taking her story to Reno. So what
could he do? He had driven out there and waited for her. Just
to talk to her, set things straight. He had held the rock hammer
tight in his fist just so she wouldn't try anything again. . . .

And then that bastard Sam had seen him drive by with the
lawyer. He'd thought for *sure* the old man had recognized
him.

All these thoughts raced through Kyle's mind as he
grabbed a third set of gear, making certain to take equipment
other than his own in case anything went wrong and he once
again had to cover his tracks. He was going to have to be
smarter this time.

He waited, giving them another minute's lead. He did not
want them to see him following them. Especially not the bitch
from the FBI.

37

VIRGIL LOADED ME INTO A HIGH-SPRUNG PICKUP truck that was parked outside the back door, where Laurel Dietz had parked her red Chevy Blazer. I glanced quickly around the lot. I saw a dark green Ford Explorer. Was it Kyle Christie's? No matter, I could leave Kyle to Tom and Ian, who would be here any minute. I had worse things to worry about just then. I was going underground.

Virgil drove up the haulage road past the mill and continued on up the side of the mountain. A huge, fat-tired yellow vehicle the size of a swimming pool lumbered past us going downhill loaded with rocks. "Ore truck?" I asked, trying to lure him into conversation.

"Thirty ton," he replied, but said no more.

We came around a last curve and there was the mine portal, the gaping maw of the tunnel that led into the earth. It was surrounded by trim masonry, the bold symbol of Virgil's pride. Carved into the cement facing above the masonry was GRANVILLE RESOURCES, and between the masonry and the mouth itself were the words, GLORIANA MINE.

"Was the mine named for a real person?" I asked, still desperately trying to make small talk.

Virgil's jaws clenched tightly, bunching his muscles, and he spat, "Some lady of the evening Chittenden knew."

We climbed out of the pickup truck. I had to run to keep up with Virgil as he closed on what looked like a industrial-sized forklift tractor without the forks. It was equipped with a heavy roll cage. He climbed swiftly into the saddle and flipped a side seat down. "You sit here," he said. "You get to feeling faint or nauseated, you let me know. It will only get worse."

I climbed into the seat and grabbed the protective bar in front of my knees, and we were off, the engine of the tractor

echoing brutally off the hard face of the mine. Just before
diving down the portal, Virgil pulled the machine to the left
and stopped at a board full of hooks. He pulled a brass tag
out of his pocket and hung it up. I noticed that it matched
the number of the tag I held in my pocket. "What's that for?"
I asked.

Virgil did not even look at me as he backed the tractor
around and took aim at the portal. "That's in case you are
killed in a rock fall," he said. "So we can identify what's left
of your body."

THE TRACTOR HURTLED past the portal, confining the din of
its engine to the space of the tunnel that led into the mine, a
decline that dove into the mountain at steeper than ten degrees
off the horizontal. Instantly, my whole world was transformed. Gone were all physical clues to what was normal, or
usual, or recognizable. We dropped quickly through the short
fetch of daylight that lapped jealously into the tunnel and
entered a world of darkness. All color fell away as the absence of light sucked up the thin beams of our headlamps like
a famished sponge. Instantly, there was no tint of pink or
yellow or blue except as a ghostly remnant on my hands. All
was simply darkness, a sucking gray without warmth, and it
was growing darker with every foot. I squeezed my eyes shut
and held them closed for several seconds, forcing them to
adjust to the darkness more quickly, but when I opened them,
the best our headlamps could raise was just a turgid charcoal
gray.

I turned and looked longingly over my shoulder at the
dazzling pinpoint of light that was the portal. Something
moved across it: a man stepping into the tunnel? The glare
was so great that I could not tell for certain. Then we went
around a slight bend in the tunnel, and even the tiny shard of
light was gone.

I turned back to face downward into the earth. I looked all
around, lacing the darkness with the beam of my headlamp,
trying to orient myself in this new world. The floor and walls
of the decline were gray, featureless rock. Along the ceiling

were strung corrugated tubes three feet in diameter. Tucked up beside them were heavy electrical cords and long hoses which I presumed to be water lines. The tunnel roared with sound. "What are those?" I asked, pointing at the larger tubes.

"Ventilation. Air blows through them at thirty miles per hour. There are places where you'll need to cover your ears."

I could barely hear him over the sound, which by itself would have been disorienting. As we jolted along down the uneven rock floor of the decline, my mind struggled to understand what I was seeing and hearing and feeling, trying madly to match this new landscape with any I had met before. I could remember nothing even remotely like this domain with no light to give form to solid objects. As I once again scanned my headlamp over the long tubes above, my brain suggested to me that I was descending the gullet of a giant caterpillar. *No,* I told it, *this is a mine. Just map it, please.* But all reference to the outside world had been obliterated, and there was only darkness.

My eyes fell into a hypnotic stare, searching for anything to look at within the limited fields illuminated by our headlamps. I saw only rock dust, which floated in the air like a thousand tiny space ships navigating the void, making the atmosphere within the tunnel seem almost liquid.

Suddenly, lurching out of the gloom far below us, I saw an array of lights. There were four of them. They bounced and swayed slightly, dull mesmerizing fireflies in the total darkness. Three seemed to move as a fixed arrangement, and one bounced just above them. *You're in the benthic deep,* my brain informed me. *This is a National Geographic special, and we are watching deep sea creatures from a diving bell. Those lights are the phosphorescent protuberances on a deep sea creature. And it's a giant! It's—*

The array now loomed close enough that I could discern what carried them. Three were headlights on another enormous ore truck, and the fourth was the lamp on the hard hat worn by its driver. Slowly, I realized that the headlights were as dim as our headlamps, so that miners, whose eyes were attuned to this eternal darkness, wouldn't blind each other as they met in the tunnel.

I told my overheated brain to take a break from interpreting what it saw.

After what seemed like hours but was probably only minutes, we came to a side tunnel and turned off into it. Virgil shut off the tractor and spoke to me.

"MacCallum didn't kill Pat," he said.

"How do you know?"

"I just pieced it all together. I recall now seeing Don sitting in his office as I left that evening, just kind of staring out the window. He couldn't have done it. When John and I got to the crash site, the dust was still settling, and Pat's blood hadn't even begun to dry."

"Are you sure? We can't be too careful."

"Yes, I'm sure. And there'd be a record in the guard station if Don had gone out and come back in. And it was at least a fifteen-minute drive down to the crash site, and dust won't hang in the air like that, and blood dries in a snap in the desert air. And Don's crazy, but not that kind of crazy."

He was beginning to relax. He pointed down a side tunnel. "These drifts lead off toward the working faces. The geologists take assays along the face to check the grade, then mark it for the miners. The miners drill the face, then set their charges. We take the ore up to the mill, then shoot the waste back in here impregnated with gunite. Then we move up a level and go again. Now; there are four levels, and five of these entries. I have men working ten faces on this vein alone, and further down the main decline there are more veins that run off at an angle. Where do you think our man is?"

My eyes went wide. I was still reeling with disorientation, every inch of my skin registering to the increased heat and humidity and the sounds of the drills and other engines that formed a steady buffeting below the roar of the air tubes. Where was MacCallum? I had divined that he was underground, but I had no idea where. "Give me a minute," I said. I picked slowly through my mind, treating it like a filing cabinet. "Do you know where a miner named Larry is working?"

"Big Paiute guy?"

"Yeah. I talked to him at a restaurant last night. The waitress said he was making extra money. I figured that meant he had an assistant."

Virgil's eyes narrowed as he reached down and turned the engine back on. He whipped the tractor around and fed it back into the main decline, and we jolted on down, sinking ever deeper into the earth.

A few minutes later, he turned into another side tunnel. Virgil parked the machine and we got out and turned the corner toward the working face. All around me, there were large metal straps bolted into the walls and ceiling. "What are those?" I asked.

"Rock bolts," Virgil shouting to be heard over the increased thundering as we neared the working drill. "We're in the vein now. This rock's unstable. The main decline runs through the competent rock. We only cross-cut into the vein where we have to. As the miner proceeds, he sets these straps and bolts to keep the back up. The bolts go way into the rock. Here's one that hasn't been set yet." He picked up an iron rod that was longer than he was tall.

The solid metal suddenly seemed puny as I considered the stresses that were being released all around me. I tensed further, recalling the stories in my college classes about rocks literally exploding as the pressures of adjacent volumes were removed.

We trudged up the stope, soon reaching a place where there were no confining straps of metal and rock bolts. The rock stuck out in jagged slabs. It was like walking into the mouth of a shark.

"Watch your footing, and don't bump your head," Virgil said. "In fact, you'd probably better wait back by the turn there. This part has just been blasted. Larry hasn't barred down the loose ore or set the rock bolts yet."

"I hear someone working up there," I said.

Virgil heard it, too. The sound of metal against rock. "Larry!" he shouted. "Is that you?"

The noise stopped.

A man in miner's garb stepped around the corner where we could see him. He was alone. He was holding a long iron bar.

"MacCallum?" shouted Virgil.

The man did not reply. But as we stepped closer, we could see that it was indeed Donald Paul MacCallum. Instead of looking startled, he grinned sloppily, a kind of welcome-to-the-party smile. But he still held the bar. I stopped where I was, out of range if he decided to use it as a weapon.

Virgil's shoulders sagged. "All the time, you've been down here?"

MacCallum's smile faded slightly, but he laughed, an almost-giggle. "Aw, hell, Virgil, sometimes you gotta get off and let the world turn around a few times without you."

Virgil collapsed against the wall of the stope. "All these days, I've been—" He clutched at his chest. I watched him closely. Confronted with a man who had hideously inconvenienced him for days and perhaps months, he had fallen back rather than storming towards him. "I thought you were dead," he said, pain tightening his voice. Then suddenly rage took over, and he began to shout. "How in hell did you do this? My people have been down here every day! No one's told me anything!"

MacCallum leaned his bar against the rock and shrugged his shoulders, foolishly relaxed, a Charlie Chaplin in miner's garb. "Oh, Larry's pretty good at knowing when folks are coming. He just gives me the high sign, and I step out of sight. No one was expecting to see me here, so no one did. It's kind of like looking for gold, Virgil; you have to open your mind to what's possible."

"You gave me one hell of a scare!" Virgil said, still furious.

"Aw, hell, Virgil, I didn't mean to worry you. I know you've got your safety record to worry about and all, but it never occurred to me that you'd . . . well, you know."

Virgil's face had turned ghostly in the scant illumination of our head lamps. "I thought something had gone wrong because we argued. . . ."

MacCallum's laughter erupted again. "What? You mean when we had words over that map you wanted? Aw, hell, Virgil, I'm more stable than *that!* I just needed a little time, was all, and . . . well . . ." His face clouded. "No, my reasons for coming down here had nothing to do with you."

Was Virgil correct about MacCallum? I decided to test the only other possible explanation he might have for hiding from Virgil, and everyone else on the surface. "I have a message for you," I said.

"Oh?"

"Sam died during the night. And the BLM agent you were worried about is gone, anyway. No one can hurt him anymore."

MacCallum bowed his head, tipping his hard hat and its light toward the ground. He said nothing for a while, then, "Did he die at Rosebud?"

"Yes."

"Good." When he lifted his head, MacCallum's eyes were shining with tears. He was not Sam's murderer.

I said, "So I guess it's okay to come out now."

MacCallum nodded.

Virgil said, "What in hell are you two talking about?"

I answered for MacCallum. "He was just down here so an old man could die in peace. You wanted to file a map of Phase Two. That's where the old man lived."

MacCallum said, "The minute you filed for that permit, that prissy, officious new jackass from the BLM would have gone out there to inspect the place. He would have thrown Sam off the place in an instant."

Virgil shook his head in confusion, then said, "Have you heard who else is dead?"

"Well, I heard about Pat Gilmore." He kicked at a rock. "Poor woman. She got to hurrying, right? And—"

"Wait," said Virgil. "If Don here didn't kill Pat, then who did?"

"Kyle Christie," I blurted. Tom Latimer was right. I did need someone to teach me a few things. Such as how to keep my mouth shut.

"Now just how in hell's name do you have that one figured?" Virgil demanded.

"Have you or John Steinhoff described the scene of the wreck to anyone?"

Virgil said, "Hell no. Obernick told us not to. I didn't, and I can vouch for John. I've known him for decades. Neither one of us said a word to anybody."

"And how long did that range fire burn?"

"Two days."

"Then, you see? Anyone who could describe the crash site the morning after it happened saw it," I said. "Kyle knew that pickup had flipped, and where. How'd he know that? And there's forensic evidence. She was killed by a blow to the top of the head with a square-ended weapon. That would be a mineral hammer. No geologist would be without one. And come to think of it, Kyle's the only man around here I've seen who's tall enough to land one on the top of a big woman's head."

I turned to MacCallum. "Umberto Rodriguez is dead, too."

MacCallum's mouth sagged open.

Virgil said, "God knows why. Someone dumped him and his vehicle down a mine shaft over on the Kammas."

MacCallum's eyes pulled into a pained squint.

Virgil shot MacCallum a look. "I'll bet that was your pal Kyle, too," he said.

MacCallum cocked his head to one side and said, "Aw, you just can't let that go, can you? This is all nonsense. Kyle's a stupid putz. He wouldn't hurt a—"

Virgil cut MacCallum off with a roar. "I tell you, he doesn't show women proper respect!"

MacCallum stared at the floor. "Nobody's perfect, Virgil."

"Perfect? Hell, he's hopeless. The two of you! You've been sitting on something out there in the Kammas! You're holding out on us!"

MacCallum spread his hands. "Holding out on you? Oh,

sure Virgil, I found something, but have I found what you needed me to find? You know just as well as I do that very few exploration targets pan out. I found a vein, sure, but hell, everybody knows there's mineralization in those mountains. We've known that for a century, before you or I were born. And yeah, I've kind of knit things together into a bigger picture, but . . . You aren't telling me you bought all Chittenden's crap, did you? Come on, Virgil! The man's a comedian!"

Clearly Virgil had. Or had let himself hope. He sagged back against the wall again, his eyes round with the vacancy of grief.

Just then, I saw a light out of the corner of my eye where there had not been one a moment ago. I moved carefully down over the rubble toward the turn to see what was causing it.

The light vanished, as if someone had turned it off from a switch.

"Who's there?" I asked, turning my headlamp this way and that.

Suddenly, my light swept across a pair of legs. In the instant it took me to sweep my light back again and up, I heard the sound of iron striking rock, and as I found my target, I saw Kyle Christie with his arms up to the rock above us. He was jamming another long iron bar home, right into the shark's teeth.

I turned and ran, screaming a warning to Virgil and MacCallum. In the next instant, the earth roared, and something huge slammed my back and propelled me forward. I hit the working face like an egg, all air instantly squeezed from my lungs. My mind jammed. My body went numb, and all fell into total darkness.

38

SLOWLY, A LOUD RINGING IN MY EARS DREW ME back to partial consciousness. I tried to breathe but could not. Fingers probed around my face, pried into my mouth, withdrew, danced down my cheek to my throat and felt along it.

"Can you hear me?" said a tiny, excited voice. "Breathe, damn it!"

Slowly, I realized that the voice only sounded tiny through the icy ringing in my ears.

"Are you all right?" the voice was asking. Begging.

I tried to speak, but could not. Bit by bit, the numbness gave way to pain, and I reasoned out which way was up. The pressure against my cheek and belly was the rock below me, and I was lying on it. But I could not take a breath. Then suddenly, air rushed painfully into my lungs as my rib cage sprung back into shape. I coughed. I opened my eyes, but could see nothing. The hand touched my face again, from a different angle.

"Oh good, you're alive," said the voice, a little louder now. "Do you know where Virgil is? Can you feel him under there? Wait, I think I found my light."

The field before my eyes turned from totally black to gray. A thick pall of rockdust roiled about before my eyes. I tried to move, but could not.

"I'll check your back and legs now," Don said, his voice still almost lost in the terrible ringing that filled my ears. "You tell me if anything hurts."

Pain shot up through my right leg. "There," I said, grabbing toward the apex of the worst hurt.

He probed along it. "Broken," he said.

"What hit?"

"The concussion of the collapse. We were lucky it spent

most of its force at the turn in the stope. Oh, hell, there's Virgil!"

Through the churning dust, I could see Virgil lying on his side, the blue of his shirt barely discernable between a mantle of rubble, and the falling pall of gray. His legs were covered with rubble, but his hard hat was still in place. His eyes were open and his lips moved feebly. I dragged myself toward him with my hands and put my ear to his mouth.

"Forgot to pray," he whispered. "She warned me. . . ."

"Hang on, Virgil!" I gasped. "We'll get you out. No more bad dreams."

MacCallum hurled debris away from his legs, slowly uncovering them. "Oh. This is bad."

I looked. There was a lot of blood, all pasty with the dust. I pulled off my equipment belt and handed it to MacCallum so that he could tie a tourniquet to stop the bleeding. Virgil's breath came raggledly. Then it stopped. I felt for a pulse at his throat. I could not find one. Then, dizzy with my own pain, I felt for broken ribs, preparing to start CPR. Finally, I realized that I was wasting time, and pulled off his hard hat, cleared his air passage, set my lips to his, and exhaled the air from my lungs into his. MacCallum put one hand over the other on Virgil's heart, and began to pump.

39

BREATHING THE TENUOUS EDGE OF LIFE BACK INTO a man is a strange way to get to know him. We heard ribs crack before Virgil's lungs remembered their job and started moving again, but his pulse remained fast and faint. His eyes did not open. He did not speak. He did not respond.

"We need to get him out of here," said MacCallum. "I'm going to see if there's a passage." He scrambled up over the tumble of loose rocks and searched, leaving me in the velvet darkness. I held Virgil's hand and watched MacCallum's tiny bobbing light, trying not to think of what it might be like if MacCallum left, or were crushed by settling rubble.

After agonizingly long minutes, he called back through the oddly muffled space. "There's no way out," he said. "And there's a big slab hanging over the top of the pile. If I touch it, or move anything from beneath it, it's going to come down on us like a torpedo. So don't move. How's Virgil?"

"He's with us for the moment," I answered.

MacCallum's headlamp began to move again.

Trying to control my rising panic, I called, "If you get crushed up there, then I'm here in the dark by myself with two dead men. Please come down."

MacCallum's light turned back toward the immense knife edge of rock that was aimed at us. He crouched, considering the rock from every angle, double-checking his analysis. Finally, he turned and came carefully down the rockfall, moving on all fours, like a spider. His light seemed to flicker.

"Is your battery wearing out?" I asked.

He nodded. "I was due to replace it. My spare's under a hundred tons of rock now. Virgil's is crushed. How is yours?" He reached down to Virgil's battered leg and gently teased the battery loose from the belt I had worn. I could see that it had suffered the same fate as Virgil's. "The good news,"

MacCallum said, "is that whatever hit this thing did *not* hit your kidneys."

"What are we going to do?" I said, my voice a half-octave higher than usual.

"We wait," he said. MacCallum eased the pressure on Virgil's tourniquet for a moment, then tightened it again. Then he stepped back over me, found himself a place to sit, took his hard hat and equipment belt off, and set them to one side. He rubbed his eyes with the heels of his hands and then pushed his fingers up through his hair. Then he reached over to his headlamp and switched it off.

"We wait in the *dark*?" I gasped.

"Yes. Save the battery."

I tried not to think of the precariously balanced tumble of rocks that rested only inches from my feet. Tried to control my breathing, not knowing how long the air would last. Tried not to think about the pain that was now pulsing in my leg.

MacCallum found my hand in the dark and held it gently, calming me. "Don't worry," he said. "There are good men who already know what's happened. They know what they're doing."

"You trust them," I answered.

"I do."

Moments ticked by in the concussive darkness. "What's that feel like?"

"What?"

"Trusting someone with your life."

MacCallum didn't answer right away, but then said, "It's like having many brothers. You might fight with them, but when you're in danger, you want them there." He squeezed my hand again. "How's your leg?"

"It hurts. I'll be all right," I said hopefully. "Have you been in total darkness like this before?"

"Many times. I find it soothing." He yawned.

"What is it that draws men down here?" I asked, trying to keep him talking. Right then, I would have asked him to recite the Gettysburg Address just to hear the sound of his voice.

He considered my question for a while. "When I'm down

here, when I drill into this rock and expose a new face, I am literally seeing something that no man has seen before. It's kind of like being there at the moment of creation."

The moment of discovery. Ever new, ever marvelous. I clung to the feeling it conjured. I had found it in a sunrise, a newly opened flower, or the right correlation between well logs just brought from the field and laid out across my desk at an oil company. In that instant, the darkness was less terrifying. But the instant did not last. "What do you think is going to happen?" I asked.

MacCallum said, "The future is an elusive thing."

"Aren't you terrified?" I panted, thinking about the tons of rock that lay before me in the dark, just waiting to settle with the first bit of shaking. I did not like to think that I might have survived this only to be killed when the rescuers knocked something loose trying to help me.

"Not as long as I'm still in the game." He laughed; just a quick, intoxicated riffle of sound.

"How can you be so calm?" I asked.

"What else should I do? The past we can map, with one degree of accuracy or another, but the future is a place of the unknown. There's nothing I can do. I have no idea how much rock is there. I will only exhaust myself if I worry about it. So I leave it to the others."

"I'm in pitch darkness with a total madman," I said.

"What are you talking about?"

"A mine collapses on you, worse yet your old partner did it to you, and you get sleepy."

"Kyle did this? You're raving. He wouldn't hurt a fly."

"You lose a million dollars in stock value, and you think it's penny-ante poker."

"No, that wasn't funny," he said irritably, "but it's a game, and I'm still a player. Hell, there's gold all around me. What do I have to worry about?"

Gold? I wanted to scream. We didn't need gold, we needed water, and food, and a medic. "You're nuts. You think gold can buy you out of anything. You think it's money, just like every other nutcase that ever wandered off up a gully with a rock hammer."

"No, I don't. It's just a metal."

"But Rudolf said—"

"The reindeer?" MacCallum laughed. The sound bubbled like champagne out of the bizarre world of detached clarity he seemed to inhabit. I could see now that he was indeed a wizard. He lived in a strange splinter zone of genius, somewhere in that narrow boundary region of detached thought that lay between my more pedestrian outlook and full-on insanity.

"No," I said. "Of course you don't know Rudolf. He's just a gold junkie I met. He told me that everyone sees gold as money. Everyone except me, apparently."

"Gold is not money," MacCallum said. "It is the currency of last resort. Come the revolution, or the plague, or whatever disaster, it's that last thing that everyone can recognize as having value."

"And it always has value?"

"Hell, no. If things break down far enough, it's a dead weight. Shotgun shells will be worth more." He yawned. "But I don't think that's going to happen. We're all too adaptable. Our technology has evolved too far. We like our refrigerators too much, and our VCR's. And even plagues leave a few people alive. Besides, gold is just chump change next to the money that flies around electronically these days." I heard him shifting around in the dark like a dog who was getting comfortable before a nap.

My voice barely escaping my lips, I said, "You aren't going to sleep, are you?"

"I think I'd better. I'll need my strength later."

In half a minute, I heard the sound of his breathing grow rougher as it eased into a gentle snore. MacCallum, the mouse who trusted, was asleep in his burrow.

But I was not a mouse. Not yet.

I tried to remember the story of the jumping mouse. I had read the story quickly one night, during my travels west. The mouse symbolized the direction of Introspection on the medicine wheel. Jumping mouse searched and searched for the mountain, so he could climb up and see the world, but on his journey, he encountered two great beasts who were ill. Only the eye of a mouse could heal them. He gave one eye to each. So when he reached the goal of the mountain top, he could not see. He lay trembling in fear, waiting for eagle to come down and eat him.

I now trembled like the mouse, and was as blind.

How had the story ended? Jumping mouse had awoken, and found that he *was* eagle. What had Peggy told me, that day at the airport? I struggled to remember, to calm myself, to focus. Eagle was the east, Illumination.

I sat in the total, featureless darkness, my hand on Virgil's pulse. He was still alive, but not by much. My leg coursed with pain. My body ached in a thousand places, not the least improved by the hard edges of the rock on which I leaned. My lungs felt full of lead.

I began to wonder about the quality of the air. It was growing hotter, and very, very close. I waited, trying not to think, trying to ignore the fear that waited like a jackal at the edge of my mind.

I squeezed my eyes shut, trying to pretend that the absence of light was only because they were shut.

Closed. Could I open them?

If there was no illumination outside my eyes, then I would look inward.

Like a lost shred of sanity, I heard Ray's voice deep inside my ears, *Your heart is like a fire. . . .*

I longed to feel him near me. In the darkness, I let my heart rise like an unseen sun and search for him. I willed it with all my soul.

Slowly, a brightness of light that eyes do not see radiated through my body. As tears flowed out between the closed lids of my eyes, I told Ray wordlessly that I was alive, and that I loved him. I told him about my strange new friend, MacCallum, and smiled about the love my friend had for his wife, and his wife had for him. I asked him if it could be the same for us. I strained to listen.

The minutes ratcheted by.

I opened my eyes. All was still darkness, and the only sound was my heart beating.

THE SOUNDS STARTED almost like the breath of the earth itself, felt more than heard. Then they grew louder than the pulse that still surged through my ears, and the gentle snoring that now came from one side of me, and the dry, shallow panting that came from the other. "Don! Wake up!" I said.

"Huh?"

"I hear them."

The sounds grew louder and louder. I prayed silently that the vibrations of the machinery would not knock that knife of rock down onto us.

I reached my hand into my jeans pocket and held the brass tag and thought of Ray.

I heard voices.

"Don!" I whispered.

I heard them call names. "Virgil!" they called. "Mac-Callum!"

The miners did not call my name. That meant that they did not know that I was down here. And that in turn meant that Kyle had gotten away. For an instant, I wanted to stay exactly where I was, in the darkness, where he couldn't see me.

I had become the mouse.

MacCallum was standing up, turning on his light, calling back to them, telling them about the loose slab. They acknowledged, and we heard the sounds move to the left to dodge around it.

"We'll shoot some gunnite in," someone hollered.

"Too slow!" MacCallum shouted back. "Virgil's not good. We've got to get him out, fast!" He turned to me. "Are you still getting a pulse?" he asked.

"Yes. Get that light back on. Let's brace some rocks around Virgil. If something rolls, it'll at least stop the small ones from hitting him."

The light switched on, blinding me. All was a bloody orange for a minute as my eyes adjusted. MacCallum bent and loosened the tourniquet for a while, then tightened it again, and began to stack stones one on top of another.

Minutes trickled by, like life's blood flowing out of us. MacCallum shone his light up into the pile of rocks, toward the sounds. And suddenly, a second, brighter light came back toward us. We were going to live.

40

STEPHEN GILES STRODE DOWN THE CONCOURSE AT San Francisco International Airport, his ticket held tightly in his sweating hand, every cell in his body taut with anticipation. *This is it, at last—thank God I thought to ask the postmaster to check that other mailbox to see if the envelope had been switched!* The world could rot in hell; he, Stephen Giles, could not have stood the infamy of being a tawdry public servant another instant! He was shedding that skin, and all the years of shabbiness, if only for this one week, and he might—he *would*—meet refined persons of power and position at the resort, and they would take him as one of their own, find a place for him, and finish his transformation into the person he was always meant to be—

A man stepped out of the crowd. "Stephen Giles?" he said.

Stephen smiled. Had they sent a welcoming party?

"You are under arrest for conspiracy to commit fraud," the man said, as he snapped handcuffs around Stephen's wrists, spoiling the crisp starch in his perfectly-pressed shirt. "You have the right to remain silent. You have the right—"

Stephen did not hear the rest of what the man said. His ears rushed with his pulse. He was drowning under a thousand screaming voices of rage and despair.

SHIRLEY COOK STROKED the soft fur of the cat who lay across her lap. It purred. Its subtle sounds were more pleasant to her than what she had just heard on her new radio. There had been an accident at the Gloriana Mine. One man was dead, another in critical condition. A third man and a woman were being treated for minor injuries in Winnemucca. "It's a strange life, kitty," she told the animal sadly.

The cat purred. Shirley stroked its fur.

*   *   *

Laurel Dietz stood beside the big leather swivel chair behind Chittenden's desk in his office at Granville Resources' corporate headquarters. Chittenden was gone, she knew that, even though the rest were still running around like rats, wondering where he had gone with his blessed company jet. He was in Switzerland, or Panama, or the Cayman Islands, one of those nifty places where men like him went to dine on the nuts they had squirreled away.

No, nuts and squirrels was the wrong image. Chittenden was a modern-day example of that more romantic human animal, the pirate. He robbed from the rich and . . . stuck it in his pockets.

A weight sat on Laurel's heart. It was not that she stood in moral judgement of him. Not she. What pressed against her chest this morning was the knowledge that she had, once again, fetched up against a dead end. She had wanted to sit in this chair one day, to claw her way up through the company and supplant Chittenden through her own cunning, not be left high and dry by his.

She riffled through her mental file cabinet for a moment, wondering if she had missed a sign along the way, or dodged left when she should have gone right. And for just an instant she wondered if, on the long flight up from Nevada, she should have sat up front in the second pilot's seat next to Chittenden and put a hand on the upper part of his thigh. But no, she knew the answer to that one. The outcome would have been the same. And she wanted to *sit* in the chair of power, not wait behind it.

Right now, that chair was empty, literally, and it stood before her, beckoning. She *could* sit in it, if only for a moment. No one would know, or care. . . .

She moved toward it, put a hand on its arm to turn it toward her, a sense of near-sexual ecstasy rising in her loins—

The door opened behind her. "What are you doing?" scolded the executive secretary. "And who do you think you are, anyway, coming into Mr. Chittenden's office like this?"

Laurel let go of the chair and stared at it. *Another time*, she told it. *The night is young.*

MORGAN SHUMWAY STOOD inert in the doorway of his bedroom as the men continued to search his closet. His entire body felt remote, as if it belonged to someone else. The men were bagging up his shoes now, but he had cleaned them, hadn't he? Could they find something on them, even after the scrubbing and reconditioning to which he had submitted them, something that could connect him with that mountain in Nevada and the remains of that hideous man he had left there? And he'd burned the clothes he had worn at the lake shore, and washed every stitch of clothing he had worn during that hellish drive with that stinking corpse. No, he was certain, they would not find a trace. They could spin nothing on him.

Now a man was removing his hat, his precious creamy-white Stetson hat, from the closet. *What is he doing with my hat? A hat can tell them nothing! Good God, the bastard's smiling!* Shumway's bowels began to churn.

The tall FBI agent with the salt-and-pepper hair was moving toward him with a smile that was quickly spreading into a grin, carrying the Stetson with hands gloved to prevent contaminating evidence. He said, "We'll be taking this hat, too, Mr. Shumway. It's the one thing people forget to wash. They put their clothes through the laundry, they go over their shoes with a hose and a scrub brush, but they forget about their hats." He carefully tipped the hat over and looked inside, up around the hat band. "You get to sweating, as you're coming down the mountain after dumping a body in a mine shaft. And even more so after the man who's waiting to take you away nearly mows down an old man on a lonesome road, and he panics and runs up behind the old fellow and whacks him on his fragile head so he'll forget. You see the tally of your crimes growing. Murder, accessory to murder . . . yes, you get to sweating. You take your hat off for a moment and mop your brow. Then you put the hat back on, and everything that was on your hands is now on this sweat band, right here."

Morgan Shumway stared helplessly into the hat, knowing that it had become a jail cell. Then he glanced up at the FBI agent to see if the man was only calling his bluff. To his horror, the man now stared at him like he was climbing straight in through his eyes.

41

MY TRUCK THREW A ROD ON THE ROAD BETWEEN
the Gloriana Mine and Winnemucca and now waited by the
roadside to be hauled away for scrap. Tom was driving it. I
was in an ambulance, and Virgil Davis floated somewhere in
the sky, hurried by helicopter to the hospital in Reno, his
grasp on life too frail to survive the long, jarring ride by road.
It seemed that the world was falling to pieces.

Tom had stopped briefly at the hospital before having Faye
fly him back to Salt Lake City. He squeezed my hand as I
lay in the emergency room waiting to be X-rayed. "They
found a body under the rubble as they were digging you out,
Em. It was crushed beyond recognition. Any guesses who it
was?"

"Kyle Christie." The room seemed to spin. "I saw him just
before the rock fell."

Tom winced, and squeezed my hand again. After a while,
he said, "Broken leg. Bruised from head to toe. Exhaustion."
His eyes ran with tears that did not quite spill over. "They're
going to keep you here at least tonight, for observation."

"Observation," I repeated foolishly. In my drug-induced
haze, the word had near-mystical importance to me. "Important to see clearly."

"This isn't what I meant to have happen," he said.

"Silly me. I learn the hard way."

"Let me teach you. Please."

Warm tears welled up underneath my eyelids.

"You'll need a new truck," he said. "So you'll need a job.
There's always a place for a scrappy little nut case like you
at the FBI."

I laughed hollowly. "Institutions. One's like another. I may
as well become a Mormon."

"Think about it," Tom said. He touched my cheek gently.

As the light of late afternoon reached in through the windows, the nurses moved me into a room. I lay in a haze, trying not to think.

Just before the end of visiting hours, a woman appeared. She never introduced herself, but I knew who she was. She had the black hair, the broad nose, the short forehead, and the high, wide cheekbones of the Northern Paiute tribe, and she carried herself with the inward quiet of the mystic.

She nodded to me. When I nodded back, she came to the edge of my bed and smoothed the air over my face and body with a brush of eagle feathers. Then she said, "You'll feel better tomorrow. I will wait for you at Double Springs. It's in the Black Rock Desert, along a trail made by your people."

I tried to tell her that my truck was dead, and that worse yet, my leg hurt so badly that I didn't think I could drive for who knew how long, but she said, "There is always a way to go where you are going," and left. Only then did I realize that the pain in my leg and my heart had lessened.

In the morning, the first rosy light of a brand new day traced the ceiling in my room as I lay trying not to panic as the painkillers and sedatives wore off. The past, present, and future all met in the cracks between the ceiling tiles, while beneath my back, the earth seemed to lurch on its axis. In my shattered, hypersensitive state, I fancied I could feel the restless energy of her crustal plates heaving and sliding beneath me, rending in new places to let the hot breath of her interior hiss new deposits of brilliant gold into her hidden caverns, an image both beautiful and terrifying.

At nine, Faye poked her nose inside my doorway. "I have someone with me who wants to see you," she said. "You need me to comb your hair? You look a mess."

I was just opening my mouth to ask who in hell could merit my combing my hair when Ray sidled through the doorway. He looked embarrassed. Faye made herself scarce. He came around to the side of my bed, bent, and kissed me softly on the lips. As he straightened up, a mischievous smile played across his face.

I smiled back. "I guess this is the only way you get to see me in bed," I said.

A wider smile and a flick of one eyebrow was all the answer I got.

"Want to go into the desert with me?" I asked. "There's this place called the Black Rock."

Ray took my hand and gave it a squeeze. Then he turned toward the doorway and loudly cleared his throat.

Faye stuck her face around the door frame again.

"Can you land that thing on a dry lake bed?" Ray asked.

Faye's eyes lit up. "Sure."

FAYE BROUGHT THE Cheyenne down gently as a feather on the impossibly flat surface of the Black Rock Desert, in the arm that runs between the Black Rock Range and the Calico Hills, and taxied to within a few hundred feet of the place where four-wheel-drive vehicle tracks led off into the hillocks of sand that surrounded the shoreline. She shut down the engines, and I got out and hobbled around on the cracked, white silty surface of the vanished lake while she and Ray chocked the wheels. The lake bed ran for thirty miles straight to the south, widening out between the tall ridges of the mountain ranges. Far away, I could see lines of dust that marked the trajectories of the crazy four-wheelers who were out there playing silly buggers in the heat. Beyond them, the sail of a land yacht slewed crazily across the terrain.

My companions shouldered the camping gear we had assembled from my poor old truck and Faye's baggage bay, and I came along behind them, shuffling along on my crutches. I had to rest many times, but oddly, the pain diminishing rather than growing.

We found Double Springs in due course. We came first upon a campsite set up by a group of college students out of Reno who said they were studying the Emigrant Trail. They had state-of-the-art tents, a propane stove, and lightweight aluminum camp chairs set up beside their brand new four-wheel-drive vehicle. We told them we were looking for a woman in a beat-up Toyota. "Oh, she's over there on the other side of the springs," they said. "Beyond that tussock."

When she saw us approaching, Hermione nodded gravely and came out from under the tarp she had strung to a bush from one side of her car. "Don't go too near," she said, as Faye bent to look into the two big barrel-shaped holes in the sand that formed the pools of the springs. "It's hot. Your people used to cook beans in there."

"What did your people cook there?" I asked, lowering my exhausted body onto the ground.

She pointed at a lidded pot that sat simmering in the water. "Fish stew," she said.

Great stands of desert brush grew near the springs, and I could see the twin ruts of the ancient wagon trains, now criss-crossed by the crazy meanderings of Jeeps and Ford Explorers. After Ray and Faye had settled our gear and I had rested, and as the day began to cool into evening, Hermione took me down this road toward the south, away from the others, and seated me on a low rise in the crumbling soil. She said nothing, but sang for a while and burned a bundle of herbs, then arranged rocks around me, four of them, set at the cardinal points of the compass.

She sat inside the stones with me for a long while, her eyes closed, deep in meditation. Then she looked at me and said, "You are ready to open your eyes and see clearly. You must first recognize that sight has always been with you. It is not strange or evil; it is only what you were born with. It is time to trust in it."

"Are you talking about some 'sixth sense?' " I asked, fear rising from the pit of my stomach.

She looked at me from several angles. "If you do not use your sight as you were meant to do, you will stay unhappy. The Spirit did not build you in parts, it made you as a whole creature. You are needed."

I almost growled with frustration. "So this is one more recruitment."

"Recruitment?"

I told her irritably about Tom, and about Shirley's presumptions.

Hermione's face softened. "I need you, yes. Shirley needs you, and this Tom, and all people need you. That mountain needs you. That lizard—"

"You've lost me."

"Don't listen to me. Listen inside." She touched her heart. "And look." She touched her forehead.

My heart quivered. My brain ached. I could not understand, but I was too tired to argue anymore.

I asked, "Why are you doing this for me?"

She answered, "It is time to knit our world together. It is always time. Someone did this for me. I do it for you. I did not get Pat Gilmore here in time, and Shirley is as blind as the people she despises. Now sit for a while with these stones, and see what comes." With that, she stepped outside the ring of stones and walked away.

I sat, and watched the lizards skitter across the soil. One stopped and did little pushups as it considered me. The sounds of the other campsite on the far side of the springs tinkled up to join the sounds of ours. A young fellow on a mountain bike hurtled past me, startled to find me there, staring at me as if I were nuts.

As the sun set, the little creatures of the desert emerged from their burrows. A rain cloud rose up from the west, threatened the earth with thunder, and moved around me to the north. I watched a kangaroo rat come out to forage, bounding along on its impossibly long hind legs, and thought about the perfect balance it enjoyed with the sagebrush under which it lived. I knew that during the day, as the creature slept within its burrow, with a plug of loose sand pushed up to close its entrance, the moisture from its exhalations gave the plant enough water to survive until the next rain. And during the night, the animal emerged and ate the seeds the shrub had made from the magic alchemy of his water combined with the minerals of the earth and the energy of the sun. I smiled at this little brother, who moved as secretively as the mouse who had found himself the center of so much trouble in the mine to the east.

Music arose from the other campsite. It was loud and

sounded raucous to my ear; at first, I cursed the other campers
for breaking my silence with their boom box. But then, as the
music meandered and ran on and my ear adjusted to hearing
it, I realized that it was not electronically-reproduced sound.
One of the college students had brought his fiddle, and was
playing his heart out to the rising stars. For a moment, the
tethers of the time into which I had been born let go, and I
experienced the wilderness with the sense of newness that had
met the Sarah Royces who had passed this way a century and
a half past. I sighed, and felt the exhaustion of my journey.
And, for the first time, I knew that I would make it to my
goal.

A mouse ran from its hiding place under the sagebrush
and disappeared into its burrow.

I contemplated the stones. I sat in the West, the Looks-
Within place, awaiting the East, Illumination. As I waited, I
listened to the Wise Thunder of the North. It warned the
Mouse—South, Trust—to run to its burrow where it would
be safe. With my eyes wide open, I glimpsed the medicine
wheel that waited within my heart. And, deeply humbled as
I was everything I had lived in the past few days, I saw that,
like most people born into this world, a spoke or two of my
own wheel was a little bit short.

Sounds of laughter arose from our campsite, and I heard
Ray's voice rise with the others. Smiling, I hitched myself up
on my crutches and limped back to join them. I found them
sitting around a campfire, warming their hands around cups
of hot chocolate, telling made-up stories about the stars. Ray
smiled to see me. He seemed at peace, and happy, and not in
the least out of place.

That night, we slept out underneath the brilliance of the
stars, Ray and I curled up in separate bed rolls, but only
inches apart. He smiled and touched my cheek before he
closed his eyes, and, many times during the night, as I lay
unable to sleep, I found his dark eyes upon me, checking on
me, watching over me.

As the stars swept across the sky, I saw a golden path
stretching before me, and I perceived a future in which all

humans embraced the earth as a treasured gift. In this world, each and every child grew into a caretaker, integrating the careful use of raw materials into a gentler industriousness, bending to touch the flowers with renewed wonder, and received the earth's bounty according to the needs of the body, not the gnawing hungers of unconsciousness. I felt a deep and abiding gratitude for all that had been given to me, every talent, every meal, every scrap of metal, and for the first time, I felt fulfilled and complete.

In the future that stretched before me, opposites came together and intertwined until they merged. In that future, I perceived a place for the disparate regions of my own aching soul.

In the morning, I left my crutches by the tent and, leaning on Ray's strong, firm body, limped down to the four stones that Hermione had placed for me. I drew him inside its magic.

We watched a flight of horned larks stitch the thin grasses with their erratic search for food. Ray held me close and kissed my hair and asked me nothing.

It was time for me to answer his question.

"Ray," I said, barely above a whisper, "you and I are good together. My courage grows when we're together, and I love you with every ounce of strength that gives me."

Ray swayed slightly, soaking up my words as if they had form and motion.

I said, "And we are different in important ways. That's why I had to come out here, to this open place where I can see more clearly. But coming out West alone didn't go very well. I found that I didn't have the courage to look at what I truly wanted. I didn't trust my heart. But when I wound up in total darkness, I had no choice but to look. And you know what I saw? I realized, as I waited in that mine, that I did not need to change you. I am hoping you can do the same for me." I looked up to see how he was taking this.

Ray met my gaze. His brow knit slightly, his indication that he needed me to say more.

I said, "I will never be a Mormon. Even if I did everything necessary to look, act, smell, and taste like a Mormon, I still

would not *be* a Mormon, at least not like you are. I can't fake
what I am, Ray. And the truth is that I don't even feel the
urge to try. So I can't say yes to what you've asked me to
do."

Ray's arms tightened around me in supplication, and his
deep indigo eyes closed tightly.

I squeezed back, and in my most soothing tone, said, "I'm
not done yet, Ray. Please look at me. Because here's my
challenge: Neither do I say no. I *would* like to marry you.
Look, here you are with me in the wilderness. And you were
with me in that mine, and in just the same sense, you've been
with me wherever I've been since the day we met. I don't
have to ask you to meet me somewhere in between, because
you already have. So even when neither of us knew it, your
heart has made room for everything I am. I'm just hoping it
has room for everything I am meant to become."

Ray opened his eyes again. "You already astonish me," he
whispered.

I buried my face against his throat. "*Please*, Ray, give us
some time, see what *we* become. I'm going to make it easier
for us. I'm going to quit running away from you. I'm going
to move to Salt Lake City. I'll find a place of my own to live
and I'll get a job; I need the money to put a new engine in
my truck."

Ray looked pained. "Em, that truck's—"

"Ray, it's plenty used, but it's still not used up! Any way
you slice it, I'll need a job. I don't know what kind of job
that can be to start with, but I know where I'm going to wind
up, at least for a while. I'm going into business as an independent consultant to forensic cases."

Ray's arms spasmed with sudden fear.

"No, Ray, this is what I *do*. But I will do it as a consultant,
not as an idiot runaway nitwit who gets squashed a mile underground! You don't see Tom risking his neck, do you?
Well, he wants to be my teacher, so I'm going to let him, but
on my terms. No FBI. Because here's my promise: From now
on, I will do what I do consciously, and humbly. With my

eyes wide open. And with you. What do you say?"

Ray loosened his embrace just enough so that he could raise my chin and look into my eyes. He was smiling as wide as the sky.

MINING SUPPORTS THE EXCELLENT STANDARD OF living that most people who can read this book now enjoy. Even the page on which you are reading these words was manufactured and contains mined materials (as well as wood pulp, which is grown), and the long process of composing, editing, printing, communications, and shipping which supported its production are absolutely dependent on mining. Without mined natural resources, we would not live as long or as comfortably as we do, nor could we become as well educated as we are, travel as far and as fast as we do, or enjoy the ease and depth of communications which now links the humblest village in the dustiest Third World country directly to the wealthiest and most advanced cultures in the history of our planet.

Mining is obviously a reductive process, and is to varying extents also destructive and dangerous. In recent decades, we have come a long way in learning to limit the destructive aspects of mining, and we have further to go. Part of my agenda in writing mystery books about geology and geologists is to provide a layperson's view into the earth science professions, so that readers can hope to make more informed decisions that influence every aspect of their lives and lifestyles.

In researching this book, I took extensive tours of two underground gold mines. As alluded to on the acknowledgments page, the first one, which I visited twenty-two years ago, was pretty dangerous. I was taken into an area containing very unstable rock, and the extent of my training was to be told, "Don't bump your head." The stope was dripping with water. We were right under a lake, which politely waited until a time when no one was underground to catastrophically drain down through the mine. The second mine, visited last fall, was by comparison extraordinarily safe and well managed. I was nervous in that mine, but only because the surroundings were strange to me. Also in preparing to write this book, I visited two smallish open-pit gold mines in Nevada. These were similarly very safely managed, and, when the ore has been removed, some may look forward to futures as landfills, which I consider to be an excellent use of old holes in the ground. The alternatives are to dig new holes for our garbage, throw it in the valleys, or build it into mounds. And by the way, solid waste insiders tell me that the trash we throw in landfills today will become a major mineable resource of tomorrow (there are already efforts under way to sort trash and bury materials in cataloged locations for easier future retrieval).

And, as I write these words, two hundred fifty representatives of governing bodies and mining interests from around the world are meeting in Reno to discuss how better to approach the problems of mining pit waters.

Having just praised some parts of the mining industry, I shall now criticize others. Some mining projects have been incredibly destructive. To take an example from the mining of gold, the hydraulic mining of the placer deposits on the western flanks of the Sierra Nevada during the California gold rush dumped incalculable cubic miles of silt into San Francisco Bay and its tributaries. This was an ecological disaster, which no one in any industry will deny. But at the time it was done, it was considered an amazing technological feat. Which mining project of today will be reviewed in the future as a similarly blind blunder? Will it be the huge open-pit gold mines of the Carlin trend? Some of them appear to have based their initial EIR reclamation modeling predictions for pit lakes on problematically incomplete data. Or will it be the newer coal mines of West Virginia, which employ the strip-mining practice of removing the mountaintops that cover the coal and shoveling this overburden into the valleys? Some of these mines are many miles wide and cover tens of thousands of acres. Do we need that gold and that coal badly enough to justify these levels of impact?

My biggest criticism regarding the fate of natural resources does not go to the mining industry. It goes to the consumer, a largely anonymous and only sketchily regulated entity of which I am of course a part. It strikes me that our lives are becoming so far removed from the genesis of the highly sophisticated materials we consume that we no longer even stop to consider that we are using mined materials, or wonder where they came from. And the corporate entities (of which I have also been a part) that mine these materials have become such vast machines, with such overwhelming political sway, that they influence the laws that are meant to govern them.

I struggled with these issues in writing this book. I had not set out to write about natural resource consumption, but by the time I neared the end of the book, it had become a blaring klaxon that kept me awake at night. I have preferred in the Em Hansen books to present information and opinions rather than judgments, and have tried my best to continue this practice in this book; it is my experience that, when educated, people make judgments of their own that are hopefully better than mine.

An old friend read the first draft of this book and accused me of having taken sides in the mining versus environmentalism argument. He has worked as an economic geologist throughout his career, and was sufficiently upset by what I had written that he insisted that I not even name him in the acknowledgments. Shaken, I cried on the assembled shoulders of my writers' group, bemoaning the fact that life seemed to have gotten so complicated and scary in this increasingly technological, corporate-culture-influenced world.

Mary Hallock, a savvy businesswoman, said wryly, "Oh sure, things used to be so much simpler. We just took and took and took because it was there. We never thought about it."

I replied, "So how are we as individuals supposed to cope with these issues?"

Ken Dalton, a telephone company executive and vintner, said, "Sarah, we don't cope with these issues as individuals. We cope with them as a society."

It is important that we continue to increase our collective awareness of what we do, so that we can make the wisest possible decisions regarding what natural resources to use, how to acquire them, and how to handle the daughter products of their acquisition and use. I think the best way to ensure that we continue to increase our wisdom in these regards is to support education, scientific research, and policy-making that are in no way influenced by financial or other special interests. We must also demand with our votes, our communications, and our consumer dollars that natural resources be used—or left in the ground—wisely and respectfully. Our world is changing. Let's make certain that it changes for the better.

And one last thing. Preparing this book has forced me to become more aware of what natural resources I personally consume. Like a great number of persons in this culture, I used to continuously hunger for more of whatever I was consuming, be it chocolate bars, new cars, trips to far-off places or any other community. I suffered from a classic cup-half-empty attitude. But in the process of contemplating what I am consuming, I have discovered how much I already have, and now find that all along, my cup has been full and over-flowing. I respectfully thank the Earth for its bounty.

And I thank you for reading these words.

Sarah Andrews
April 6, 2000

HERE'S AN EXCERPT FROM
FAULT LINE—
SARAH ANDREWS' NEW MYSTERY, AVAILABLE
IN HARDCOVER FROM ST. MARTIN'S PRESS!

*A bad earthquake at once destroys our oldest associations:
the earth, the very emblem of solidity, has moved beneath
our feet like a thin crust over a fluid;—one second of time
has created in the mind a strange idea of insecurity, which
hours of reflection would not have produced.*
    —Charles Darwin, *Voyage of the Beagle*, from his journal
    entry made after experiencing the devastating February 20,
    1835, earthquake that reduced Concepción, Chile, to rubble

THE EARTHQUAKE THAT SHOOK ME—AND THE REST
of Salt Lake City—awake at 4:14 A.M. that wintry Monday
measured 5.2 on the Richter scale. That's a modest quake by
California standards, and if you live in Japan, or Mexico City,
or Turkey, or in any other place in which violent shaking of
terra firma is more common, you'd be done chatting about it
by lunchtime. It would only re-emerge in your thoughts if
someone mentioned it again, or if you lost a favorite knick-
knack in the fracas, or if you saw the follow-up in the next
day's paper.

But in Salt Lake City, Utah, some of us thought life was
ending. The girls who lived across the hall from me greeted
the experience with screams of terror and a great deal of
howling about Armageddon and other biblical references of
doom. For them, the Earth had just become a place that had
to be reconsidered: a place that might drop them, or cause
something to drop *on* them.

Being a geologist, my experience of the event was somewhat different. I found it exciting, once I got over the dis-
appointment of waking up from the dream I was having. That
dream and I didn't want to let each other go, so it translated

the motion Salt Lake City was experiencing into the blissful experience of rolling around on that self-same bed with my boyfriend, Ray. This was definitely wishful. Ray's a devout Mormon, and, as we ain't hitched, his policy had been to say good night after the lingering tease of a smooch. But my body, having entirely different ideas . . . well, hated to wake up. I can be forgiven for hoping, damn it, because stranger things have been known to happen than for a handsome, healthy thirty-two-year-old male to finally decide to just plain go for it.

But the earthquake did wake me up. Something deep in my brain stem finally got through to the pleasure section of my gray matter and said, *Hey, honey, this isn't just someone bouncing the springs next to you, and aren't those your neighbors screaming?*

As I surfaced fully from my dream, I heard not just my neighbors losing their wits, and the rattling of books, jam jars, pot lids, and the crashing of other miscellaneous chattel falling off of shelves, but the sound of my slatted window blinds slapping against the glass. And then it was over. Perhaps ten seconds total.

There were a few seconds of complete silence; then Greta and Julia, the college girls who lived across the hall, caught their breath and started in again with their howling.

I rose up onto my elbows, my heart racing with both the happy and unnerved varieties of adrenaline, still struggling to sort out what my neighbors were trying to tell me. Had the house just been hit by a Mack truck, or were they flipping with jealousy because they'd somehow gotten a glimpse into my dream?

I switched on my reading light and discovered that I was indeed alone. But the shade on my desk lamp was swaying, all by itself, and my jacket was sliding off the chair onto which, tired from the previous afternoon's solo cross-country skiing, I had dumped it. A rolling pencil toppled off the table that doubled as a dining surface and desk. Then more silence, except for the otherworldly ruckus of my panicked neighbors.

The racket suddenly got louder as the door beyond mine

crashed open and Greta and Julia thundered out into the hall. They took the stairs at a gallop, ululating like a couple of banshees and wailing prayers to Jehovah. Their voices streamed off in a wild Doppler shift of terror as they flung open the street door and hurried out onto the frozen sidewalk.

I swung my legs out from under the covers and lurched onto them. One leg twanged with pain, and I wobbled, arms whipping around in search of something to grab hold of. That leg had until recently been encased in a nice fiberglass walking cast, having gotten itself broken during a mine cave-in, and to celebrate I had overdone it with the cross-country skiing, trying to convince myself that I was whole again. But that's another story.

I staggered across the small bed-sitter room I was renting and opened the front window, letting in the biting breath of winter, and hollered, "It's all right! It was only an earthquake!"

They rounded on me, staring wide-eyed, as if I were some hideous gargoyle come to life.

Which got me to wondering what in hell I was saying. *Only? An earthquake? Hey!*

I suddenly felt a little exposed there hanging out of the window and summarily backed off and slammed it shut.

In some abstract corner of my reckoning, I understood their concern perfectly. Those of us who grow up in the great solid interiors of continents tend to think of the Earth as something that holds still. Oh, it might crumble underneath our boots as we climb a steep hill on adobe soil, or the passage of a summer's cloudburst might carve a steep gully through it, and we have the occasional landslide, but on the whole, our experience is that, at depth, Mother Earth stays put. Which is good, and comforting. Floods we've got, and tornadoes, and plagues of locusts, so who needs earthquakes? Those are for idiots who live by volcanoes and steep coastlines, right?

Wrong. As a Salt Lake City resident, I was living right on top of the Wasatch fault, and it had just awakened from a half century's nap.

The phone rang. *Ah*, I thought. *Ray, calling to check on me. How dear. Kind of makes up for his distance lately.* I picked it up and said, "Hi, sweet pea."

A female voice on the other end shrieked, "Jesus! What was that?"

I let out a laugh, embarrassed to be caught spilling my love name to the wrong ears, but relieved that it was, at least, a very close friend who got to hear it. "Oh, ah . . . hi, Faye. What's up? Certainly not you, at this hour?"

"The hell! That was an earthquake, right?"

"No, just a routine bit of maintenance on the Earth's sub-structure, the laws of thermodynamics bringing about a little reapportionment of stress translated to its crust, as it were. Yes, that was an earthquake. What's the deal—you got to call up a professional to have it certified?"

"Em, my dear," Faye intoned frostily, "I am a pilot, not a geologist. I know turbulence. When the Earth shakes, that's *your* department." Muttering, she added, "Leave it to Em Hansen to intellectualize a near-death experience."

I realized that I was grinning into the phone. Yes, I had just experienced my first earthquake. I whooped, "Wasn't it great?" Because it was. I felt excited, even gleeful. I guess that's part of what sets a geologist apart from normal people: We find natural disasters stimulating. Hell, from a professional standpoint, riding out an earthquake is a rite of passage.

"Great?" Faye said. "Woman, you are insane. My favorite Acoma water olla just bit the dust. Or turned to dust."

"Sorry to hear." Much as I admired Acoma pottery, I was certain she could afford another twenty like it. Faye Carter was filthy, stinking rich. She flew a half-million-dollar air-plane on errands at break-even rates for her buddies and called it a delivery service.

"You don't sound suitably sympathetic," she growled.

"Hey, any geologist worth her salt wants just four things in life. One is to witness a volcanic eruption, another is to see a flash flood, a third is a landslide, and a fourth is to feel a real live earthquake. Coming from Wyoming, I've seen a flash flood already, and now here's my earthquake. So that means I'm halfway there."

There was a moment of silence at the other end of the telephone line. I expected her to come back with some rejoinder about finding a saner profession, but instead, very softly, almost at a whimper, she said, "Em, can you come over?"

It was not unheard of for Faye Carter to sound grumpy, but nervousness was not in her nature. "Um, are you okay?"

"Of course I'm okay!" she shrieked, which was also out of character. She was silent for another long moment, then said, "I . . . aw, hell, Em, the earth just kind of wound up somewhere different, you know? I mean, not all of us find these kinds of things as entertaining as you do! I mean, is it done? It could be a foreshock, right? There might be something bigger coming. Should I run outside? Should I—"

"Is it a foreshock? I have no idea. Not my specialty. More likely there will be aftershocks, but small ones. Very small. Your olla collection won't so much as jiggle."

"You need to get out more," she grumbled, then muttered something about scientists having been fed turpentine with their pablum.

To which I replied, "I went into geology precisely because I could be outside more. And it's just your house jumping around on you that made the earthquake feel so big. If you had been outside, you—"

"Em, you're sick," she muttered, then gasped, "I wish I hadn't said that," and dropped the phone. It hit something hard with a deafening *thunk,* and a moment later, I heard the distant but unmistakable sounds of vomiting. I heard also a man's voice: "Faye? You okay, love duck?"

Love duck? Well. I decided, that puts sweet pea all in perspective, but Tom Latimer, Zen FBI agent and curmudgeonly cradle-robber, calls Faye "love duck"? I decided to revise my diagnosis. There had been no earthquake. Instead, my species had gone collectively insane.

I waited for the phone to be picked up again. Waited two minutes, in fact, because I was concerned about Faye, and not for the more compassionate reasons alone. I had been living in Salt Lake only a few months, she was the closest friend I had in the city, next to Ray, and, love between a hardheaded cop and a harder-headed geologist being what they sometimes were, she topped a short and essential list that might be entitled "Without These People, I Implode." Funny how something like a little natural disaster can leave you feeling more dependent than you're immediately willing to admit.

While I listened to Faye's distant vomiting, I walked around my apartment, switching on lights, inspecting the place for broken crockery. I sniffed slightly over the shattered saltshaker I found in the kitchen and put away my jacket. I glanced out the window to make sure Greta and Julia weren't freezing to death on the front lawn, and saw that our landlady, Mrs. Pierce, was out there wrapping quilts around them, fussing over them like an old hen pecking at june bugs. I waved to let her know I was all right. Finally, I gave up and put the phone back on its cradle. Tom was with Faye, so I could relax and go back to sleep, right?

Wrong. It was too early to be up, but it was also too late, and I was too wired, for getting back to sleep. I thought of phoning Ray, then remembered that he was out of town, down in Saint George with his mother on family business.

Which means that Ray doesn't yet know about the earthquake. . . .

I stopped short in the middle of the room, wondering how I'd known that. Well, because Saint George is at the opposite corner of the state is why. He would not have felt it.

Fine. But how do I know that? How did I know that the shaking would not be felt that far away?

Because the motion was sharp, chattery, a quick jolting followed by a high-amplitude rolling sensation.

I have this kind of conversation with myself all the time. Geologists are emotional introverts, but intellectual extroverts, which means that they like to keep to themselves, but, contrary wise, like to think out loud. Which frequently results in . . . well, talking to ourselves. But the fact was that somehow I knew—instinctively, intuitively—that I was very close to the epicenter of the earthquake. It was a kinesthetic evaluation of the amplitude and frequency of the vibrations. The initial chattery vibrations would attenuate over a very short distance, leaving only the big rollers, and even they would feel more liquid, less jolting.

I had to think a moment to remember my freshman Physical Geology course, in which the professor had explained the differences in the kinds of shock waves set off by the slippage along fault planes that we call an earthquake. I remembered that they had differing senses of motion—some push-pull, some side to side, some up and down. First came the fast, short-amplitude P waves (for primary), then the slower but bigger S waves (for secondary). But there my memory fizzled out. It had been too long since college. I couldn't recall which wave was which. One had a push-pull sense of motion and the other an up and down, and one was surficial and the other traveled at depth, but . . .

But I trust my gut sense, I decided. The epicenter might have been felt ten miles away, but not one hundred, and certainly not as far away as Saint George. I am a geologist down to my deepest neurons, and I know these things.

About then, certain possibilities began to hit me. Geology had just happened in a big way, and right under my feet. Perhaps, in the aftermath of this event, there will be work for me! Maybe the Utah Geological Survey will need me part-time, even, so I can keep going to school. Enough of this job-hunt merry-go-round! If—no, when—I find work, I can even tell Tom Latimer to take a hike with this training he's putting me through. This thought in particular appealed to me. Tom and I had been getting together on the odd evening and weekend. He was training me to be a detective, or operative, or whatever he liked to call himself. He was teaching me how to detect things formally, through the old-fashioned routes, and without risking my foolish neck. But low risk meant life in a laboratory, looking at bags of dirt shipped in from the remote places I'd prefer to be, and old-fashioned seemed to mean the same thing as tedious. I'd begun to tire of the whole idea. "Give me a good field job in geology," I'd told him.

"Out there by myself. Working out geological puzzles, not human ones. That will keep me out of trouble." For the first time that day, Tom had laughed.

Laugh while you can, cloak-and-dagger boy, I told him now in the privacy of my own head, because the earth has moved, and I am going to do some geology! I grabbed my jeans, some wool socks, and a pair of boots—my favorite old pair of red ropers, for luck—and wiggled into them. Did the rupture come to surface? I wondered. Will I be able to see the scarp? No, it wasn't that big. Well, maybe some chimneys have fallen, or maybe there's even a house off its foundations!

I stopped, my right boot halfway on my foot, chagrinned at what I'd been thinking. I was a student of the Earth, but Faye had been right: My excitement was everybody else's tragedy. I began to wonder about the damage in a different way. Wondered if anyone had been hurt. Wondered if any cornices had fallen on people's heads. These thoughts kept me frozen for several seconds.

Well then, I'll just go out and see if I can help, I told myself. I pulled my boot the rest of the way onto my foot, slipped into my down parka, checked its right-hand pocket for my keys, and hurried out the door.

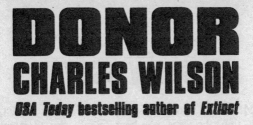

DONOR
CHARLES WILSON
USA Today bestselling author of *Extinct*

Young ER Dr. Michael Sims feels that too many of his patients are dying without cause. Shannon Donnelly, the Congressman's beautiful daughter, believes the police are wrong in ruling her father's death a suicide. Now they're teaming up to uncover the truth about a terrifying medical experiment involving nerve regeneration and organ transplants. It's backed by millions of dollars. It's protected at the highest levels of government. But there are no volunteers, no donors. There are only ordinary people who check into this Mississippi hospital . . . and discover that death wasn't the worst thing they had to fear. Getting "chosen" is. . . .

> "With his taut tales and fast words, Charles Wilson will be around for a long time. I hope so."
> —John Grisham

> "Charles Wilson is a wizard plotter."
> —*The Los Angeles Times*

DON 6/01

SKEPTIC
HOLDEN SCOTT

DR. MIKE BALLANTINE is a man of science, fact, and logic—until he sees his best friend, the Governor of Massachusetts, obliterated before his eyes. Until a bizarre specter appears before him. Until a beautiful CIA agent named Amber Chen tells him about an executioner emerged from the depths of the Chinese Revolution, bringing to America a murderous art that is part magic, part science, and pure evil. Now, as Mike and Amber desperately try to unravel a mystery of biomedicine and murder, they face the most chilling revelation of all: that the worst weapon ever invented is not a bomb, a missile, or a toxin—it's a ghost . . .

"A truly original thriller—part medical, part paranormal, and totally gripping."   —Nelson DeMille

"Riveting . . . Brilliantly told. The suspense is relentless and builds to an ending that leaves you astounded and wondering why someone didn't think of this before . . ."
—Jack McConnel, M.D., cofounder of
the Institute for Genomic Research

"Ingenious, fascinating, and thoroughly original . . . SKEPTIC raises the bar for the medical thriller. Holden Scott ventures into exciting new territory."
—F. Paul Wilson, author of *Nightkill* and
The Barrens and Others

**AVAILABLE WHEREVER BOOKS ARE SOLD
FROM ST. MARTIN'S PAPERBACKS**